NIGHT
FLYING
AVENGER

NIGHT FLYING AVENGER

Pete Grant

NEWMARK PUBLISHING COMPANY

c.2

Published in 1990 by
Newmark Publishing Company
South Windsor, Connecticut 06074
(203) 282-7265

Designed by Irving Perkins Associates, Inc.
Typeset by Pagesetters Incorporated
Printed and Bound by The Book Press
Manufactured in the United States of America

10 9 8 7 6 5 4 3 2 1

Library of Congress Cataloging in Publication Data

Grant, Pete
Night Flying Avenger
1. Night Carrier Flying   2. Night Raids Over Tokyo   3. Saratoga

89-064418

ISBN 0-938539-02-7

Author's Note

This book is autobiographical historical fiction. Many of the events are true and are described from personal experience. The author has added fictional episodes, places, and characters. All the pilot's names have been changed except for that of the pilot to whom this book is dedicated. Some of the occurrences and incidents are stories told to the author by other pilots. Many of the historical events are true and have been researched from numerous books for accuracy of detail, although their interpretation is strictly the author's. If there are any inaccuracies, they should be considered fictional additions.

Epigraph

He shall cover thee with his feathers, and under his wings shalt thou
trust: his truth shall be thy shield and buckler.

Thou shalt not be afraid for the terror by night; nor for the arrow
that flieth by day; nor for the pestilence that walketh in darkness;
nor for the destruction that wasteth at noonday.

A thousand shall fall at thy side, and ten thousand at thy right hand;
but it shall not come nigh thee.

Psalm 91:4–7

Dedication

This book is dedicated to Lieutenant Doty, a pilot from Night Air Group 53, who gave his life flying off the U.S.S. *Saratoga* on the night-carrier raids over Tokyo, February 16, 1945, trying to save his flying companions.

This book is also dedicated to all Navy Air Corps pilots who served as night-carrier pilots during World War II. It was their pioneering efforts in taking off and landing on navy carriers at night in the Atlantic and Pacific oceans that established continuous protection for the ships. They were instrumental in destroying the threat of the German submarines in the Atlantic and played a significant role in the fight against the Japanese in the Pacific.

Prologue

A young Connecticut man leaves college after
Pearl Harbor to become a Navy pilot and sees
action in both the Atlantic and Pacific.

Ensign Pete Grant (P.G.) climbed into the cockpit of his torpedo
bomber that had its wings folded, and took a quick glance at the
dimly illuminated instrument panel. He hooked his parachute harness and safety belt on and connected the plug to his helmet earphones. Through the constant chatter on the radio, P.G. received
the signal from the flight deck crew to start his engine. He checked
his throttle adjustment, pushed the rudder brakes down, and hit
the starter switch. The propeller caught with a single cough and a
puff of exhaust. As Grant slowly advanced the torpedo bomber
deftly up the deck of the carrier, the ship rolled from side to side.
P.G. was seventh in line for the front catapults. The night fighter
planes (F6F-3Ns) were on the deck ahead of his plane, being hurled
one by one into the night sky. The U.S.S. *Saratoga* and her planes
were in the hottest combat zone in the Pacific.

The plane he was flying was a brand new, midnight blue
TBM-3N. Enclosed within a bubble on its right wing was sophisticated radar gear that could penetrate bad weather and, in particular, could see surface vessels and aircraft at night.

The instrument panel was equipped with red lights so the illumination would not interfere with the pilot's night vision. P.G. constantly watched the deck crew as he maneuvered the plane up the deck of the carrier U.S.S. *Saratoga*. The ship was now designated CVN-3 and was one of three carriers with a complete night air group aboard. The *Independence*, a CVL carrier, and the *Enterprise* CVN-6 were the other two.

This was no ordinary flight that P.G. was taking. It was a night-flight off the deck of one of the navy's oldest and largest carriers, affectionately called "Sara, the Queen of the Flattops."

There were reports of enemy submarines in the area, so the ship was completely blacked out. There was no illumination on the deck except for the edge lights, visible only from above, outlining the edges of the carrier to give the pilot some depth perception as he attempted to land his plane. The only other visible light was the slight blue glimmer from the plane's exhaust stacks on the engine cowling.

P.G. rapidly checked his flight instruments as the plane slowly moved up the flight deck. He knew his entire cockpit blindfolded; at night there was no time for groping for a lever or handle. More than 50 different instruments had to be memorized and etched in the pilot's brain.

"Get the hell away from there," a voice called out. "Now!"

The warning was drowned out by the roar of the plane's engine. As P.G. surveyed the deck in front of him, a shrill whistle pierced the air and the ship's bullhorn screamed, "Stop engines."

"Move . . . move . . . get out of the way!"

A sudden movement off to the bomber's right caught the pilot's eye. He peered through the darkness, straining to see what it was.

"Abort. Abort. Abort."

The command rang through P.G.'s radio set. He immediately backed off the throttle and shut down the engine.

"What the hell's going on?" he shouted.

"Crewman down. Hold your position until further orders."

This was not the first time "crewman down" had delayed a take-off. P.G. knew exactly what it meant. One of the deck crew hadn't moved fast enough and had been clipped by the propeller of one of the night fighters. The lucky ones generally escaped minus a hand or an arm. Those less fortunate could easily have the tops of their skulls sheared off. At nighttime it wasn't easy to see those whirling propellers.

Over the radio he heard the command, "Restart engines."

He also heard from the flight control officer that the projected position of the ship's Point Option had been changed. Point Option is the latitude and longitude where the carrier would be located when he returned. The Point Option had already been changed twice and he was getting pissed off. All those figures had to be written on a navigation board and then replotted in order to find the carrier sailing on a black night in the vast Pacific Ocean. Sitting in a dark cockpit and plotting vectors to get home was no easy chore. Usually the pilot put his plane on automatic pilot when he did this, but even then figures weren't completely accurate because at night it was difficult to determine wind velocity and speed over an open ocean.

Landing aboard a bobbing cork at night was an ass-tightener. A night pilot never knew whether the flight deck was coming up at him, going away, or pitching sideways. Usually there was no horizon to help the pilot orient himself in space, so he had to be like a cat, piercing the darkness with his eyes.

P.G. was no ordinary night-flying ensign. He had been a top naval air cadet in athletics and academics, but more important, he had better eyes than a cat. He had 20/15 vision in both eyes and his depth perception was incredible. Using dioptric measurements to test depth perception, he could align objects perfectly. The examining ophthalmologists were amazed at his visual acuity. This was one of the main reasons he had been selected to fly in the night air group.

He had flown earlier with the Night Hunter Killer Groups in the Atlantic against the German submarines. The German submarines would surface at night to recharge their batteries, out of range of the land bases in the Mid-Atlantic Gap. The navy's night torpedo bombers, the Avengers, would make radar runs, scanning the ocean's surface for the U-boats. Once located, the planes would blast them out of the water with their wing rockets. The Avengers had all but eliminated the German submarine threat to merchant vessels as they sailed to support the European conflict.

As P.G.'s plane approached the aft elevator just behind the catapults, he quickly checked the mags to make sure the dual electrical system in the plane was working. There was little to no dropoff as he checked the left and right magnetos. If the mags dropped off too much, the plane would be in unsafe flying condition, and the pilot would have to down-check the plane. He also made a mental checklist and ran it down.

As he did so, the plane finally reached the port catapult of the *Saratoga*. The flight deck crew hooked the catapult launching attachment to the undersurface of the plane. The launching officer waved his lighted wand in a circle to signal him to bring his engine up to full power. He pushed the throttle forward, adjusting his rudders to hold the brakes. As the bow of the big carrier came up onto the crest of a wave, the launching officer thrust the wand forward and P.G. released his brakes. The catapult pulled the plane down the track, accelerating it from zero to 150 knots in 120 feet.

There was a jolt as the plane left the deck. Grant felt like a one-armed paperhanger as he hit the handle to raise the landing gear. He kept the nose of the plane up and slowly raised the flaps, trimming the plane as he went. He constantly watched the artificial horizon to make sure the wings were level as he ascended rapidly into the black sky.

Flying at night off the deck of a carrier is completely different from day flying. The pilot has to be an excellent instrument pilot and must trust his instruments completely. If the weather is bad, or if there is no moon, it is a bitch to fly at night, no matter how skillful a pilot you are. Night flying in bad weather really tests the tentacles of your nerves. It quickly separates the men from the boys.

As the plane reached 5,000 feet, his night fighter partner for the evening, Domkowski, a buddy of his, flying a F6F-3N Hellcat, pulled up on his starboard wing. Dom flicked his wing lights three times as a recognition signal.

The two planes headed on a vector toward Chichijima, a small Japanese-held island about 500 miles from the Japanese mainland. American intelligence believed there was a small airstrip with Japanese fighter planes based there. The planes lowered their altitude and flew fifty feet above the water, using their radio altimeters to avoid radar detection. The *Saratoga* was about 150 miles from the island. The mission for his radar operator was to try to read the signals of the Japanese radar on the island to determine their characteristics and geographic positions. The torpedo bomber plane he was flying had special Racon (radar) equipment on board for this purpose. Once they located the radar station they were to home in on the radar beam and destroy the setup. The night torpedo plane and the fighter plane were both equipped with MK rockets that could sink a destroyer or wipe out a base.

Stewart, the marine radar officer, announced that he had determined the frequency the Japanese radar was using and he was ready to home in on the target.

"You better drop some CHAFF," said P.G., "just in case the Japanese have radar-controlled guns that can fix in on us."

"Roger," said Stewart. He pulled a release handle in the back of the plane that dropped large quantities of metal tinsel (CHAFF) into the air to act as a bolus to confuse the Japanese gunners.

After about 15 seconds P.G. shouted into his mike, "Okay, Dom, let's go get them. Let's give them hell. We ain't gettin' paid by the hour."

Suddenly, antiaircraft fire lit up the island. It was more than they expected from the small island. A few bullets ripped through the wings of the planes as they dove over the target. P.G. reached down on the starboard side of his cockpit and grabbed the handle, releasing the parachute flares to illuminate the base. The night-flying team banked their planes around and shot a full salvo of eight rockets at the target. An oil tank blew up and caught fire, lighting up the sky. P.G. opened the bomb bay doors of the torpedo bomber and made a sweeping turn back toward the target. He switched on the mechanism in the front of the cockpit for arming the bombs. Fires were now spreading over the area. He pressed the automatic release button on his pistol-grip stick for the 500-pound bombs. The bombs were spaced to fall 150 feet apart. There were tremendous explosions as the bombs hit the ground. The wings of his plane shuddered. Most of the antiaircraft batteries were silenced.

"Scratch one radar station!" said Domkowski triumphantly.

"Hot shit!" said P.G., "we got 'em!" Both pilots knew their mission was a success.

"Let's head for home, Dom," said P.G. Dom joined up on his wing, and P.G.'s radar operator located the *Saratoga* on the scope.

"The *Sara* is at 125 miles; vector is 240 degrees."

"Roger," replied P.G. "Notify Domkowski."

As they approached the task force, they picked up the destroyer picket boats and checked their IFF (Identification, Friend or Foe) gear in the cockpit, to make sure it was on. IFF gear is an electronic radar box that sends out a coded signal that identifies planes on the ship's radar. Another method of identification was also used. They avoided being shot down as enemy planes by approaching the destroyer at a designated vector. This vector changed every day and had a secret code. The radar gear on the destroyers would check to make sure there were no followers, for it was a favorite trick of the Japanese flyers to follow the American planes back and let them guide them to the American fleet. Some of these Japanese planes had kamikaze pilots aboard who would blow themselves up to destroy their targets.

P.G. got permission to enter the landing circle and, as the plane flew on the downwind leg, he couldn't see the surface of the water. In the daytime, he could anticipate a difficult landing in rough weather, but it was now almost midnight, and landing was three times as hazardous. As his plane approached the landing groove, he sighted the landing signal officer, who was using his brightly lighted wands. He looked out the left side of the cockpit for his arm signals. The plane's canopy was open in case the plane missed the deck and hit the water and he had to get out in a hurry. The L.S.O. had his wands stretched out laterally, indicating the plane was flying in the right attitude for landing.

He received the cut signal and pulled his throttle all the way back, hoping to catch a wire with his tail hook. Suddenly his front wheels hit the deck with a jolt and the nose of the plane headed for the sky. He instinctively pushed the control stick forward to get the nose down and the plane back down on the deck. He gently pulled back on the stick, trying to catch a late wire on the carrier's deck. The night was as black as a witch's tit. He felt a quick jerk, and his neck snapped back as the plane rattled around and came to a complete stop. He climbed out of the cockpit, his legs shaking a little bit. He looked around. The big torpedo bomber plane had caught the top wire of the crash barrier. A flight deckhand, seeing what had happened, shouted, "You were lucky on that one, sir!"

"I'd rather be lucky than dead!"

1

College and the Day of Infamy

Pete Grant's family had been hit hard by the Depression. His father lost most of his money in the 1929 stock market crash and the family home was taken over by the bank. There were six children and there was no money left for college. No one had to sit him down and tell him that he had to go to work to make a living. After graduating from high school, he got a job working for an insurance company in Hartford. He was given the title of junior underwriter, and although the pay was practically nothing (seventy dollars a month), he struggled to save as much of his paycheck as possible. He walked four miles to and from work in order to save the dime that was necessary for the trolley. He was also a brown-bagger and proud of it.

In early September, an incident at work propelled him into a better-paying job. The assistant secretary of the insurance company called P.G. into his office and asked him to work with some college trainees who were coming into the home office. In particular, he was to work with John Sourgrass from Louisiana, and explain the ins and outs of home-office operations.

During the next month he tried to teach John how fire insurance policy rates were figured. He showed him how the rates go down if a person lives near a fire department or if the town has sufficient fire equipment. He also showed him composites of "firebugs," people who take out fire insurance and then burn their homes or offices to collect on the policy.

One day John Sourgrass took him out to lunch. In the course of the conversation, John asked Pete how much money he was making. Pete stuck out his chest and said, "I'm making $70 a month, and I've been promised a raise in six months."

John started laughing. "Hell, boy," he said, "I make that in one week. I'll never be as smart as you are. My daddy sent me to a state university down south so I wouldn't flunk out. Look at me now."

P.G. turned red, a combination of embarrassment and anger creeping across his face. "You make $70 a week?"

"I'll show you my check when I get it today."

Sure enough, John Sourgrass was earning in one week what P.G. was making in one month. "That does it!" he said. When he got back to his department, he went directly into the assistant secretary's office. "Mr. Clark, I quit."

"What's wrong?" asked the assistant secretary.

"When you pay that nincompoop, Sourgrass, the same amount in one week that I earn in a month, there's something wrong with the system."

"I'll give you a ten-dollar a month raise," said Mr. Clark.

"You've got to be kidding! That's peanuts! I won't take it!"

That night, when he got home, he went into the house and slammed the door behind him. "I'm not going to take that crap anymore. They're paying that jerk, Sourgrass, as much in one week as I make in a month. I told Mr. Clark what he could do with his lousy job!"

His father said, "You go back and apologize."

"I won't do that."

P.G.'s older sister joined in the conversation. "I agree with Dad."

His father shouted. "How are you going to eat? You can't stay here if you don't help foot the bills. We've had a Depression, you know. You still have to pay $20 a month board. Where do you plan to get that?"

"I'll find something. I'm strong, healthy, and willing to work."

"If you don't pay board, you can't live here," his father replied.

His sister spoke up. "I'll call Mr. Clark and apologize for you."

"No way. My mind is made up. They're a bunch of crooks."

The next day he went to the State Unemployment Bureau to look for a new job. He stood in line with unshaven derelicts, alcoholics, and an unsavory variety of unskilled laborers; most of them didn't speak English. He was the young squirt in the crowd. He was slowly finding out what life was all about.

An older man standing in line spitting tobacco juice said, "Son, what are you doing around here?"

P.G. replied, "I quit my job because they weren't paying me enough."

"You've got to be stupid. You never quit a job until you have another one lined up."

"What are you doing here then?" asked P.G.

"I'm too old to get a job. They keep turning me down. I have very few skills," the old man said with tears in his eyes.

Suddenly P.G. started to worry about whether or not he'd be able to get another job, after seeing all those men standing in line. Finally, after standing in line for two hours, he got up to the front desk.

"What are your skills?" asked the secretary.

"I don't have many. I've worked for three months in an insurance company."

The young girl smiled and let out an exasperated sigh. "Are you willing to take any kind of job?" she asked.

"Yes."

"Do you know what a trucker is?" He shook his head. She rolled her eyes. "Well, you put heavy metal parts in pans on a hand truck and deliver them to different departments in the factory. Colt Patent Firearms needs a trucker today," she said.

"What do they pay?" he questioned, voicing his main concern.

"Twenty-eight dollars a week for a 48-hour week."

"I'll take it," he said.

He started work at 6:00 A.M. the next day, pushing a hand truck loaded with metal parts to different departments in the factory. His back, arms, and shoulders ached from lifting the metal parts, but he didn't care. He was making at least forty dollars more a month.

His father and sister wanted to know what he was being paid. He refused to answer because he was afraid that his board might be increased. He was ready to carry his own weight and had plans for his own paychecks.

One morning when P.G. was delivering parts to the production line, one of the workers hollered out to him.

"Hey, Grant, I wanted a rotator gauge. What the hell is this?"

"Rotator gauge? If that's what you wanted, why didn't you write that down?"

"I did, you little shit. Why don't you learn how to read?"

"Who can read this slop? Why don't you learn how to write?"

"Well, maybe you need to have your eyes opened up, boy."

With that, Jim Campbell moved menacingly toward P.G. This wasn't the first time a delivery had caused problems. The scrawl that passed for handwriting was often illegible, at best. Campbell threw a looping roundhouse right that caught P.G. on the chin. He staggered backward, regained his balance, and charged. He was met with a left hand which dropped him to the seat of his pants. He shook his head, and pulled himself to his feet. Lowering his shoulder, he leaped toward the machinist, and drove him backward into a parts bin. Seconds later, he felt several hands pulling him away as the two combatants were separated. Minutes later, the inevitable call came, "Grant, report to the supervisor's office immediately."

Charlie Townsend stood up from behind his desk. "What the hell was that all about? Since when does a trucker attack one of my machinists?"

"The parts were wrong, again. It happens three or four times a day. They think they're telling me what they want. I think I'm getting them what they asked for. I show up with the wrong parts and they get mad. This time we both got a little too mad. But if this keeps up, it'll happen again. Something has got to change!"

Townsend peered over his glasses at P.G. "Listen, son, we've run this company for a lot of years, and we've had more than a few brawls. I'll tell you what. The machinists always win. Why? Because without machinists, there's no production. Without production, there are no orders being filled. With no orders being filled, there are no jobs. Got that? Now, if you have any ideas that will help out, I'd be glad to hear them. But, if I hear that you're mixing it up with any more of my machinists, you're out of here. Now, what did you have in mind?"

"Why not just number and color-code the slips in the metal parts pans; for example, pink for .45-caliber revolvers, blue for machine guns, yellow for rifles, and so on?" P.G. asked.

Townsend paused. "I'll get back to you," he said.

Three days later, he was called into the supervisor's office. "We're going to try your idea for the .45-caliber pistols. If it works, we'll do the other guns," he said. "I'll try anything to keep my machinists happy and not sitting on their butts."

For the first few weeks, nothing seemed to change. Eventually, however, people got used to the system and the entire production line seemed to improve. Meanwhile he continued to save for his college tuition.

It wasn't long before P.G. was back in Charlie Townsend's office. He was given a small office and a new job at double his salary.

Knowing P.G.'s academic aspirations, Charlie Townsend talked to him. "Son, why do you want to go to college? You can do all right just working with us."

"How do you tell someone that enduring is not enough?" thought P.G. Not wanting to start a lengthy discussion on the matter, he simply smiled at Charlie and walked down the corridor back to work. That night, he got a second job working on weekends as a coat- and hat-check boy at a country club.

Between both jobs, he was able to pay his board and save $1,500 toward college. Accepted at the state university, he started his freshman year in September of 1941, majoring in business. He wanted to take a premed course but, with only enough money to get through his freshman year, that was a dream beyond reality.

Things started to fall into place for him. He got free meals by working in the cafeteria and was elected president of his freshman class.

The state university had fraternities and sororities and his status as president of his class meant that he was rushed by many of the best fraternities. He joined Phi Mu Delta fraternity and soon learned that fraternities were a good place to socialize and have bull sessions and also a good place to take your favorite girl on weekends. Liquid refreshments included a keg of beer and snacks to munch on. There was even a nickelodeon that played the latest records of Tommy Dorsey, Glenn Miller, Benny Goodman, and Lionel Hampton. You didn't even have to put a dime in it to make it play. P.G.'s dream had come true. He was now at college pursuing an academic career.

Suddenly, that dream was shattered. On December 7, 1941, the Japanese bombed Pearl Harbor. The student body and faculty at the University were stunned when the news came over the radio. There was mass confusion on the campus. The message amid this chaos came through loud and clear—male students old enough to volunteer or to be drafted would be entering the armed forces to pursue a different kind of education; for some, a lethal one.

The Japanese had cleverly chosen an early Sunday morning for the attack on Pearl Harbor. It was designed by Admiral Isoroku Yamamoto, the Commander in Chief of the Japanese Imperial Navy. He felt that a surprise aerial attack would deliver a crushing blow to America's sea power, and he was right.

The initial radio reports about the attack were scanty. The base was quiet and the usual weekend leaves were in effect when the Japanese planes hit Pearl Harbor at 7:00 A.M. When the bombers thundered over Ford Island in Hawaii not a shot was fired in opposition.

American seamen and officers on the decks of the ships gave them little attention, for they assumed they were friendly planes. Screaming dive bombers and torpedo bombers shattered that moment as Japanese planes swooped over the army, navy, and marine airfields, destroying the unmanned American planes on the ground and successfully bombing the "sitting duck" battleships and cruisers in the harbor. Initially, not one American gun opened fire—nor did any American fighter planes take off. Five of the battleships, the *West Virginia, Arizona, Nevada, Oklahoma,* and *California* were hit by torpedoes and dive bombers.

Once the Americans recovered from the shock and realized what was happening, the crews manned the remaining guns and shot down several of their attackers. There was no air resistance to slow the attacking bombers because all the American aircraft on the ground had been destroyed. Survivors instead worked feverishly to control the damage to the ships, which included the battleships *Tennessee* and *Maryland.* The men labored courageously, fighting fires and counter-flooding the ships to keep them on an even keel and to prevent them from sinking. Heroics could not salvage the U.S.S. *Arizona,* which settled on the harbor bottom with more than one thousand of her crew trapped below in a watery grave.

The Japanese carriers launched almost four hundred planes to attack Pearl Harbor. Their loss was approximately thirty aircraft and their crews. It was a small price for the damage inflicted; the attack wiped out a major portion of the United States fleet. Fortunately, when the Japanese planes withdrew to return to their carriers and then to Japan, the oil tanks on Pearl Harbor were still intact and the United States Navy's two carriers based at Pearl

Harbor, the *Lexington* and the *Enterprise,* were at sea. The other large navy carrier, the U.S.S. *Saratoga,* was on the West Coast.

Late Sunday night and Monday morning the news reached the American people. Newscasters Edward R. Murrow, H.V. Kaltenborn, Lowell Thomas, and others dramatically recounted what had happened. Newspapers had extras out on the streets announcing the vicious attack. Americans were shaken and angry.

The next day P.G. was in the cafeteria busing tables when President Roosevelt delivered his war address and declared the December 7 attack on Pearl Harbor a "day of infamy." Radios were turned up loud so everyone could hear the news. Eating stopped and everyone listened intently. When the speech was completed, the entire student body present stood up and started to sing the "Star-Spangled Banner." Very few students knew all the words, but they would learn them before the war was over. Foul epithets were spoken by the students concerning the day of infamy.

"Those slant-eyed, yellow bastard Japs, they'll regret bombing Pearl Harbor. We'll get revenge."

"We'll avenge what they did tenfold."

"They'll regret tackling the Americans."

"They're a bunch of shrimps who want to dominate the world."

"God is on our side."

"Justice will prevail."

Mass confusion and anxiety spread across the college campus. The young men were frustrated by the start of a war; their education plans were completely disrupted. From the onset of hostilities, there were realistic fears that the Japanese would attempt to invade the coast of California. The National Guard was immediately called up to defend our country. America was no longer just a co-defender of Europe; America's homeland and very existence were being threatened. ROTC students were sent away to army training camps, and the male students who remained either enlisted or made plans to enter the various services. Some students, however, got deferments.

On the night of December 8, 1941, at the state university, young men gathered to shoot the bull. The beer flowed, and even though the students were in the midst of their first semester finals, little studying was done. P.G. lived in a building called the Barracks, which were the least expensive dormitories on the campus. A group of freshmen got together in his room to discuss how they were going to cope with this new development. There were many unanswered questions. What branch of the service are you going into? Are you going to join the army, the navy, or the marines? Are you going to volunteer or are you going to wait to get drafted? Do you want to fight the war on the land, on the sea, or in the air? Do you really want to fight? Should you try to dodge the draft?

Present at that meeting were six men who would participate in the war. In that group was a six-foot, five-inch, 245-pound football player by the name of Brett Groppo. Also a five-foot, ten-inch scat-back football player, Ray Schultz, who would go into the marines and become an officer fighting on the islands of the Pacific. There was a thin, tough, intelligent Swede by the name of Bert Frederickson, who would lose his life as a navy pilot. A senior Barracks counselor, Carl Main, joined them and he would become an army captain serving in the Battle of the Bulge. Pete Grant and his roommate, Jim Dougherty, completed the group.

P.G. led the discussion. "Hey guys, we got one hell of a problem facing this country. We're in big trouble. Ray, what do you think about this Japanese attack?"

"What do I think? I think this country got caught sleeping in the shithouse. That's what the hell I think!" said Ray. "I think we were unprepared and we have a lot of catching up to do. Right now we don't have enough military equipment to fight a war with Mexico. Those bastards caught us with our pants down."

Groppo was seething. "I'll kill them with my bare hands," he said.

"Your bare hands won't help you if a machine gun mows you down," said Carl. "Besides, you're an easier target to hit because you're the size of a goddamned tank."

"I never thought of it that way," replied Groppo, subdued by the remark.

"How the hell do we decide which branch to join?" asked Frederickson.

"How about one we won't die in?" said Schultz.

"Listen to Schultz," said Groppo, getting back into it. "There's a war on and he's looking for guarantees."

"I wonder if I could stick a bayonet into someone?" said P.G.

"You might have to stick it into more than one," said Schultz. "Hey, you've seen one dead Jap, you've seen 'em all. Once you kill one in the infantry, you might have to kill 20 more on the next hill to survive."

"I don't think I'd like that," said P.G.

"You'd never make a marine," said Schultz. "If someone comes at you with a bayonet to kill you, you've got to kill him first or you're dead. You don't give any quarter. It's either you or him. You flinch, you die. It's that simple."

"Maybe the navy would be better," said Frederickson.

"Only if you want to be eaten by the sharks," said Carl Main. "If you like to swim and go down with the ship, by all means, join the navy."

"What about the air force?" asked Groppo. "You wouldn't have to stick a bayonet into someone's guts."

"No shit. But one shot can turn your plane into a ball of fire."

"You mean you burn up?"

"That's exactly what I mean," replied Frederickson.

"Groppo, you're too big anyway. You wouldn't be able to fit in a fighter plane," said Schultz.

"How about submarine duty?" asked Groppo.

"You're too big for that, too."

"It stinks down there, anyway," said Schultz. "If you fart, it stays there for a week, until you surface. And incidentally, the way you fart, everybody would suffocate."

They all started to laugh.

"Well, we all have to enlist to help this fucking country out," said Groppo. "Obviously our politicians screwed up, so it's up to us, gentlemen. As far as I'm concerned, the sooner the better."

They filled their glasses with beer and stood facing each other. They raised their glasses together in a toast of friendship. Schultz said it most aptly. "We've got to beat those fucking Japs or we're all dead."

The next week P.G. did very little studying, even though it was exam week. He gave a lot of thought to his options. He was a freshman in good standing and could ask for a deferment. If he became an engineering or premed student, he could get deferred and complete his college requirements. He probably could get out of the war completely. He might still have to go into the service after the war in order to qualify for the deferment. That would be a hell of a lot safer than being shot at.

He thought about his family. His brother had been in the ROTC program at the university and was called up immediately when the war broke out with Germany. He had been assigned to one of the army's crack outfits, Division One, "The Red One." He eventually served as a company captain in North Africa and then was wounded in Sicily.

His father had repeatedly told P.G. that he didn't want him to go into the service. After all, his oldest son was in the service and might be killed, and someone had to carry on the family name. If you were the only male in the family, you could qualify for a deferment. His sister told him that he could avoid the draft and get a deferment by going to work in a defense factory. He had worked at Colt Patent Firearms, and they might give him his job back.

Sitting under a tree on campus one day, he realized he was not seriously considering deferment or waiting to be drafted. He knew he wouldn't be able to look at himself in the mirror if he took that route. He decided to volunteer for one of the services, but which one? If the Japanese won the war and took over, there would no longer be a free America.

His mind was made up, but doubts persisted. Someday, he thought, he might regret not having asked for a deferment because those who got one wouldn't be shot at and would survive the war. They'd also end up three or four years ahead of him in achieving their goals. When the war ended, service in the armed forces would soon be forgotten and wouldn't get you a job. It had happened to the World War I veterans, and P.G. was sure it would happen again.

P.G.'s mind was made up for him. All the students constantly listened to the radio to hear the news about the war front. The local newspapers and *The New York Times* were read cover to cover. The news got progressively worse. It became obvious that the Japanese had prepared themselves diligently for success in controlling the entire Pacific and Far East. A major disaster was unfolding.

The day after the Pearl Harbor attack, Japanese troops landed north of Luzon in the Philippines. They also bombed Hong Kong and destroyed its air force, committing numerous atrocities. Thailand was invaded by Japanese Lieutenant-General Yamashita with his highly mobilized mechanized Fifth Division Units. There was no resistance. Just before Christmas (1941) the Japanese invaded the Philippines en force. Japanese Zeros destroyed B-17 bombers on Clark Field in Luzon, taking over control of the air.

The last bastion of American troops on Bataan in the Philippines were ingloriously defeated as General MacArthur and his wife and four-year-old son fled aboard a PT boat under cover of darkness.

Many of the American troops left behind would eventually die of hunger, fever, disease, and torture by the Japanese. Since the Americans did not surrender quickly, the Japanese high command ordered a death march of 60 miles to a concentration camp to teach them a lesson. If the men fell out of step or were weary and wanted to relieve themselves they were hit with rifle butts and bayoneted or shot in the head. Many died from untreated intestinal infections from drinking contaminated water. As the news of these atrocities reached the States, the American people became more united and swore revenge.

The well-trained Japanese armies easily destroyed all British, Dutch, and American resistance in Singapore, Malaya, and the Philippines and anticipated invading Australia.

Panic was setting in on campus among the male students. Fraternities and other groups of men on campus enlisted en bloc in specific services so they could serve together. The fraternity that P.G. had joined decided to enlist in the V-5 Naval Air Training Corps. P.G. and about forty of his fraternity brothers went to 120 Causeway Street, Boston, which was the nearest navy enlistment center.

To qualify to be a navy pilot, a rigid physical exam had to be passed. All but five of the fraternity brothers passed this exam. P.G. was one of those who did not pass, even though he had the best ratings on the eye exam. He was called into the office of the senior medical officer. He knew right away something was up. "Son, have you ever injured your nose?" asked the doctor.

"Yes, I hurt my nose in a sledding accident when I was five years old. I also hurt it playing football," he replied.

"Well, you have a deviated septum that could cause breathing difficulties at high altitudes," said the doctor. "If you get that nose of yours fixed, you'll qualify for the Naval Air Corps Cadet Program. You can't enlist in the Program unless you get it taken care of."

He was depressed. Almost all the other guys had passed. They would receive traveling orders at the end of the semester. He went home and talked to his mother and father about what had happened. His father refused to pay for the operation. Instead, he suggested that he try for a deferment because of his nose problem. P.G. wasn't interested in a deferment. He couldn't understand his father's attitude.

P.G.'s grandfather was a farmer in the territories of northern

Europe. His farm was on the border of the constantly disputed territory of Russia, Poland, and Germany. Since the tenth century the land had changed hands numerous times after wars and partitions. It was a constant battleground. One century it would be occupied by Poland, the next by Russia, and the third by Prussia (Germany). It was not an ideal place to live if you hated wars.

His father had come to America when he was sixteen, before World War I, because he didn't like what was happening in Europe and didn't want to go into the armed forces. He saw another war developing and decided to leave. He left home and sailed on a boat, steerage class, to America. Arriving in New York City, he worked on the Bowery to be able to feed himself and eventually settled in Connecticut. P.G.'s father was a pacifist and he felt that P.G. would be killed while flying.

His father exploded. "Son, I don't want you to go into the service and fight a war."

"Dad, you can't see past the nose on your face. This country, the one that took you in and gave you a home—it *needs* me! It needs me now more than you or this family ever has."

His mother looked down at her hands. She was obviously disturbed by the argument between her husband and her son. There were tears in her eyes. His father was visibly shaken and started to speak, but stopped. In that moment—as father and son stared at each other—Peter realized he'd spoken the truth. And his father knew. But the elder Grant, the avowed pacifist set in his convictions, regained his composure and said, "If you want to be shot out of the sky in one of those goddamned newfangled airplanes, you go right ahead!" He walked out of the room and slammed the door.

P.G.'s mother was crying. "You have to try to understand your father," she said, "he's very set in his ways."

His mother acted as an intermediary and was more supportive of P.G. "I'll sign the papers for you," she said. "I don't know where the family will find the money to pay for the operation." P.G. said he would pay for it out of the money he had saved to go to college. Finally, his mother signed the form authorizing the operation.

He went into the hospital, and the surgeon opened up the air passages to his sinuses and lungs. His nose was packed with gauze, and a pressure dressing was tightly applied. Both of his eyes became black and blue and so swollen that he couldn't see. He had trouble breathing through his mouth, and wondered whether what he had done would be worth it. He had to apply ice packs to his eyes and his cheeks for two weeks to get the swelling down. He looked like he had been in a street fight. Fortunately, he didn't get an infection from the naso-septal operation.

There was some good news. The ear, nose, and throat specialist from Boston charged him half price when he found out why P.G. was having the operation. The fee depleted his college money, but that didn't matter since he was going into the service. The operation was a success, and P.G. was accepted by the Navy Department for the V-5 Naval Cadet Training Program.

2

Learning to Fly

It was the latter half of 1942. P.G. and his fraternity brothers were V-5 naval air cadets. They received orders to proceed to Arkansas State Teacher's College in Conway, Arkansas, for pre-preflight training. It was an evaluation program to determine whether the cadet could fly an airplane.

The cadets were a hand-picked group of college students with keen minds and athletic backgrounds. Their eyesight had to be perfect and their reflexes honed to react rapidly to changing conditions.

The men teaching them would be civilian pilot instructors, recruited from private life, to indoctrinate the college students. Training was to be done on the Piper Cub, the simplest training plane available.

Most of the cadets could hardly wait to begin flight instruction. They were anxious to get into the air and try to fly that little airplane. It really was a primitive plane, and the cadets wondered if there was a sewing machine engine under the cowling. The apprehension and anticipation of trying to learn to fly an airplane was overwhelming. Everything they had heard about flying they had read about in newspapers or books. They were true novices. About all they knew was that Charles Lindbergh was the first man to fly across the Atlantic and that Wiley Post had flown around the world. Now, they too had the chance to become pilots.

The day after the cadets arrived at Arkansas State Teacher's College, they were taken on buses to a small airfield on the edge of town and were shown the Piper Cub they would be flying. It was a single-winged aircraft, painted yellow, with a wooden propeller. The wings had a paper-thin cloth covering. It looked very fragile sitting on the ground. It weighed only 750 pounds. It carried 18 gallons of fuel and had a 50-horsepower engine with a maximum speed of 100 mph. The propeller sometimes had to be started by hand, occasionally causing an accident when the prop kicked back. All the controls of the airplane were operated by a single, centrally located stick. The movement of the plane in the air was controlled by the deflection of air passing over movable surfaces on the wings and the tail.

Foot pedals with brakes controlled the rudders, and the ailerons on the wings moved in opposite directions, pushing one wing up and the other down, thus causing the plane to roll. The elevator attached to the rear of the plane's tail pushed the tail up or down, causing the plane to climb or descend. The tail rudder, which was mounted vertically and hung onto the back fin, controlled the plane's rotation about its vertical axis, called "yaw." This moved the plane to the right or to the left. The three working together— the ailerons, elevator, and rudder—allowed the aircraft to execute its varying flight patterns.

As a cadet sat in the cockpit of the plane, his right hand held the stick and his left controlled the throttle that was pushed forward to increase the power; pulled back to decrease it. His feet were placed on foot pedals that controlled the brakes and moved the rudders.

Flying in the Piper Cub, the aspiring pilots wore helmets, flight goggles, brown leather flight jackets, and parachute harnesses. But to look like a pilot is not to be one. To become a navy pilot, a cadet needs excellent depth perception, excellent muscular coordination, and a keen mind with strong motivation to succeed.

"Airport" was a kind term for the large grass field the cadets used as a takeoff and landing strip. There were two hangars where the planes would be repaired when they became damaged. Engine changes and mechanical repairs would take place there as well. After a certain number of hours in the air, each engine needed a thorough overhaul. There was also a gas filling area, but no control tower. A large windsock and flag were flown from the highest point on the hangar to determine the direction of the wind. "Brother, this is going to be interesting," thought P.G. when he first surveyed the scene.

Before the fledgling cadets could get into that primitive, low-winged, yellow plane they had to complete ground school instruction. They learned the mechanics of airplane engines and underwent a simplified course in aerology to understand the weather and some of the risks of flying in bad weather. Navigation and a course in radio signals and communication were also requirements.

The indoctrination program included a taste of military training. Green uniforms that were formerly used by the Civilian Conservation Corps (CCC) were issued. The men began an exercise program and were taught marching formations. It was extremely confusing to many of them, since they were only a few weeks removed from a college campus.

The flyers got their introduction to reveille the first day. P.G. practically jumped out of bed. The brassy blaring of the bugle sounded like it was coming from under his pillow. He looked around, and noticed the other cadets had the same groggy, confused look about them.

Reveille had barely faded away when the door to the barracks burst open, allowing one Lieutenant Roger Weathers to barge in. He was a tall, imposing figure in a military uniform with a booming voice. The lieutenant's voice had the same quality and tone as the bugle.

"Welcome to the navy, ladies. It's now 5:30 A.M., which will be the time you will hear that sweet melody each and every morning. It's our little way of saying rise and shine. Drop your cocks and grab your socks. Now bust out of those beds. Get dressed. Let's go. Move your ass. Move it. Move it."

After assembly, the cadets were sent out for a five-mile jog to get their bodies in shape. It was quite obvious that the instructors meant to get the cadets in fighting strength as soon as possible.

The squadron of the naval air cadets was split into two groups. One half of the group took ground instruction in the morning, while the other half had flight instruction. They changed places in the afternoon. The cadets were eager to start their flight instruction, which began with an hour and a half of daily flight time. It was not only the highlight of the day, but for some a greater physical thrill than anything else in their young lives.

The cadets were told that after seven or eight hours of flight instruction, some of them would be allowed to solo. Successful candidates would then go on to preflight school. Each cadet was assigned an instructor, and there were also check pilots who would determine whether or not a cadet would be washed out of the program.

Like many young men who flew over that grassy Arkansas field, P.G.'s first flight with his instructor became rooted in his mind. "Do you know how to drive a car?" asked the instructor, Jim Taylor.

"Sure," P.G. lied. He knew his family had never been able to afford a car. He thought back to the first time he tried driving. Rich Pettimore had his father's '39 Dodge, and he gave P.G. a very brief lesson before turning him loose. P.G. nearly put the car in the Connecticut River. Fortunately, it ended up in a ditch. He hadn't had much interest in driving since then.

"Well, forget everything you know," the flight instructor said. "An airplane is not on a concrete highway. It goes up, down, and side-ways, and sometimes the power shuts off. I'm going to teach you some basic rules today. First of all, keep your head and eyes moving around from side to side, and always watch the instrument panel. If you're lucky enough to complete flight training, you may face the enemy, and the enemy is everything out there: another plane, high-tension wires, the weather, buildings, even a flock of birds."

Jim Taylor continued his serious lecture. "If you're a good pilot, the muscles in your neck will develop because when you fly, you'll constantly be looking around. If your plane gets too low and you don't know where you are, you can hit high-tension wires and that's the end of you and your airplane. In bad weather, sometimes you can't see ahead of you. You have to know your instruments and trust them. Memorize that panel so that if something goes wrong, you'll instinctively pick it up. Investing a little time may save your life someday. If you complete the Naval Air Cadet Program, you'll learn instrument flying so you won't be afraid to fly in bad weather. There's no horizon to help you in bad weather, so you can't fly by the seat of your pants."

P.G. spoke up. "Can I ask some questions?"

"Absolutely," replied Taylor. "The navy grades me on how well you fly and whether you graduate from the program. I want you to know all the answers."

"Did you have any trouble learning how to fly?"

"You bet your ass I did. All of my sphincters got tight. Once I soloed and got confidence it was the most exhilarating experience of my life. You'll know what I mean when it happens to you. One word of caution," Taylor added. "Remember to turn your instruments on before you take off, or else they're useless. The instructor who spun in the other day in bad weather hadn't turned on his vertical and horizontal altitude directors, which we call the artificial horizon and the direction gyro. They're useless unless turned on and set prior to takeoff."

P.G.'s ground school training seemed to drag on. Like everyone else, he wanted to get in the air. When assignments were finally posted, he was like a little kid in a candy store. He was up almost an hour before reveille. He was dressed and ready to go long before formation was called. Finally, however, the time came. He went down to the flight line and met Jim Taylor at the hangar. Taylor ran him through a quick mental checklist.

P.G. climbed into the plane. Taylor started the engine, and P.G. immediately froze. He went to say something, but his jaw was locked. He literally couldn't lift up his arms. For a second, he thought his heart was going to rip through his uniform. His face paled and his skin became clammy. He didn't want to fly. It was crazy, he thought. How can 750 pounds of steel stay airborne? They were going to get up in the air and crash—if they got up in the air at all. His father had been right. He should have gotten a deferment. He started to sweat. He felt his body begin to shake. He was sure Taylor noticed this also, but Jim just looked over at him, grinned, and said, "Up we go!"

Jim pushed the throttle forward and away they went. The plane bounced down the field and leaped into the air.

Taylor took the plane up to 6,000 feet. "I'm going to show you a controlled stall," he said. "Watch the way I pull the nose up and then see what happens." As the nose of the plane went higher, suddenly it dropped off and started to spin. The instructor quickly pushed the stick forward and nosed the plane down to pick up airspeed. He then leveled the plane off and said, "At 6,000 feet that maneuver is relatively safe, but the plane's nose has to be in perfect position when you level the aircraft."

"Shit!" said P.G. as his head seemed to spin a little. He realized he would have to regain his equilibrium in some way in order to respond properly, as did his instructor.

"Remember though, you can't do these maneuvers close to the ground. This plane is not built for aircraft acrobatics. Now you take over with your stick." P.G.'s muscles tightened up suddenly; the plane seemed to fly more roughly. "You'll have to learn to relax under stress, cadet," said Taylor. "Learn to caress the controls but keep constantly alert. Make believe you're stroking your best girl-friend's rear end and you'll do a better job. Take us back to the airport now."

P.G. made a slow turn, dropping the right wing down and level-ing off the plane. "Take us down to 2,000 feet." He pushed the stick forward and the plane sped up. Jim said, "Pull the throttle back so you don't have such a fast descent. Cadet, you're heading in the wrong direction. You're supposed to be heading for Conway, Ar-kansas, not Memphis."

P.G. made a 90-degree turn to the left and the instructor said, "Good, I didn't think you were watching the compass. I'll take it back and land." After landing the plane Taylor said, "I think you've got a little potential. I'll see you tomorrow. Start memorizing the instrument panel. Tomorrow, we'll go over the preflight checking of the plane before you leave the chocks."

"What are chocks?" P.G. thought to himself. He asked one of the mechanics in the hangar, who started to laugh.

"Chocks are the wooden blocks put in front of the aircraft's wheels to keep the plane from moving when the plane is on the ground."

"Well, hot diggity, I've learned another word for my vocabulary."

He walked back out to the plane and climbed in. He sat in it for more than an hour and a half trying to memorize the location of each instrument on the panel. It looked complicated to him; much more complex than any automobile panel he'd ever seen. There was an ignition key and a gas gauge. However, there were two magnetos (electrical systems) in the plane to make sure the ignition was always firing the engine. Checking the magnetos, or "mags," prior to take-off was a must, because both had to be working properly.

There was also an altimeter. On the left side of the cockpit was the throttle, which controlled the engine's power and was pushed forward at takeoff for full thrust. A magnetic compass mounted on the top of the dashboard, an airspeed indicator, a clock, and a simplified type of directional gyro added to the complexity. There was also a mixture control to lean out the gasoline, usually used when cruising over 3,500 feet, and an RPM gauge. P.G. remembered that Taylor suggested he always watch the manifold pressure, because if it drops, the pilot is in big trouble. A manifold pressure gauge measures the actual pressure in the engine manifold in millimeters of mercury and reflects a healthy engine performance. If the carburetor starts to ice up at a high altitude, the engine may start to run rough, but if the manifold pressure drops, the pilot had better start looking for a place to set the plane down.

Since P.G. was in the morning instruction group, he was at the line at 6:30 A.M. He checked the flight board to see what plane he was assigned to fly and went out and stood by the plane.

When Taylor arrived he squinted at Grant and asked, "Have you checked the airplane over?"

"Not completely," he replied. He really didn't know what to look for.

"Well, your life is going to depend on how well you check your aircraft. What goes up comes down and sometimes it comes down like a rock in peculiar places," he said as he smiled.

"I looked at the prop and it looks O.K. It doesn't look like it's been nicked or cracked."

Taylor had his hands on his hips, waiting patiently as he took the rookie through the drill. "Did you check to see if the gas gauges register full? And, did you check the oil level and the engine mounts?"

P.G. hesitated and finally answered, "No."

"Sometimes a hard landing can injure the engine mounts. This is an important area to check for damage. You also have to check to see that the ailerons, elevators, and rudders move well. What you do is move the stick around and press on the rudder pedals and watch the wings to see that the controls work properly before you start the engine. Got it?"

"Yes."

"Okay, cadet. Remove the chocks from in front of the wheels and let's get into the airplane."

P.G. and his instructor climbed into the Piper Cub, put their seat belts on, and checked the movement of the plane's controls.

"Look around and make sure no one is near the propeller when you turn on the ignition switch," warned Jim. "You should crack the throttle forward a little bit, and then turn the key to start the engine. If the engine doesn't sound right, you can down-check the aircraft and tell the mechanics to fix it. Remember, your life depends on that engine pushing that propeller around as you fly. Any questions?" asked Jim.

"Yes," answered P.G.. "For starters, how do you turn these instruments on, and what do you use for settings?"

"There's a little knob on the side of the artificial horizon that you turn on. The rpm gauge has to be set for warm-up and the oil pressure gauge checked to make sure it has come up to the green normal range. Remember that," said the instructor. "I'll taxi the plane down to the end of the field. Take a look at the windsock on the roof of the hangar to determine which way the wind is blowing and then turn the plane into the wind.

"Once a pilot gets down to the end of the field for takeoff, facing the wind, he locks his brakes, revs up the engine, and checks the mags. To make sure the duel magneto system is working, he switches from "both" to left, then back to "both," and then to the right."

Taylor paused, then continued. "If the electrical system is not working properly and the engine fuel is firing improperly, the engine can cut out, and the pilot has a real problem. That's why the duel magneto electrical system is a backup system. If the plane's engine drops off more than 100 rpm in either mag, the pilot takes the plane back to the hangar, or he'll be landing it in a cornfield somewhere, if he's lucky. If the mags check out all right, the plane is ready to fly," Jim explained further. "When you get to the end of the runway, be sure to look around to see if any planes are coming in to land. A landing plane has priority over a takeoff plane. Okay, we're all set and ready for takeoff." Jim pushed the throttle forward and as the power increased, the engine roared and the wings began to quiver. As the airspeed increased, the plane started to bounce and the wheels left the ground. They flew off into the blue sky.

In the Piper Cub plane used for training, there were dual controls so that cadets could follow the instructor through the maneuvers as he took off and landed the plane. This way the instructor taught the young trainee how to climb and glide the plane and how to handle engine failures, set the throttle, and lean out the fuel.

Eventually, the instructor would allow the cadet pilot to land the plane, although the instructor would still be on the dual controls. He would also allow the cadet to take off. When the cadet pushed the throttle forward, he noticed a tendency for the nose of the plane to move slightly to the left; the torque of the propeller caused this because the propeller turns in a clockwise direction.

After three or four flight lessons, the instructor took his hands off the stick and his feet off the rudders and allowed the novice pilot to take the plane up. At this point, the cadet pilots experienced a lot of apprehension. When his instructor did this, P.G.'s first thought was, "Taylor must have a death wish." And on the heels of that he thought, "Maybe I do, too," and shoved the throttle forward. His plane seemed to go to the left and started heading for some trees.

Taylor didn't move. "Shit, I'm going to hit those trees and he's not going to do a damn thing to help me," thought P.G. "I've got to stop this thing."

He hit the right rudder and the plane swerved back toward the center as the plane gained airspeed. It suddenly leaped into the air as he slowly pulled back on the stick.

"Easy as we go," said Taylor, "you're not milking a cow." As the plane started to climb, he said, "Make a gentle left turn at 400 feet. Never make a sharp turn at a low altitude. When you reach 1000 feet, make a gentle ten-degree bank to the right and take the plane out to the practice area. I'm going to give you some compass headings and I want you to hold to them.

"Fly 15 degrees east," he said. After a pause, "Now 30 degrees west. Hold your compass heading. I want you to make a 180-degree turn next." P.G. did as he was told. "That's pretty good," responded the instructor to his movements of the plane. "What do you think about the sound of the engine?"

"It sounds a little rough," P.G. responded, as he looked at the throttle adjustment. Taylor had leaned out the gas and had pulled the throttle back somewhat. "I think we should put the throttle back on rich," said P.G.

"Good!" said Jim. "Always listen to the sound of the engine. It should have a constant hum. Okay, let's get back to the airport."

The next day he and his instructor spent an hour and a half in the air. He made 15 landings, each followed by a comment from his instructor.

"Watch the nose of the plane closer when you land. It's better to come in a little fast than too slow." Grant felt that Taylor was particularly hard on him, always correcting and giving compliments infrequently. When they got back to the airport, the instructor said, "Leave the engine on. I'm getting out. It's all yours. Take the plane up, but don't spend longer than 30 minutes in the air. Try a couple of stalls at 6,000 feet and be careful."

"Goddamn," he whispered to himself. "He's got more confidence in me than I have in myself." He felt a cold sweat break out over his face and he had a strange sensation in the pit of his stomach. "This is a life-or-death situation," he thought. He didn't have to worry about defecating because his sphincters were tighter than a hawk's asshole in a nose dive. He gulped a few times. His breathing increased and his pulse was pounding. What if the engine conked out?

He knew his biggest problem was pushing the throttle forward, but as he did he realized he wasn't going to end up in the trees. When the plane became airborne, and he was up to 6,000 feet, he suddenly realized how beautiful the sky and countryside were. He decided to try some turns and glides to get the feel of the plane, and finally got up enough nerve to even stall the plane. He was quick to recover, however, and after flying for 45 minutes, he flew the plane back to the airport. He was amazed that he remembered all the compass headings and brought the plane in with a perfect landing.

Taylor was waiting for him at the hangar. "Okay, P.G., you did a good job." He had soloed, and it felt good.

3

It Isn't All Peaches and Cream

That night in the barracks, P.G. was dozing when he felt four pairs of hands clamp down on his arms and ankles. He panicked, his body thrashing, as the hands lifted him from his cot. Then he realized his captors were heading for the showers to administer a ritual soaking—he was the first in the group to solo, after just seven hours of instruction. "You sons of bitches," he howled as they turned on the spigot, "you're no better than the Japs!" After he was sopping wet, P.G. sat laughing in the shower with the cadets. "Thanks, fellas," he said. "But remember, payback's a bitch." The next night he helped soak four other cadets to balance the scales.

News of John Kelly and his airplane crash quickly brought the group back to reality. Cleared for solo by his instructor, Kelly had no difficulty in taking off, but when he returned to the field, he came in too hot, overshooting the grass runway. Instead of taking off again and going around for another attempt at landing, he cut the throttle, put on his brakes, and crashed into the trees at the end of the field. He was taken to the local hospital and then transferred to a larger hospital in Little Rock, Arkansas, for more intensive care. One of the cadets who witnessed the accident said Kelly was unconscious when the medics put him in the ambulance. The only good news was the plane did not burn up. In a bad crash, aviation fuel is usually thrown all over the place, and the heat of the engine or the impact of the crash ignites the fuel.

That night the cadets, sitting around the barracks, were quite concerned about their buddy. Would he make it? And if he did survive, would he be thrown out of the program?

The next day, as P.G. stood before his plane, he was surrounded by thoughts of John Kelly. What had caused the accident? Why Kelly? Were the planes safe, or were the cadets some kind of guinea pigs? He went through the check-off list very carefully.

The wreck of Kelly's plane hadn't been taken out of the trees because a Navy Investigation Board was coming to review the events that had led to the crash.

The cadets could not put the accident out of their minds, for it was still in sight. Seeing the plane broken up in the trees, with one wing off and the motor hanging out, was a grim reminder of the unexpected tragedies that can occur. "There but for the grace of God, go I," P.G. mused as he flew by.

A few days later the damaged aircraft was removed from the trees and put in the hangar to be inspected by the Navy Investigation Board. The cadets heard that Kelly had regained consciousness but had several broken bones and internal injuries. The Board would question Kelly to see what happened and would interrogate the instructor who cleared Kelly for solo flight. Flight operations at the base would be scrutinized. This was the routine procedure followed when any serious airplane accident occurred. As a result of the accident, the crash and fire equipment at the field were upgraded.

During the next three weeks, the instructors flew with the cadets every fourth flight to evaluate their progress. They also intensified the navigation course and after about 20 hours of solo time the instructors scheduled a short cross-country flight for each of the cadets. P.G. prepared to fly to the naval base at Millington in Memphis, Tennessee.

"Get your flight maps out, and compute the distance, flight speed, time of arrival, and possible gas consumption tonight, so we can get off early and be back in the afternoon," said Taylor as he left him the day before his excursion.

That evening, he worked on navigation for the trip. He knew that he and his instructor, Jim Taylor, would be flying a Piper Cub with a radio communication system to assist in landing at the navy base in

Memphis. Calculating the time of arrival with different airspeeds and wind directions had to be done before his arrival at the flight line at dawn. Numbers and calculations did not intimidate P.G.; he enjoyed this part of the preparation.

In class that afternoon, the instructor began by emphasizing the importance and practicality of navigational skills. "Look at each other," he said. "You are a select group of student cadets. You have been given the opportunity to become naval aviators. It is going to cost the government thousands of dollars to teach you to fly. You will be quite different from the Army Air Corps Cadets, because some of you will become carrier pilots and will be flying over water and landing airplanes on the decks of carriers. You will have to be proficient in navigation skills. There won't be a big land base for you to set down on if you run out of fuel; all you have is the ocean with sharks in it looking for dumb pilots.

"This is the most important course you will be taking as you go through flight school. I want you all to get 4.0s, because all you need is one mistake in hitting Point Option, and you're in big trouble."

"Remember the plane flies in different directions at high speeds; but also remember the carrier down below moves in different directions as well. Sometimes radio silence cannot be broken, and you have to get back to the carrier with only your navigational skills. I'm not trying to scare you, I'm just trying to keep you informed. Graduate Naval Air Cadets are the best pilots in the world, because they are pilots and navigators. If you stick with it, you can become one of those elite." The instructor paused to let his message sink in.

"Now, here's a little dictum that all navy pilots should know: Never fly down a railroad track."

"Why?" asked one of the cadets.

"Because you'll have a head-on collision, that's why; an Army Air Corps plane will be coming in the opposite direction, completely lost, because the pilot doesn't know his navigation. The only way those dumb army pilots can find their way home is to follow the railroad tracks." Suddenly there was a burst of laughter.

The next morning, P.G. was at the flight line at dawn. He performed his routine preflight check of the plane. Before taking off, the instructor told him that he would allow him to call the control tower in Memphis when they came close so he could determine whether he could enter the landing pattern without any trouble.

The plane's takeoff was uneventful. He and Taylor decided to fly to Memphis at 3,500 feet so they could see the city of Memphis and some of the sights. It was not a long flight, about 145 miles one way. They had to cross the Mississippi River to get to the naval air station, so they had a good reference point. Visibility was unlimited, and they saw Memphis and the river come into view, sprawling over the southern flatlands.

"You'd better radio Millington Tower and ask how they want us to approach the field," said the instructor.

"Millington Tower, Millington Tower, this is Navy AST 56 approaching the field. Request landing instructions," he radioed.

"Navy AST 56, this is Millington Tower. Identify yourself. We do not have your flight plan."

"Millington Tower, this is Navy AST 56, we are a Piper Cub from Arkansas State Teacher's College Preflight Program," he responded, wondering if they would turn him away.

"Navy AST 56, this is Millington Tower. Prevailing wind is from the west at 12 knots. You are cleared to enter landing pattern. Beware of other planes entering the pattern."

"Roger, Millington Tower," said P.G., feeling more like a responsible pilot than a fledgling cadet. But when he looked down at the Millington Air Field, he became confused. No runway went east to west or north to south as they did on the field he was used to, but instead a large asphalt circle with runway additions like the spokes of a wheel covered the ground.

Sensing his momentary confusion, Taylor interrupted his thoughts. "Take her into the wind and land her in the circle."

He did as he was instructed and made a perfect landing. "That was nice," said Jim. "Taxi up in front of the tower and we'll have the plane tied down. They have a good dining hall here. I'll buy you dinner, then we'll gas her up and head back home."

They ate in the officers' dining hall, where the food and service were good, much better than the usual slop he survived on as a cadet. Late that afternoon they flew back to Arkansas and landed just before sundown. Before they landed, Taylor spoke out of a long silence: "Sundown is one of the most dangerous times to land an airplane. Your eyes aren't adapted to the darkness, and you can have a rough time seeing. It's also more difficult to see other planes in the area, so you should be extra cautious."

"Thanks."

The next week, he worked with his instructor on airport patterns.

Most airports use left-hand patterns, he learned. He was taught the correct way to approach a strange airport. He soon learned that not all airports are the same; some are much larger than others and some more sophisticated. Other airports are like cow pastures and have small runways. He learned how runways are numbered. For example, Runway 260 means 260 degrees on the compass.

When approaching an airport, the pilot requests landing instructions, and is told which runway to land on and which way the wind is coming from. He usually circles the airport first and enters the traffic pattern on the downwind leg, which means the plane is running with the wind and parallel to the runway he is going to land on. He then turns into the second leg of the landing, the base leg, at almost 90 degrees. The wind plays a role in blowing the plane further downwind. The final approach is made when the plane is lined up with the runway for landing and the motor power is diminished gently so the plane descends slowly and lands on the runway.

Jim Taylor reviewed this pattern repeatedly with him, and every time they landed the plane, he emphasized landing it smoothly and deliberately. He also advised him to move his eyes from the side of the plane to the front to get a sense of depth perception so that he wouldn't try to land the plane up in the clouds or knock off the landing gear by coming in too low.

Taylor told him that he felt that the most hazardous times in flying were on takeoff and landing. "If a power failure occurs at takeoff, you should land directly ahead; if you try to turn around with no power on, you'll spin the airplane in." Taylor emphasized that landing could also be extremely dangerous because the plane's power was being reduced: "Don't be afraid to go around again if your calculations are off. Pride does not make a good pilot. Pour the throttle to the firewall and make another pass." P.G. sensed a finality in what this man was telling him, as if this was parting advice.

When they landed, Taylor squared with Grant and said, "You're cleared for preflight school. Good luck. I think you'll make a good pilot, Grant. I like a lot of what I see in you. You're steady on the stick and you've got good vision. And you've got something else, but I'm not sure what to call it. It's a feel for the air. You seem to be able to anticipate the next movement of the plane, and I've never seen that in a fledgling cadet. I hope I'm not wrong about you."

"You're not," said P.G. They shook hands and then P.G. took off to celebrate.

Of the original 60 cadets who had entered the class with him, only 42 made it to the next stage. Not everyone was celebrating.

That evening when he lay on his bunk, he thought about his experience learning to fly. He realized that flying an airplane can be mind-boggling. How do you make quick decisions while flying at high speeds? What happens to your reflexes if you're too tired? What if you don't remember the rules of the road? He wasn't too sure about the planes he was flying. Some of the aircraft equipment didn't look very good. What if the equipment is bad or is damaged or worn out? The human body wears out and dies; how about the plane's engine or parts?

The next morning, he and the remaining cadets got on a bus to Little Rock, Arkansas. When they got to the railroad station, he picked up some newspapers, magazines, and sandwiches; and boarded the train for the 500-mile trip to Athens, Georgia. On the train, he looked at the Arkansas newspaper first and as he read he was startled by what he saw. The headlines announced that Admiral Yamamoto, the architect of the Pearl Harbor attack, had been killed.

The Army Air Corps, flying new twin-engine P-38 fighter planes, called "Lightnings," had flown 400 miles from Henderson Field at Guadalcanal to Bouganville for an intercept. Admiral Yamamoto was flying from Rabaul to Bruin in the Shortland Islands on an inspection tour. He was in a sleek, new Japanese Betty, the fastest Japanese bomber available, and had an escort of six Zeros. The ambush took place at 9:34 A.M. on April 18, 1943, and Admiral Yamamoto's Betty bomber was shot down by the American P-38 Lightnings.

Peter wondered about the extent of the damage to the Japanese high command. Admiral Yamamoto was the Commander in Chief of the Japanese Fleet. He was the individual given credit for the surprise attack on Pearl Harbor and for the capture of many Pacific islands and the Philippines. He virtually was a god to the Japanese military hierarchy.

P.G. slowly read the article, then stood up and hollered, "Hey fellas, they finally got the bastard responsible for Pearl Harbor!"

"Who are you talking about?" asked Jesse, one of the cadets.

"They shot down Admiral Yamamoto in the Pacific," said P.G.

"Who the hell is he?" asked Jesse.

"He's the top man in the Japanese Navy," said P.G.

"There'll be a lot of cheering in our navy high command now," said one of the cadets. "They finally got the son-of-a-bitch!"

"Admiral Halsey and Admiral Mitscher would have given their left nuts to get that guy," said another.

"Well, they got their revenge. I wonder if there will be enough of the war left for us to fight?" asked Jesse.

"I wouldn't worry about that," said P.G., "some other Japanese admiral will take his place."

"Their morale has got to be affected by his loss," said Jesse.

"Not much," said John Canfield, another cadet. "They're fanatics."

"Well, the Jap deserved what he got," said Jesse. "He authorized a sneak attack on Pearl Harbor without a declaration of war. He's considered an outlaw among civilized nations. I'm sure he understood that he was fair game for what he did. He got what was coming to him. Good riddance!"

4

Preflight School in Georgia

Ninety-five-degree heat from the oppressive July sun welcomed the cadets as the group arrived for their preflight training at the University of Georgia in Athens. The cadets were issued khaki uniforms with officer epaulettes and given officer-like caps. It was quite obvious their status had been upgraded. Marine sergeants and shore patrol personnel covered the base.

The new group of cadets was divided into rookie squads. Once again a complete physical examination was done, and measurements of all areas of the body were taken. It quickly became evident to the cadets that the emphases at this preflight school were to be physical fitness, strict discipline, and regimentation. Most of the officers in charge of training the naval air cadets were former college athletic directors who had been given officer status, such as lieutenant or lieutenant-commander. There were also one or two Annapolis graduates who were supervisors.

To the cadets, the first week of preflight school was a living hell. Reveille was blared at sunup, a decidedly different way to say "time to get up." Cadet Orson Miller didn't feel like answering the call of dawn his second morning of school, and that turned out to be a big mistake.

"Boy," a marine sergeant bellowed, "what in the hell are you doing?"

Miller obviously took too long to answer, because the question was punctuated by the whack of a wooden board across the bottom of the cadet's feet. The sergeant then moved to the side of Miller's bunk.

"Boy, it's almost noon!"

With that, the cadet tried to scramble out of bed. Too late. The sergeant grabbed the frame of the bed and flipped it, pinning Miller underneath.

"Now, boy, the next time you hear that horn, what are you going to do?"

"Mmmph," came the muffled reply.

The sergeant stepped on the overturned bunk and pressed down. "I can't hear you."

"Mmmph."

The sergeant pressed harder on the overturned bunk mattress. "Louder."

"MMMPH."

"Shit," muttered the sergeant, "someone teach this boy to speak English."

With that, the sergeant took his foot off the bunk, gave it a swift kick and marched out. Cadet Orson Miller never slept through another reveille.

That demonstration in front of the cadets revealed that there was a toughness to the marines that no cadet would dream of testing.

After a quick brush of teeth, a shave, and possibly a shower, cadets ran out for company lineup in front of their barracks. Combing hair was unnecessary because there was no hair to comb—everyone had a butch.

After sounding off for muster to make sure that everyone was present and accounted for, each man marched with his company to the mess hall. Southern military breakfasts were interesting in that there were no choices. Men were served either eggs or pancakes or oatmeal with or without grits, but none of that mattered because it all tasted the same. After a week of swimming and running for many miles, the food took on some flavor, and very little was left on the plates. Grant even learned to like grits.

Physical training began immediately, whipping the men into top condition. Timed runs, including the 100-yard dash, 440 meters, and the mile took place, and cadets were given a time they had to achieve in order to successfully complete the program. The pressure to perform was real. At the end of each week, stopwatches were brought out and times were recorded.

Since this was a navy organization, every cadet had to learn to swim, one of the toughest obstacles to overcome. Each man was required to remain in the water, swimming constantly, for more than an hour; if a cadet tried to put his hands on the side of the pool, the marine sergeant would discourage him by stepping on his fingers. They were told the swimming part of their training would increase and get more difficult as their courses progressed, for a naval air cadet had to learn all the strokes; freestyle, breast stroke, backstroke, and side stroke. They also had to learn how to rescue another seaman. Ways to use clothes to help stay afloat were demonstrated—filling pants or a shirt with air to help support each man's body. The hardest tests were treading water with clothes on for 40 to 60 minutes, swimming a mile, and jumping off a 35-foot platform.

The obstacle course was also difficult. Cadets had to climb ropes over large fences, jump over hurdles, and crawl on their bellies under wire while live ammunition was sprayed over their heads. The swimming part of the course was the most difficult for P.G. He had never learned to swim, and each cadet was expected to keep up with the squad regardless of his level of expertise. Only motivation and determination made him pass all the tests.

Wrestling and boxing were integral parts of training an air cadet as well. P.G. thought this method of training was unfair. The men were told to line up, and the squad leader would say, "Right turn, hup." The man each cadet faced was the man he wrestled. A 135-pound cadet might have to wrestle a 230-pounder. Scoring depended upon pinning the individual and the amount of time it took to do so. Although the marine sergeants said they would eventually be separated by weight and the winner in each class recognized and rewarded, that never happened. In the gym in Georgia, in the middle of August, the temperature ran as high as 104° F. The men still had to wrestle. The gym was stuffy, and the importance of showering became clear. The navy didn't issue deodorant.

Boxing was another ballbreaker. The only saving grace was that cadets had to wear leather headgear which, although it stank from overuse, protected noses from being flattened by bigger or stronger opponents. Low blows were also prohibited. The smart guys always pulled their boxing shorts up as high as possible to avoid them. Still, low belly blows and knockouts occurred even with the leather head-gear, rules, and hiked-up shorts. Heavy gloves were also part of the uniform, but they still hurt on impact and didn't prevent the occasional knockout.

Leadership qualities were continually being assessed by the commanding officers, and inspections of uniforms, shoes, and nails were monitored closely by the marine sergeants. After a couple of weeks, squad leaders were chosen, and P.G. was selected. Although a squad is the smallest military unit, usually made up of ten men, he was moving in the right direction. Someone thought he might be a leader. He decided to keep working hard. Leading beat the hell out of following.

The intensity of the competition increased markedly after a few weeks. When the rookies had completed half the program, the base commandant announced that the top 10 percent of the cadets would be given five days' leave upon completion of the preflight program before reporting to E Base in Memphis, Tennessee. The five days' leave was quite a motivator, and it became dog-eat-dog after that.

The difficulty of the physical tests was matched by that of the academic courses. Navigation in particular was emphasized, and all sorts of problems were presented when Point Option moved from one location to another. Wind and air speed changed, and estimated gas consumption and time of arrival had to be recalculated. Grant's mathematical ability proved invaluable for this subject; he had very few problems with the navigation course. He finished near the top of his class in navigation, and he would often be called upon in the barracks to help some of the cadets. He did this willingly; these were his buddies.

Aerology was also important in the naval air cadet courses. There were no weather stations out in the stretches of the ocean, and if bad weather came up, the pilot's interpretation of the conditions was a crucial determinant of his survival. Pilots developed a healthy respect for weather and its variations. For example, wind velocity changed depending on the height of flight. Whitecaps on the sea assisted in determining the direction of the wind. Types of clouds, such as cumulus, cirrus, and cumulonimbus gave some clue to the approaching weather or a possible squall line.

Courses in gunnery using live ammunition and courses in aircraft recognition were also taught. The latter helped pilots differentiate American planes from those of the Japanese. Ground school courses in Morse radio code, blinker lights for signaling messages in flashes, and semaphore, a system of signaling by the use of flags, were included along with seamanship and the essentials of naval services and first aid.

In ground school, the cadets were told that they would have to become experts in instrument flying because of the unpredictability of weather when flying over the vast expanses of the ocean. Being on instruments for as long as ten hours at a time would be necessary.

This was immediately questioned by one of the cadets. "I thought they had automatic pilots that you could switch on in the new navy planes?"

"That's true, cadet," said Elmer, the instructor, "but if the automatic pilot doesn't work or if you have to fly instruments on your own for any length of time, you better know how to do it. Turn the instruments on, too. A cadet got killed recently at Whiting Field in Pensacola, Florida, in bad weather, and when investigators examined the aircraft, they found the cadet had forgotten to turn on the artificial horizon. He tried to fly by the seat of his pants in bad weather and spun in."

P.G. remembered his first flight instructor in Arkansas telling him about that.

"All cadets who graduate will train in a general aviation simulator trainer. In these flight simulators, you learn how to fly using instruments."

A cadet raised his hand and asked, "How can the instructor tell if you're flying those simulators properly?"

"A graph of the entire flight is made and it records how the pilot responds. If the pilot makes a lot of mistakes, it's right there on the tape."

"Are we checked out in instrument flying any other way?" asked another cadet.

"Of course," said the instructor. "You'll fly real airplanes on instruments. The instructor will sit in the front cockpit and the cadet in the rear. A canvas hood will be pulled over the cadet's cockpit so that he can't see outside for orientation and then the instructor will place the plane in an unusual attitude. The cadet will then have to use his instruments to straighten the plane out."

"Mr. Baker, what do you mean by that?"

"It means that when the weather and visibility are good, the eyes and ears help the pilot to fly the aircraft in the right attitude. In bad weather, or flying at night, the pilot's eyes are not as helpful, so he needs instruments to keep the plane properly oriented in space."

"Sounds tough," remarked one of the cadets.

"It is," said the instructor, "but it's a hell of a lot easier than swimming 20 miles back to your carrier in the middle of the Pacific Ocean because you couldn't figure out how to get back in a storm. You'll have to get a real feel for flying the plane on instruments. You will also have to possess complete faith in what your instruments tell you. At first, when you try instrument flying, you'll find that you wildly over-control, ending up in dives, stalls, steep banks, and even spins. When that happens, go back to your ground schooling and study the basic artificial horizon, directional gyro, and other instruments. Once you gain confidence in instrument flying you'll be a better pilot. It could save your life someday.

"If there's any doubt about the weather or approaching weather, don't hesitate to go on instruments. Also watch the altimeter, and if you're flying in unfamiliar territory, don't hesitate to go to a higher altitude to avoid an obstacle that may be in your path. Fortunately, in the navy you'll be over the ocean most of the time, but not all your flying experience will be over the water."

His answers were greeted with absolute silence. He had total command of his listeners, for whenever flying was discussed in the classroom, the attention span of the cadets increased. They were all trying to learn how to fly; any tips to help make them better pilots were greatly appreciated, for becoming a naval aviator was not just a patriotic exercise. It had become a personal challenge for each cadet.

Two weeks before the end of P.G.'s preflight training program, he was presented with an unexpected scare. The barracks sergeant called him into his office and told him to report to the commandant's office. His heart started to pound. Usually, being called to the commandant's office meant disciplinary action, or failure in one of the courses, or possible probationary status. He searched his mind to try to remember where he might have gone wrong. His class grades were good. He passed all his athletic tests, except that he wasn't the greatest swimmer in the world. What could he have done wrong?

When he arrived at the commandant's office, the marine sentry told him that Captain Perkins was waiting for him. P.G. entered the office, came sharply to attention, and saluted the captain.

"At ease, Cadet," said Captain Perkins. He noted the apprehension on P.G.'s face. "The news is either good or bad depending upon how you interpret it." Somehow, that statement did not soothe P.G. or his pounding heart.

"Cadet Grant, Cadet Captain Bill Johnson broke his leg on the obstacle course today. He'll be out of the program for four to six months. You've been selected to lead your company, Company K. I know it's kind of unfair to you because the company competition in parade marching for the battalion flag and banner is in one week. The winners of the competition get an extra five-day vacation between bases."

"I know that, sir. When do I take command?"

"Tomorrow morning at reveille."

"Can I tell the men why I've been selected?"

"Of course. You'll be allowed to practice two evenings after dinner since you have not had command of Company K. Good luck to you. We have a retired admiral who will be reviewing the battalion in two weeks; he'll select the winning company."

He saluted the captain and left. "Great!" he thought. "An admiral is coming to review and judge the competition and there are only two weeks to get the company ready. How the hell am I going to get those guys to recognize my voice commands in that short time? Will they respect my authority?" The pressure of leadership set upon P.G. He could feel it in his chest, his gut, and his shoulders.

That night in the barracks, P.G. called the cadets of Company K together. "Each one of you birdmen is going to learn your right foot from your left foot in the next two weeks. I've been assigned to take over Company K in the morning. I want to win that battalion banner for all of us and for that guy who broke his leg. I think you all appreciate that we'll get five days' extra leave if we win. We've been given two extra evenings to practice so you can recognize my commands. We're going to win. I've given it a lot of thought. Here's how: We're going to do our whole marching program for the admiral without a command from me. That means you won't have to learn my voice commands. If one of you goofs up, it will be your own mistake. That means you're going to have to memorize each move and lock it in your brains. We're going to do some razzle-dazzle too, and we're going to make it look like a walk in the park.

"Tonight we start. We'll outline what we're going to do. Each one of you will be given a sheet to memorize. Thursday and Friday nights we'll practice until sundown, if necessary. We'll also be going over the marching formation in the barracks every night. I'll use spoken commands so the rest of the companies don't know what we're up to. If any of you give the secret away, it'll be the last thing you do! A week from Sunday is graduation, and Saturday night is the military ball. Let's go to both as winners!"

After he had outlined their marching pattern, their use of rifles, standing at attention, and splitting off into different patterns, he knew there was bound to be some complaints—and there were. The complainers were shouted down, however, because the cadets all wanted those extra five days for fun and frolic.

One of the cadets got a coed to type copies of the complex marching plan to hand out to the cadets in Company K, and that Thursday and Friday they marched in formation until midnight. Observing Company K's extra marching and their seriousness, the other cadets thought they were being disciplined by the commandant.

There was a bit of illegal betting between some of the companies as to which company would win, and Company K, with a new captain, was picked for the bottom of the heap. With bets set and dress uniforms on, the cadets welcomed the day of the competition. Each company was given five minutes to demonstrate their marching abilities. Company K was the last company to perform. P.G. started Company K's performance by giving one order, "Company K, perform."

For the next five minutes Company K marched without a sound being issued by the company commander. They did the silent march without a flaw. It was eerie to watch the entire company march through intricate maneuvers without a command. They moved forward, and then turned sharply to the left. They moved rapidly through three changes in direction, and headed past the review stand. When it was all over, the admiral in the reviewing stand turned to the commandant and said, "I see you saved the best for last. Company K wins the competition hands down. Hell, they put on a show as good as our Annapolis cadets. Commandant, I want to meet the cadet captain of Company K."

"You will," said the commandant. "The battalion commander will announce the winners. They will present arms in front of you to accept the banner and then will pass in review."

Peter Grant smiled softly to himself as he turned to his troops. There was one thought in all their minds—Ah, a five-day vacation.

5

The Military Ball

There was a further attrition of Naval Air Cadets at the Georgia Preflight School. About 10 percent of the cadets did not graduate from the program. Their failure was usually due to physical defects, such as eye problems, obesity, or inability to complete the various physical tests, such as the obstacle course, running, swimming, climbing ropes, or push-ups. A few cadets were lost because of academic problems. The navigation course was usually their undoing.

Every three months, a military ball was held for the graduating cadets. White dress uniforms with gold epaulettes were worn, and the cadets were allowed to remain out until 2:00 A.M. They were cautioned to be naval gentlemen at all times, because a choice group of young female coeds from the University of Georgia usually signed up to be the companions for the evening. Some of the officer's daughters and volunteers from the Atlanta area colleges completed the group.

Each graduating cadet drew a number that was assigned to a coed, whom he would escort for the evening. The marine sergeant in charge of the barracks gave out the numbers. Since this was an ongoing project—it happened every three months—the sergeant knew some of the young ladies. When a cadet approached him about his date for the evening his replies were sometimes helpful, sometimes cryptic: "She's a bombshell. I'm not sure you'll be able to handle that tiger." Or, "She's the sweetest girl this side of the Mississippi." Or, "She's the fastest roller-skater in the South."

"What the hell does that mean?" the cadet would ask.

The sergeant would smile and say, "It means that none of the cadets have been able to catch that doll yet."

The night of the dance, there was a different odor prevalent in the barracks. The shower room was overcrowded, new underwear had been purchased, and aftershave lotions and colognes made the barracks smell like a French whorehouse. All the cadets had fresh haircuts, shoes were brilliantly shined, and uniforms were spotless. There were also some bets placed as to which cadet would end up with the best-looking girl, since a queen of the ball was to be selected at the end of the dance. Some of the cadets were switching numbers—which was perfectly legal prior to the dance.

"Hey, Maynard, give me that roller-skater, fat boy. I'll track her down."

"Okay," Maynard replied. "I'll trade."

"Jones, number 21 is a dog. It's a bad luck number. I'll trade you right now," said Cadet Roberts.

"What's your number?" asked Jones.

"My number? Why it's . . . uh . . . 13," Roberts responded.

"Forget it!"

"Hey, Kelly, are you really going to wear those shorts? You look like a goddamned fairy. Do you plan to take your pants off on the dance floor?"

"No, but maybe I will later in the evening."

"Lucky, lucky seven, boys, lucky, lucky seven. I got the good number. What am I bid for it?"

"I hear she's five-by-five," said Petrofsky. "Count me out."

The shouting and chattering went on right up until it was time to head to the gymnasium. The cadets marched as a batallion, and entered the gym in squads. The young ladies were already lined up. Each one had her number on the side of her dress. They all wore corsages of gardenias, camelias, or other flowers of the South. The cadets fidgeted nervously, almost afraid to see who was wearing a matching number.

The numbers that were given out to the cadets were based on

their class standing. P.G. had number 37, which meant that he had earned a five-day vacation. The top 75 of the 750 cadets were to get the vacations.

The cadets' anticipation was overwhelming. They were like a bunch of young horses that had been in the barn too long. The air was electric as they approached the young belles. Necks craned. Eyes popped. P.G. was lucky. Wearing number 37 was a beautiful redhead with bright green eyes. She was slender and athletic looking, in a green strapless evening gown that left little to the imagination. She greeted him with a big smile and a kiss on the cheek.

"Daddy told me you were a handsome cadet," she said. "My daddy is the executive officer of the base. I'm Sarah Tomkins, and I already know your name."

"Oh, shit. Now I have to behave," thought P.G. He felt his heart sink. "Of all the rotten luck. Why do these things have to happen to me?"

His date must have seen the look of disappointment on his face. "Relax, P.G.," said Sarah. "Daddy told me to have a good time, and I plan to, after seeing you. I'm a Georgia peach and my family has lived in Georgia for three generations. Where are you from?"

Things were moving right along. "I'm from Connecticut. That makes me a Connecticut Yankee, I know, but I'm from the southern part of Connecticut." He smiled. "Would you like to dance?"

"Love to." The band was playing a Glenn Miller piece called "Chattanooga Choo Choo."

He and Sarah danced well together; they did some jitterbugging and slow foxtrot dancing. Sarah obviously knew how to dance and enjoyed it. She cuddled up on the slow pieces such as "I'll Be Seeing You" and "Begin the Beguine" and "String of Pearls." The body contact improved as the music progressed.

Some of the cadets wanted to switch partners between songs because some girls were prettier than others. It was obvious to P.G. that Sarah was in everyone's sights. She was a knockout. The band played a few group dances in which Sarah danced in the crowd, and it was obvious she enjoyed all the attention she was receiving.

At intermission refreshments were served, and there were two different punch bowls. One was spiked and one was not. P.G. opted for the spiked punch, which was made with champagne and fruit juice. Sarah reached for the unspiked punch, and glanced coyly at

P.G. "I want to have a level head for the rest of the evening," she murmured.

"You can't leave until the chaperoning officers leave at twelve midnight," said Sarah. "The band plays until 1:30 A.M. and the cadets have to be in their bunks by 2:00 A.M."

"That doesn't leave too much time for us to have some privacy," he said. "Do I get to take you home?"

"Of course," said Sarah. "I'm looking forward to it. I live on the campus. However, you're one of the lucky cadets." She smiled, her green eyes flashing and her beautiful white teeth showing. "I've got a red convertible outside and we'll sneak out around 11:30." His heart started to pound in anticipation.

"I'm ready right now."

"Don't be too anxious," she said. The band started to play again and they went back on the dance floor. It was a South American rumba, and Sarah danced seductively to the beat. Very few of the cadets were familiar with the rumba, and as the music increased in intensity, most of the cadets and their escorts dropped out. Soon there were only a few couples on the floor, with a large group of interested observers.

Sarah enjoyed being the center of attention. She led P.G. through some of the more difficult maneuvers, and soon they were dancing by themselves. Finally the music stopped and there was a burst of applause.

"You're a great dancer," said P.G.

"You are too," said Sarah. "I think we're going to get along just fine."

He was surprised how friendly and warm Sarah was toward him. He heard that southern belles had to be "sweet talked" and courted delicately if you wanted to get to know them. Sarah was much different from what he expected.

Around 11:00 Sarah started cuddling up even closer. The lights had been dimmed and she pressed her body against his thighs as she danced. At the end of one of the dances, she pulled him closer to her and gave him a warm lingering kiss. When they separated, he looked directly into her sparkling green eyes.

"I like that," he responded. "I really like that!"

"Why don't we leave the dance floor and see what else you really might like?" she suggested.

"We're not supposed to leave until midnight."

"I know a back way out. My car's parked behind the gymnasium."

"Sounds good to me."

They went to where the restrooms were and went out the back door of the gym. When they got into her car she gave him another long kiss. She finally started the car and drove until they got to the gates where a marine sentry stopped them. "Do you have a pass to leave the base?" he asked.

"I'm Sarah Tomkins, the executive officer's daughter," she replied.

"Okay," said the marine sentry, "but get that cadet back on the base by 2:00 A.M. or he's AWOL."

"I'll be sure and do that," she replied, and smiled. She drove for about ten minutes and turned up a dark, winding road. "Let's get out of the car," she said. "Grab the car blanket."

"I can't remember when I've enjoyed a dance as much as this one," said Sarah. "I wish I'd met you sooner. Will you be coming back to Georgia? You're the type of man I could fall in love with."

He, on the other hand, was thinking other thoughts. "Oh, boy. I think I hit the jackpot." They spread the blanket out under the blue Georgia sky and she slid into his arms. As they kissed, she opened her mouth and her tongue slid into his mouth, vibrating spasmodically.

He thought his tonsils were being vacuumed as he was overwhelmed by her kisses and her aggressive attitude. "Oh, well, I'll just relax and enjoy it while it lasts," he decided.

Sarah crushed her body against his. They rolled as one on the blanket. She sat up and unzipped the back of her dress revealing two gorgeous breasts and a magnificent athletic body. Her breasts were firm with two sharp-pointed, erect nipples showing through her bra.

A quick thought came into his mind. What would happen if he got caught making out with the executive commander's daughter? That thought was quickly thrown out when Sarah grabbed his hand and placed it on her breast. "I think I could fall in love with you," she said as she unhooked her bra.

"You're gorgeous. Your body is unbelievable."

"Why don't you get comfortable and take your clothes off?" suggested Sarah. "I'll help you."

She unbuckled his belt and then slipped out of her gown. Their nakedness only increased their passion for each other as their hands explored each other's body.

"Oh, P.G., I want you. Why don't you come into me?" Their bodies became entwined into one and there was a sudden burst of energy as their backs arched and he drove into her. A moan of happiness came from Sarah as her body responded to his. Her hips and thighs pushed against him. The youthful drive of their passion was spontaneous. Not a word was spoken.

The exquisite feeling of sharing each others' love with their bodies suddenly ended with a spasmodic climax, as Sarah cried out. They both became limp and exhausted from their heated passion.

"I think I love you," said Sarah. "That was beautiful."

As they lay under the sky as one, P.G. felt overwhelmed by this young gorgeous Georgia belle. "This could be the beginning of a beautiful relationship," he thought.

They drove back to the base and he got to the barracks just in time to avoid being AWOL. Sarah gave him a big kiss. "I'll be in touch," she said.

P.G. had his doubts about that, but the next morning, he was awakened by the sergeant at arms telling him that he had a phone call. It was Sarah. "Cadet, I plan to see you before you leave," she said in her Southern drawl. "Why don't we have breakfast together? I'll pick you up at the gate."

"You can pick me up anywhere, anytime. I'll meet you at the gate," said P.G. He had checked out of the base the day before and was due to catch a train at 4:00 P.M. She picked him up in her red convertible wearing a low-cut pink summer dress. Her red hair shone in the sunlight. They drove to a local country inn for breakfast. En route she stopped on a shady lane and gave him a big kiss.

"I wish you weren't leaving," said Sarah. "I was just getting to know you. If you think I'm going to let you go after what happened last night, you're crazy," she said. "I don't know about you, but I enjoyed making love. It's too bad you have to catch a train today. I worry about you. I don't want those Memphis belles to get their hands on you. I want you to be my private property. I expect you to call me once a week," she said. "You can call collect if you don't have the money."

"Oh, I'll call all right," he said, as she smiled at him.

"I'm going to visit you in Memphis," she said. "You know, that was my first experience. For all we know I could be pregnant. We'll have to keep in touch. I'm only 16, and if you don't call or write me, I'll have the military police come after you. I could get you for rape."

"You wouldn't do that, would you?" asked P.G.

"Of course not," said Sarah. "I have bigger plans for you. You see, I happen to feel I'm falling in love with you. I don't plan to wait forever to be with you again."

P.G. was stunned by her remarks. No protection had been taken, and now he would really have to keep in touch. He started to sweat, remembering that the navy frowned on cadets getting married. But then, the navy hadn't made love to Sarah. He certainly was going to keep in touch with her, for a lot of reasons.

6

E Base

E Base is called Elimination Base by the cadets because it is where most potential naval aviators are eliminated from pilot training. Cadets know how important and crucial E Base is.

P.G. received orders to proceed from Georgia preflight school to E Base training at Millington Naval Air Base in Memphis, Tennessee. He was now a true athletic cadet, bronzed from the Georgia sun. He had lost approximately 25 pounds from his six-foot frame and weighed in at a muscular 185 pounds.

Of course, even athletic cadets were bound to be unnerved by what followed.

"Okay, next. Move up. Let's go."

P.G. hustled up to the empty chair and sat down. He heard the buzzing of an electric razor near his ears. Moments later, he could feel the metal blade plowing across his head, pushing his hair forward and onto the floor. At home, a haircut and small talk with Frank the barber could take about 20 minutes. This one took about 30 seconds. P.G. got up and ran a hand through the bristle that now passed for his hairstyle. As he was doing this, he was grabbed by the shoulders and steered toward a second line.

"Delousing, boy. Just in case you came in contact with any army types, we need to make sure you're all cleaned up before you get into one of our planes."

Once P.G. was deemed sufficiently clean, he was pointed in the direction of his barracks. As he stepped into it, he was struck by the sparseness and the total lack of privacy it afforded. The barracks consisted of a quonset hut that had about 60 cots in one large room with mattresses about as thick as a daily newspaper, and footlockers in which to stow gear. There was also a head with open stalls and a few mirrors. Sleeping at night in a large group was an experience; everyone had to contend with a symphony of various levels of snoring and an occasional howling nightmare.

E Base Flight Training School in Memphis had both ground school and flight training. Ground school training was a step up from what they received at Arkansas State Teacher's College. Half the cadets went to ground school in the morning while the other half had flight instruction; the process was reversed in the afternoon.

When P.G. arrived at the Naval Air Base in Millington, just outside Memphis, he could hear the droning buzz of the planes overhead. The plane that the cadets would fly was a Stearman N2S-3 biplane. It was considered the most effective primary trainer of World War II. It was sometimes called the "Yellow Peril" and nicknamed "The Washing Machine" by the flying cadets because of the large numbers of cadets who were washed out of primary flight training because of their inability to master it. If a pilot didn't land the Stearman just right, he could easily ground-loop it on landing and add the cost of a broken wing to the government's investment in the cadet's training. When this happened, the cadet ended up going before the Flight Board to determine fault and would sometimes be washed out.

The Stearman N2S-3 had a wingspan of 32 feet and was 25 feet long. It had a Lycoming R-680 radial engine with 220 horsepower and could fly 124 mph at sea level. A great plane if a pilot could master it, the N2S-3 was also perfect for doing stunts and acrobatics. The navy felt that if a man could fly this plane well, he would be adequately prepared to go on to Pensacola, Florida, or Corpus Christi, Texas, to fly the larger SNV-1 trainer or the SNJ, with retractable landing gear.

As P.G. toured the grounds, trying to acclimate himself to his new home, he wandered through the line of planes. He casually looked over the Stearman, but then stopped short when he saw what followed.

"This," he thought, "is for me."

He gazed up reverently at the Ryan PT-22. It had an open cockpit and single, low wings. His thoughts drifted, and he pictured himself flying the sleek, high-performance fighter into the sky at nearly 200 mph, knocking Zeros out of the air. The Ryan could fly to 17,000 feet, although bringing it in was not a task to be taken lightly. It had to be brought in hot in order to land it safely. Of course, there was a lot of classwork, and a lot of air time, to be put in before he would even get near the Ryan.

The next morning, all cadets were gathered in the base's main auditorium. Sergeant Orvis Jennings stood up before the group and cleared his throat loudly. An immediate silence fell over the crowd.

"Cadets," he began, "There are nearly sixty of you in this hall. You'll notice there are not that many planes in that hangar. It will not pain us greatly if, by the end of training, there are only enough cadets to fill those planes. If you drop out, if you are kicked out— that's fine. However, there is one thing you will not do here, and that's ruin one of my planes. Unlike cadets, there are only so many planes to go around. You'd better be damn careful with each and every plane. Since we expect you to be quality pilots, you're going to dress like it. Fall out and line up. Uniforms will be issued through the door on your left. Dismissed."

For a moment, no one spoke. Then the cadets scrambled to form a line, and waited for their names to be called.

The uniforms were a big improvement over the CCC green uniforms they wore in pre-preflight school. P.G. was issued dress blues with a dash of gold and dress whites with epaulettes. Khaki uniforms similar in design to the navy officers' were worn for work or everyday use.

Flight gear was also issued to the cadets. A snug khaki uniform that fit from the ankles to the shoulders, like a jumpsuit, was worn. It zipped up the front and each cadet had his name imprinted in gold and black over the left breast pocket. Cadets wore tight-fitting helmets with earphones that could be plugged into the plane's radio. Flight goggles that fit snugly around the eyes were issued and were extremely important eye protection, for the planes had open cockpits. A parachute harness, which could be hooked onto the seat-type parachute in the cockpit, was also issued.

The intensity of the flight training and ground school training increased. The entire base was more militarized, discipline was much stricter, and there were greater penalties for misbehavior. Weekend liberty was taken away if a cadet stepped out of line. If shoes weren't shined, clothes weren't neat, or attitude was bad, the penalty was a demerit. Demerits resulted in a cadet marching in front of the commandant's office. Too many demerits and the cadet would march right out of the program.

The biggest fear was not of the cadet military establishment but of the flight school instructors. Most cadets who failed the flight training program were washed out not because of bad behavior but because they were unable to fly the planes adequately and safely, making them a risk to their fellow pilots.

In order to make the grade and become a pilot, reflexes had to be perfect and the men's eyes and depth perception could have no flaws. Each naval air cadet was being trained to land a high-speed aircraft on the deck of an aircraft carrier, in rough or smooth seas, on a strip no longer than 200 feet. In combat, a plane might be damaged to the point that it becomes impossible to control. Landing a plane aboard a carrier, a navy pilot does not have a 5,000-foot runway to land on. He has a moving, bobbing target going into the wind, while he tries to catch a wire with a hook dangling from the plane's tail, traveling at more than 100 mph. It is a controlled crash.

After two weeks of introduction and indoctrination, with the emphasis on learning specifically about the Stearman, the cadets were allowed to sit in the cockpit of the plane so they could memorize the instrument panel and the flight controls.

The first flying day at E Base dawned warm and clear. P.G. put on his new flight gear, replete with helmet, goggles, and a parachute harness strapped to his shoulder. He went to his assigned plane and met his instructor, a short, cocky naval aviator named Hayes who had a reputation as an excellent instructor. He was a full lieutenant who had seen combat in the Pacific and seemed to be a friendly guy. P.G. liked him immediately. There was a quiet confidence about him. Grant looked at the cut of his flight suit, and how he carried himself. He noticed the creases around the eyes of the aviator's face and thought, "So, this is one who was good enough to survive."

Hayes strapped him into the back cockpit of the plane, plugged his earphones in, and climbed into the front cockpit. P.G. was nervous and sweating, but happy that his flight instructor was a combat veteran. The motor started, the prop began to whiz around, and Hayes taxied the plane to the edge of the field. The plane tore across the field, wheels bouncing on the ground surface. It gained speed, its wings slicing through the air, and suddenly, delicately, left the ground. "This is what it's all about," said P.G. in the sudden realization that he was flying again. His fears dissipated.

He immediately noticed the difference in flying the Stearman biplane as compared to the Piper Cub. Even though there was a small windshield on the top, the wind rushed by his face. It was much noisier flying in an open cockpit. It was harder to hear the instructor. He had to holler through a tube from his cockpit to the cadet's. The roar of the airplane engine often drowned out his voice. All this was compensated for by the feeling of freedom, of really flying, that engulfed P.G.. He was not in an enclosed cabin—he was actually up among the clouds, with nothing between him and the sky.

Hayes took the plane up to 7,000 feet and demonstrated some power stalls. After two or three demonstrations, P.G. tried. By tapping his head and throwing his hand back in P.G.'s direction, Hayes signalled P.G. that he now had control of the aircraft. If at any time Hayes wanted control of the stick, he would shake the stick while P.G. had it. Grant would then release control of it to Hayes. After one flight with Lieutenant Hayes, he liked him even more. Hayes let him take the stick. He felt Hayes trusted him. Grant realized an affirmation he never experienced—the quiet acceptance of a proven war pilot.

P.G.'s thoughts quickly flashed back to the commandant's final words of the previous day. "Think of what you're doing up there, gentlemen, but don't think too much. If you do, you'll realize that you're flying a large chunk of metal propelled by a lawn mower engine. Don't think what will happen if that engine fails, or if the metal begins to snap off and drop away. Let your training and instincts take over. You're in a situation where too much thinking is very dangerous. In fact, we've had pilots freeze on the stick because the thought of what they were doing totally overwhelmed them, to the point where their muscles just shut down and froze. I don't have to tell you what happens when a man's muscles become locked on the control stick of a plane that's in a stall or a spin that he can't work his way out of. Panic can set in. If it is not controlled, the result is one less instructor, one less cadet, and one less expensive aircraft. Just make sure it doesn't happen to you. The best way to do that is to know your plane, so when something goes wrong, you instinctively make the right decision."

This advice reverberated through P.G.'s head quite often, and it made an impact. It certainly helped him now, as he demonstrated two perfect power stalls. Hayes gave him the signal to return control of the plane, and he did. The lieutenant brought them safely back to the base.

During the two weeks of ground school, P.G. was told there would be five stages of flight instruction. "A" Stage was a frontline introduction to the aircraft and simple landing and takeoffs. "B" Stage was learning to fly a figure eight around pylons that were placed on the ground. Introduction to more difficult flight maneuvers was then taught. The instructors demonstrated the techniques used in doing these maneuvers; the cadets learned by feeling the stick and rudders lightly as they went through the maneuvers.

During this period, P.G. performed his first vertical roll. The maneuver started by pointing the plane's nose down to gain speed and then putting the aircraft into a vertical climb. The ailerons on the wings were then used to roll the plane over on its side. The rate of the roll was reduced, and the stick was pulled back to start moving the plane's nose down toward the horizon. As the plane became level, the rate of the roll was once again reduced, and the wings were positioned into level flight. He also learned how to do a loop-the-loop, which is a 360-degree turn in a vertical plane. This was an easy maneuver as long as power was maintained throughout the loop. If the loop was made too big, a pilot could lose power and spin in. This was particularly dangerous if it was attempted too close to the ground.

After the vertical roll, P.G. learned how to do a barrel roll, in which the plane rolls through 360 degrees while the nose of the aircraft traces a circle. The maneuver that was his greatest challenge was the slow roll. In this stunt, the nose of the plane is rotated 360 degrees on a point, rather than around a circle, as in the barrel roll. This maneuver is the "pièce de la resistance." If a pilot is able to do this maneuver without a mistake, it means he's really wired into the aircraft. The slow roll employs the function of each flight control in the rolling attitude. The elevator and rudder exchange functions and the movements of the controls must be exaggerated in order to execute a slow roll smoothly.

Hayes knew how to do the slow roll to perfection. One afternoon after flying with his instructor for two hours, when they were down on the ground again, P.G. said, "Lieutenant Hayes, how about giving me a shot at a slow roll tomorrow?"

He smiled. "So you're hungry, huh? Okay, Grant, tomorrow's the day."

The next day, at 6,000 feet, Hayes demonstrated a slow roll. "Point the nose of the plane down to increase your speed before you start," Hayes shouted. "This will help keep the nose of the plane on a point. Use the ailerons to start the roll. Now you try it," said Hayes.

P.G. tried it, but when he got the plane upside down and was hanging by his seat belt, he had trouble keeping his feet on the rudders. He couldn't keep the nose of the plane up and the plane almost went into a spin.

"Tighten your seat belt so you're held tightly in the seat," hollered Hayes. "It'll help keep your feet on the rudders when the plane is upside down. Try it again."

P.G. tightened his seat belt, pointed the nose down to increase the plane's speed, and did a perfect slow roll.

"That's the way to do it," said Hayes. "Practice that maneuver when you're flying up here by yourself and make damn sure your altitude is high enough. Also remember your brain has to function properly in the upside-down position. You can't fly by the seat of your pants if your ass is off the seat."

The next day P.G., flying the plane alone, did ten slow rolls. His equilibrium adjusted steadily and each one got easier.

Some of the cadets could not master this maneuver and were either washed out of the program or assigned to become transport pilots, flying planes like the PBY-2.

"C" Stage flight was predominantly acrobatics and learning spot landings. A whitewashed circle was painted in an open field, and cadets tried to bounce-hit the circle in landing the aircraft. Once their wheels touched the circle, they had to push the throttle forward, take off again, and try hitting the circle from a different direction. It was easy to do if a pilot's coordination was good and if he was shooting spot circle landings by himself. It was difficult if there was a gusty wind. Sometimes there were three or four cadets using the circle at the same time and the likelihood of a collision increased.

"D" Stage was the final line, for this was the point at which check flights were performed. No matter how good a cadet felt he could fly the aircraft or how good a pilot his instructor thought he was, each cadet had to get by the check pilot in order to advance in flight training.

Apprehension in "D" Stage was overwhelming. The rules were quite simple. Pilots were checked in all types of flying by a senior instructor. If they received a down-check, which was shown by a thumbs down, they were given one more chance. If a pilot received two down-checks in a row, he was washed out of the program. If he received an up-check after a down-check, he had to fly and get one more up-check. Thus two up-checks in a row had to be earned. The confidence of the cadet was sometimes destroyed by the first down-check. In fact, some of the cadets left the program without even attempting to go through the rigors of two up-checks.

All the check pilots were known by the cadets, and a book was kept on each of them, with the number of up-checks and down-checks that had been given to previous cadets. Most cadets felt that it was a roll of the dice. If you were lucky, you got an easygoing, honest check pilot. If you were unlucky, you got a check pilot with a bad reputation. Not only each cadet, but also the instructors who had flown with them through all their stages, were checked and evaluated according to the ability of their trainees to get through the program.

"P.G., you're ready for 'D' Stage," Lieutenant Hayes announced. "You're as good a pilot as I am," he said. "Almost," he added with a grin. "Good luck."

The next morning P.G. went to the flight line to look at the board to see who his check pilot was—his heart went up into his mouth. He started to sweat just as he had before his first flight. He drew "Down-Check" Jones for his check pilot. The book showed that Jones had washed out his previous four cadets.

"Okay, cadet, let's see what you've got," Jones yelled over the noise of the engine. "We'll start with some spot landings."

P.G. turned the plane into position, and located the whitewash mark on the ground. He brought the plane in smoothly, touched down on the spot, and took off again. He repeated this exercise three more times.

"Good, cadet. Now, give me a chandelle."

P.G. took a deep breath. A chandelle is a maximum-performance climbing turn. It starts with a shallow dive and ends with a 180-

degree turn, completed with the wings level and the aircraft near a stall. P.G. started the plane downward, and let his instincts and training take over. He executed it perfectly, as he did the slow roll moments later.

"Do you know how to do an outside loop?" grumbled Jones.

"No," said P.G. "We were told never to try that because we could tear the wings off."

"That's wrong," said Jones. "I'll show you."

He flew the plane up to 7,000 feet and tried to put the plane into an outside loop. Starting the outside loop flying down wasn't bad, but as the plane started upward, Jones lost control of the plane and it went into a spin. It felt as if the wings were coming off. The plane went around three or four times in the spin Jones didn't appear able to come out of it. P.G. grabbed the stick, pointed the nose down, and leveled out. The instructor looked as if he had passed out up front. After a full minute he came to and seized the stick from P.G.'s hands. "You bastard! You almost killed us! You're through. You're all done."

Flying back to the base in complete silence, P.G.'s only thought was that it was good to be alive. Jones refused to admit it, but P.G. knew he had saved both of their lives.

When they got to the ground, P.G. was given the thumbs down, a down-check. He had had it, but decided he'd stick it out nevertheless, because he knew he was a good pilot. But getting slapped down by a naval superior—someone he should be able to trust—killed some of his new-found respect for the navy.

After eating that evening P.G. saw his flight instructor, Lieutenant Hayes, as he was leaving the mess hall. P.G. tried to avoid him. Hayes blocked the hallway. "What the hell happened up there?" he asked. He was fuming, his brow a dark and ominous cloud.

"I don't want to talk about it," said P.G., barely looking up.

"Well goddamn it, you're going to talk about it because I won't let it go. You're one of my best flight cadets and you got a down-check. Why?" Hayes' piercing stare was hard to take. P.G. hesitated about telling him what happened, but finally decided to tell the truth.

"Why, that bastard," said Lieutenant Hayes, "that'll be the last time he pulls that crap."

The next day, P.G. had his second check pilot test. The check pilot's name was Dixon, and although the book on him was much better than for Jones, P.G. was still downhearted. When they got into the air, as before, they went up to 6,000 feet. Here, the instructor told P.G. he was going to put the plane into a spin and he wanted him to get them out of it. The instructor started the spin. P.G. pointed the nose down, picked up speed, and pulled out of the spin with ease. "Is that good enough?" Grant thought, his anger directed at no one in particular.

"Show me some acrobatics," said Dixon. P.G. figured he'd do a slow roll; it was a difficult maneuver, but he felt that if he was going to flunk out he might as well do it in style. He did a slow roll and kept the nose right on the point.

"I've seen enough," said Dixon. "Fly me back to the base." When they got on the ground, he got an up-check. The thumb was pointing to the sky.

"Cadet," said Dixon, "that was a good flight. Keep your confidence up, and you'll get through. Put what happened yesterday behind you. That's where it belongs."

The next morning, P.G. went to the flight line to see who his next check pilot would be. His gut clenched when he saw the assignments on the flight board. His check pilot was the executive commander of the base. "Oh brother, they've got it in for me," thought P.G.

After they got up to 7,000 feet, Commander Young gave him control of the plane and said, "Do you think you can do a slow roll without trying a few other maneuvers first?"

"Yes, sir," he replied.

He pointed the plane's nose down to gain speed before going into a slow roll and rotated 360 degrees on the point. He thought it was excellent, but it wasn't his thoughts that counted. He stared at the back of Commander Young's head and wondered what was going on in there.

Commander Young said, "Okay, that's enough. Let's head back." When they landed, P.G. got his second up-check. He came to attention and saluted Commander Young. "Lieutenant-Commander Dixon told me you did the best slow roll he had ever seen done by a cadet. I agree with him. Good luck."

When P.G. walked into the barracks, the cadets gave him a big cheer and pounded him on the back. Tears came to his eyes. Screw Jones, that bastard. Nothing could stand in his way now. However, he still had to complete "E" Stage.

"E" Stage was the introduction to night-flying at the naval air station in Memphis. Even if a cadet was able to learn the intricate maneuvers—acrobatics, spot landings, and formation flying—there was still another obstacle. The naval cadet had to learn how to fly the Stearman at night.

At night, depth perception was extremely difficult and important. The horizon was often invisible, especially if the moon was obscured by clouds. On some nights there was no light whatsoever except for the lights of Memphis which projected an eerie glow in the distance.

Most of the Stearman planes had primitive radio equipment and no radio homing device to tune into if the pilot got lost. There were also no railroad tracks at night up in the sky to guide the pilot; there were many potential enemies to look out for.

At night, a pilot first had to have the confidence and ability to keep the plane flying in a good attitude even when he couldn't see half the instruments in the cockpit. This was where the blindfold test prior to soloing was reinstituted. A pilot had to be able to sense and feel the location of the throttle, rudders, and the stick, because the dimly lit instruments were difficult to see.

The cadets who got to "E" Stage were briefed in the hangar before going to the flight line. "Be sure to follow the plane ahead of you after takeoff," said the instructor. "We don't want two planes landing on top of each other. Do any of you have any questions?"

"Yes," said one cadet. "Is it better to come in fast or slow when landing a plane at night?"

"I'd say it's better to come in a little fast," said the instructor. "If you are too slow, the plane could stall and spin in. Are there any more questions?" he paused. "If not, man your aircraft."

P.G. called the tower for takeoff instructions. "Memphis Tower, this in Navy 33, request takeoff instructions."

"Navy 33, wind direction is from the west. Proceed to runway 240."

After getting airborne, he noticed how difficult it was to see the runway at night and considered asking the tower where the hell it was but thought better of it. He was apprehensive about taking the Stearman up. The plane was tough to land in the daytime and would be tougher to land at night. He decided he'd bring the plane in fast.

P.G. also noticed that the planes became almost invisible at night except for the wing and tail lights. Sometimes the engine exhaust flame helped in identification, but God help the pilot who didn't keep his eye on the plane ahead of him. Before he knew it, he could be following a distant light that was actually a car on the road. As the car disappeared into the distance, so would the pilot's concentration and the realization of his whereabouts. Panic would set in.

Usually, during night-flights, pilots shot six or eight landings, each one a new experience. Chances of injury increased in the dark, for ground loops occurred more often at night and wing tips were frequently damaged. Night-flying was the toughest test of the flying skills of the naval aviator, and it eliminated its fair share of fledgling cadets.

Depth perception was doubly important at night. It was very difficult to tell exactly where the runway was even with lights spaced apart on each side of the runway in use. As pilots approached the end of the runway and got lower to the ground, the space between the lights got progressively smaller until only one solid light presented itself. Thus, if a plane was too high coming in for a landing, the lights would appear to be spaced out more. The tendency was to come in fast at first because of the fear of stalling the plane and losing control. A three-point landing with the tail touching first was the ideal each cadet strived for.

One night, one of the navy air corps cadets got lost by following a car light in the distance. When he realized his error, he panicked and almost ran out of gas. The cadet ended up landing the plane in the center of a local racetrack while a race was going on. It was the only lighted field the cadet could find and he made a perfect three-point landing, but the horses on the track bolted and some of the jockeys were thrown. No one ever found out which horse won the race.

If a pilot was a drinking man, heading for the bar after night-flying was mandatory. Drinks did not calm everyone, though; a few cadets just quit after night-flying, certain that they would kill themselves if they continued.

P.G. completed night-flying successfully without a mishap. He also got to fly the low-winged Ryan PT-22 before departing from Memphis.

One week before leaving Memphis, Lieutenant Hayes invited him over to his home for dinner to meet his wife, Sally and their three-year-old daughter. Hayes' wife, who was from Indiana, was a pretty brunette with big brown eyes and a great smile. Their daughter, Amy, looked just like her mother. P.G. got along fine with Sally and Brad and was invited back for a farewell dinner the night before he left.

That evening, after dinner, instructor and cadet walked through the cool Tennessee night air.

"You've got a lot to live for," said P.G.. "Your wife, your baby . . . it must make going to fight the Japs awfully tough."

"Harder than you know," said Hayes. "But when I'm in the air they give me strength. They're what we're fighting this war for. What about you Pete, you have anyone?"

"Maybe. I hope so." He thought of Sarah.

"I hope so too, for your sake. A pilot has to be a cold, bloodless son-of-a-bitch on a mission, but if flying's all he has, he's in trouble. I know you can fly like a demon, and I believe you can fight the enemy. But when you come down to earth you're a man with a family, and a future."

"My family is against me flying," said P.G.

"That's too bad," said Hayes, "but it doesn't change anything I said. To survive this war you have to be ice cold in the air. But down here, you're a man. Do what you have to do to stay sane. By the way, Pete, 'Down-Check' Jones is no longer a check pilot. His test pilot record was reviewed. He gave very few up-checks. He was reprimanded by Commander Young and relieved of his instructor's duties. He's shipped out."

"What a shame," replied P.G.

7

After Memphis

Sarah wrote to P.G. every week. She had every intention of marrying this handsome cadet from New England. She always added a little perfume to her letters. He enjoyed getting her letters; it made him feel great to be loved by someone. "Southern girls are more precocious than northern girls and certainly more aggressive," he thought. "She's only 16 years old, and I'm only 19. Hell, I could be nailed for rape if she wanted to turn me in." He laughed quietly to himself, thinking how he had been seduced by the executive officer's gorgeous redheaded daughter.

Sarah had no intention of having P.G. arrested for anything, however. In fact, after their first encounter, she wanted to spend as much time with him as possible—as intimately as possible. P.G. had taken to referring to her as "carrot top." Sarah was proud of her red hair, and pointed out to him that Mary, Queen of Scots was a vivacious redhead. She went so far as to speculate that since she had quite a bit of Scottish blood in her, they might be related.

Sarah had always been very athletic. She played tennis, jogged, bicycled, and was an excellent swimmer. She was blessed with a great figure, and she was determined to keep it. When that figure was combined with her flaming red hair, sparkling white teeth and flashing green eyes, she attracted attention wherever she went. She had a keen mind, was in the top 10 percent of her senior class, and was planning on attending the University of Georgia—if she didn't get married first.

P.G. wasn't the greatest letter-writer in the world, and Sarah often had to prod him to write to her. If he didn't write, she'd get on the phone and talk to him at length and tell him how much she loved him. He would get a letter off to her once every three or four weeks, usually sending it the day after she called.

He remembered the first letter he received from her. When the sergeant at arms delivered the mail by hollering out the cadet's name, he put the letter up to his nose and said, "This letter smells like it came from a whorehouse. I wouldn't mind meeting this girl myself."

"You couldn't handle her," P.G. said under his breath, his face reddening as he went up to get the letter. He felt like nailing the sergeant at arms in the nose but thought twice. He took the letter, put it in his pocket and went to the john to read it in privacy.

Dearest P.G.,

I miss you very much. I keep dreaming about how much I love you since we were together under the Georgia moonlight. It was the first time I made love to anyone and I'll always remember it.

My heart, mind, and body ache to be with you. Although you're not far away in Memphis, it's still too far away from me. I know our first meeting was much too short to get to know each other. It was mainly physical, but I enjoyed every second. You can be sure of that.

It may seem to you that I'm too young to consider a commitment for the rest of my life. My mother thinks it might be puppy love, but I don't.

I really want to get to know you better and to spend more time with you. I want to know what your plans are for the future.

I pray that your thoughts about me are similar to mine about you. I can't help but feel you enjoyed being with me as much as I enjoyed being with you.

I almost feel as though fate brought us together and

I pray that God will bring us together again. I pray every night that he will keep you safe for me as you fly those planes. Please be careful and think of me. I miss you.

Please let me know when I can see you and spend some time with you in Memphis.

XXXXXXXXXOOOOOOOOOOO—These are hugs and kisses from me.

Sarah—"Your Carrot Top"

My address is 18 Hunter Drive, University of Georgia, Athens, Georgia.

Sarah also remembered the first letter she got from P.G.. She was disappointed because it wasn't as warm as her letter had been to him.

Dear Sarah,

I received your letter and want to thank you for writing to me. Please don't put so much perfume in your letters because it's embarrassing for me. A little is fine because it reminds me of you, but don't put quite so much.

You, too, were my first experience in making love, and I honestly did enjoy it. The time we had was too short and the next time we should spend more time together if your parents will let you see me.

I want to get to know you, too. I remember our dancing together, having fun, and making love. Behind that red head of hair and shining green eyes I want to know what makes you tick. I also want to know about your plans. I miss you!

Sincerely yours,
Peter Grant

P.S. Send me a picture of yourself for my locker.

Sarah thought the best part of the letter was the P.S. when he asked for her picture. She had just the one for him. She had a beautiful photo of herself in a bathing suit and planned to get it blown up to send to him. She made up her mind. She was going to Memphis even if her parents disapproved.

Sarah's letters made P.G. realize she was serious about him. He also recognized that she had a good mind and knew how to write and express her thoughts. He remembered her beautiful youthful body, and how vivacious and lively she was. When he wrote to her, he often told her about his experiences and how much he enjoyed flying. He felt he could open his heart to her. She wasn't just a morsel; She had a lot going for her. But marriage? For God's sake, he didn't even know if he'd survive the goddamn war.

He didn't tell her anything about his down-check in "D" Stage at Memphis until it was all over and he was about to complete E Base. He had three days' travel time to get to Pensacola, and two of those days were to be spent with Sarah in Memphis. She was coming by bus from Atlanta. He arranged for a room at the Peabody Hotel for her.

Sarah had a fight with her father and mother about going to Memphis without a chaperone. She decided she was going anyway. Her mother, in particular, objected to her going. Her father was more understanding and insisted she call them as soon as she arrived so they could be sure she had gotten there safely.

P.G. finally finished E Base on a Wednesday and Sarah arrived at about 5:00 P.M. He met her at the bus depot. She ran from the bus and gave him a big hug and kiss. "I missed you so much," she said, "and I plan to spend every minute with you while I'm here."

"Great. Would you like to get something to eat first," he asked, "or should we check you into the hotel?"

"Be serious," she murmured softly, "I'm going to check into the hotel first."

They got her bags and took a cab to the Peabody and she signed the registry as Sarah Grant. "This is my brother. He'll be visiting with me a good deal of the time," she bluntly told the desk clerk, as he looked at her over his eyeglasses.

"Hmmph," he said.

When they got up to the room and shut the door, she put the chain on the door and gave him a warm kiss. She unzipped her dress and started to unbutton his shirt as he fondled her body. "Don't rush," he said. "We both want to enjoy this."

She slipped out of her dress. Her entire body was bronzed tan and magnificent. She told him that she had inserted a diaphragm. "I went to the doctor to get one because I knew I wanted to be close to you."

"That's great," said P.G., thinking, "This girl knows what she's doing," as he slipped out of his clothes. He touched her breasts with his fingertips as she caressed his back. She gently pulled him down on top of her on the bed.

"Oh, darling," she said, "I love you so much. I've waited so long for this." Their bodies began to move as one in rhythmic motion as she responded to his advances. Her nipples hardened and pressed against his chest as her back arched against him. Her hips moved against his. The intensity of their lovemaking increased as she forced him over onto his back. He responded by arching his back upward as she pressed her body into his. Their passionate lovemaking ended in a climax that left both of them completely exhausted.

P.G. felt as though he were in heaven for two days. She felt the same way and told him. He became the aggressor in their physical relationship. They really got to know each other for the first time, both physically and mentally. He realized her love was unconditional. This was the first time they really had a chance to talk to each other at length.

They went dancing at the Starlight Room of the Peabody Hotel and went to Basin Street to listen to jazz bands. He told her how much flying had come to mean to him. She told him that she was going to college until he would think about marrying her. She said she was not interested in anyone else and wanted to spend the rest of her life with him. She also told him she wanted to have three or four children.

He found out that Sarah's ancestors had strong roots in the South. They had landed in Williamsburg, Virginia, in the late 1600s and had moved to Atlanta. Her great-great-grandfather had owned a plantation and slaves during the Civil War. The family dynasty was wiped out when General Sherman put the torch to Atlanta.

"I worry about you flying," said Sarah. "I pray for the war to end. Do you plan to stay in the navy after the war ends?"

"I don't know."

"I don't plan to date anyone else but you," said Sarah.

Very little sleep was obtained those two days, even though they spent much of the time in bed. He knew he loved her and would marry her if he survived flight training and the war.

There was nothing left undone when P.G. boarded the train for Pensacola. They knew where they stood, alone in the world, a war raging far away. Sarah cried as P.G. held her. The uncertainties of their lives made their parting seem absolute. The war had brought them together. Would it tear them apart?

8

Philippine Sea Battle, June 1944

Lieutenant Brad Hayes kept in touch when P.G. went to Pensacola. The lieutenant was interested in him as a cadet and potential naval officer and hoped that someday they would fly together.

When P.G. started intermediate flight training in October 1943, he received a letter from Lieutenant Hayes. Hayes told him that he would be taking a refresher course at Jacksonville, Florida, and would then be returning to combat in the Pacific. It would be his second tour of duty, as he had been to the Pacific in 1942, during the early part of the war. That experience accounted for the respect that most of the cadets at Memphis Naval Air Station had for Brad Hayes. He was a combat-proven pilot who had flown off the big carriers, so he knew what he was talking about. He would be a valuable replacement pilot in any air group and would probably become executive officer of a squadron. After taking a brief six-week refresher course in fighter planes on the East Coast, Hayes received orders to fly to San Diego to join an air group in the Pacific.

In April 1944, Hayes joined the air group assigned to the U.S.S. *Enterprise,* which was operating with Task Force 58, and during the next three months he flew in some of the most exciting and rewarding battles for the United States fleet. He participated in the Marianas Turkey Shoot, a fight that killed most of the experienced Japanese carrier pilots. Admiral Spruance was the fleet admiral in charge, and Vice-Admiral Mitscher, whose flag was on the *Lexington* at the time, was in charge of the carriers. Mitscher's *Lexington* stayed alongside the *Enterprise* in the Marianas Turkey Shoot and the battle of the Philippine Sea, the latter a battle that almost killed Lieutenant Hayes.

Admiral Spruance, in charge during the battle of the Philippine Sea, held the responsibility of capturing, occupying, and defending Saipan, Tinian, and Guam. The primary objective for Vice-Admiral Mitscher, in charge of the carriers, was to have the flattops act as a defensive screen to shield the amphibious forces at Saipan and make the invasion possible. U.S. Navy brass predicted that Japanese planes from Guam would participate in the battle. The Japanese high command felt that their land-based planes on Guam would help equalize the battle, since they were outnumbered two-to-one by the American carriers. When Japanese aircraft based on Guam attempted to attack Task Force 58 on June 19, 1944, Hellcats from the American carriers intercepted them. They destroyed 30 fighters and seven bombers. The Japanese strategy had backfired. The fight continued and raged on for eight hours on June 19th. Mitscher ordered every available fighter into the air.

The Marianas Turkey Shoot earned its name when the American Hellcats vectored out at high altitudes against the Japanese Mobile Fleet. They encountered their poorly trained Japanese flyers, and had a field day destroying the Japanese planes. Over 300 Japanese aircraft were shot down. Since most of the Japanese planes were wiped out in the Marianas Turkey Shoot, the Japanese carriers were no longer considered a threat to the American Fleet. Admiral Spruance felt confident that it was a good time to go and try to finish the job.

However, American search planes had difficulty finding the surviving ships of the Japanese fleet. At 4:00 P.M., a search plane sighted the fleet approximately 220 miles away from the American force.

Vice-Admiral Mitscher, not only a powerful commander, but also a pilot, always tried to protect his pilots. He had a difficult decision to make. Should he put his pilots at risk by creating a situation that would force them to land on the carriers at night, or should he pass up a great opportunity to attack? The enemy was within striking distance and not well protected.

It was a difficult, heart-rending decision that he had to make. That was why he had a difficult time explaining to his pilots what he wanted them to do.

"Gentlemen," he began, "we have a golden opportunity to put the Japanese fleet away for good. Their planes have been virtually eliminated, their pilots shot down, and their defenses weakened. The time to take advantage of this opportunity is now! By 10 A.M. tomorrow, they will have had sufficient time to replenish their forces or go into hiding, and our opportunity will be lost." He paused for a second. The men were listening intently.

Mitscher started again, "After much deliberation, I have decided to go after the Japanese fleet and finish the job. You will hit them fast, hit them hard, and then return to our carriers. I realize that you will be returning at night and a night landing is probably the toughest thing for a navy pilot to accomplish. This is a once-in-a-lifetime chance to knock out the Japanese fleet. We would be making a grave mistake not to take advantage of it. I know this is a calculated risk, but if anyone can do it, my pilots can."

The room was quiet. Then the air exploded with cheers. These men were determined and confident, and they were willing to participate in eliminating the Japanese threat—regardless of the risk —even though they knew some of them would die.

Over 200 fighters, dive bombers, and torpedo planes were launched. Later reports indicated that the search pilot who initially found the Japanese fleet had made a mistake as to its location by about 60 miles. This meant that the American navy pilots flying off the carriers would have to fly an even greater distance from their own carriers to attack and return. It also meant that pilots surviving the attack would assuredly be returning at night. Most of the pilots had never landed a plane on a carrier at night. Some of the planes would be running out of fuel and others would be shot up or have injured aboard.

The Japanese fleet had also intercepted the American search pilot's message and was racing away as fast as they could, creating more distance for American pilots to cover, and leaving less fuel for their return to Point Option.

Before launching, all the American pilots were given a clear battle plan: They were to sink the Japanese carriers. They ultimately succeeded in setting fire to the Japanese carriers *Chiyoda* and *Zuikaku*. They also severely damaged a battleship and a cruiser. The Avenger TBF-TBMs sent the *Hiyo*, one of Japan's largest carriers, to the bottom of the Pacific Ocean.

Once the air groups completed the mission, the survivors headed back toward Task Force 58. The problem of getting back home now faced the American pilots. They had done their job well, but they did not relish the thought of trying to land their planes on the carrier's decks at night. They knew that they had no alternative except to land in the water. Their nerves were spent from taking and giving fire. Fatigue was setting in. The pilots were ill prepared, and knew it, for landing their battle-scarred aircraft on the decks of the carriers at night.

It takes a lot of guts to land a plane in the water. The pilot has to try to hit the crest of a wave into the wind. He knows when he hits the water at over 100 mph, it's a sudden stop. If he doesn't hit just right, the plane can cartwheel and he's dead. At nighttime, it's much more difficult to make a safe belly landing because he can't see what the water's doing or where the crest is. His depth perception is gone and the chance of serious injury is much greater.

Some of the fighter planes that were in the air and sea battle had used up a lot of fuel in the fight and their tanks were down. Some were close to empty. Other planes were shot up and badly damaged, and the pilots knew they wouldn't be able to get back. A few of the pilots and crews had been shot down and were in the water. The survivors had fought a grueling battle at sundown, and weren't looking forward to the long return trip at night to reach a flattop.

Most of the pilots flying back to the task force detected the fleet's radio beacons at 70 miles and were picked up by the ship's radar. The radio airwaves were filled with foul language and expletives as some of the planes ran out of gas and had to ditch. A few pilots wasted their fuel trying to speed up to get back so they wouldn't have to attempt a night-carrier landing.

Vice-Admiral Mitscher knew he would lose some pilots who had just battled the enemy so valiantly. He was visibly disturbed; he knew the price of victory. He wanted to save as many of his pilots as he could. He gave the order to turn on the lights of the ships of Task Force 58. This had never been done before, and put the task force at great risk. Crewmen pointed searchlights up toward the sky, fired star shells from the five-inch guns to help the planes find the carriers, and switched on lights to outline the flight decks. The carriers in Task Force 58 also spread out so they could take the planes aboard easier.

As darkness set in, some of the planes started arriving and entering the landing circles. Many of the planes were almost out of fuel and their pilots were looking for any open deck. Ships radioed the pilots that they could land on any available flight deck. Some planes ran out of gas before they could land and destroyers attempted to pick them up. A few pilots with sputtering engines refused to obey wave-offs and landed on top of other planes that they couldn't see on the deck. On the *Enterprise,* two planes landed almost simultaneously; the fighter's tail hook caught an early wire, and the bomber a late cable. Some flight deck crewmen died trying to get the planes and pilots aboard.

Since there were so many planes returning and running out of gas at the same time, there was complete chaos. The pilots made passes at anything that was lit up and floating. None of them wanted to ditch their planes in the water.

In that group of fighter planes and torpedo bomber planes that fought the Japanese fleet was Lieutenant Brad Hayes. He was flying with a fighter air group off the carrier *Enterprise.*

He had shot down a Jap plane and had used up a lot of his fuel in the fight. He leaned out his remaining fuel, hoping to get back—he would have pissed in the gas tank if it would have helped. His options included making a power-on landing in the water while it was still light or running out of gas trying to get back. With no gas or power, he could spin the airplane in and lose control. Bailing out at night and hoping to be picked up could also be a problem in the vast Pacific Ocean.

A sputtering engine finally forced him to bite the bullet. He put his wing lights on and decided to ditch the plane. He was lucky that his plane hit on the crest of a whitecap. His body was snapped first forward and then backward. The impact of the plane hitting the water dazed him—he couldn't remember where he was or what he had to do. Water gushed into the cockpit as the plane tilted to one side and started to sink; the ocean's cold water brought him back to his senses. Quickly he released his seat belt and struggled to push back the canopy, which had been jammed forward on impact. At last he scrambled out of the cockpit into the pitch blackness of night. He moved rapidly, automatically, but had no time to extricate his life raft from his plane. Instead, he inflated his Mae West and slid into the cool Pacific Ocean. He knew he had to conserve his energy. He kept moving to keep up the circulation in his legs and throughout his body. His only chance was to be picked up the next morning when the ships began looking for pilots. Hayes wept a little and prayed a lot, thinking during the entire experience that he had to stay alive for his wife and child in Tennessee. He was determined to live. He hoped the fleet would not get into another battle and leave the downed pilots to die. He continued to pray and struggled to stay afloat all night.

After recovering as many of the planes as possible, Task Force 58 headed toward the scene of the battle, in the direction of the path of the returning flyers. Many of the pilots were missing. It was hoped that some were still alive.

There is nothing quite like seeing the sun come up when trying to stay afloat, swimming alone in the middle of the Pacific Ocean. All Brad had on as survival gear was his Mae West life jacket, which barely kept his head above the water. He tried to fire his Very pistol flares, but they were wet and didn't work. He also had a whistle pinned on his Mae West which he decided not to detach and use until he saw a ship, hopefully an American one. Finally, after being in the water for ten hours, a ship appeared on the horizon. He unpinned his whistle and started to blow with as much strength as he could muster.

It seemed forever before the ship drew closer: It was an American Fletcher-type destroyer. Although it appeared to make no difference, he continued to blow on his whistle. The destroyer looked as if it was going in circles around him. "Don't they see me?" thought Hayes, for they refused to come closer. After what he felt was an endless period of time, he became exhausted and lost the strength to blow on the whistle. At 7:00 A.M. a motor launch from the destroyer dropped over the ship's side and came to pick him up.

"For God's sake, why didn't you guys pick me up sooner?" he asked. "Couldn't you see I was almost out of breath?"

A chief petty officer in the launch spoke up. "We were afraid there were Japanese subs in the area, sir, and we didn't want to catch a torpedo. Besides, the way you were blowing on that whistle, we knew you were doing fine. We had you in sight the whole time."

"Remind me to kick someone's ass later on," said Hayes.

9

Intermediate Flight Training School, Pensacola, Florida

After completing E Base at Memphis, the cadets proceeded to the naval air stations at Pensacola, Florida, or Corpus Christi, Texas, to receive intermediate flight training; the last phase before obtaining the gold wings of a naval aviator. Though both bases offered similar instruction, cadets preferred orders to Pensacola, because the first navy pilots flew there and each man wanted to be among the aviators continuing the historic tradition.

Pensacola, on the Gulf Coast, was a small, unpretentious town, warm and full of palm trees. Virtually all its activity centered upon the navy and its personnel. The town's merchants provided opportunities for the satisfaction of diverse appetites: various bars, brothels, and restaurants catered to the navy men. Cadets came to know the town quickly, for when they received time off, they would trek into town for whatever action they could find.

Initially, all naval cadets checked in at the main station in Pensacola and were then assigned to the outlying fields for additional training. The outlying field that most of the cadets were assigned to first was Whiting Field. It was way out in the boondocks, and the runways were asphalt on top of mud flats.

At Whiting Field the cadets would be taught the art of instrument flying. At this stage in their careers, the cadets used SNV-1s or SNVs; these were training planes with fixed landing gear. They were low-winged aircraft with closed cockpits equipped with canvas curtains that could cover the rear-seat pilot. The curtain prevented the cadet from peeking out to see what attitude the plane was flying. The plane was ideal for instrument training, but it seemed to vibrate incessantly both in the air and on the ground. Most pilots wondered whether a mechanic had left a part out in the construction of the engine. The cadets called them the "Vultee Vibrators."

During instrument flying, the instructor sat in front and the cadet in back, with the canopy pulled over his head. It was here the cadet learned to fly not by the seat of his pants, but by using only his plane's instruments—the turn and bank indicator, altimeter, and airspeed indicator—to guide him in flight maneuvers.

The young cadets also learned how to take off and land relying completely on their instruments, how to fly the radio ranges, and how to use instruments in making a landing approach with a radio beacon. They learned to use location markers, which are radio beacons located along a runway in an instrument landing system, that transmit a characteristic signal to provide position or distance information to the aircraft. The pilot then knows where the plane is in relation to the runway. If a pilot gets fogged in and can't see anything, he can use the system to find the runway and land the aircraft.

Instrument flying was frustrating at times. Cadets felt as if they were locked up in a birdcage trying to flap their wings.

One of those birdcages was the Link Trainer that simulated actual flying in the air, although it sat on the ground. It was an enclosed cockpit with a canopy and all the instruments of a regular airplane. One could compare it to some of the rides at an amusement park, except that it had much more expensive and sophisticated instrumentation. The Trainer mimicked takeoffs, landings, cloud cover, altitude, airspeed, and produced a record of a cadet's maneuvers while he sat in the cockpit. The experience was often boring, but it was a necessary evil, because instructors monitored the records and awarded pass or fail grades.

The cadets realized that the navy was trying to train them to use their instruments properly so that if they got into a cloud bank or storm or were flying at night, they wouldn't end up flying upside down, or spin the airplane in.

P.G. distinctly remembered his first instrument flight in one of those Vultee Vibrators.

"Have you ever played 'Pin the Tail on the Donkey?'" asked instructor Connors.

"Sure. My girlfriend and I play it all the time," said P.G.

Connors looked at P.G. and decided to let that one pass.

"If you remember, you're blindfolded and spun around and then have to pin the tail on a donkey. Your head gets a little dizzy. In instrument flying the stakes are a little bit higher. I'm going to spin the plane around up in the air and then see if you can straighten it out by using just the plane's instruments. You'll be blindfolded, because the canopy will be over your head, but you'll still be able to see the instruments. Let your equilibrium return, trust your instruments completely, and you'll do all right."

"Great," thought P.G. to himself. "I'll be up in the air with a new plane and a new instructor with no idea where the hell I'm going."

P.G. climbed into the back cockpit, and away they went. When the plane got up to 8,000 feet, the canopy was pulled over P.G.'s head. It was a very uncomfortable feeling. He hated being in tight, closed places. The instructor put the aircraft through a series of violent maneuvers. P.G. thought he might vomit.

Connors' voice blared in his earphones. "Okay, Cadet, see if you can straighten this thing out."

P.G. looked at his instrument panel. The bank of flickering lights and the bucking motion of the plane did nothing to ease his queasiness. He blinked his watering eyes several times so he could see the panel clearly. The artificial horizon showed the plane was diving and the right wing was in a bank. He straightened the wings out first. As he did so, he could taste the bile in his throat. He gagged, trying desperately not to be sick. He gently pulled back on the stick to level the plane off. The smooth ride did nothing for his stomach. If Connors asked him to do the same move again, he'd refuse.

"Good job, Cadet. Try not to be so jerky next time."

"I think we better go back up to 8,000 feet," said P.G. "You left my stomach up there."

When they got the plane on the ground P.G. had a pounding headache. He didn't like being penned up in a closed space. He wondered how cadets who were claustrophobic would make out with instrument flying.

Check pilots evaluated cadets in instrument flying and some men were washed out just for failing to turn on the instruments prior to takeoff. After some flights, a cadet would appear from under the canopy wondering whether he had flown the plane adequately. It was a real guessing game sometimes, but once the cadet learned to trust his life to the instruments it wasn't too bad. P.G. had no trouble passing the grade in instrument flying at Whiting Field and was soon transferred to Barin Field for advanced flight training.

Most of the cadets who reach Barin Field for their last training period before graduating know that if they keep their noses clean and don't goof up, they will wear the gold wings of a United States Naval Aviator within a few months. That thought sustained many of the men and motivated them to continue.

All the schooling prior to Barin Field prepared each cadet to fly more sophisticated airplanes. At Barin Field, the cadets flew the SNJs, North American Aircraft's low-winged training plane with retractable landing gear and a closed cockpit like the navy fighter planes. Usually brightly painted, it possessed a variable pitch propeller and was an excellent plane for acrobatics. The plane was used for introducing the cadets to dive bombing and its front-mounted guns were used to shoot at canvas sleeves towed by other aircraft, to test the pilot's ability to shoot accurately in the air. The cadets really enjoyed flying the aircraft because it was highly maneuverable.

Formation flying played a big part in the final training of the naval cadet, and there was an art to flying on the wing of another plane. Flirting with death happened every time a pilot trainee coordinated the movement of his eyes, hands, and feet to manipulate his high-speed plane next to another plane for formation flying. Although it was frowned upon, pilots actually touched wings at times. Formation flying required intimate dependence between participants: Every cadet learned to become a part of the flying team.

When bad weather made flights unusually dangerous, formation flying became impossible because other planes' positions were unknown. Sometimes pilots were killed during formation flying. When a pilot approaches a formation of planes, he slides his plane straight across and under the tail of the plane he is going to join up with. If he comes in too fast, he can overshoot the mark and then has to make another approach in order to join the formation. Occasionally a cadet will throw his wing up to stop his plane, creating a blind spot. With the wing up, the pilot can't see the formation he is trying to join and goes barreling in, causing a mid-air collision. Like a bowling ball hitting the first pin and knocking the rest of the pins down, the disaster continues through the rest of the formation. He might cut off the tail of the plane that he's joining up on, causing both planes to crash. Sometimes, the culprit is able to bail out and save his own life while the plane he's joining up with is cut in two. Although such occurrences are rare, they demonstrate the total interdependence of all pilots flying in formation.

Seven of P.G.'s college buddies made it to Barin Field. They had all signed up together in Boston with the hope of flying together. As he was going out on maneuvers one day, P.G. ran into Charlie Stockman, one of the seven.

"Hey, Charlie, how's it going?"

"Good, P.G., good. I'm doing formation flying today, if you want to see how an expert does it."

Charlie wasn't just bragging—he was one of the base's top cadets and he could hold a plane in formation like very few experienced pilots could. P.G. walked over to the hangar with a few other cadets to watch the formation. Charlie lifted off, and banked gracefully to join up with the formation. Behind him, Cadet Bobby Averill was preparing to join the group also. Averill and Charlie had developed a friendly rivalry, and there was always a bit of showmanship when they were in the air together.

"Hey, Averill," Charlie called over his radio, "what are you flying back there, a Model T?"

"Hey, big shot, you had a little head start. Now it's time to clear the way for a real pilot," Averill replied.

With that, Averill pushed his throttle forward and poured on the coals in an attempt to catch Stockman. P.G. and the other cadets watched in amazement from the ground. The planes disappeared from view into a cloud bank, with lots of friendly wagering going on as to who would emerge in the lead. They would never know.

Once they entered the clouds, the pilots couldn't see each other. Each had to assume where the other was heading, and adjust accordingly. As Charlie veered to get out of the clouds, the propeller of his buddy's plane chewed up his tail. Charlie's plane began to spin uncontrollably and he tried to bail out, but he was too low to the ground for the chute to open. The next day there was a wooden crate with the cadet's belongings in front of the barracks.

The final obstacle for the naval air cadet to overcome before graduation was being checked out in SNJ night-flying. The SNJs flew much faster, were more sophisticated, and proved more difficult to land at night. They also had retractable landing gear. Since accidents were common during night-flying, a flight instructor usually went up with the cadet and shot three or four landings with him so the cadet could grasp the procedure. When the instructor felt the cadet would be safe on his own, he would land, get out of the front cockpit, and the cadet would move up in his place. The cadet would then call the tower for takeoff instructions and taxi out in the dark to the runway in use. Cadets memorized the runway patterns of the field, because at night it was hard to tell which direction to take for taxiing.

Visibility was better from the front cockpit. Once in the air, the cadets were told to stay close to the field so they wouldn't get lost, because other cadets were flying in the area. The cadets had to be extremely alert, because at night the chance of a mid-air collision increased tremendously. What appeared to be a bright star on the horizon often ended up being a plane coming head on at high speed.

The most common accident involving night-flying cadets, however, was not a head on collision but a "wheels up" landing; failure to drop the wheels into position for landing. The cadets were so nervous they didn't remember the essentials of flying, and neglected to use their check-off list. The tower was no help at night because they couldn't see whether the wheels were up or down.

Ground looping, when the plane goes out of control on the ground and turns around in circles, often caused problems as well, including wing tip and wing flap damage. Occasionally, a cadet pilot coming in too fast and applying the brakes too heavily would damage the propeller by causing the plane's tail to go up and the prop to hit the runway. This bent the propeller and caused serious engine damage.

Fortunately, on the night that P.G. was checked out in night-flying there was a full moon. He periodically reviewed the airspeed, rpm, and oil pressure gauges, knowing the importance of the instrument panel at night. The green fluorescent lights of the instrument panel had an effect on his night vision and interfered with his eyes' adaptation to darkness; like every pilot he quickly realized that flying by the seat of one's pants at night is virtually impossible. After making three or four good night landings, he was cleared to take the plane back to the line. At this point, he began to enjoy night-flying, perhaps because his fears had disappeared and experience replaced them. That night, however, as P.G. later learned, one of the cadets strayed away from the landing pattern, became lost, and landed in the Gulf of Mexico.

Weather often determined when cadets flew, and if it was foggy or the field was locked in with bad weather, a day of rest was called for. Heavy rain, electrical storms, and threats of hurricanes coming up the Gulf occasionally grounded all the planes on the flight line. Near graduation, inclement weather produced extra sack time because by then the cadets had finished ground school and were spending most of their time in the air.

Three days before P.G.'s graduation, bad weather developed. At 8 A.M., fog as thick as cotton enveloped the base, and the weathermen forecasted no clearing. The cadets were grounded. This relieved some of the instructors from any teaching obligations for the day, and five of the senior instructors decided to go aloft and test their navigation and instrument flying skills. The instructors, some of them combat veterans from the Pacific war, hated the boredom of teaching recruits; they all had instrument ratings and were confident flying in inclement weather. So they planned a flight into Texas and back. Once they got airborne, the weather changed rapidly and the Gulf Coast got locked in the grip of a hurricane. Three of the five instructors didn't make it, crashing their planes in attempts at blind landings or running out of gas. One of the instructors flew north as far as his gas supply would allow, broke through the overcast sky, and landed safely in Kentucky.

The other surviving instructor took the airborne water route. He flew out into the Gulf, called "Mayday," and radioed his approximate position before he ran out of gas. He parachuted into the Gulf of Mexico. Although presumed dead, three days later he showed up at the base; after he had been in the water for 12 hours, an oil barge picked him up, his body intact. Only because he was a seasoned combat veteran with some battle stars did he escape a court-martial. When the local newspapers and the Associated Press heard about the incident the story was spread around the country, and Walter Winchell labeled Barin Field as "Bloody Barin."

The next day, a bizarre and tragic turnabout: Instead of wooden boxes containing the belongings of deceased cadets, the dead officer's belongings sat in front of the Bachelor Officer's Quarters.

That afternoon, the executive officer of the base addressed the entire battalion of cadets and officers. He ended his lecture by saying: "Use your head when you fly, especially in bad weather. I don't care who you are, cadet or officer, don't take stupid chances. Remember, each of you is the captain of his own ship when you fly, so you'd better keep your head screwed on right or you'll end up in the deep six.

"Now, I have an announcement to make. Admiral Radford will be pinning the wings on the next graduating class." That was P.G.'s class. With that remark, the executive officer dismissed the battalion.

Discussion after the meeting turned away from the tragedy and toward graduation. Some of the cadets spoke with excitement about the arrival of relatives for the graduation, but not P.G. Since he came from a poor family with no money to pay for the long train trip, he knew he'd receive his wings without any family present. They had been informed about the graduation, but they couldn't afford to attend.

On graduation day the weather was beautiful. Because the admiral was going to be pinning on the wings, the entire battalion of cadets participated in the parade and graduation. Dress whites were the uniforms of the day. The press came, and the admiral spoke concerning the progress of the war. Photographers were everywhere.

The graduating naval cadets marched to the podium according to class rank. P.G. was surprised to see that he was in the top third of his class, and when he went up to salute the admiral and receive his gold wings, the flash of cameras recorded the event as the admiral pinned the wings on his chest. The best surprise for P.G., however, was when he stepped off the podium. A beautiful redhead was waiting for him. Sarah had taken a train to be at Pensacola for his graduation. She had tears in her eyes, for she was so proud of him. "Oh, Peter, I knew you could do it. You're the best pilot in the navy. You're going to be an admiral some day."

"You're prejudiced, but probably correct," said P.G. as he took her into his arms, embracing her, and gave her a long kiss. They were obviously glad to see each other. He realized he had accomplished his goal of becoming a pilot. Sarah was also beginning to play a bigger part in his life.

10

Operational Flight Training School, Opalacka, Florida

Graduation was a day of exhilaration, celebration, and reflection. Receiving the gold wings of a naval aviator was the greatest achievement in the lives of these young men. Most of them did not comprehend what the future would hold for them. Nothing could be worse than what they had just been through. They are ready for tomorrow, but feared the future may make them long for the past.

As P.G. traveled to Opalacka, he thought long and hard about what the admiral had to say at graduation.

"Each of you cadets has had to live with the daily stress of not knowing if you were good enough to become full-fledged naval aviators. You all knew that one small mistake could wash you out of the program, or worse, end your life. Those of you who are here today represent a select group of individuals who have learned to work together toward a common goal—defending our country. I salute you, and I wish you luck."

Quite abruptly their lifestyles changed, and they gained some interesting fringe benefits. P.G.'s cadet income increased to that of an ensign, and since he had become a full-fledged flyer, he would receive a 50 percent hazardous pay increase.

Because he did well in aerial gunnery, the navy selected him to become a carrier pilot, and consequently he received orders to report to Opalacka, Florida, for instruction in flying torpedo bombers. This postgraduate training period would be his last preparation before joining the fleet.

At Opalacka Naval Air Station, the new pilots roomed in the Bachelor Officer's Quarters. It was obvious that their status had been upgraded. The changes permeated all aspects of their lives. No longer were they required to make their beds. A laundry service picked up their clothes. Even the smell in the living quarters, previously redolent of dirty socks and sweat, seemed to improve. Overall, the new ensigns noticed a new respect for the gold bars they wore on their shirts or epaulettes. Enlisted men now saluted them. They found dates easier, too. As officers, they had their own private dining room and were given a choice of food. There was a restricted bar at the Officer's Club that offered reduced prices for drinks. It was considered proper for ensigns to get married if they so desired. Cadets were discouraged from marrying because their wives could easily become widows overnight.

With the promotion, the men learned quickly that the work and effort required of them increased as well; flying became more complicated and suddenly more like a business—a risky business.

Opalacka Naval Air Station was near Fort Lauderdale, Florida, and was one of the main training stations for dive bomber and torpedo bomber pilots. It was here that the men would now be flying big operational carrier planes.

Unfortunately, most of the airplanes at Opalacka Naval Air Station were old; any torpedo bomber planes that were in good condition were active with the fleet. Some of the air station's planes were patched-up former combat planes. This meant that equipment failure was a real possibility every time a plane took off.

P.G. was assigned to a training unit for carrier pilots who would be flying torpedo bombers. There were twelve pilots assigned to the unit. A training instructor who was a full lieutenant was in charge. His name was Lieutenant Rottenburger, and he was aptly named. The foulness of his disposition was matched only by the endless stream of profanity that issued forth from his lips, which were permanently contorted into a snarl. In the locker rooms he was aptly called, "Rotten Burger." He had not been selected for combat duty and ended up as an instructor for those pilots who would be seeing combat. He was understandably bitter about this, and showed it in his attitude toward the young recruits. He had two younger officers as his assistants. They had been in combat and understood what pilots needed to learn in order to survive. Without them, the training would have been a disaster.

Lieutenant Rottenburger was a strict disciplinarian and allowed no nonsense. His concept of flying was all business, and his countenance and demeanor demonstrated this. He had a constant frown on his face and his eyes seemed to pierce through your backbone like a sword. In the air he was constantly berating the pilots over the radio and, when the flight session was over, terra firma was a welcome sight. Rottenburger was one of the reasons the pilots headed for the bar after a strict flying workout.

Advanced ground school instruction took place early in the morning and then the graduate pilots would take to the air as a group at 10:00 A.M.

The early-morning ground school instruction was to teach the pilots about the plane they would be flying, the TBF-1. The plane had a 2,000 hp engine and weighed 17,000 pounds. It was the largest stick-controlled aircraft built for the navy during World War II. The number of instruments on the control panel had doubled and the power of the engine had escalated dramatically over the previous training planes. Before the young pilots would be allowed to fly the expensive aircraft, they would have to memorize the flight control panel.

For each ensign, the first solo flight of a torpedo bomber elicited the most fear. P.G.'s first solo came after a blindfold check-out by Lieutenant Hanson, one of the flight instructors. He sent him up with the advice, "Don't be afraid to use the whole runway for takeoff."

The plane was so large that in the cockpit P.G. felt as if he was looking out a two-story window. He was. He locked the fold-back wings in place before leaving the flight line and adhered to the formality of asking the tower for takeoff instructions. Sitting at the end of the runway in the mammoth plane and cleared for takeoff, he asked himself, "What do I do next?" He hesitated. Then he remembered the advice of a marine flight instructor. He threw the throttle forward, all the way to the fire wall, hollered "Shit," and started the plane moving down the runway.

Because the plane was so big and slow to respond, he wondered if the controls were functioning properly. The gigantic plane lumbered down the runway like a pregnant turkey. "When the hell is this thing going to get airborne?" he asked himself. The plane's flaps were down, but there appeared to be no airlift. A fence at the end of the runway seemed to race toward the nose of the plane. A wave of panic raced through his mind. He yanked hard on the stick, and finally the plane lifted off the ground. Immediately, he pulled the wheels up to avoid hitting an approaching tree.

"God, this thing handles like a drunken ox," murmured P.G. under his breath. When he reached 6,000 feet he tested the ailerons and rudder and gradually tried putting the plane through various turns and dives. It seemed to take hours for the plane to respond to his commands. His flight instructors at E Base had told him to caress the stick, but to P.G. this control stick felt like a heavy billy club. "This is ridiculous," he thought. He quickly learned to use the control tabs on the left side of the cockpit behind the throttle. The tabs mechanically aided the use of the stick.

He took the plane up to 9,000 feet and decided to see how fast it would fly. As he pushed the throttle forward, the plane felt slow in responding but the airspeed indicator showed 275 mph. He pointed the nose down and dove the aircraft. The airspeed indicator read 375 mph. Diving this heavy-weighted plane obviously increased the airspeed. "If the engine cuts out, this thing will drop like a heavy lead sinker," thought P.G.

He decided to take the plane back up to 9,000 feet to see what would happen if he dropped the wing flaps. He slowed the plane down and dropped the flaps. The airspeed slowed and the nose came up. He retrimmed the plane. Then he tried dropping the wheels and flaps down at the same time. The plane really slowed down and he had to push the throttle forward to maintain airspeed. He raised the wheels and flaps and noticed the forward burst of speed. He continued to fly the plane for about two hours to get a "feel" for its flying characteristics. The plane was obviously not built for acrobatics.

Finally, he got up enough courage to request permission to enter the landing circle. He reminded himself, "For God's sake, remember to put the landing gear down." He felt the jolt in the cockpit when the wheels locked in place. Like most new torpedo bomber pilots, he brought the plane in fast, but he was pleasantly surprised when the plane sat down easily on the runway. The large wingspan and heavy weight of the plane helped make it a smooth touchdown. To increase his confidence he shot several more takeoffs and landings.

One positive aspect of postgraduate training at Opalacka was that most of the instructors were combat veterans from the Pacific War. Some were given instructor duty to give them a rest from the stress of being in combat. They were also there to use their experience in teaching the new young pilots. Some were eligible to wear the Navy Cross, Distinguished Flying Cross or Air Medals, but most of them didn't except on special formal dress occasions.

After a few drinks at the Officer's Club one night, a marine instructor who had once been recommended for the Congressional Medal of Honor, Captain Trowbridge, spoke of those most deserving of medals: "The real heroes are those pilots who die in combat, the ones actually shot at and killed. There's no way this nation can adequately honor them." Many of the veteran combat pilots, like him, related their experiences to the rookie pilots. Through casual conversation, the veteran instructors told the new aviators how to survive. They explained how to stay calm in combat, perform like a professional, destroy designated targets, and take evasive action properly so the pilot could live to fight again.

"Sometimes, in aerial combat, the odds may be stacked against you," said Captain Trowbridge, "but you'll fight like a bulldog. Some of you may die. If you're lucky, you'll live to talk about it. It's like the roll of the dice. If your number comes up; you lose."

Combat veterans with numerous battle experiences taught methods of attacking enemy ships. The instructors told it like it actually happened. One of the combat instructors was a Lieutenant Gregory Thompson. He was one of the senior instructors and had seen a lot of action. "When attacking a task force or fleet of ships, a coordinated effort is necessary if you hope to succeed," said Thompson. "Usually, the dive bombers come in high, taking advantage of any cloud cover, and dive out of the sun. The pilots fly the SBD Dauntless dive bomber at 10,000 to 20,000 feet and then they dive straight down like a bat out of hell because the plane is harder to hit that way.

"Their job is to disable the designated battleship or carrier, knocking out the guns, so the torpedo bombers can come in to finish the job. The torpedo bomber pilots are like the fullbacks on a football team trying to get a touchdown on the three-yard line. It is their task to complete the job."

Chuck Strong, one of the trainees, raised his hand. "I heard our torpedoes don't always work right. Is that correct?"

"Unfortunately, that's right," said Thompson. "The gyroscope, the instrument for keeping the torpedo on a steady and straight course toward the target, sometimes malfunctions, making the torpedo 'porpoise' or turn 180 degrees. It's a waste of a torpedo and often a waste of the pilot."

"Are they still dropping torpedoes?" asked Chuck.

"Yes, but not as often," said Thompson. "The navy air corps is now using the torpedo bombers to skip or glide bomb. Four 500-pound bombs are put in the belly of the torpedo bomber when the plane is used for skip bombing. This is a form of dive bombing. As the plane approaches the side of the ship from a high altitude, it starts its pull-out after the bomb either directly hits the top of the ship or its side. Of course, the closer the bomber descends toward the water, the easier it is to hit the target. While this is going on, the enemy's pouring shells into the air and it's like flying through a buzzsaw.

"A pilot has to have a lot of guts to be a successful torpedo bomber pilot," said Thompson. "The skill, daring, and tolerance of the pilot is extremely important. Dives don't always work according to the book because when a pilot pulls his plane out of a dive, the pull-out can cause the pilot to black out. The blood leaves the pilot's head for other parts of his body by centrifugal force—often referred to as Gs. Since the pilot becomes unconscious for a short period of time, the ability to come out of this state rapidly is important. The pilot needs to maintain control of his aircraft and get the hell out of the target site after bombing. The navy considers pilot blackouts unavoidable hazards in high-speed dives, and accidents and causalities do happen. Some pilots think blackouts contribute to getting hemorrhoids."

"Is that what happened to Rottenburger?" P.G. whispered to Chuck. "It would explain his lousy disposition."

The next day, the 12 trainee pilots flew out to the target area and started practicing skip- and glide-bombing techniques. The target was a wooden sled being towed behind a destroyer.

Since P.G. was now flying combat-operational aircraft, he was introduced to blackouts when doing these high-speed dives. It was a physical sensation that he had never experienced before. As he started to come out of the high-speed dive, he could feel the blood drain from his face and head, tightening up his facial muscles, before he lost consciousness. His facial muscles felt like hard leather. As he leveled off, the blood returned to his head and he became alert again. It was a strange sensation.

During the war, doctors and engineers searched for ways to prevent blackouts. They tried to develop a device to control the rush of blood from the pilot's head to his feet. The experimental anti-G suit exerted pressure on arterial pressure points and the stomach area to retard the flow of blood from the pilot's head. Also, pneumatic pads that inflated at the end of the dive helped reduce, or at least delay, the normal tendency to black out. The pad, like the anti-G suit, compressed the abdomen. In addition to blackouts, dive-bombing pilots faced the problem of punctured eardrums or nosebleeds while coming out of a dive. In order to survive, the pilot had to be in perfect health.

At Opalacka, rumors abounded that the Grumman Corporation was coming out with a more sophisticated torpedo bomber plane called the TBF-3 that would replace the dive bomber SBDs. Also, the new Grumman fighter planes, the F6Fs, had the capability to carry a bomb load. Most of the pilots liked the Grumman airplanes because they were rugged, reliable, and stable in the air. Eventually, the carrier air groups consisted of Grumman airplanes only, the F6Fs and the TBF-TBM-3s.

After completing dive- and skip-bombing exercises off the coast of Florida, most of the new torpedo bomber pilots got the opportunity to drop one torpedo at a target 300 miles off shore.

For the practice drop, the torpedoes had dummy heads so that no explosion resulted. Getting a good drop demanded a proximity to the sea that intimidated many pilots. To hit the target, a pilot had to be nearly skimming the waves before he dropped his load. A trial run took some guts but to drop a live torpedo with all the guns of an enemy battleship focused on shooting down the bomber took either nerves of iron or a brain of stone. P.G. couldn't decide which.

The torpedo bomber pilots were getting a taste of the real thing. Training intensity was turned up a full notch. To blow off steam, the pilots often went to the Bachelor Officer's Club late in the afternoon or on weekends. Late one afternoon, P.G. met Chuck Strong at the bar. They were getting to be good buddies.

"These planes we're flying look like they're ready for the grave-yard," said Chuck. "I hope I don't go there with them."

"Yeh, I agree with you," said P.G. "They sound like popcorn machines sometimes. The other day I tried to lean out the fuel mixture and the handle came off in my hand."

"What did you do?" asked Chuck.

"I flew the plane right back to the base. Rottenburger got mad and hollered at me."

"What did you tell him?"

"I wanted to tell him there's always hope for hemorrhoid suf-ferers," said P.G.

Chuck laughed. "Well, I downed two planes the other day and my instructor got his balls in an uproar. But I had the last laugh."

"What happened?"

"He got a flat tire taxiing out to the runway, and it took the crew two hours to get the plane out of the way. We had a great time in the air without him."

"So what have you heard?" asked P.G.

"We're going to be shooting field-carrier landings next week," replied Chuck. "I hear it's kind of risky, especially in the clunkers we're flying."

"The whole deal is risky," replied P.G. "What's new?"

Sure enough, the next week they started practicing field-carrier landings in preparation for landing on a real ship. This consisted of flying the torpedo bomber 200 feet above the ground with the flaps and wheels down in landing position. The object was to hit a spot on the runway that had been painted the approximate length of the landing area on an aircraft carrier. A landing signal officer, with brightly colored flags, stood at the left of the marked area on the landing strip and signaled a cut of the engine if he thought the pilot had established optimum position for landing.

One day, P.G. almost killed himself practicing field-carrier land-ings. The plane assigned to him was an old clunker on its last legs. Shot up in action in the Atlantic and repaired two or three times, it barely coughed up enough power to get off the landing strip. He didn't want to entrust his life to this old maid, but he had no choice.

Usually, a pilot shot 15 to 20 practice field-carrier landings and then returned to the base. After shooting about five landings and hitting the spot area accurately, he gunned the plane to take off again. He circled the field, made a good approach, and got the plane into the groove. Watching the landing signal officer, he received the signal to cut the throttle for landing. The plane was slow and in a good stall position. His airspeed was about 100 knots.

As soon as the plane hit the ground, he knew he was in big trouble. The right front tire was flat. The right wing was going to dig in, and the plane would flip over. He quickly threw the control stick to the left and forward to try to get the plane up on its left wheel as rapidly as possible. He kept the right wing from digging into the ground and starting a cartwheel. The right wheel rim was already digging into the concrete and pulling the plane to the right. Luckily, he got the mammoth plane up on the left wheel and tire. He quickly decided to try to blow the tire on the left side by stepping hard on the left wheel rudder and brake. With screeching brakes and the smell of burning rubber, the left tire blew. The speed of the plane was much slower now. The plane went up the runway grinding the wheel rims. Then the tail came up, the propeller hit the concrete, and the engine stopped dead. He scrambled out of the cockpit before a fire started. His legs were shaking, and he felt cold sweat soaking his flight suit. The only damage to the plane was a bent prop and two flat tires.

When he got back to the base, he was ordered to fly again by the executive officer and was in the air within three hours in another plane. This was standard procedure so the pilot would maintain his confidence. The next day he was told there would be a Flight Board inquiry concerning the crash. Whenever there is an airplane crash, a Board of Inquiry is convened to determine cause and fault.

Two days later, the Flight Board made their inquiry. The landing signal officer was an honest man and took responsibility for the accident. On the record, he stated that the tire was flat before landing, but he didn't notice it until too late. Only after signaling a cut had he seen that the tire was flat. "Ensign Grant did a remarkable job of flying to prevent injury to himself and to his aircraft," said the L.S.O.

The chairman of the board, a navy captain, came up to P.G. after the inquiry, shook his hand and said, "Get back up there, Ensign, you did a good job in a tough spot. We're glad you weren't hurt."

He wasn't the only one who was glad!

11

Atlantic Fleet Operations, Norfolk, Virginia

After completing field-carrier landings at Opalacka Naval Air Station, P.G. and the pilots in his group were given orders to proceed to Glenview Naval Air Station to be checked out in carrier landings prior to assignment to the fleet.

Most of the pilots who came to the Glenview Carrier Qualification Training Unit had completed their operational training in carrier-based fighter planes, dive bombers, and torpedo bombers. Glenview provided them with their first real taste of landing an airplane on a flight deck. Two converted cruise ships, the U.S.S. *Wolverine* and the U.S.S. *Sable*, resided on the Great Lakes for use in checking out the pilots. These former cruise ships had flight decks constructed on them. Each pilot was required to land safely on the converted carriers eight times before he would receive a letter from the commandant clearing him for carrier duty.

The planes used for qualification were SNJ trainers similar to the ones used at Barin Field in Pensacola, although tail hooks were added to the fuselage. The navy wisely decided to use the cheaper training planes for carrier qualifications. Numerous accidents, such as blown tires, damaged propellers, and unscheduled baths in the Great Lakes, were common.

P.G. qualified for carrier duty and was ready to move on. He hit his eight landings right on the nose. Before leaving Glenview he took advantage of the chance to read the reports of the landing signal officer. His report said he had had a tendency to come in too high and too fast. "What did they expect a pilot to do?" he thought. "Did the navy expect a guy to come in too low and hit the rear end of the carrier, or come in too slow and spin the plane in and get killed?" Though a little annoyed, he couldn't get too upset. He qualified, and managed to avoid dumping a plane in the Great Lakes.

He then checked into the commandant's office and received orders to report to the Norfolk Naval Air Station in Virginia. Many of the postgraduate pilots traveled to Norfolk; it served as the home for one of the largest diversified naval bases in the country and for the Atlantic Fleet Command. The Newport News Shipyard was close by, and served as the manufacture and repair site for many of the large naval vessels. The Naval Air Station in Norfolk was a way station for rookie pilots before they went into combat for the first time. It also provided a place for seasoned veteran pilots to wait for reassignment.

The pilots became part of a pool of men awaiting assignment to carrier air groups. To maintain their flying expertise, they continued to fly planes at the Norfolk Naval Air Station or secured ferry duty, flying new planes out to the West Coast for transfer to carriers in the Pacific.

All through 1943 and 1944 the conflict in Europe raged and the war was fought in two main theaters against the Germans in Europe and the Japanese in the Pacific. The war effort in Europe was supported by the enormous capacity of the United States to manufacture new weapons in large quantities. However, delivering those weapons often posed a problem. The Merchant Fleet was frequently confronted by the highly successful German Submarine Fleet operating in the Atlantic. Hundreds of thousands of tons of Allied cargo needed for the build-up in Europe were sunk by German U-boats.

Admiral Ponitz, in charge of the German U-boat fleet, had cleverly placed his U-boats in an area known as the Mid-Atlantic Gap. This was the area where the submarines could operate beyond the range of land-based aircraft. Here, free from the threat of American planes, the U-boats roamed at will, searching out and destroying ships. They could safely surface at night to recharge their batteries.

The United States Navy Atlantic High Command stationed in Norfolk realized that a new type of aircraft carrier was needed to close this Mid-Atlantic Gap problem. They decided to try the escort carrier (CVE). This was a small carrier that had a composite squadron of 28 aircraft aboard, each plane manned by a trained carrier pilot. The TBF-TBM Avenger was the backbone of the new antisubmarine attack force. A smaller group of planes, Wildcat F4Fs and later F6Fs, would be on board to act as carrier aircraft patrol.

The Atlantic was an extremely dangerous place for the small carriers to operate because of the rough seas and inclement weather. It was equally tough duty for the pilots who were assigned to them and several pilots were lost—some in combat, many from operational accidents. They didn't enjoy this duty because they were fighting a very impersonal battle. Most pilots wanted to participate in naval air and sea battles in the Pacific rather than trying to find an enemy submarine operating under the surface of the Atlantic Ocean.

Initially, the CVE small carriers protected the Merchant Fleet by serving as escorts along with destroyers in the Atlantic convoy lanes. The technique did little to diminish the number of German submarines operating successfully in the mid-Atlantic, so eventually the navy organized the escort carriers into Hunter Killer Groups. A Hunter Killer Group was a CVE carrier with destroyers, usually three in number. They operated independent of the convoys and the Hunter Killer Groups stayed with a submarine contact until they scored a kill. About a dozen such groups operated in the Atlantic with their air group squadrons, and the tide suddenly changed: The United States began to sink German subs. The list of the CVE escort carriers that scored kills in the Atlantic included the U.S.S. *Boque*, the U.S.S. *Block Island,* and the U.S.S. *Guadalcanal.* Through the concentrated efforts of the Hunter Killer Groups, many German submarines were sunk and others were crippled.

One of the stumbling blocks facing the United States Navy was developing a way to prevent submarines from operating at night. Under the protection of darkness, German submarines surfaced and sank merchant vessels with surface guns and recharged their batteries. They stayed in the Mid-Atlantic Gap to be out of range of land-based planes. In 1943, the navy developed a radar system for the TBF-TBM Avenger. ASD-1 radar used a parabolic disk antenna mounted in a dome-like structure on the leading edge of the

Avenger's right wing. It could detect both surface and airborne targets at a greater range than other radars, and by adding extra fuel tanks to the bomb bay, the plane's operational range was increased to almost 2,000 miles.

Because of the success of these planes in detecting German submarines during the day, the navy chose the Avenger, equipped with new radar equipment, for use in night operations. Initially the pilot, with his radar operator, took off at sundown and remained in the air all night searching for submarines. If the plane's radar picked one up, the pilot contacted destroyers on the surface and guided them toward the enemy. The extra fuel tanks in the Avengers allowed the planes to stay keyed in on the target until contact was made, and then they returned to the ship at sunrise to make a daylight landing.

Because of the rough seas in the North Atlantic and losses in the past when pilots had attempted to land on carriers at night, no one conducted routine night operations early in the war. Planes consistently went up at sunset and returned at sunrise, but they never tried to land on board ship at night.

Captain Dan Gallery, the commanding officer of the escort carrier U.S.S. *Guadalcanal,* wanted to try night patrols with fully armed TBF-TBM Avengers. He presented a plan to his pilots proposing full 24-hour operations off the deck of his ship, and they were willing to try it.

To train carrier pilots for night-flying, he first sent them up at sundown to try landing at dusk. He then sent them up for night-carrier flying when there was a full moon. Later, as their skills in night-carrier landings improved, they flew in the worst weather and the blackest of nights. A few accidents befell pilots and escalated the risks for the flight deck crew as well; whirling propellers could cut a man in two. But the navy pilots soon mastered the difficult technique of making night landings while the ship's crewmen learned how to launch and land planes safely.

The development of night-flying demanded some adjustments. For example, blue-gray surface paint over a gray camouflage worked well for daytime flights but clearly failed for night operations. To reduce chances of detection, midnight blue replaced the gray on the night torpedo bombers.

Flame-dampening devices covered the plane's exhaust to obscure any light emitted by the engine. The cockpit lights were changed to red to improve the pilots' vision. Special edge lights, visible only from the air, outlined the sides of the carrier's deck. With these changes and the developing expertise of the men involved, Captain Gallery's pilots eventually flew and landed Avenger planes all night long. In a short period of time, the air group aboard the U.S.S. *Guadalcanal* sank two German submarines.

TBF-TBM Avengers proved to be the ideal planes for operating off the carriers at night. Besides carrying 350-pound aerial depth charges that would go off under water, Avenger planes were equipped to carry aircraft rockets. These rockets were mounted on firing rails under the wings of the plane, usually four on each, and the five-inch warheads could penetrate the thick steel of most submarines or surface vessels. The first use of these aircraft rockets was in January 1944, when they were fired against a German submarine. Shortly afterward, these aircraft rockets were used in the Pacific against Japanese submarines. The escort carriers, with their midnight blue Avengers, were eventually credited with more than ten kills against Japanese subs in the Pacific.

Navy pilots flying Avengers off the U.S.S. *Guadalcanal* were also credited with capturing a German submarine. The U.S.S. *Pillsbury* towed the German U-Boat 505 to port before it could be scuttled. It was the only German submarine captured during World War II. The composite Hunter Killer Groups began to eliminate the German U-boat threat in the Atlantic. The TBF-TBM Avengers had established themselves as versatile aircraft.

Replacement pilots for the Hunter Killer Groups usually came from the Atlantic Fleet Command at Norfolk Naval Air Station. Volunteers would be asked for. In the late spring and early summer of 1944, about 150 pilots waited in the Norfolk pool to be reassigned to carrier duty, and while stationed there, most of the carrier pilots lived in the Bachelor Officer's Quarters on the base. Their requirements included periodic flights to keep their skills intact, and weekday early-morning musters at the flightline of one of the hangars. Usually, when the air operations officer arrived, the senior officer present called the pilots to attention. The arriving officer then put them at ease and announced those pilots receiving orders for duty and the reassignment of those chosen to ferry aircraft out to the West Coast.

One day in June of 1944 stood out for P.G. The air operations officer asked for volunteers to act as replacement pilots for one of the Hunter Killer Groups in the Atlantic. He was forthright and honest about the assignment, stating that night-carrier landings on the small escort carriers would be part of the deal and would be risky. If not enough pilots volunteered, he would designate those pilots who would be checked out in night-carrier landings on a carrier operating out of Norfolk, either the U.S.S. *Solomon Islands* or the U.S.S. *Block Island.*

Some of the carrier pilots in the pool had been sitting around at the Norfolk Naval Air Station for three or four months waiting for assignment. They were trying to pick their slots, but unless they had girlfriends in the Norfolk area, most of them wanted to get the hell out of there and see action. Still, night-flying off a jeep carrier in the rough seas of the North Atlantic was not the duty they were looking for. The seasoned pilots, ones who had seen action and were in the pool, always told the others, "Don't volunteer for anything." So none of the pilots raised their hands to volunteer. "Hey, give me a chance," they replied to the officer.

Hoping to generate affirmative responses, the operations officer, a commander, made the statement, "If you have some buddies in the crowd, this is an opportunity for four or six of you to stay together and fly together. It will be a short tour of duty because the escort carrier that needs the replacement pilots has been out there in the Atlantic for four months and will be coming into shore in three months. Think it over," he said, "especially you torpedo bomber pilots. I will talk to all of you tomorrow."

That evening, in the barracks, arguments for and against volunteering were hotly debated by the pilots. All sorts of scuttlebutt was heard. Four of the torpedo bomber pilots decided to join up together: Bob Johnson, Tom Coy, Chuck Strong, and P.G. They were tired of ferrying planes to the West Coast and wanted to get back into the challenge of flying off the carrier deck. They would have preferred the opportunity to join an air group that flew off the deck of a large carrier, but volunteers couldn't be choosers, and besides, they reasoned the landing area on a jeep carrier was almost as large as the landing area on a large carrier. The big difference was that the pilot had to locate a smaller cork bobbing in the ocean.

The next morning when they mustered at the hangar, the men got a big surprise. The air operations officer had an announcement to make. "We have just received a directive from the Navy Department in Washington, D.C., that all torpedo bomber pilots not already assigned to duty will be checked out in night-carrier landings. There are 34 of you here now. If any of you decide to volunteer, you still can, and will be given preference for operational carrier duty. In other words, those who volunteer first will be first assigned. Are there any here who wish to volunteer?" Eight of the torpedo bomber pilots raised their hands. P.G. and his three buddies were in the group.

12

First Night-Carrier Landings

During the next week, the eight pilots got in more flight time than they had during the previous three months. They flew to outlying fields around the Norfolk Naval Air Station and practiced field-carrier landings with a landing signal officer standing at the end of the runway. After a solid week of practicing, the men flew out to a jeep escort carrier and successfully landed aboard.

Tom Coy spotted P.G. on the flight deck. "Piece of cake, huh, P.G.?" Tom needled him. "Just like landing on the carrier in the Great Lakes."

"Yeah, right, Tom. Except the Great Lakes didn't have 20-foot whitecaps, and the carriers didn't bob around as much."

P.G. and Tom both laughed, because they knew that regardless of where they were, at least they were back doing what they did best. They also knew there were several major differences they were going to have to get used to.

Flying aboard a real carrier for the first time, flying an operational aircraft, was a new experience for the young aviators. Practicing on land was nothing like the real thing. They were in the big time now. There was no room for error. As a pilot approached the landing area at the back of the carrier, it was necessary to get the plane into proper position. The pilot couldn't tell which way the deck was going because of the high speed of the plane. It could be coming up, going away, or could be rolling sideways. Wires were elevated across the width of the deck on the back of the flight deck, and the length of the landing area was only 200 feet. The landing approach had to be perfect so that an extended wire hook on the back of the plane's tail could catch the wire and jerk the plane out of the air. When the tail hook became engaged, the landing gear on the front of the plane was usually jammed down on the deck. It had to be sturdily built to withstand the jolt of the landing. Sometimes the gear collapsed. Flying at 120 mph, the plane would be pulled to a stop by the wire cable in about 30 feet. The dead stop usually snapped the pilot's head backward against the cushioned headrest. If the pilot missed the elevated wires in the landing area, there was a raised wire-cable barrier that could also stop the plane by entangling the propeller in its cables. This was the pilot's last chance to keep his plane on the deck. Some pilots were saved from going into the water when their plane's hook caught the top cable of the barrier. Pilots who walked away from that landing felt as if they had cheated death.

The pilot quickly learned to depend on the landing signal officer. As the pilot approached the deck of the carrier with his plane in the groove, he watched the L.S.O. The L.S.O. wore a brilliant-colored suit and held two brightly colored paddles indicating the position of the plane in preparation for landing. If the plane was too low, the signal officer would hold the paddles low, near his ankles. If the plane was too high, he would hold them over his head. If the plane's position was perfect, the paddles would be held straight and extended laterally at chest level. If the plane was in a dangerous position, he would receive a wave-off with the paddles being moved rapidly back and forth over the landing signal officer's head. If the pilot received a wave-off by the L.S.O. it was mandatory. There might be a damaged plane on the deck entangled in the barrier cables and one plane could land on top of the other. The pilot had to receive a "cut" from the L.S.O. in order to land on the deck. To indicate that the plane was in position to land, the L.S.O. would bring his paddle across his neck in a cutting motion.

There was also a steel net below and to the right of the flight deck that the landing signal officer could jump into if the approaching plane placed his life in jeopardy. The fast-approaching plane would seldom hit the back end of the carrier's deck, but when this happened, it usually resulted in a fatality. Sometimes, if the plane caught the hook too close to the outside edge of the flight deck, the plane would be pulled over the side into the water.

No doubt, flying off a jeep carrier was a challenge. At least that's how P.G. felt. After he made four or five landings on the flight deck, he gained a greater respect for the Avenger. Although heavy on the controls, the plane was easy to bring aboard ship, the wide wingspan and its great weight made the plane settle quickly on the deck once the hook caught the wire. He eventually found the plane could also sustain extensive battle damage and still fly.

Another week of day-carrier landings perfected their skills and familiarized them with catapult launches. There were two catapults on the front part of the deck. When a pilot catapulted off, he held his brakes and threw the throttle full forward with his flaps adjusted. The catapult then released and the plane traveled down the track going from zero to 120 mph in less than 150 feet.

Sometimes, problems developed when planes were catapulted. Depending upon the velocity of the wind and turbulence of the sea, the deck could go up and down from 30 to 70 feet in front of the plane. It was the catapult launching officer's job to make sure the planes were launched with the ship's nose pointing up. As the plane was catapulted, the pilot had to react quickly and gently pull back on the stick to avoid hitting a wave.

During daylight operations, the flight deck crew wore brightly colored helmets and shirts to distinguish them according to their duties. They would usually be crouching on the deck against the wind trying to avoid the air streams from the plane's propeller. The crew had to be as quick as scampering cats, for when the plane landed and caught a hook, they would run to unhook the wire so the landing plane could advance on the deck and leave space for the next plane. During an accident, they were all over the crash scene, ready to pull the pilot out of the plane because of the possibility of fire. If the plane skidded and bounced over the side, a bullhorn would sound to alert the destroyer coming up behind to pull the pilot and crew out of the ocean.

The pilots shot day-carrier landings for three weeks, perfecting their skills. There were a few accidents such as blown tires, damage to landing gear, and a couple of planes bounced over the side. The pilots were all rescued and no harm was done except for the loss of the planes.

At sundown General Quarters would sound, and everyone would go to their assigned battle stations. Darkness enveloped the ship and the stillness of the night felt menacing. The ship's hatches were closed, and the ship was blacked out in preparation for a possible submarine attack.

As the expertise of the carrier pilots improved, the time approached when attempts at night-carrier landings would begin. Finally, on a bright, moonlit night, it was time.

The landing signal officer came into the ready room and showed the pilots the special suit that he would be wearing. He would also use lighted wands at night similar to the paddles used during the day. His uniform was transformed into a glowing suit, lit up by a special light so the pilots could see him on the platform.

P.G. and the other pilots donned their red goggles, to acclimate their eyes to the darkness, while the group discussed methods for the landings. The pilots were all apprehensive.

Once the planes cleared the deck each pilot was called into the landing circle by a code name. Using a landing approach like the one used for any airport, the pilot entered a downwind leg; only here the landing field, the carrier, moved forward as the plane progressed downwind. Upon arriving opposite the carrier's fantail, the aviator then started his cross leg and made his approach behind the deck. Usually on the first pass, the planes were much too fast and the L.S.O. gave them a wave-off.

It soon became obvious to the pilots that in the daytime the horizon was helpful. At nighttime, the pilot had to rely on his instruments to fly. The radio altimeter was extremely important because the fliers had no visual way to gauge their height above the water.

It was the pilot's responsibility to have the tail hook and wheels down in place, because the landing signal officer could not see them. The L.S.O.'s role was critical to these night landings, and along with the pilot, he was evaluated at this new and dangerous exercise.

As P.G. directed his plane into the groove for his first night landing, he reminded himself not to come in too slow. He wanted to avoid a spin or stall as he approached the carrier's deck. A perfect landing had to be performed. He saw the landing signal officer, got the cut, and suddenly felt a jolt as the tail hook caught the wire and his head was thrown back against the headrest. Bingo. The crew quickly unfastened the hook, thus freeing him to taxi his plane up to the front of the deck, where he lined his plane up with the others to be catapulted off the deck for more practice.

"Hell, this is going to be easy," he said.

His second night landing was a true ass-tightener. He got into the groove behind the carrier's deck perfectly and received a cut from the landing signal officer. He then got the scare of his life. When he pulled back on the throttle to cut the power and try to catch a wire, instead of the flight deck going away from him, it was rushing up at him. His front wheels slammed the deck first and the nose of the plane bounced toward the sky. He had to get the plane back to the deck rapidly. He slapped the stick forward, hard, and then gently pulled back on it so the plane could catch a wire. He caught a late wire and the Avenger settled down. P.G. sat dead still in the cockpit and caught his breath.

"Goddamn! It ain't going to be easy! I could easily kill myself."

He made two more night landings that evening and each one was a new experience. The many variables involved were incredible, and it seemed almost unjust that with all his training, all his skills, he and the other pilots were throwing darts at a board when it came to night landings. P.G. realized it was the ultimate test of the pilot's reflexes, visual acuity, and flying ability and there was no room for error. "Fine," he thought. He could make no mistakes. Not one. Otherwise he could be dead.

Landings progressed quite well until late in the evening. One of the planes failed to catch a wire and went over the side. The bull-horn went off. The pilot, dazed by the crash landing, almost went down with the plane because he had forgotten to release his seat belt and shoulder parachute harness after he hit the water; a swimmer from the destroyer pulled him out of the plane as it sank.

All the pilots were scared shitless before making their first night-carrier landing, but after making six or eight successful landings, their confidence returned. Some were unable to conquer their fears and were eliminated before they killed themselves or someone else. The eight volunteer torpedo bomber pilots passed the test and were cleared to join the night-flying Hunter Killer Groups. Only four were needed, however. Bob Johnson, Chuck Strong, Tom Coy, and P.G. got the assignment.

P.G. stood on the deck at dawn, unable to sleep after that first night of landings. He looked out over the heaving gray whitecaps and saw the expanse of the ocean. His pulse quickened and he felt his heart beating; he knew the part of him that was a pilot had to rise to the challenge. It was a new experience for him, and he sensed that a pilot's life must be led in fear and arrogance. There was no room for anything else.

13

Night Submarine Attack

The next day Lieutenant Bob Johnson, Ensigns Tom Coy, Chuck Strong, and Peter Grant were passengers in two TBF Avengers as they flew out to the Mid-Atlantic Gap. They were replacement pilots for one of the jeep Hunter Killer Groups.

It was a new adventure for the pilots to be passengers in the belly of the torpedo bomber plane. The planes had their bomb bays loaded with extra fuel tanks and were to fly 800 miles out into the Atlantic and then land aboard the jeep carrier that would serve as their base.

The pilots had never been in the belly of the torpedo planes before, and after being shot off the deck they preferred sitting in the cockpit, where they could see all the action. Landing aboard the jeep carrier in the Avenger's belly was no picnic either. When the hook engaged, P.G. and company were slammed forward, then aft, then forward as the plane settled on the deck.

"Goddamn," said P.G. "this is worse than riding with no hands on a roller coaster!"

Once aboard the jeep carrier, the pilots were assigned to living quarters which consisted of a bunk and a locker. All the pilots slept near the ready room, which became the focus of most of their attention, for it was here that they received their daily flight instructions and if they weren't logging sack time, they spent most of their time there.

The four replacement pilots quickly fit in with the other pilots in the air group and were welcomed. They were soon playing poker, acey deucy, and hearts with the other pilots when they weren't flying or stacking Zs.

The day after their arrival they were assigned to daytime flight search lines. Lieutenant Bob Johnson was a former combat pilot and was permitted to fly with his buddy, Ensign Tom Coy. The day and night search lines were usually flown in pairs. Because Chuck Strong and P.G. had volunteered together, the torpedo bomber skipper said he would let them fly as a team.

During the first three weeks, the fresh pilots had a chance to take in the complexities of maintaining carrier operations 500 miles out in the Atlantic, an ocean as rough as any in the world. The destroyers were usually refueled first, since they carried the smallest tanks. A line was attached from the tanker to the destroyer and sometimes it looked as if the destroyer was underwater as it was being refueled. The oil tankers were very large ships and were much more stable than the destroyers. They had a very low center of gravity, heavy displacement, and relatively small superstructures. When the sea was rough and ships had to be refueled, the fuel lines would sometimes break and thousands of gallons of fuel would end up in the ocean.

After P.G. and the replacement pilots were at sea for three weeks the jeep Hunter Killer Group ran into a severe storm. All flights were cancelled and the skippers of the four navy vessels had to detach themselves from the formation and spread out so that the ships wouldn't hit each other. Waves reached a height of 40 to 60 feet and from the carrier deck, the destroyers would seem to disappear under the waves. The pouring rain and hurricane winds tossed the ship around. Swells smashed against the bulkheads.

The carrier experienced the worst problems. Some of the steel pad eyes that were welded to the decks to anchor the planes got torn off with the heavy rolling of the ship. A few planes broke loose. They crashed against other planes on the flight deck and hangar deck, and the danger of fire was imminent. Security watches had to be increased to monitor the lines.

With the heavy rolling and gale-force winds sweeping across the flight deck, it was almost impossible to work topside. Men swept overboard usually were not recovered. Sometimes the rolls created by the waves became so severe the ship seemed certain to roll over.

Below decks, P.G. and Chuck were nauseous and scared, concentrating very hard on not getting sick in their bunks. The rolling motion of the ship was tough, but when the ship's screws came out of the water they spun crazily without the resistance of the sea and rattled every plate on the carrier. They hoped the welders who put the ship together had taken their time. The worst that could happen was the ship could pop a plate. That would be just as bad as catching a torpedo.

The storm lasted for a long time, and hot food could not be served. The plates would break and besides, the food wouldn't stay down anyway. Sandwiches and coffee were available and even some of the most seasoned members of the crew had queasy stomachs.

Two planes were washed overboard by the mountainous seas, rolls of the carrier, and the brisk wind. The ship was lucky that no fires were started. The planes that were torn from their moorings slid off the flight deck into the water.

After three days, the storm let up as quickly as it had begun. The sea suddenly became smooth as silk and the sun broke through the clouds. The bright sun hurt one's eyes at first after three days of darkness. It was a welcome sight. The next day, the three destroyers joined up and a full damage report was issued. Except for the loss of the two planes on the flight deck, the four ships survived. The skipper of one escort destroyer thought the stability of his ship was suspect. Some of the seamen hoped there would be enough damage to at least one of the ships so they would be allowed to head to port, but that never materialized.

Routine day- and night-flights commenced that afternoon and Lieutenant Johnson and Ensign Coy entered action quicker than they anticipated. They were first given daytime search lines, which were boring. The pilots of the two planes remained in sight of each other and flew near the surface of the water to prevent detection by the enemy's radar. With each bomb bay loaded with an extra fuel tank, they traveled from 400 to 600 miles away from the escort carrier. Sometimes wing tanks were also used. Unless the weather was bad, the two planes kept visual contact; only under unusual circumstances was radio contact employed. For communication, the pilots used a flashing signal light.

Throughout the flights, the radar operator constantly searched the water surface for unusual blips, but the German submarines usually stayed under the security of the ocean's surface during the day.

The automatic pilot was frequently used, particularly when a change in Point Option was announced in code by the carrier. The navigation board would be pulled out in the front of the cockpit and the new vectors and positions (latitude and longitude) would be placed on the board. The pilot would then have to recalculate his position in relation to the carrier.

After flying for two weeks on daytime search lines, Bob and Tom were assigned to night duty, and they found flying search lines for enemy submarines at night no less tedious. It wasn't too bad flying at night if the moon was out. The galaxy of stars could be downright rapturous. If the pilot concentrated on his work and didn't think about the hazards of flying over the big Atlantic Ocean with a single engine plane, that was okay, too. Without enemy action, flying at night was boring. Four weeks of frustrating flying crept by before all hell broke loose.

One night, during bad weather, the two pilots decided to fly formation on one another, wing tip to wing tip. They also flew a little higher off the water, not trusting the radio altimeter. They took turns flying wingman on each other because the lead pilot could go on automatic; the wingman had to fly by sight and the seat of his pants. Flying in formation at night was nerve-wracking.

Bob Johnson's radar operator was the first to detect a blip on the water. "I've got an unidentified blip 70 miles at 30 degrees on the surface of the water," said Bill Jones, his radar operator.

"Notify Tom and see if his radar operator can confirm," responded Bob. "Use the signal light." He felt his pulse come up a step, bringing his body into readiness.

The radar operator signaled to the other plane. "They got it, too," he replied.

"Okay, tell Tom we're going down on the surface of the water. Tell him to arm his aerial depth charges. We'll use our rockets if we can catch them on the surface. We'll drop some lighted parachute flares or a float light on the surface of the water to mark the spot if we need to. Tell him we're going full throttle ahead. I'm going off automatic." They were quite a distance away from the escort carrier, but Bob's check of the fuel gauge showed enough left for the attack and return.

The radar blip brightened on the scope as they got closer. Pushing the throttle to the fire wall, Bob knew that he and his buddy would have one quick shot at whatever was on the surface. "Ten miles to target, continue at 30 degrees," announced the radar operator.

Bob figured that he was within two or three minutes of being over the target. Suddenly, out of the dark blue, bullets ripped through the sky as the enemy ship opened fire. It was a submarine on the surface recharging its batteries: Bob and Tom had caught the Germans with their pants down. The German gunners didn't realize they were lighting up their sub for the midnight blue Avengers.

Johnson was now flying at an altitude of 400 feet so he could point the plane's nose down and aim his rockets at the sub without going into the water. He pulled the pistol trigger for the rockets and let all eight go in one salvo. An explosion tore up through the sky as he scored a direct hit amidships. Tom followed up with his rockets and suddenly there was silence on the water. The planes circled the area. A float light and dye marker were dropped to mark the spot, and parachute flares were used. Aerial depth charges were also dropped to make sure they had finished the job.

The attack occurred so quickly that the command base at the escort carrier had not been informed. The latitude and longitude of the attack were calculated, and Bob called the Combat Information Center on the escort carrier to announce the kill. There was rejoicing in the command center.

After the call to the carrier, Bob Johnson looked at his fuel gauge; his fuel was running low, and his prospects for a safe return to the escort carrier were diminishing. He leaned out his fuel mixture and headed home with Tom on his wing. The escort carrier and destroyers were vectored to the area, sailing in the direction of the planes to close the distance. With a probable kill behind them Bob and Tom began their two-hour journey back to the escort carrier, hoping they had enough fuel.

They made it. After being debriefed by the air operations officer, they repeated their account of the attack for the pilots in the ready room. Crews on the destroyers later spotted an oil slick and debris in the attack area, which confirmed the kill.

P.G. and Chuck were elated that their buddies from the Norfolk pool had sunk a German submarine. The entire ship's crew and air group were proud of them. The Atlantic Fleet Command was jubilant.

One week later, P.G. and Chuck were on a night search line in the Mid-Atlantic Gap, when Chuck's radar operator spotted a blip on his radar screen. They raced full speed ahead to blast another sub out of the water. At 5 A.M., they shot all of their wing rockets into the target with no response from the enemy. They thought the sub had dived and got away. The next day, a destroyer reported two whale carcasses floating on the surface. What a way to kill fish!

Although they did not see combat on this short stint of duty flying off the CVE jeep carriers, P.G. and Chuck felt they had increased their expertise and would be better pilots. Suddenly, they too felt more like veterans.

With little difficulty, they mastered the prescribed recognition signals and shackle code, carrier operating instructions, deck signals, and belly tank or wing tank release methods.

After the four pilots had served aboard the CVE carrier for eight weeks, the captain of the ship announced that the ship was being detached and would be going back to the Norfolk Naval Base. It had been a successful Atlantic cruise for the CVE jeep carrier, for it had sunk another German submarine.

14

Virginia Beach Interlude

Sarah was not happy when she found out that P.G. was flying out over the Atlantic in search of German submarines. She constantly asked her father about P.G.'s whereabouts and the danger of this type of operation. Unfortunately, her father couldn't do much to find out about P.G.'s mission, due to its classified nature.

"You really love that guy, Sarah, don't you?" he remarked.

She looked at her father and held his gaze. "I want to spend my life with him," she said.

"You're that sure? How long have you known?"

"Since I first saw him at the ball."

"Love at first sight, is that it?"

"The very words for it. You don't believe me, do you?"

"I'm not sure. I do believe you're young and impressionable."

"And you're old and cynical," said Sarah. Her father closed his eyes and took a deep breath. Sarah recognized the warning and regretted her words. If anyone would side with her in her love for P.G., it would be her dad. "I apologize," she said softly. "You didn't deserve that."

"Apology accepted. And maybe you're right about me. But let's say skeptical instead of cynical. It sounds better."

Sarah smiled and looked down. "Fair enough," she said.

"There's one rule in war, Sarah: Young men die. You're a freshman in college and you must understand. Your beau took on one of the most dangerous jobs in this war. He's got guts. He lives one day at a time. If he dies, Sarah, your life will have to go on."

"Yes, I realize that," said Sarah, a little too quickly. She wanted out of this conversation.

"No, I don't think you do," her father said quietly. "You're a young lady on the brink of becoming a woman. There's great joy in growing up, but the stakes are high, especially in wartime. If you want to love someone, you have to be able to take the pain of losing him. I hope you're that strong."

"Daddy," she said, "I know what I want and I'm going after it. I'm determined, and I think I come by that trait honestly."

Her father grimaced and thought, "The girl knows how to get what she wants, doesn't she?"

"Does your mother know how you feel?"

"Not really. She's holding out hope that I'll marry a southern gentleman."

"Hm. Well, I can't blame her. You do have roots in the South."

"Can you talk to her?"

"For you?"

"Yes."

"I can try. That's all I can do. I know you, Sarah, and I know you'll find a way or make a way to do what you want. But the bonds of family come first. Harden your heart to us and a part of you will die as surely as if you lost Peter Grant."

Sarah stood there and felt the weight of her father's words. She breathed shallowly and felt her eyes burning. She stepped into her father's arms and buried her face against his chest, feeling the rough cotton of his shirt on her cheek.

"I could never . . ." she mumbled, "I could never do that."

"Okay, baby, okay," he said. "Take it easy. I'll talk to your mother." She gave him a big hug. "Tomorrow I'll see if I can find out when P.G. returns to his base." Her arms tightened around him and he thought, "Oh, the things we do for the love of our children."

The next morning at breakfast, Sarah's father told her the news: He'd called Atlantic Fleet Command in Norfolk and found out that P.G. would be returning soon. "I'm going to Norfolk when he comes in," said Sarah immediately.

"You'd better ask your mother first. You'll miss some of your classes at the university."

"I can make them up. I'll study on the train going up there so I won't fall behind."

"Your mother won't approve."

"I know, and I'm sorry," she said, "but I'm still going." Her green eyes flashed.

"Well, you've got a few weeks to convince your mother."

During that time, Sarah worked on her mother and begged for her blessing to go on the trip. Her persistence paid off.

"If you're going to Norfolk, you'll need some new clothes," she said. "Your father has some officer friends up there who will help to keep an eye on you while you're there. Perhaps you could stay with one of them."

"Oh, mother, I don't want to be chaperoned by one of daddy's officer friends. Besides, I have my own money, and I'm sure I can find a nice place to stay."

"One of your daddy's friends has a cottage at Virginia Beach," said her mother. "You can stay with them."

"We'll see. But I don't want to be chaperoned."

During the next week, Sarah and her mother went shopping. Her mother wanted to buy her a lot of frilly dresses. Sarah wasn't interested. She was more intent on finding new bathing suits and fancy lingerie. She sneaked away one afternoon and found a shop that had bathing suits styled with low-cut backs; and bought a pretty emerald green one. A lingerie shop was harder to find, but she finally located one in downtown Atlanta. As she selected the sheerest nightgown she could find, she thought, "Okay, P.G., I'm not holding anything back. Let's see what you've got."

Sarah had been in touch with P.G. only through her letters and hadn't decided whether she should surprise him or tell him of her plans. She decided she would surprise him.

Word came to Sarah's father that the jeep carrier would be coming into Norfolk in two weeks. Her parents were amazed at the frenzy of her activities. She got up and jogged every morning, played tennis with her girlfriends, and swam at the university pool.

"What's she up to?" her mother asked her father.

"She's just a healthy, athletic girl who wants to be in good shape when she sees her man," said her father.

"Well, I hope she can handle that ensign," said her mother.

"I'm sure she can," replied her father. "I was able to handle you."

"That's different," she said, as she looked at her husband over the top of her glasses.

When the jeep carrier pulled into port at Norfolk, the ship's crew and officers were all on deck. A booming cheer rose from the ship and was matched by the crowd. Wives and children of all ages cried with gratitude and relief.

P.G. and Chuck shouldered their way through the crowd, grabbed a cab, checked into the Bachelor Officer's Quarters at the Norfolk Naval Air Station, and made plans for the evening to raise hell and get drunk. P.G. planned to call Carrot Top since he had five days off. He figured he'd head in her direction the next morning.

The two ensigns took "real" showers, shaved, and headed for the Officer's Club. Quite a few of the pilots and single officers had beat them there.

After P.G. and Chuck had a couple of highballs, a page came over the loud speaker. "Ensign Grant, report to the front lobby."

"What the hell is that about?" asked P.G., a bit put out that he was being pulled away from his friends.

"You'd better go find out," said Chuck.

P.G. went out to the front lobby and, standing there with red hair shining like a sunset was Sarah. "My God," thought P.G. in disbelief. She looked stunning in her white high heels and white dress. She ran toward him. He was speechless. They ran into each other's arms and clung to each other.

"Oh, God. Oh my God," said Sarah.

"Save your 'Oh God's' for later. Kiss me." And she did—long, softly, and tenderly. When they finally stopped, P.G. looked down and said, "Let's go find a place to be alone."

"Daddy's officer friend is letting us use his beach cottage at Virginia Beach for three days," said Sarah, "if that's all right with you."

"All right? Are you kidding me? You and three days at a beach cottage? Is anyone else going to be there?"

"Not if I can help it," she laughed.

"Great! I'll go tell Chuck I won't be back, and then I'll go to my room at the B.O.Q. and get some clothes. I'll have to get a rental car so we can drive to Virginia Beach." His brain was at full throttle.

"I've already taken care of that, too," she replied with a big smile.

"Well, it certainly seems like you've taken care of everything."

"Just wait," Sarah thought to herself. "You haven't seen anything yet."

P.G. got some clothes and packed his bag. He and Sarah got into a Chevy rental car and started driving to Virginia Beach. It was about 7:30 P.M. and Sarah hadn't eaten all day. "Would you like to eat first or make love first?" asked P.G.

"Make love," she said as she smiled at him.

They stopped for a quick bite to eat and arrived at the beach about 9:00 P.M. The cottage was dark and dusty so they opened all the windows to let the fresh air in and then started to look around.

"Not a soul on the beach," said Sarah. "Why don't we take a swim?"

"Might as well," said P.G. "I've been on dry land for almost six hours. Hey," he said, startled, "I'm not sure I brought my bathing suit."

"Just wear your skivies. We can go skinny dipping if you want," she said.

"Sounds good to me!"

Sarah quickly got into her new low-cut, tight-fitting emerald green bathing suit. Her muscular, athletic figure looked as if it were poured into the suit.

"Hey, Sarah," said P.G., taking in her figure. "Come here." She did. He slid his hands around her waist and pressed his hips against her. He was speechless. Then he managed to blurt out, "You're beautiful!"

She smiled and grabbed his hand and they ran out to the beach. She dove into the water and he dove in after her. Sarah was an excellent swimmer, but he was not to be denied. He caught her and crushed her wet body to his. The water was shallow and warm. The moon was full, outlining her beautiful figure. He slipped the straps of her bathing suit off her shoulders and gently cupped her breasts. She pushed him away and slipped out of her bathing suit. With one big heave, the suit was thrown on the beach. He quickly stepped out of his sopping shorts and flung them after her suit.

"Catch me if you can," she yelled, as she ran through the surf away from him.

He dashed after her. Finally he caught up with her and pulled her to him. Her body was pale white in the moonlight, and her red hair glistened. He touched the beautiful jewels of her nipples. She gently arched her body against him. They fell together in the shallow water. She sighed and gently squirmed as she aroused the young officer's body. Her hips rotated rapidly into his as his mouth reached for her nipples. She sighed in deep passion as her legs wrapped around his. He drove harder trying to answer all her bodily movements. She felt his muscles flex and harden as she drove against him furiously. They moaned with ecstasy as they reached the climax together.

"Oh, Peter, I love you so much."

"I love you, too, Sarah, and someday I hope you'll be mine. I wish the war would end right now."

"So do I," Sarah murmured. "So do I."

During the next three days they nurtured the growing closeness of their relationship and their frequent exchange of love built a strong bond between them. There was time for frank discussions and the exchange of ideas. Behind that veil of Sarah's beauty was a human being with a keen and imaginative mind. P.G. learned that she had been brought up by her parents in the classic southern tradition and it had been instilled in her that she must marry a southern gentleman. It became obvious that in her relationship with him she had rejected this concept.

Her mother, he learned, did not relish the fact that she was falling in love with a Connecticut Yankee. Sarah's father was willing to compromise for his daughter's happiness and realized that the deep southern traditions were rapidly changing and the ideological boundaries between the states were being erased by the war. Blacks and whites, northerners and southerners, were fighting side by side trying to protect this great country of ours.

In the daytime, they spent most of their time at the beach, soaking up sun or swimming in the surf. He found out that she loved classical music and was a constant book-reader. She said reading a good book cleared her mind of cobwebs. Their conversations explored the depth of their thoughts and sometimes invaded the inward strengths of their convictions. He found out that she had a definite mind of her own and quite a temper and that her green eyes brightened or dimmed in response to favorable or unfavorable comments. Her temper did not diminish his love for her, however.

The time grew short for them. Sarah would have to return to Athens, Georgia, and he would have to go back to flying torpedo bombers. Their last evening together at the beach was traumatic.

Lying in bed, exhausted, they both had fallen asleep. He was awakened by soft sobbing from Sarah. She was dreaming and tears were rolling down her cheeks. P.G. decided to awaken her. He gently pulled her to him. Sarah lurched forward and gasped. Then, realizing his presence, she clung to him.

"P.G., hold me tight. I had a horrible dream. I dreamed that we would never see each other again. You were killed in an airplane crash. It was horrible."

"Sarah, I'm right here and I'll do everything in my power to stay alive."

"Oh, Peter, I'm scared. I hate that dream!"

He gently caressed her as she pulled him closer to her. Their bodies melded together in another shared moment of exquisite happiness. "P.G., please, please, don't ever leave me."

"Sarah, I think we should get engaged soon." He was shocked at hearing his own words and even more surprised that he'd spoken what he felt in his heart.

After hearing that, Sarah smiled and hugged him even tighter. She fell asleep in his arms with a smile on her face.

15

Night-Flying in the Northeast

After the five-day break, Ensigns Pete Grant and Chuck Strong were assigned to the pilot replacement pool at Norfolk. They weren't too happy about the prospect that they might have to go back out into the Atlantic with a jeep Hunter Killer Group. They were more interested in joining a large air group that might be going to the Pacific.

Because of the success of the night Hunter Killer Groups in the Atlantic, the navy command decided to expand the use of night fighters and night torpedo planes. In the summer of 1944, the navy sent a directive to all naval air stations asking for volunteers for night-carrier duty. The plan was to form night air groups that would operate from large carriers. The groups would have pilots completely trained in day and night landings to allow for 24-hour protection for the fleet. P.G. was in the pilot pool at the Naval Air Station in Norfolk at that time and since the directive requested volunteers, he and Chuck decided to apply so they could fly together.

They were interested in becoming part of a full-fledged air group heading toward the Pacific. The operational risks were greater flying from carriers at night, but flying skills good enough to survive landing at night provided a better chance of surviving the war.

The group, including P.G. and Chuck, received orders to proceed to the Naval Air Station at Quonset Point, Rhode Island. The site was selected because of its inclement weather and fog. Northeast weather would be ideal for putting the night pilots through the mill. The weather conditions would help simulate flight conditions that a pilot would encounter while night-flying off a carrier.

When the pilots arrived at Quonset Point, they had to retake their physical examinations and also underwent additional extensive eye tests. There was a new dietary aspect to their training. Carrots were frequently on the menu and meals were adjusted to contain additional foods high in vitamin A. Its presence was necessary for the production and regeneration of the visual purple of the retina in the back of the eye. The doctors told them they had to have adequate vitamin A in their bodies because its deficiency caused night blindness.

During the next three months, the navy pilots received additional instrument training on the ground and in the air. A night fighter squadron and torpedo bomber squadron were formed. They were later joined to form Night Air Group 53. The group was being trained for a specific purpose. The night fighter planes and their pilots were being trained to protect the fleet at night. They would be used primarily for night combat air patrol and were taught how to use their planes' radar to identify enemy aircraft and ships at night. They were also taught how to use their flight instruments to complete an interception and how to follow radar ground control instructions.

There was a big difference in the training of the torpedo bomber pilots. They would be a strike force acting as an offensive unit, rather than a defender or a protector. They were also being trained in long-range night scouting patrol. Because of the size of the torpedo bomber, a more powerful and sophisticated radar could be carried in the belly for air-to-surface detection of enemy ships and air-to-air combat.

The night-fighter and torpedo bomber pilots were eventually trained to work as a team. If a bogey was detected on the carrier's radar scope, the information was transmitted to an Avenger equipped with night radar. The Avenger would then give out vectors to the fighter pilot for the intercept. Visual contact would be made, and the plane engaged and shot down.

The pilots of Night Air Group 53 were told that the first attempts at night intercepts were made in the Gilbert Islands Campaign in November 1943. The carrier *Enterprise* had been bombarded, taking fire from Japanese Bettys for two nights. The commander of Air Group 6, Ed Butch O'Hare, took to the skies when a large group of bombers came back. There were three planes: two fighters and one TBF Avenger. The Avenger found the targets on the radar scope and opened fire on the Japanese Bettys. One Betty caught fire and exploded, and a second was shot down.

This was the first successful night interception and attack by the radar-equipped fighters and torpedo planes working as a team. In the confusion that developed during the night battle, Butch O'Hare was lost. No one knew how. The loss of Butch O'Hare was a tremendous loss to the United States Navy. He had earned the Congressional Medal of Honor and had become the navy's first Ace of World War II.

The planes assigned to P.G.'s outfit were the latest navy planes, namely TBM-3Ns. These Grumman Avenger torpedo bombers had been adapted for night-flying with a bubble on the right wing that had a radar antenna. The radar had been improved from that used by the torpedo planes with the Hunter Killer Groups in the Atlantic.

At the Quonset Point Naval Air Station, Night Air Group 53 did most of their flight work beginning at sundown, flying from 7:00 P.M. to 2:00 A.M., and sometimes all night long.

Most of the night landing and takeoff bounce drills were done at the outlying airstrips in Charlestown and Westerly. The offshore scouting line flights and bombing exercises usually originated at the main Naval Air Station at Quonset. It was often difficult to determine what the impending weather would be, but flights were seldom canceled.

P.G. and the pilots of VTN-53 were taught day and night tactics by experienced combat veterans who had flown in the Pacific, and others who had flown off the CVE Hunter Killer Groups at night in the Atlantic. At the ground school at Quonset Point, where the pilots learned flying strategies, question and answer periods between the veteran combat instructors and the newer pilots followed each teaching session. The question most often asked was: "If you have an air fight at night, how do you tell your own planes from the enemy's?"

"It can be difficult," said the combat instructor, "because the plane is just a blip on the screen. However, if he's a friendly, he should have his IFF (identification friend or foe) gear turned on, and this can be checked. If there's any question, you'll need visual contact before shooting him down. This puts you at greater risk, though, because Japanese Bettys and other planes have rear-firing 20-mm cannons. The more sophisticated radar gear in the Combat Information Center back on the carrier can help you sometimes if you need it."

"What if the weather is really bad and you can't make visual contact? What do you do?" asked P.G.

"That type of decision probably has to be made back at the base. The Combat Information Center should know if any enemy planes are in the area. If you can't see them, you have to rely on radar equipment back at the base and hope that the technicians and boss in the command center know what they're doing. Don't be afraid to ask for instructions. A blip on a radar screen can be one of your own or the enemy."

One of the ensigns raised his hand. "What if you don't have time to get instructions from the Combat Information Center? Let's say, someone is shooting at you."

"You're on your own. You either take evasive action or try to destroy your opponent. In the air you're the captain of your plane, and it's your decision as to how you respond. You have every right to defend yourself."

Most of these sessions with the instructors provoked prolonged conversations and bull sessions in the dining hall. It was obvious that there weren't answers to all the questions. Something new was being developed—night-flying off the carriers.

P.G. and Chuck Strong had become close friends in Norfolk, Virginia, and were now rooming and flying together at Quonset Point, Rhode Island. Usually before flying at night, they would eat in the dining hall at the B.O.Q. The food was excellent and often had a New England flavor to it; clam chowder, swordfish, or lobster would sometimes be on the menu. Chuck Strong, who grew up in the midwest, really enjoyed New England seafood and could wolf it down.

After eating, they would take the shuttle bus to the hangars and check in at the ready room. On the flight board, the pilots flying that night would be listed with their assignments.

One evening P.G. and Chuck went out to the flight line. They didn't think they would be flying because the fog had rolled in over the coastline.

"What do you think, Chuck, we going up tonight?" asked P.G.

"I don't think so. The ceiling is close to zero and I can hardly see my hand in front of my face."

"Well, maybe we can get a card game going. It would be better than flying in this soup."

When the twosome arrived at the hangar's ready room, the torpedo bomber skipper was there. "Only half of the group will be flying tonight," said the skipper. "We don't want too many planes in the air in this lousy weather. We're still going to fly some scout lines and search missions. The bomb bays will be loaded with extra gas tanks in case there's a serious weather problem that you have to fly out of. We all have to learn how to fly in this bad weather, you know."

P.G. and Chuck looked at the flight board and sure enough they were assigned to fly.

"I don't like it," said Chuck.

"Neither do I," said P.G.

The two were assigned an offshore search line of 400 miles toward Newfoundland. Aerology had reported a severe storm in the area. P.G. and Chuck knew that storms off the northeast shores of New England could be fierce.

"Gentlemen, because of the foul weather tonight, you'll probably have to take off together so that you won't lose contact with each other. If the weather gets too bad, you're to return to base," said the skipper. The two pilots stared at him until he looked up. "Now, get moving, you guys," he said.

P.G. and Chuck walked out to the flight line together. "For God's sake, what are they trying to do to us?" asked Chuck.

"They want to see if we're good instrument pilots," said P.G.

"I'm not ready to meet my maker," said Chuck. "And I certainly don't want to meet him in the Atlantic Ocean. I noticed the skipper isn't flying tonight."

"Yeah, I saw that too," said P.G. "We'd better stay close together. You never know what's going to happen. I'll take off from the runway flying on your wing because once we get airborne, we could get lost in the fog."

"Okay," said Chuck. "Maybe we can fly high enough to get above the overcast. One consolation is that we're going to have our bomb bays filled with auxiliary gas tanks. Hey, maybe we'll end up in San Francisco."

"I wouldn't mind that," said P.G.

They walked out to the flight line together. When they got to their planes, they walked around the TBM-3Ns to make sure there were no problems with the equipment. The planes they would be flying were parked next to each other. Their code names for the evening were Fox 6 and Fox 7. The field was fogged in and visibility was reported at about 800 feet with a 500-foot ceiling.

P.G. climbed up onto the wing of his plane and got into the cockpit. He put his seat belt on and plugged his helmet earphones in. There was a lot of static. He checked his radio with the Quonset Tower and then checked with his crew.

"Skeeter, how's the radar working?"

"Okay, sir, the screen lights up. It looks like we may have to use it tonight."

"As long as we don't have to use a Mae West. I wish the stars would come out," commented P.G.

"Amen, sir. We'll do fine."

"Dominic, how about you in the turret?"

"All set, sir."

P.G.'s number-one man was really Dominic and not Skeeter. If they got into trouble, Dominic usually helped the most. He knew how to use the radar scope better than Skeeter. P.G. turned the switches on for the artificial horizon and the radio altimeter. He pushed his navigation board into the slot on the control panel and pressed the button to light up the instruments. A red glow emanated from the dashboard. He looked out over the right side of the cockpit and saw the ground crew chief wave his wand in a circle, indicating that it was okay to start his engine.

He checked in with Chuck. "Fox 6, this is Fox 7. Do you read me?"

"Fox 7, loud and clear. Looks like we got our work cut out for us tonight."

"Fox 6, we'll take off together. I'll fly wing on your right wing for the first leg of the scout line."

"Roger, Fox 7. We'll raise our wheels and flaps when we reach 300 feet. Then we'll make a left turn and try to break out above the overcast."

"Okay," said P.G. "I don't want to lose you in that fog."

When Chuck's plane got to the end of the runway, he called, "Quonset Tower, this is Fox 6, request permission for takeoff."

"Fox 6, cleared for takeoff."

P.G. pulled up along side Chuck's plane at the end of the runway and as Chuck poured the coal to his plane, P.G. did the same and the two planes lifted off together. He kept his plane tight on Chuck's wing, almost touching, as they ascended. They were soon in a solid overcast and he had trouble flying safely on Chuck's wing. All he could see was the pale blue flame from the engine's exhaust.

They broke out of the overcast at 9,000 feet. The stars and moon shone brightly above the blanket of gray clouds. Chuck radioed to P.G. "I think we ought to stay up here heading for Newfoundland. I think we'd kill ourselves getting down in that fog."

"I agree," said P.G. "We're going to do a high search to-night."

As the night flight team headed out on their search line 400 miles off the northeast coast, the weather got progressively worse. After flying for two hours, visibility was near zero. Lightning could be seen in the distance and there was a lot of turbulence.

"I don't like the looks of the weather. I think we ought to head back," said P.G. "Chuck, why don't you check in and see what's happening back at base."

"Okay, P.G. Quonset Point Tower, this is Fox 6. How's your base weather?"

"Fox 6, this is Quonset Tower. Weather is getting progressively worse. Visibility is 700 feet and decreasing. They're talking about closing the field."

"That's nice," said Chuck.

"The torpedo bomber skipper will be coming up to the tower in a few minutes to make a decision. We'll call you. Do you copy?"

"Roger, Quonset."

Back at Quonset Point, the air group commander and torpedo bomber skipper checked in with the tower. "How many pilots are out there in this soup?" asked the commander.

"There are eight torpedo bomber pilots and six night fighters," said the air operations officer.

"What's aerology predicting?"

"They think the whole East Coast may be closed down in the next two hours."

"Can we get most of them back before we have to close the field?"

"All except the two pilots on the scout line up in Newfoundland. They're three hours away."

"Who are they?" asked the skipper.

"Chuck Strong and Peter Grant. Two of our best."

"Do they know G.C.A.?"

"I think they've both been checked out at least once."

"Call all the pilots and tell them to get their butts back here as soon as possible."

"Fox Flight, this is Quonset Tower. Return to base. I repeat, return to base. Acknowledge."

The fighter pilots were only 150 miles away when they received the call and they were back at the base in 15 minutes. They all landed safely.

P.G. and Chuck heard the message. P.G.'s radio receiver had a lot of static and he didn't think he'd be able to land using the G.C.A. runway at Quonset. He notified Chuck.

"Fox 6, my radio reception is poor. I'm not sure I can use the G.C.A. to get back to base."

"I'll bring you in using my radio," said Chuck. "When I get 100 yards from the runway I'll flick my wing lights. You'll be on your own then," said Chuck.

"Okay," said P.G. "But don't come in too low."

Chuck and P.G. descended into the thick clouds together. "I hope Chuck knows what the fuck he's doing," said P.G. His stomach felt heavy and tight. "Skeeter, your job is to watch that goddamned altimeter. If I get below 300 feet, you're to scream as loud as you can on the intercom. I want you to call out the altimeter changes every 50 feet below 300."

P.G. tried to listen to the G.C.A. signals as Chuck approached the runway. His radio was useless—continuous static.

"We're at 500 feet," said Skeeter. They still hadn't broken out of the overcast.

"Four hundred feet," shouted Skeeter. "Three hundred feet."

Suddenly P.G. saw Chuck's wing lights flash on and off. His plane broke through the overcast. They were overshooting the runway. P.G. made a sharp left turn and stayed at 200 feet altitude, just under the clouds. It was just like doing a field-carrier approach, or landing on a carrier.

He took his plane back on the downwind leg, made a turn toward the runway on the cross leg, and set the plane down gently on the runway. Chuck set his plane down five minutes later. When the two pilots got back to the flight line, the torpedo bomber skipper was waiting for them. "You two guys did a great job getting those planes down safely in that soup. I'm proud of you."

Chuck replied, "You ought to try it yourself some night, Commander."

The skipper stopped and turned. He walked up to within a foot of Chuck and stared at him for a solid count of five. "I have, shithead. More times than you and this whole crop of rookie pilots put together. So don't cry and stomp your feet."

"I'm standing here, Commander."

"Yeah, and from where I stand I see a decent pilot who's getting a fat head about what he's worth to the navy. Remember this, tadpole—you may have seen some action in that jeep group in the Atlantic, but that don't mean shit to me."

"So what does it mean to you?" Chuck fired back. "Sending your men out into that goddamned storm on nothing but a scout line? The Germans couldn't find ship or shore out there if Hitler's balls depended on it."

The commander stepped in tighter, his chest touching Chuck's. "I'll tell you what impresses me—a pilot who can take orders and fly in any weather without a goddamned chirp. A pilot who can do it night in and night out, Ensign, because doing it right once is yesterday's news come dawn."

"Let it go, Chuck," said P.G. "He's a lot bigger than you with a lot more rank."

Chuck's face was hot. "Yeah, and we could've been history come dawn."

The commander stared at Chuck and said, "Strong, if you ever see real action you may understand what I just said. But right now you're just a pilot who thinks he's a goddamned stud. Dismissed."

Chuck took a deep breath and was about to swing at him. P.G. grabbed his arm and pulled him away. As they walked away from the commander, who stared after them, P.G. said, "Don't say it. Just keep your mouth shut. Say it later. Say it to me. But right now just shut up and walk." Chuck did as he was told. He didn't want to spend his navy career in the brig.

A week later, a jeep carrier, the U.S.S. *Solomon Islands,* pulled up alongside the docks at Quonset Point, Rhode Island.

The pilots of Night Air Group 53 were told they were going to practice day- and night-carrier landings on the flight deck of that jeep carrier. The deck looked awfully small to some of the young pilots who had never seen a jeep carrier before.

At first the pilots of Night Air Group 53 would operate out of Quonset Point Naval Air Station. The jeep carrier would leave the docks at Quonset and the pilots would fly their planes out to the carrier, and practice day-carrier landings. They would have to learn how to land in the daylight before they would be allowed to try it at night.

The men realized why all those previous spot landings they practiced at E Base and in advanced training were so important. Some wished they had practiced more often. After two weeks of daytime carrier landings, it was time. There was a full moon and the ocean was calm.

The torpedo bomber pilots were the first ones off the deck. The group did very well. Except for a few wave-offs, all the pilots landed aboard safely. After the torpedo bomber pilots had made three or four night landings, the fighter pilots took over. The fighter group was less fortunate because they were flying F6F night-adapted planes with a radar bubble on the right wing. Their planes were much lighter than the torpedo bombers. When they hit the deck they bounced around more.

The landing signal officer was having trouble with the group. The F6F-5N Hellcats were much smaller planes and the landing speed was faster. As many as three wave-offs would take place before the L.S.O. could get a pilot aboard. One pilot received nine wave-offs before making a successful landing. It was stressful and frustrating for both the pilots and the L.S.O. An accident was bound to occur, and when one of the planes almost knocked off a five-inch gun near the bridge, the captain said, "I've had it. Have the fighter planes return to Quonset Point. They need more practice." The rest of the night-carrier landings were canceled that evening.

The next morning, a strategy session was held to discuss the previous evening's mess. The pilots who had flown the night before and the landing signal officer congregated in the ready room. The L.S.O. opened the discussion with a statement describing the difficulty he faced due to darkness, in determining the speed and flight position of the planes moments before they landed. The pilots complained that they couldn't see the L.S.O. and suggested that he wear brighter clothing.

To help the pilots see the L.S.O. better, engineers devised a stronger Woods light. This helped, but one fighter pilot died and another was seriously injured during the training period of night-carrier landings. Lieutenant Parker came in too slow, and just before getting to the flight deck spun his plane into the water. Parker was probably knocked unconscious on impact and drowned as the plane went down like a stone. The landing signal officer was visibly upset. By putting his paddles down by his ankles he had tried to tell Parker he was too low, but Parker either didn't watch him, or the position of his plane obstructed his view and he didn't realize what was happening.

Training on the East Coast at Quonset Point proceeded. The volunteer pilots, with guidance from seasoned veterans, soon mastered the art of night-flying. Constant night-flying in bad weather conditions and landing aboard jeep carriers in the North Atlantic with rough seas honed their skills for landing on the carrier deck.

Flying continued in even more adverse weather as the air group's proficiency improved. The radar operators inside the planes were constantly tested in picking up enemy surface vessels at night. They also practiced picking up their own carrier at night when the ceiling got down to 500 feet and the weather and darkness were so bad that visibility was zero.

Near the end of the five-week stint at sea the scuttlebutt in the ward room was that soon the night air group would be observed by some big shots from Washington, D.C. The following day a torpedo bomber plane from Norfolk Naval Air Base, flown by a famous navy captain, landed and a rear admiral emerged. That evening, the majority of the air group was to fly, and the pilots knew they were being scrutinized by a flag officer.

The intensive practice paid dividends. The fighter pilots and torpedo bomber pilots landed safely without a hitch. The next morning, as the ship headed for port, all the pilots were told to assemble in the ready room. The admiral entered.

"Gentlemen, you put on an exhibition last night that was amazing. To be able to fly off a carrier at night and return safely gives the navy a new weapon, and we need that weapon badly. Your air group is shortly being sent to the Pacific. The navy will be able to apply your expertise in many different ways. I'm proud of you, but more important, the navy is proud of you."

P.G. breathed a sigh of relief. He had finally gotten his wish. He was going to war in the Pacific. As the carrier headed for Quonset Point he had time to think about Sarah. He worried about how she'd feel about his going to war. For the first time he felt the enormity of the conflict he was part of. There had been so much training, so much procedure in his life as a soldier. The time was coming to fight for his country and for his own life. He felt very lonely and decided he'd call Sarah when he got to Quonset Point.

When the ship docked he headed straight for a phone and called her. He wasted no time on a preamble or pleasantries. "Sarah, I just got orders to ship out to the Pacific." There was a silence. "Can you come up to Rhode Island for a few days before I leave?"

He then heard the voice of a frightened girl. She was teary. "I can't. I have exams. I've been expecting this. That dream I had won't go away. Talk to me, let me hear your voice," she said.

"Sarah, it's my duty and I have to accept it. Talking to you only hurts more. I don't like it any better than you do. I love you, Sarah. Don't ever forget that. Write to me often. When I find out what ship I'm assigned to, I'll send you the address. Until then you can write to the San Francisco Navy Post Office. They'll forward my mail. I'll miss you."

"I'll love you forever, P.G." said Sarah. "I don't want to say good-bye."

P.G. was alone again, holding the dead phone.

16

Barber's Point, Hawaii

The air group received top-priority orders to proceed to the Pacific. While some of the air groups traveled by ship through the Panama Canal to the West Coast and then to Pearl Harbor, Night Air Group 53 received orders to proceed to the West Coast via air transport. The navy wanted them in the combat zone as soon as possible.

With only three airlines flying around the United States during World War II, passengers had to be fairly important to get aboard these planes during wartime. Commercial airlines were still in their infancy, and their planes were primitive but reliable. It took from 18 to 24 hours to fly coast to coast, depending upon the layovers. Most of the airlines flew the DC-3, which carried about 21 passengers and had metal bucket seats without leather cushions. An open area above the seats held small pieces of luggage.

Three or four stops for refueling were made on a trip. Stops were also necessary for passengers to get up and walk around after sitting in the cramped seats for four, five, or six hours, and since there were no pressurized cabins, the planes had to stay below 12,000 feet. Instrument flying was in the development stage and radio range stations had not been set up so planes could not fly in inclement weather.

The DC-3 was noisy. It vibrated terribly and ventilation was poor. Passengers tolerated the long flight because they had to. The flight from New York's Floyd Bennett Field went to Atlanta, Dallas, Phoenix, and then San Francisco.

As P.G. walked out to board the plane, he had to step up on a wooden stool and climb into the plane. Once he found his seat and the engines were started, the roar of the twin radial prop engines became deafening.

"Hey, Tom," he yelled to his traveling companion, Ensign Coy, "I felt safer in one of those rust buckets back on the Great Lakes."

"You've got that right," Coy replied. "These planes look awfully flimsy and sound worse. Imagine dropping one of these on a carrier deck."

Once the plane was airborne, it got worse. Fifteen minutes after taking off, the plane began to get knocked around. A young lady across the aisle from P.G. began to sweat and fidget uncomfortably. P.G. looked around and noticed she wasn't the only one who was doing so. Shortly afterward, she lurched forward and threw up into a paper bag. P.G. heard a few other muffled sounds that he could only assume represented the same actions from other passengers. A foul smell permeated the cabin. He wondered why they didn't use the bathroom, but a quick look at the line of three or four people probably discouraged that. Right about now, P.G. and Tom could have both used a cold drink, but they were out of luck. They wouldn't be able to get anything to eat or drink until the next refueling stop, about an hour and a half away. They knew it was going to be a long flight. . . .

Finally the pilots of Night Air Group 53 landed in San Francisco after a bone-shaking 26 hours. The next day they were en route to Hawaii.

Some of the air group pilots flew on four-engine C-54 transport planes, while others flew Pan American seaplane clippers from San Francisco to Hawaii. It was cold and bumpy on the flight, which took 18 hours. There was always stress and trepidation involved in making a trans-ocean flight. Once the plane gets beyond the halfway point and reaches a point of no return, if it has severe engine trouble, the pilot must proceed with the engines that are still functioning or ditch in the water. P.G. and his group landed, relieved and starving, at Hickam Air Force Base in Hawaii, after having nothing but sandwiches and a few candy bars en route.

After they landed, navy transportation took them to Barber's Point Naval Air Station, and they checked into the Bachelor Officer's Quarters. Barber's Point was the base for the Night Attack and Combat Training Unit. The pilots would receive their final training prior to going to a fleet unit.

The following morning the pilots assembled at the hangar and received orientation about the local area, since they would start flying soon. They took ground school courses with emphasis on identification of enemy aircraft, since there were both navy and army air force planes flying in the area.

In 1944 Pearl Harbor still showed signs of the damage done by the Japanese, with a few of the damaged ships still half submerged in the harbor.

Within 72 hours the air group was flying. Live bombs, torpedoes, and .50-caliber ammunition were now loaded on the planes, and target practice off the Hawaiian Islands took place daily.

P.G. had an interesting experience flying one night over Barber's Point Naval Air Station. The group had been told to practice night formation flying. He was to lead a section of six torpedo bombers. After takeoff the planes were to rendezvous 20 miles off shore. Float lights would be dropped in the water as a reference point. A replacement pilot flew with the group for the first time that night: He would be baptized into night formation flying. If the planes flew in two sections of three planes, there would be a blind spot for the wingmen. The wingmen had to watch the lead plane constantly in order to avoid a mid-air collision. The exhaust stacks were a reference point at night, yet it was impossible to watch two planes right next to each other.

As the planes joined up in formation with P.G. flying the section lead, the last group got into difficulty. One plane threw his right wing up to try to slow down his aircraft, thus creating a blind spot. The planes in formation couldn't see what was happening because they were watching their lead aircraft. P.G. screamed at the pilot over the radio, "For Christ's sake, dive low out of the formation. You're going to hit one of the planes. Don't ever throw your wing up if you overshoot. You're fucking up the whole formation."

Shortly thereafter, on the radio, a meek female voice interrupted the radio transmission. It was the control tower at Barber's Point which had WAVES working as control tower operators. "Navy aircraft using foul language, give your flight number and pilot's name."

P.G. was pissed off. "Lady, we may be fucked up out here, but we're not that fucked up. What we're trying to do is keep our tit out of a wringer, which is something you might appreciate."

At the meeting the next morning, the air operations officer had a surprise for the pilots. "Gentlemen, we're not going to be doing any flying today." This bit of news immediately caught the pilots' attention. A few of them wondered if they were going to be given a day off. The officer continued. "Instead, we're going to take you out in a PT boat and drop you in the middle of the ocean."

The silence erupted into a cacophony of questions, protests, and howls. The operations officer waited for the uproar to end.

"We're going to put each of you through an ocean survival test. I would like you to return to your quarters and dress in the same uniforms you wear in the cockpit of your planes. Be back here in 20 minutes. Dismissed."

Suddenly, all the pilots took a long, hard look at the uniform they would be wearing. P.G. had a .38 Smith and Wesson gun with a shoulder holster and an ammunition belt. He also had a machete strapped to the upper part of his right thigh and a helmet with goggles and a parachute harness. A Mae West life jacket was also worn and a battery float light was attached to the upper part in case the pilot was in the water at night. A small waterproof Very pistol for sending flares was attached to the left belt line. A whistle for signaling was attached to the upper left Mae West straps. It all added up to a good deal of weight.

The pilots were taken out in the PT boat in groups of 30 and were told to jump overboard when they were about 40 miles off shore. The first thing a man had to do when he hit the water was to get rid of all the heavy equipment that weighed him down or he'd never stay on the surface. The gun, the belt filled with ammunition, and the machete all went. Not all of the life jackets inflated after the pilots hit the water, and it became a cooperative effort to keep everybody afloat. Some pilots had to blow up their own life jackets through a tube attached to the Mae West. They formed a chain of hands, and the stronger swimmers helped those who were not so good.

The PT boat took off over the horizon after everyone was over the side and the general feeling of all the pilots was the same. "Why, those bastards have left us out here to drown." It wasn't too bad trying to stay afloat for the first two or three hours, but after that, it truly became a survival challenge. The pilots were in excellent physical shape and fatigue was not a problem. There was some anxiety about sharks being in the area but, fortunately, no one was injured or bleeding; that might have attracted the unwanted visitors.

The group tried singing songs and telling dirty jokes, but humor came hard. The songs stopped after a while because of fatigue, and some of the pilots had difficulty staying afloat. A few got muscle cramps and had to be supported by the group; some started vomiting. After being in the water for about five hours, they all realized that the navy's survival test was to be graded pass/fail. Occasionally they'd see a plane overhead but the aviators' screaming and waving did no good. By this time the men were ready to surrender to anyone. If a Japanese sub had surfaced to pick them up, there would have been little resistance.

"Can you believe this shit?" asked one of the pilots. "They train us for months, teach us to kill Japs, and then throw us in the ocean. Makes a hell of a lot of sense, doesn't it? I'll tell you, if any of you have guns, hang on to them. When those bastards come back to pick us up, we'll blow their goddamned heads off."

That little speech was met by a rousing chorus of cheers.

About this time, a PBY flew over the group, circled around, and then dropped some large gear into the water. The group swam toward the yellow-colored gear, but swimming to it was no easy chore because the sea was getting rough. There were three large rubber life rafts in the package. These were inflated, and the lucky ones got in. The life rafts could not hold all 30 pilots. It was decided to tie the three life rafts together and to take turns resting inside. The others held onto the sides of the rafts.

Each raft had an emergency kit, and these were opened. The men found canned rations and concentrated candy. There was a cheese-cloth concoction to help take salt out of the water, and a cloth chart the size of a bandanna that had the prevailing tides for the ocean for the area. The chart was for the Atlantic Ocean, however, not the Pacific. There was a needle with squeezable medicine for pain and a Very pistol for firing colored sparklers into the air so that air-sea rescue would be able to find them. They decided if they got back safely to Honolulu they would redesign the survival kit.

Around 4:00 P.M., the PT boat came back and picked them up. No one was lost. They all climbed aboard, wrinkled, sick, completely tired out, and pissed off at the United States Navy. The pilots all slept soundly that evening.

After the swimming lesson in the middle of the Pacific, the pilots were assigned to groups that would go out on submarines from the base at Pearl Harbor. The purpose of the exercise was to show the pilots how the submarine picked up downed pilots during combat operations. If a plane was in serious trouble and had to ditch into the ocean, the pilot was to holler "Mayday" and give his estimated mileage and direction to submarine reference points determined prior to takeoff. It was usually a name with a letter code for the vector on the point of the compass.

To be on a submarine for any length of time requires a certain temperament. Quarters are cramped and every inch of space is utilized. P.G. and his group were assigned to the U.S.S. *Hoe*. The pilots were briefed by the executive officer as soon as they came aboard. The SS 250 *Hoe* was a Gato Series submarine, which displaced 1,825 tons when surfaced and 2,410 tons submerged. It was 311 feet long and 27 feet wide, with four diesel engines, four electric engines, and a speed of approximately 20 knots surfaced and nine knots submerged. It had a long range of 11,800 miles when surfaced. It also had ten tubes and carried 24 torpedoes.

The outer armament consisted of two five-inch guns and two antiaircraft 20-mm cannons. A radar antenna was behind the two periscopes, which were equipped with protective sleeves. The periscope-radar complex also housed a folding whip-type radio antenna and two small blackout bridges. The radar outfit gave adequate warning of an enemy approaching.

To calculate torpedo launch data, the U.S.S. *Hoe* had a small mechanical computer that was accurate when used with the radar. The acoustic devices, sonar, and hydroplanes were likewise effective. The commanding officer was Lieutenant-Commander Refo.

During P.G.'s stay on the submarine it made two or three dives. Silence prevailed unless the sub was running under the sea; then the motors could be heard churning.

A simulated nighttime pickup of a pilot was demonstrated. A PT boat dropped off a pilot and his position was given to the submarine. The submarine then lifted its periscope and searched the area with sonar and radar until the pilot was located in the water. The sub surfaced. A crew member in a frogman suit with a rope attached to his waist was sent into the water to pick up the pilot, who, if American, was usually in a yellow rubber life raft. Once the pilot was recognized as friendly, the swimmer would grab the life raft, and the submarine would pull the line in. This wasn't easy if the sea was rough.

The pilots felt uneasy about submarines. They had cramped, tight quarters and a man had to have a butt the size of two apples in order to sit on the john. The taller pilots could be heard swearing as they slammed their heads on low bulkheads. Staying below the surface for more than a week was mind boggling. The air had a peculiar odor, and the best deodorant or air fresheners couldn't change it. If the enemy was above and searching for the sub, silence for long periods of time had to be maintained. It could test a man's nerves and his patience.

The pilots' orientation on the functioning of the submarine in air-sea rescue took about five days, and then they returned to Pearl Harbor, resurfacing at night to enter the bay. Most of the pilots were happy to know about the function of the submarine in air-sea rescue, but when they got ashore and smelled the fresh air, they were glad they had chosen the Naval Air Corps.

During the next two weeks, the pilots of Air Group 53 had the opportunity to fly over the eight major Hawaiian islands. They saw Diamond Head, Waikiki Beach, Pearl Harbor, and the active volcanoes fuming. They saw the lush, green vegetation that blankets all the mountains, and the sugar cane and pineapple plantations in the lowlands. "In all," thought P.G., "the Hawaiian Islands are magnificent and not a bad place to be stationed."

They relaxed in town on weekends and were invited to social gatherings by the natives. The people of Hawaii were a fascinating mixture of Polynesian, Oriental, and Caucasian races. Some of the most beautiful women in the world were in Hawaii.

One night, one of the chaplains on the base asked P.G. if he could fly with him the next day. "Sure," said P.G. He had frequent requests from flight surgeons and chaplains asking for a ride. Most of them had to get four hours of flight time in, in order to get flight pay.

P.G. took the chaplain up while he practiced bombing runs on a floating target with six night torpedo planes. The plane he was flying was a replacement plane and not in top shape. The evening was calm and everything had gone well until they returned to

Barber's Point Naval Air Station for landing. As P.G. turned his plane into the downwind leg to make his approach, he pushed the lever to lower the landing gear. Skeeter, the radio-radar operator, checked through his window to see if the landing gear was down. He called P.G. "The right wheel hasn't locked in place, sir."

"That's great," replied P.G. He pulled out of the landing circle and took the plane up to 5,000 feet and tried to hand pump the landing gear into place. The right wheel still flapped in the breeze.

He decided to try to knock it in place by dive bombing the plane and rapidly rolling the wing. No dice. The wheel still flapped in the breeze. He notified Barber's Point Tower of his problem and was instructed to fly by the tower to see if the wheels were properly down before landing.

By then the chaplain was alternately vomiting and saying the rosary in the plane's bomb bay area.

"Christ," said P.G. "Have faith, father."

P.G. activated the handle to pull the landing gear up, but only the left wheel would come up and lock in place. He hoped that both wheels would come up and then he would be able to make a belly landing. He decided to put the left wheel down again and it did go down, but the right wheel still hung like a piece of wet laundry on the line.

The crash crew was alerted at the field and, because the gas gauge was getting close to empty, P.G. decided to try to land the plane on the one left wheel. He came in hot to keep the plane's weight up on the left wheel and, as the plane started to slow down on the runway and settle on the right side, he felt the right landing gear click and lock in place. He heard a big cheer from the back of his cockpit as he taxied the plane back to the hangar, smiling, thinking, "Hey, if the navy doesn't drown me or kill me with lousy planes, I may actually make it to fight the Japs."

When he stopped the plane at the flight line and got out of the cockpit, he had to carry the chaplain out of the back of the plane. He was soaked with perspiration and trembling. "Thanks be to God, Ensign," he said. "My prayers were answered. Now I've got to go back to the barracks and change my trousers."

That weekend P.G., Chuck, and Domkowski, one of the fighter pilots, had time off and decided to raise hell. P.G. let the recent episode roll off his sleeve. He realized that he had handled the emergency quite well. The chaplain talked about it for the next six

months but still had the guts to fly with P.G. to get his four hours in
for flight pay.

The three navy pilots, however, did not invite the chaplain to go
with them on weekend leave. They had seen a few of the attractive
natives and were looking forward to meeting them. They decided to
head for Waikiki Beach and the Royal Hawaiian and Moana Hotels.
Chuck had tried to reserve a suite of three rooms for the weekend at
the Moana, but only three separate rooms were available. Each pilot
was eyeballing for a female companion to share his room with;
besides, Domkowski snored like a drunken ox and usually kept the
others awake.

The three pilots put on their swim trunks and decided to see if
there were any girls on Waikiki Beach. The beach had crystalline
white sand and extended from in front of the hotels to Diamond
Head. The air was dry and hot and the swimming was world class.
The Pink Palace (the Royal Hawaiian Hotel) housed some of the
wealthiest people of the islands and the international set. The
Moana Hotel, where the pilots were staying, was right next door.
The Royal Hawaiian had a Mai Tai Bar right on the beach. The
drinks were tropical and deceptively strong. Going down they
tasted like fruit punch. Coming up they looked like a Hawaiian
sunset.

Chuck was the first one who seemed to be getting an evening
escort. A very attractive young lady in a tiger swimsuit struck up a
conversation with him at the Mai Tai Bar. The next thing he knew
they were splashing around in the water together and seemed to be
heading toward an intimate aquatic encounter. Her name was Kiki.
They had two or three drinks at the bar together, and things moved
right along. Chuck's face was lit up like a Christmas tree.

Suddenly, a tall, bronzed lifeguard waved at Kiki and she ran over
to meet him. She told Chuck that she had a surfing date with the
lifeguard. "I'll see you at the beach tomorrow," she hollered back
at him.

"Hell," said Chuck, "a lifeguard. A damn lifeguard. I didn't train
to be a pilot to let a lifeguard bird-dog a girl right out from under me."

"Well," said Domkowski, "she wasn't quite under you yet. Besides,
is getting girls the reason you joined the navy?"

"Absolutely," said Chuck, and paused, looking down the beach.
"It certainly wasn't just to fly airplanes."

"*C'est la vie*," said Domkowski. "The day is still young. Maybe you'll find another fish in the stream."

That evening they headed for the International Marketplace, where there was shopping, dining, and entertainment. They ended up being drawn into the Aloha Bar by American and Hawaiian dance music. The Marketplace didn't have good-looking women on the market that evening, although some of them sure knew how to dance. The three pilots tried to hula and developed a new respect and desire for the hips of the Hawaiian girls.

Following their attempts at the hula, the pilots sat down for another round of drinks. "Man," Chuck spoke up, "all the pretty women in Hawaii must be home in bed."

"Yeah, but they're smart. At least they're not with you." Domkowski raised his glass at Chuck and laughed.

"Oh, excuse me, Casanova, I see they're just falling all over you," he answered.

"Any time I want, Chuck, any time I want."

"Okay, hotshot, what do you say the three of us each puts up 50 bucks. Whoever winds up with the best-looking lady and makes out takes the cash. One-hundred fifty big ones. Deal?"

The three pilots clinked their glasses in agreement.

Around 1:30 A.M., three girls came into the Aloha Bar. One was a beautiful Hawaiian, with a gorgeous figure and long brownish red hair done up in a pony tail.

Chuck said, "Boys, better bring some tens to chow time tomorrow," and approached the young women from behind.

"Hello, ladies, what can we help you with?" asked Chuck.

The girls looked at each other and giggled. "We've just come in to do some dancing," said the pretty one, "and maybe just a little drinking on the side."

"What a coincidence," said Chuck. "That's exactly what we're here for."

Chuck grabbed the pretty one. Her name was Koko, and he found out she was one-tenth Hawaiian, one-tenth Portuguese, and one-tenth Irish. The remaining seven tenths were a mystery. They danced. She told Chuck that her name meant red earth.

He told her his name was Chuck which meant "brave bull." She laughed and they swung around the dance floor.

Domkowski and P.G. were less successful. The other two girls were attractive but not very cordial. They were like Dresden

China—don't touch or we might break. The men tried to get them to have more of the exotic drinks, but they refused. One said she never touched the stuff. Koko and Chuck did most of the dancing and drinking. After a while, Chuck told P.G. that he and Koko were heading back to the hotel for the evening. "Since you and Dom are obviously sucking my propwash, you can each give me 50 now, if you want," boasted Chuck.

"Or we could kick you in the ass now, if we want," said Domkowski. "You'll get paid in the morning, just like we agreed." He was pissed.

P.G. and Dom headed back to the rooms at the Moana and decided to get some sack time. P.G. viewed the whole event with a sort of detached amusement. His thoughts were confined to Sarah when it came to romance.

The next morning they went down to the dining room to have breakfast. While they were there, Koko showed up. She looked depressed.

"Did you, ah, enjoy yourself last night?" asked Domkowski.

"Sure," said Koko, "until we got back here."

"What happened?" asked P.G.

"Your buddy spent the night in the john vomiting and yorking. What a mess. He should have told me his name meant 'Upchuck.' The next time I'm going to pick up a marine."

P.G. and Domkowski looked at each other, laughed, and slapped palms. They both thought of the $50 they saved, and decided to splurge a little on breakfast. They never had a mimosa that tasted quite as sweet. . . .

17

Kiki

Kiki, the pretty young Hawaiian in the tiger bathing suit, called Chuck at the Bachelor Officer's Quarters the next afternoon. Chuck was surprised to hear from her. He was hung over from the previous night's escapade with Koko, the Hawaiian redhead, and was trying to forget the whole thing. He hadn't performed well. He had reported in sick at the flight line and was trying to sleep off his hangover. He was in no condition to fly.

"Ensign, I'm available this evening if you'd like to go out with me," said Kiki.

"Kiki, I'm on duty tonight, but I would like to see you tomorrow if that's okay," he replied. Chuck didn't want to tell her that his head felt like a rotten melon and he didn't want another fiasco like the one the night before.

"Okay, I'll meet you tomorrow afternoon at 4:00 in the lobby of the Royal Hawaiian Hotel. When does your ship go out?" she asked.

"I'll be around long enough so you and I can test the waters before that happens," said Chuck.

"I'm looking forward to it. See you tomorrow at 4:00."

Chuck hung up. Right now all he was looking forward to was sleep—and more sleep.

The next afternoon Chuck met Kiki in the lobby of the Royal Hawaiian Hotel. She wore a low-cut, short dress with spaghetti straps, and her darkly tanned body was beautiful. She was short, but her spiked heels made her almost as tall as Chuck; he was only five-feet, seven inches tall. She gave him a big hug and a peck on the cheek when she greeted him.

"How would you like to go out for a speedboat ride around the island?"

"I don't think the navy will let you do that when we're at war," said Chuck.

"It's okay if we stay close to shore," she replied. "We could anchor the boat and have our own little swimming party."

"I'm not a good swimmer," said Chuck.

"I'll have my friend, the lifeguard, skipper the boat for us. He's a good swimmer."

"That'll make a great threesome. Forget it!"

"He's only a good friend. Really! Our relationship is purely platonic."

"Not interested. I have other plans for the evening."

"Just what are your plans?"

"Well, it's not a threesome. I'd like to take you out to dinner, do some dancing, and then check into my hotel room with you."

"You certainly don't mince words. How do you know I'll go with you?"

"Well, after we spend a few hours together, I think I can convince you. Besides, it didn't take you long to snuggle up to me in the water a couple of days ago."

"Why don't you come to my place tonight? My girlfriend won't be home and we could have lots of privacy," said Kiki.

"How far is it from Barber's Point?"

"About 25 miles, near Kaneohe Bay."

"We'll see. That may be too far from the base for me."

They had a few Hawaiian drinks at the Mai Tai Bar. Chuck drank a few more than Kiki. Chuck called a cab and they decided to go into the hills to a fancy restaurant called the Moana Loa Inn, which featured Hawaiian food, a floor show, and a dance band. The restaurant had an open-spit cooking area set up in the center of the room with a large, two-sided fireplace. A suckling pig was being roasted on one side, with chicken and beef on the other side. Chuck and Kiki had a few more drinks and ate baby ribs roasted over the open fire. Fingers, rather than utensils, were used for eating. The delicious food, combined with the company, hit the spot.

The floor show was hula girls and jugglers. The band leader invited the audience to participate, so Kiki got up and performed the hula with the band. Her hips and hands expressed the message. She really knew what she was doing, and Chuck got up and joined her. They obviously enjoyed dancing together.

Kiki was an inquisitive young lady, asking many questions. "Are you married?"

"No," replied Chuck. "Does it matter?"

"Do you have a steady girlfriend?"

"Not yet, but I'm thinking about it."

A broad smile lit up her face. "What outfit do you fly with, Chuck? Have you been assigned to a carrier yet?"

"That's confidential information," he said. "Besides I hardly know you, Kiki."

"Well, perhaps we can get to know each other better before the evening's over."

"I sure hope so," said Chuck.

After dancing for a couple of hours and cuddling up to Chuck, Kiki invited him to spend the evening with her at her apartment.

"We'd better use the room at my hotel," said Chuck.

"No, let's go to my place." She was quite insistent.

"I may have to fly in the morning. I don't want to have an auto accident driving back 30 miles after drinking all this Hawaiian stuff. I'll take a rain check for tomorrow night at your place, if you come back with me to the hotel."

"Okay, if you promise."

"I promise," replied Chuck.

They took a cab back to the hotel and when they got into the room, Kiki excused herself and said she'd get ready in the bathroom.

"You can pull the covers back on the bed, Chuck, and take your clothes off."

"This is better than I planned," thought Chuck. "Hell, no preliminaries, go right to the action."

After waiting for about five minutes and still no Kiki, Chuck knocked on the bathroom door. There was no answer. He knocked again louder. "Kiki, are you all right?"

"Don't be so impatient. I'm just getting ready for you. I'll be out in a little while. Go back to bed and turn the lights out."

Chuck turned all the lights out but one. He had heard about sailors being rolled and robbed in hotel rooms, and although he was in a stage of undress and excitement, he was on guard.

When Kiki came out of the bathroom, Chuck's eyes bulged in anticipation. She had taken all her clothes off. Her bronzed body gleamed in the dimness, revealing her high, firm breasts, curvaceous buttocks, and tapered legs. She licked her lips in anticipation of his kisses as she slowly walked over to the side of the bed and straddled him.

"Okay, navy pilot, let's see what you've got. See if you can handle this tiger!"

"I'll tame you in five minutes," said Chuck.

"Not long enough. Make it 20 and I'll do whatever you want until dawn."

Kiki wrapped her legs around Chuck as she pressed her hips on top of his. She was muscular, lean, and athletic. Chuck weighed only 135 pounds. Her mouth descended on his and responded to his kisses. The oral expression of her lust left nothing to the imagination. Chuck had never met such an aggressive woman in his life. Usually he was the aggressor, and the girl was often too passive. Now he was on the bottom of the pile and he felt as though she had command. As she rubbed her body against his, slowly grinding her hips against his thighs, her mouth left his and began caressing his body in areas that had never been touched by anyone's lips before.

"My God, what are you doing?" asked Chuck. Suddenly Kiki became rigid and pushed his shoulders down on the bed.

"Do you want me to stop?"

"Oh, no. I've never felt like this before."

"Neither have I," she replied. "So relax and enjoy it." Chuck had some doubts about that. She slowly spread her legs and opened her thighs for his entry as he arched his back. She began to rotate her buttocks against him and pushed deeply into him. Chuck tried to respond to her lovemaking expertise.

"Hell," he thought to himself, "I can't let this gal take advantage of me." He forcefully rolled her over onto her back and decided to drive as hard as he could into her. Kiki began to moan and seemed to enjoy his aggressiveness.

"Oh, darling, I knew I could get you to make love to me," she said. As their passion increased their rhythm became as one, each driving against the other. Suddenly the climax was reached in a spasm of heat and sweat. They were both completely exhausted. The silence was broken by Kiki saying, "I could really learn to love you, Chuck."

"You're something special," he replied, as they fell asleep in each other's arms.

Three hours later they awoke and Kiki said that she had to leave, but would see him the next night. Chuck said that was okay if he didn't have to fly. He also thought he'd need some time to recover from this bombshell. They agreed to be in touch the next evening.

Chuck hailed a cab and paid the fare for Kiki to get home and then took a cab back to Barber's Point Naval Air Station. He was due to fly at 2:00 P.M. the next day and felt he needed a rest. Kiki had completely exhausted him.

18

A Surprise

At 8:00 A.M. Chuck received a phone call from the air group commander. "Strong, roll your ass out of bed and get to the flight line. I have to talk to you about something important."

"What's it about?" asked Chuck.

"I can't discuss it over the phone," answered Commander Brennan. "I'll tell you in my office at the hangar in 30 minutes."

Chuck took a cold shower to wake up, brushed his teeth, used lots of mouthwash, and found some mints to freshen his mouth. It was only eight to ten hours since he had had alcohol and, although he had been drinking vodka, he could still smell it. There were rigid penalties for flying after drinking heavily.

When he got to the air group commander's office, there were two armed marine guards outside the door. "Oh shit, what the hell's going on?" thought Chuck. The marine guards stopped him from entering the door. "I'm Ensign Strong," he said.

"We'll tell the commander you're here," one of the marines replied.

After a short while, he was escorted into a large room. The air group commander was with a gold-braided captain. "Ensign, this is

Captain Standish. He's head of Naval Intelligence on Ford Island at Pearl Harbor. He wants to talk to you."

"Ensign Strong, you are probably unaware that naval intelligence has had 24-hour surveillance on you for the past three days. That young lady, Kiki, whom you met on Waikiki Beach, has been confirmed as a Japanese secret service agent. We have reason to believe that she relays information to the enemy through that lifeguard she calls her buddy. We think she solicits information concerning American fleet movements out of Pearl Harbor and relays it via short-wave radio to Japanese submarines off the coast at night."

He got red in the face. Kiki certainly fooled him. "Why don't you just put her in jail?" asked Chuck.

"Good question," said the captain. "She's dangerous; in fact, three months ago she had an affair with a navy pilot who is now missing. However, she now serves a purpose for navy intelligence." The captain paused.

"We have a job we want you to do. That chance meeting she had with you was planned. You probably told her that you were with a night-carrier outfit. Is that correct?"

Chuck paused. He thought of all the time and work he had put into becoming a pilot. Was it all going to be washed away because of one lying Hawaiian bitch? The captain obviously saw the concern on his face.

"Don't worry, Ensign, you're not in any difficulty—yet. We just need to know what she knows so we can plan accordingly. Now, did you tell her you were with a night-carrier outfit?"

"I guess I did tell her. I probably shouldn't have."

"You're no different from any of the other pilots," said the captain. "Did she ask you where you were going and what your next target was?"

"Come to think of it, she did, but I didn't know."

"Do you have another date with her?"

"Yes, I'm supposed to fly this afternoon and then go out with her tomorrow night. I'm kind of beat, however."

"Well, the air group commander will give you the day off. You have a more important mission to do for the navy. It will put your life at risk, however, in a different way than flying does," said the captain.

"You're to go out with her tomorrow night, as planned. But if she asks you to go on a boat ride or to her apartment, you're not to go. You're also to watch what you drink, because she may try to slip you a Mickey later in the evening. We'll give you the name of the night-club you're to take her to. The bartender is a naval intelligence agent. If you have any trouble, you're to contact him. Don't order or take any drinks from any other bartenders. He has a full black mustache and is missing the tip of his left index finger.

"We want you to tell Kiki that you're going aboard one of the largest navy carriers that will soon be coming into Pearl Harbor, and tell her the scuttlebutt has it that the air group will be partici-pating in the invasion of Formosa, in preparation for the invasion of Japan. The navy chiefs want to divide the Japanese forces so they won't know where the next major strike will occur."

"I thought we were going over to the China Sea area anyway," said Chuck. "Are we really going there?"

"That's classified, Ensign. You don't need to know that. You're being asked to do what you're told. Besides, you will be doing a special service for your country."

Chuck thought about that. He also thought about Kiki. The bitch was a good actress.

"There's something else you should know about," said the captain. "Kiki carries a small derringer pistol and a switchblade in her pocketbook. We don't believe she'll use it on you unless she suspects that you know she's a spy."

"Can I carry a gun?"

"No. You'll be under protective surveillance the whole time you're with her."

"Is there anything else?"

"Yes. You can refuse to do this if you want. Naturally, the navy hopes you won't."

Chuck paused. What they were asking him to do sounded very risky. He hesitated and gave it some thought. He wondered if he could prevent showing his emotions to Kiki. He wasn't a trained secret agent. He could get killed. He finally replied, "I'll do it. Just make sure I get out alive."

The next night Chuck picked Kiki up at the Royal Hawaiian. God, she was a beautiful spy. But now he had to watch her in a different way. She was dangerous, possibly deadly. Sure enough, she insisted on going for a boat ride. Chuck told her that he got seasick in small boats.

She acquiesced. "Then let's go to my place this evening and I'll show you some new tricks," she suggested.

"We'll try to work that out," Chuck replied.

They went to the bistro in Honolulu that the navy had picked out and sure enough, there was a bartender with a mustache and a short left index finger. Chuck went to the bar and ordered drinks for the two of them. "Nice evening, Ensign," said the bartender. "That's a lovely lady you have with you."

"Yeah, she's a piece of work, isn't she?" said Chuck. "I'll be ordering a few more drinks from you."

"I wouldn't drink too much," said the bartender.

"Never," said Chuck.

Kiki and Chuck did a lot of dancing and, just as predicted, Kiki wanted to know all about Chuck's outfit and where he was going.

"I'm not supposed to tell you," said Chuck.

She snuggled up closer to him. "My family has been as American as yours for four generations," said Kiki. "I don't think a big pilot like you has anything to worry about from a little lady like me. Now, tell me what you're up to."

Chuck looked at her for a long moment, assessing her. She held his gaze as she held his hands.

"I'd like to, Kiki, but I really can't."

She reached up, put one arm around Chuck's neck, and pulled his head down to meet hers in a long, slow kiss. She then whispered something in his ear, and leaned back.

"Chuck, I'm worried about you. We have such a good time together, I certainly don't want anything to happen to you. At least you can tell me where you're going."

He hesitated, hoping for a repeat performance of her last kiss. He was not disappointed.

"Okay, Kiki. But keep a lid on it. I don't know tactics but I do know some of the strategy. I've got a friend in the CO's office who hears things. The rumors are that we're heading to Formosa, and we'll use that as a staging area to take Japan. I don't know the specifics, but it certainly makes sense to me. But, Kiki, remember this stuff is secret and," Chuck smiled, "if you let it out, I'll have to kill you."

"Oh, Chuck, I won't tell. I don't want you to go to Japan, I want you here." She seemed genuinely upset.

Once he told her his plans, he noticed that she cooled her advances toward him.

"I've got a very bad headache. I've got to go home and lie down," she said.

"I'll get you a cab."

"But I want you to lie down with me."

"If I do that, Kiki, I'll be late getting back to the base."

"I want you to make love to me in my own apartment tonight."

"As much as I'd like to, I can't do that tonight. I'll call you tomorrow. Besides, you wore me out the other night. I'm flying tomorrow and need to rest up."

Kiki kissed Chuck full on the lips, held it, and got into the cab. Instead of going to her apartment she met the lifeguard, and they went to a bungalow on the far side of Oahu. That evening, a coded message was sent to Japanese intelligence that a task force would be invading Formosa in the next six weeks. The message was intercepted by United States Naval Intelligence at Pearl Harbor.

19

Old Veteran Returns

The R&R at Waikiki was great for the pilots. The next week they were back at work, honing their combat skills. One evening the air operations officer told the night torpedo bomber pilots that Japanese submarines had been sighted in the area that afternoon and that their planes would be armed with live depth charges and MK rockets. A submarine was last seen just 200 miles north of Maui.

Since Air Group 53 was the night outfit based on the island, some of the torpedo bomber pilots were vectored out on a search line to try to find the subs. P.G. and Chuck, who were now flying together as a team, were sent out northwest of Maui. When they were 300 miles out, Chuck's radar operator picked up a blip on his radar screen.

"Sir, I have an unidentified object on the water at 22 miles," said Rocco.

"Notify P.G. and see if he can pick it up," said Chuck. "Use the signal light."

Rocco sent the message. He notified Chuck that P.G. was unable to confirm on his radar screen. "He thinks you may have picked up another big fish on the water," said Rocco.

"That's a crock of bullshit," said Chuck.

"Tell him that I'm taking over and leading our flight toward the target. Tell him to arm his MK rockets and depth charges."

Chuck cut back on his throttle and backed off of P.G.'s wing. P.G. then joined up on Chuck's wing and he told his radio operator to notify Chuck to get clearance for the attack. Chuck called the Pacific Air Control Center on Oahu and told them that he had a possible enemy sighting.

The control center checked to see if any of their own ships or subs were in the area. There were none. "Proceed to attack," was the message from the Pacific Air Control Center.

The pilots dropped their bombers down to 50 feet off the water, using their radio-altimeters. When they got about ten miles from the target, the blip on the radar screen disappeared.

"It's gone," Chuck radioed to P.G.

"I know. Must've dived. Keep looking. I still think it was a big fish."

"That's still a big crock," replied Chuck.

They closed in on the area where the blip was last sighted and dropped a float light.

"Let's drop our depth charges anyway," P.G. suggested.

"Why not? It might shake them up if they're down below."

The two planes dove directly over the target area and released their cargo of aerial depth charges. A series of explosions ripped through the calm Pacific air, sending towers of water skyward. The planes dropped more parachute float lights, but neither P.G. nor Chuck could spot anything. They searched the area with radar for about an hour and then returned to the air base at Barber's Point, wondering what the hell had happened.

The next day an oil slick, wooden cartons, and debris were found by navy destroyers searching the area, but a kill was not confirmed. The air group skipper told the pilots that they had done a good job, but that it wasn't worth a medal.

Because of the possible sighting, the air groups at Barber's Point were put on full alert. A few of the torpedo bombers had their bomb bays filled with gas tanks so the search lines could be extended. The PBY float patrol planes were activated, too.

It soon became obvious why the Japanese had increased their submarine activity around Hawaii. A massive, grey-blue carrier had steamed into Pearl Harbor, along with a large cruiser. It didn't take long to find out which carrier it was, since scuttlebutt traveled fast.

It was the battle-scarred U.S.S. *Saratoga,* one of the largest carriers in the fleet. The old veteran and Queen of the Flattops had returned and was preparing for a fight.

P.G. and Chuck were sitting in the Officer's Club when the news about the *Saratoga* hit. They were joined by Lieutenant Willis Stevens, who had flown off the *Saratoga* during its last campaign.

"Well, I'll tell you," Willis began, "the Saratoga is quite a ship. It's almost 900 feet long. She's pretty heavy, too, if you consider 40,000 tons a little overweight."

"Hey, Chuck, that sounds like one of your dates," P.G. cut in.

"Just as hard to get at, too," continued Stevens, "because it's got a triple metal hull. Nothing can penetrate that baby. It's got four drive shafts, and can get up to 35 knots. She can really move. And guns? Try eight eight-inchers on for size. She's also equipped with 40 mm antiaircraft batteries up and down her flight deck. The *Sara's* put down so many enemy planes and ships, her sides look like an art museum. The Japs keep trying to sink her, but they just can't do it. They'd give their eye teeth for that baby. They've even put two torpedoes in her hull, and it didn't budge her. Yeah, I'll tell you, if there's trouble brewing, *Sara's* not going to be far away. There must be something big cooking."

"It sounds like that ship is really something," said Chuck.

"You'd better believe it," replied Willis.

The next morning the pilots were assembled in one of the hangars, and the air group commander confirmed what had been scuttlebutt. Air Group 53 had been assigned to the *Saratoga* and was to fly its planes out in a couple of days and land on the ship. The group was also told that some brand new, specially equipped night fighter planes and night torpedo bombers were already aboard the *Saratoga.*

The tension increased. For those who had girlfriends or wives on the island, farewells were in the offing. Some of the air group's officers and sailors who were not flyers were told to collect their gear and report aboard.

The Stars and Stripes and the ship's ensign flew at one end of the ship. Another flag flew above the bridge, signifying that a flag officer was aboard, an admiral. This suggested that a task force would be forming in the near future.

The day for the air group to fly aboard the *Sara* finally came. Sixty planes would be landing aboard. The extensive training of the night air group was evident to the captain of the ship and the flag officers as the air group planes landed safely on the deck, one by one.

"That looks like a hot air group coming aboard," said the captain.

"They ought to be," said the air operations officer. "They're one of the few air groups that can fly day and night. They're the cream of the crop."

Three destroyers were out in front of the carrier as picket ships to help locate potential enemies. The large cruiser *Alaska* sailed off the starboard side of the carrier, her armament looking formidable. From the air, the landing strip on the carrier's deck looked much bigger than that of a jeep carrier's. The landing wires on the deck covered the same distance as the jeep carrier's, but the *Sara*'s deck looked much wider. It was almost 160 feet wide. This meant the potential for a safe landing was increased since the pilot had a wider deck to land on.

The *Sara* also had a T-shaped lift elevator for moving the aircraft from the flight deck to the hangar deck and another T-shaped lift elevator abeam of the mast and control tower.

At the bow of the *Sara,* there were two catapults, each 155 feet in length, that could hurl the heaviest aircraft into the air at flying speed within a short launch space. In the front, on the starboard side, were powerful derricks for lifting seaplanes and flying pontoon boats from the water.

The pilots' ready room of the *Sara* was elaborately furnished. The chairs were beautiful brown leather recliners with a writing board that pulled out in front. A small galley was nearby, and coffee and sandwiches were available at all times. A control center and blackboard were in the front of the ready room where final instructions for the pilots were posted prior to take-off.

The constantly changing data in the control center included the temperature, dewpoint, recognition signals for the picket boats and destroyers; radio calls, codes for air-sea rescue submarines; and YE high-frequency radio signals. For the aviators, the exact position of the carrier when the plane was launched and the anticipated position of the ship on return (Point Option) were the most vital pieces of information that had to be written down on their portable chartboards.

If the pilots thought they were through navy ground school, they were wrong. Classes took place every day. Gunnery skills were kept up. The men used shotguns to shoot clay pigeons launched from the stern of the ship. Aircraft recognition slides of enemy aircraft were also shown.

Air Group 53's fighter squadron was put to work the first night at sea. They were sent out on combat air patrol over the carrier and its escorting vessels. The torpedo bomber pilots flew air search lines mainly in the daytime to adjust to the characteristics of the *Sara*. It was easy to recognize the ship. She had an incredible superstructure with a large, wide funnel built along the starboard side.

After being at sea for five days, General Quarters was sounded at 6:00 A.M. Bells rang and, "Man your battle stations" was announced over the bullhorn.

Many of the pilots were sound asleep in their racks. "What the hell is all that noise about?" asked Chuck, as he jumped out of his bunk.

"It's General Quarters," said P.G. "Rise and shine."

The pilots donned their flight suits and ran to the ready room. The air operations officer was posting data on the blackboard. The pilots quickly wrote the information on their chartboards. The command, "Man your planes," was given.

P.G. ran to his plane on the back of the carrier and climbed up on the wing and got into the cockpit. The plane's wings were folded. His gunner and radio-radar operator were already in the plane. On the flight deck, men garbed in brightly colored green, yellow, and blue or red jerseys moved stealthily about. There were plane directors, firefighters, plane handlers and arresting gear crews. The bullhorn on the bridge blared out commands.

The planes on the back of the flight deck had their restraining ropes quickly untied. The signal for starting engines was given and there was a roar as the propellers turned over with a puff of smoke.

The fighter planes were in the front of the flight deck. It was the fighter pilot's job to get into the air as quickly as possible and protect the carrier. The giant carrier had already turned into the wind in preparation for launching the planes.

P.G., in his mammoth torpedo bomber, still had the wings of his plane folded as he moved his plane forward toward the catapults. It wasn't easy to taxi the plane up the flight deck as the carrier rolled with the sea waves. He was checking his instruments and writing data on his navigation board as new instructions concerning the ship's position were given. He particularly checked the magnetos to make sure there was adequate power for take-off. The planes were much heavier now with 2,000 pounds of bombs in their bomb bays. The pilots were told that an enemy task force had been sighted 200 miles to the west.

"Game time," he muttered. "What the hell are the Japanese doing in this part of the Pacific, anyway?" If they wanted a fight, he was ready to give it to them. There were eight MK rockets mounted on rails on the wings of his plane. He had control of a formidable fighting machine and his body was pumped up and ready for action.

As his plane approached the catapult, he received the signal to open the wings and lock them in place. He was guided by signals given by the launching officer so the plane would rest directly over the catapult. The deck crew hooked the catapult mechanism to the underbelly. P.G. was given the signal to rev the engine up to full power. He put his feet on the brakes and pushed the throttle forward. He felt the plane pulsing and rumbling underneath him.

The launching officer swung his wand around in circles. When the ship's deck was on the rise, P.G. received the signal to release his brakes. Suddenly the Avenger shot over the bow. The heavily loaded, large torpedo bomber settled slightly as it rose off the deck. He gently pulled the stick back, used his trim tabs and the plane responded. Once off the carrier's deck, he hit the lever that pulled up the landing gear and flaps so the wheels would not hit the water. He kept the nose of the plane high and banked it away from the ship. He had just gone from zero to 120 knots and had to do four jobs at once; handle the flight stick, throttle, flaps, and landing gear. His hands and feet moved in sync, a coordinated blur of activity.

As the plane rose in the air, he adjusted the flaps and pushed the throttle forward and rendezvoused with the formation. He flew into the slot on the skipper's wing. Eighteen torpedo planes had been launched. It was quite an awesome sight.

After flying for an hour in the direction of the target, the air group commander announced, "Return to base."

"What the hell is going on here?" thought P.G. "Did someone else get to the enemy first? All this for nothing?"

After the planes had landed, the pilots were told that the General Quarters and flight launch had been a trial run to see if the air group was combat ready. A full dress rehearsal had been ordered by the admiral in preparation for going into action. The 54 planes that were on the flight deck of the *Saratoga* had been launched in less than 30 minutes. That meant that a plane had flown off the *Sara*'s deck every 27 to 30 seconds.

The pilots were disappointed. That rush, that extra squirt of adrenalin, had been wasted. But what they didn't know was that the *Sara* would have her belly full of combat action soon enough.

20

Hawaii to Ulithi

The U.S.S. *Saratoga, Alaska,* and three destroyer picket boats continued to sail at full speed to Ulithi. The small task force traveled at 30 knots, sailing 700 miles per day. The ships altered course only for turning the *Sara* into the wind for launching and retrieving planes. Refueling the destroyers en route slowed them down somewhat, particularly if there were rough seas.

Ulithi, a group of islands in the southwest Pacific, had been captured by the marines and used as a navy forward staging area. It was also used as an area of rehabilitation and relaxation for the combat troops.

On the way from Hawaii to Ulithi, off-duty pilots exercised on the flight or hangar decks and continued their ground school instruction. One of the courses added to the curriculum for the night pilots was a simplified review course in radar. This was essential, because the fighter pilots were their own radar operators, and the torpedo bomber pilots had a radio-radar operator in the bellies of their planes. Each plane had a radar antenna on its right wing, and it was important that each aviator understood the mechanics of working this equipment.

Developing a way to see through bad weather and darkness became a major goal for the armed services during World War II. The country that first developed the ability to detect objects invisible to the eye could prepare for enemy attacks. If the range and bearing of the advancing object could also be identified, then a proper military response could be given. Such an advancement would be invaluable.

Interest in this problem of hampered vision, induced by night or poor weather, led to the development of radar, used for the first time by the United States at Pearl Harbor in 1941.

A blip on a big radar receiver screen does not specify the nature of the craft—friend or foe. Only an identifying signal from the plane itself can do that. For example, the blip read on the screen the morning of December 7, 1941, at Pearl Harbor was misinterpreted as American B-17 bombers returning to their bases. If that blip had been correctly interpreted as approaching enemy aircraft, there is no telling what would have happened at Pearl Harbor.

United States scientists, working at many technical colleges, such as M.I.T. and the California Institute of Technology, eventually perfected the radar equipment and it was ready for installation on American combat ships in 1942. Radar advanced to a more sophisticated level rapidly, but even in its beginning stages it gave the United States a significant edge over her opponents. In 1943 and 1944, researchers developed radar for aircraft such as the Avengers to be used in night missions against German submarines in the Atlantic. Further improvements prepared the radar equipment for use on fighter and torpedo planes on the U.S.S. *Independence, Saratoga,* and *Enterprise.*

Radar in the 1940s consisted of a system that reflected radio waves from targets, thereby determining their positions. On the ship, a transmitter generated radio frequency oscillations that were sent out as a narrow beam of radio waves through an aerial, which rotated and scanned the surrounding area. This aerial, called a scanner, could be fixed in space or rotated through 360 degrees, and was used for reception as well as transmission. The electronic echoes returning from the target became displayed on a screen in the air plot or Combat Information Center of the ship. Vectors and distances calculated from the highlighted position on the screen enabled the crew to pinpoint both the bearing and range between the target and the ship.

It was soon discovered that radar is not infallible, for its accuracy can be affected by fog, rain, hail, or snow. Both the amount of precipitation present in the air as well as the temperature influence the clarity of the signals transmitted. The farther a radar wave and its returning echo have to travel through fog, rainstorms, or clouds, the more difficult it is to determine vectors and distance accurately. Blips on the radar receiver or scanner do not discriminate between a large group of aircraft or just one plane. The screen defines the direction from which the blip emanates and its relative speed, but not much more.

American navy planes used a system called IFF (identification friend or foe) concurrently with radar. The equipment permitted a friendly plane to emit its own radio wave at a specific frequency, so that the Combat Information Center could recognize its own planes and not shoot them down. It had to be in working order and turned on by the pilot flying the plane.

After 1943, the United States began to see their system as a distinct advantage over the Japanese. They were still completely reliant on visual sightings, and thus could search effectively only in daylight. To detect enemy ships or planes, their carrier aircraft employed a two-phase search method. The first phase of the search took place at sunup at the end of their search line. The Japanese would launch their planes in the dark and when the sun came up, they would be two or three hundred miles away from their base carrier.

Therefore, the planes could not report on the areas they traveled during the night on the outward leg. Because they did not have radar, a second phase repeated the flights over those areas of the ocean in daylight. The Japanese fleet was vulnerable with this method, for it left parts of the sea unobserved.

An ironic twist to the development of radar was that a Japanese professor, Dr. Hidetsuga Yagi, had perfected a radar directional antenna in 1932, publishing a report concerning the device in several scientific journals. The Yagi antenna, first developed for operation in England and the United States, was used extensively by American forces in the Pacific throughout the war; the Japanese, however, neglected to explore the possibilities of Yagi's product.

Once the night pilots understood the principles of radar, they picked the rest up fairly easily. The scanner needed only to be turned on and proved very helpful to pilots returning from a long flight or raid. The instrument enabled them to find their carriers at night and in unfavorable weather.

When the U.S.S. *Saratoga, Alaska,* and supporting destroyers dropped anchor at Ulithi and pulled up alongside the carrier *Enterprise,* they joined a mass of ships of all sizes and shapes scattered throughout the harbor. The sheer number of large ships indicated that something big would soon take place. Before long, the air group pilots would know their destination and their roles in the encounter.

In the forward staging areas, the enlisted men and officers of the ships anticipated going ashore for relaxation and recreation. The forward staging area was where the task force would assemble to discuss strategy, and to assign targets and duties for each ship and its personnel. The carrier pilots had to be briefed; they made up the forward attack group. The torpedo bomber pilots were to drop the bombs, and the fighters were to protect the fleet, although some would be used to strafe and use rockets on Japanese airfields.

For the enlisted men and officers who were permitted to go ashore, relaxation meant drinking booze, shooting craps, and getting together with friends who served on other vessels. There were no girls around, so unless a navy man got a big thrill out of another sailor's butt, gambling or watching card games became the biggest excitement. Men routinely gambled large sums of money because they never knew whether they would survive the next battle to play cards again. In their minds, survival, not winning at games, was the primary concern.

While the young men relaxed, the flag officers, admirals, and captains sequestered themselves to study their orders. Scuttlebutt concerning the fleet's next move penetrated every corner of the ships. Signal officers and enlisted men who worked in communications became particularly popular; in some cases, the extremely curious attempted to bribe them or get them drunk, hoping to loosen their tongues and garner a hint from them concerning future destinations.

The relaxation area at Ulithi was called the Island of Mog Mog, although most men referred to it as Grog Grog. At this oasis, prices for drinks were low, and there were no limits. Only one's bladder and tolerance limited consumption. The cheaper brands of whiskies were popular. Carstairs and Seagram's Black Label never ran out; in fact, Black Label earned the title "Black Death" from the heavy drinkers, who knew well its destructive power. The overindulgers in both drink and gambling were usually the navy pilots on liberty.

The officer's bar on Mog Mog acquired many labels that seemed to change depending upon the bartenders, among them Crowley's Tavern and the Green Spigot. One tavern was named for the chief bartender, Crowley, who had a heavy hand in mixing drinks. The Green Spigot referred to the contents of a man's stomach after drinking too much.

There was an enlisted men's beach. A makeshift officer's club had a thatched roof over the bar; the club was piled high with stacked cases of whiskey, beer, and wine. LSTs that were used by the marines for the invasion of the various Pacific Islands were used to transport the enlisted men and officers to the beach. The front of the ship would pull up to shore, drop the forward doors down, and the men, hollering and whistling, would go ashore.

The trip from the ship to the beach took about 30 minutes. Coming back proved to be a chore. Many of the men, drunker than hoot owls, floundered in their attempts to climb up the ramp on the side of the ship. Sober crewmen brought some of their buddies aboard in nets because they couldn't stand up. Men in this condition neglected to salute the flag on the bridge and then lost the opportunity to go ashore the next day. Painful headaches followed the excessive drinking, and the men concocted all sorts of remedies for relief: Tomato juice, aspirin, black coffee, Alka Seltzer, and sometimes even another alcoholic drink for those who could find it. The navy prohibited alcohol on the ships, so such a search often proved fruitless.

At the bars of Ulithi Lagoon, the sailors, marines, and officers continuously exchanged rumors as to where this incredible armada of ships was headed. Many of the men had been at sea for a long time and relaxation and recreation to recharge their batteries were welcome. Friendships were reestablished with men from other ships.

One afternoon at Mog Mog P.G. met his former instructor, Brad Hayes, from E Base in Memphis. Hayes was a lieutenant-commander now and had his own torpedo bomber squadron on one of the Essex Class carriers. P.G. saw him at a distance and gave out a holler. There was a big hug and they shook hands firmly. "How the hell are you, Peter?" asked Brad.

"Itching for a fight. What about you?"

"I've been in a few fights. I'm not as eager as you. You can get your belly full, you know. I wondered if I'd ever run into you again. Let's go have a drink."

"Good," said P.G. "Brad, this is Chuck Strong, a flying buddy of mine." The two shook hands and they all sat down at a table. The table was an old crate with a tablecloth thrown over it.

They exchanged stories of their flying experiences. Hayes topped them all when he described his experiences in the Philippine Sea Battle and how he spent the night in the water, alternately praying and cursing his bad luck.

"The important thing is that you made it," said P.G.

"That's right," said Brad. "The man upstairs is keeping an eye on me."

Someone had obtained a nickelodeon for the officer's bar and stateside music filled the air. Recordings from the bands of Glenn Miller, Benny Goodman, and Tommy Dorsey played continuously. The men drank, cursed, laughed, and howled. Tomorrow didn't exist.

That afternoon the three navy pilots drank continuously. The concoctions available were limited only by the imagination of the bartender.

After consuming quite a few drinks, the three went out to the beach to watch a wrestling contest. Tables for card games had been set up and all sorts of crap games were being played, with a lot of money changing hands with each roll of the dice. An occasional fistfight took place over arguments about placed bets, but these were broken up quickly by the Shore Patrol.

Off to one side of the beach was a crowd of about 60 sailors and officers hollering and cheering. P.G., Brad, and Chuck strolled over to see what was going on. When a bunch of young men get together with no women present, the ingenuity of the male mind can be quite resourceful.

There stood eight guys with their pants down standing in front of a white sheet that had been placed on the ground. It looked as if they were chug-a-lugging beer. A chief petty officer was running a parimutuel betting pool, and contestants stood by ready to take their turns.

Some bright guy had made T-shirts with numbers on them so that bystanders could pick a number and bet on the contestants. Numbers one through eight were on the backs of the shirts. Sailors and officers could place their bets, and the odds changed right up to post time.

"What the hell's going on here?" asked Chuck.

"They're having a pissing contest," said Brad. "Didn't you ever do it when you were a kid? It's a riot. You can even bet on one of the guys."

"You've got to be kidding me," said Chuck. "Last time I entered a pissing contest I was five years old. The one who had the longest stream of piss won the contest. Clara, the little girl who lived next door, dropped her pants from under her skirt and tried to compete. She didn't have a pistol like we did and finally went running into the house crying to her mother. She wanted one of those things too."

"If you want to be a contestant, all you have to do is put up the dough," explained Brad. "If you finish first or second you can go on to the next contest. You get 25 percent of the pool if you win. The rules are simple. The contestant is allowed to drink up to three cans of beer just before post time. Each one lets the piss fly and the one that pisses the furthest gets the prize. It's just a little bit different from a horse race: You can bet on yourself if you limit it to $100."

"Any big winners yet?" asked P.G.

"Yeah, there's a big black chef's mate who's been pissing like a racehorse. He's got a 12-incher that works like a howitzer and when he lets go, the game's over. He's getting drunker all the time but he's won the last two contests."

"Can anyone get in?" asked Chuck.

"Sure," said Brad. "Just sign up and put your name on the list. That warrant officer over there has the list."

Chuck went over and signed up. By now, the crowd was getting bigger. A lot of money was changing hands.

The black chef's mate won the next contest; he let the piss fly like a volcano and outshot his nearest opponent by two feet. He collected $1,000 by betting on himself.

Chuck finally got into the contest. He was a cocky little guy, an excellent pilot with a chip on his shoulder who considered himself a world beater. When he dropped his pants, a big boo went up from the crowd. He had a short stub for a pistol. The odds on his winning suddenly went from ten to one up to 50 to one, and almost no one was taking action on him. P.G. and Brad decided to put five dollars on Chuck, although it looked as if he would be a sure loser.

Chuck drank three of the largest cans of beer he could find. He had already consumed a lot of liquor and was plastered. Each contestant had to piss from a line separately on the white sheet, and the newcomers pissed last. The chef's mate had outpissed everyone again. It was Chuck's turn next. He was alternately standing on one foot and then the other, trying to hold his beer. He knew that when you see someone else pissing, you have to piss, too. "Hurry up you guys," said Chuck. Finally it came his turn, but he couldn't piss. A contestant had 30 seconds to shoot or be disqualified.

"Squeeze it," hollered the crowd, particularly those who had bet on him. "Squeeze it hard."

Chuck grabbed his right nut and shaft and squeezed it hard. He gave a big grunt and farted. Mt. Vesuvius couldn't have done better. He leaned back to put an arc on the stream and won by three feet. Everybody cheered! P.G. and Brad made $250 apiece and Chuck made $1,200. Sailors and marines shook their heads in awe, and the crowd wanted to see the short guy with the little pistol perform again. Chuck said he couldn't—his nuts were sore. The crowd chanted and insisted. He finally gave in to the crowd and the betting increased in intensity. There were six new contestants, plus the black chef's mate.

After pounding three more beers, Chuck was ready to lead off. He had trouble pissing again. The effort was less than spectacular. It was hardly a dribble and the crowd booed.

"Why didn't you squeeze your balls, the way you did the first time?" asked P.G.

"Cause they're swollen and they hurt," said Chuck. "I'm saving them for a more useful purpose."

"The big black guy beat you," said P.G.

"I know," said Chuck. "I bet on him."

21

Mission Announced

The rumor mill continued to hum on the *Sara*. Ashore at Mog Mog, young men heard the veteran pilots speculate about an imminent island invasion. What was left of the Japanese Fleet had gone into hiding after the Marianas Turkey Shoot. To counter this, the United States Navy decided to start leapfrogging Japanese-held islands, cutting them off from supplies.

Just what island was the navy brass planning to invade next? Most theorized the navy would focus on some island closer to Japan. Many rumors said the fleet was to invade Formosa. One of the chief petty officers who worked in communications said he had seen the plans for the invasion, and that Formosa would be a staging area for the invasion of Japan.

"How come you saw the plans, Chief?" asked one of the pilots. "MacArthur and Nimitz would like to see those plans, too."

"Okay, hot shot, you want to make a bet? We're going to hit the Japs hard, and it's going to be right next to their homeland. Guaranteed," said the Chief.

"That's not much of a limb you're going out on," said Chuck. "There must be a hundred islands out there." He suddenly remembered his affair with Kiki in Hawaii. Could those navy intelligence people possibly be all screwed up, and the United States really was going to invade Formosa?

"Okinawa," said Domkowski. "It's gotta be Okinawa."

"Why Okinawa?" asked P.G.

"It's closer to Japan than Formosa," said Dom. "Strategically, it's more valuable."

"We'll find out soon enough," said Chuck, "because we're going to need to know what targets to hit."

After about a week at Ulithi and two or three trips for the men to the beach, the *Saratoga* lifted her anchor one evening and headed out to sea, where the *Enterprise, Alaska,* and a flotilla of ships that could only truly be appreciated from the air joined the *Sara.* This armada, called Task Force 58, was at the time the largest collection of ships assembled during World War II.

One morning, as the armada steamed westward, the captain's voice blared out over the bullhorn.

"Attention all personnel. Attention all personnel. This is the captain speaking. I know all of you have been wondering what our destination is. Our ship with Task Force 58 is heading directly for Tokyo."

This statement created an undertone of excitement among the men. After days of rumors and indecision, at last they had a destination. Not just any destination; they were going for the kill—Tokyo, the capital city of Japan.

"We will be under the command of Vice-Admiral Marc Mitscher," the captain continued, "and we will be holding a series of briefings to alert you to our next move. That is all."

Over the next few days, a very businesslike atmosphere surrounded the ship. The men had a mission, and they were going to be ready for it. Daily meetings among the fighter pilots and torpedo pilots were mandatory. The air group commander began to meet with the pilots to prepare them for the strike. The flyers were issued preliminary targets and orders. The *Saratoga* and *Enterprise,* both of whom carried specialized night squadrons, received orders to travel in the advance attack group. They were responsible for night surveillance for the fleet.

As the task force headed for Tokyo, the fighter pilots flew combat air patrol at night. The night torpedo bomber pilots flew air search lines with their bomb bays filled with additional fuel. Every man was involved in one way or another.

To prepare for the night raids over Tokyo, the fighter and torpedo bomber pilots had to take a survival course. It began with a
briefing from intelligence officers telling them how to behave if shot
down over Tokyo. They were taught to give their name, rank, and
serial number. Most of the pilots knew what their fates would be if
they survived a crash over Japan—torture for information, and
finally, before being killed, a parade through the streets of Tokyo as
war criminals.

That is exactly what happened to the downed pilots of the first
raids over Tokyo on April 8, 1942, four months after Pearl Harbor.
Lieutenant-Colonel James Doolittle and a band of army fliers were
launched off the carrier U.S.S. *Hornet,* 800 miles out at sea. The
raid, a daring, heroic mission was carried out by 16 B-25 medium
bombers and served to deter possible assaults on the west coast of
the United States. Unfortunately, the Japanese captured some of the
flyers and crews. They were tried for murder, herded through the
streets of Tokyo like animals, and publicly executed. Emperor
Hirohito could have stopped the executions, but did not. His military high command would not tolerate such lenience. The Japanese
believed that this public display would teach the American barbar-
ians a lesson.

For the pilots who would fly over Tokyo, the navy issued a survival
kit containing a cloth map showing the prevailing tides around the
coast of Japan in case they were shot down over the ocean. The map
served little purpose because the water was so cold at that time a
person could survive for 15 minutes at most. There also carried ten
thousand yen for bribes, and a Japanese-American dictionary.

The February 1945 attack would be carried out by the largest war
fleet in history and the plan was to sail within 300 miles of Tokyo.
The carriers would be protected by a fleet of battleships, cruisers,
destroyers, and planes. It was not to be a hit-and-run attack, similar
to Pearl Harbor. It would be a challenge to the Japanese fleet to
come out for a showdown.

The pilots were also told that two days before Task Force 58 was to
hit Japan, American Superfortress B-29s would be bombing Tokyo.
The planes of Major General Curtis LeMay's 21st Bomber Command of 70 to 80 B-29 Superfortresses were to fly from Tinian and
Saipan. The Superfortresses would also take pictures of the ships in
Tokyo Bay and of the planes in the outlying airfields. The photos
would be relayed to Task Force 58 for targeting.

The crew of the *Saratoga* soon discovered that the new torpedo planes that were taken aboard at Pearl Harbor would be used along with those on the *Big E* for special reconnaissance and search lines.

Five civilians—experts in radar-jamming equipment—had also been taken aboard the *Saratoga* and they would be flying in the special planes equipped with this new gear.

The equipment was called ECM, or Racon gear, and could detect enemy radar emissions and identify them. Once identified, the radar station could be jammed, creating false images and electronic specters for the Japanese operator. The operator would know that there was something out there but would not know its direction. He might recognize it as interference, an effect similar to that produced by dropping metallic fibers from planes. The fibers would show on the enemy's radar screen, but if there were enough of them floating in the sky it would be impossible to lock on to.

The night fighter group aboard the *Sara* was also to play an active role. They were to attack a Japanese airstrip south of Tokyo that had planes which would be used to defend the homeland. The night torpedo squadron was assigned to hit Yokosuka Naval Air Base at the tip of Tokyo Bay. The fleet-carrier group was to launch planes in both day and night attacks on Tokyo.

The success of massive fleet movements, such as the strike on Tokyo, depended heavily on the weather. A large front of low pressure was to be over Tokyo two days before the attack so the fleet could approach the Japanese mainland under cover of rain and squalls. Hopefully the bad weather would prevent Japanese planes from detecting the American Fleet. This meant that the planes of the *Big E* and *Saratoga* would be doing extra duty. The night pilots were told the anticipated arrival off the coast of Japan was either the 15th, 16th, or 17th of February 1945.

As the days before the attack were counted down, the intensity level aboard the ship increased. Finally, the captain called the crew and pilots together for a final briefing.

"Gentlemen," he began, "what we are about to do will have a lasting impact; not only on this war, but on the entire future of the civilized world. I'm not being dramatic. I'm simply telling you that this is far and away the most important assignment any of you have ever and probably will ever be involved with. The success of this mission will go a long way toward putting an end to any future

Japanese threats. A failure will only serve to make them more dangerous and confident, and will prolong the war."

The captain went on for a few more minutes, but the implication was crystal clear. This mission had to succeed. Period.

The night torpedo pilots from VTN-53 took off from the *Saratoga* on the long-distance search lines. They were told that radio silence was not to be broken unless the enemy was sighted. With the added fuel in the bomb bays of the torpedo bombers, the planes had enough fuel to go on a search line of 600 miles and return. The fighters would escort the torpedo planes for about 200 or 300 miles and then the bombers were on their own. The planes took off late in the afternoon with the radar experts in the back compartments of the planes to pick up the Japanese radar frequency. With the Racon gear in place, this was accomplished and the radar on Japan's coast was jammed.

The torpedo bomber search line was uneventful, but if the pilots hadn't been trained in night-flying, they never would have made it back to the carrier. The weather worsened. Task Force 58 had moved Point Option slightly, trying to find an open slot for the planes to land, but could not. The bad weather meant the pilots were on their own and their flying skills would be measured by Mother Nature. The torpedo bombers' surface radar was not the best, but it was a hell of a lot better than they used to have. Having a civilian expert in the back of the plane didn't hurt either. YE radio gear, a high-frequency radio beacon sent out by the *Saratoga,* proved most helpful.

P.G.'s gunner, Dominic, was invaluable. He picked up the *Sara*'s signal and as it got louder, P.G. dropped his plane down to 100 feet. The ceiling was around 300 feet with rough seas and P.G. could feel a bitch of a carrier landing coming up. Eventually he found the *Sara.* Found it, shit, he came close to hitting the damn bridge. Luckily the task force was still quite a way from the Japanese homeland and he wasn't fired on by the destroyer picket boats. He felt like he was back in Rhode Island and thought, "Hell, these South Pacific storms aren't any worse than a nor'easter." He passed the bridge on the downwind leg and made a sharp turn, trying to get into the groove. He picked up the L.S.O. Even though he was in good position to land, he received a wave-off. He was worried about his gas supply and wondered what was going on. Then he found out. By light signals and Morse code he was told to orbit because there had been a crash on the deck. He started to circle but he wanted to keep the carrier in sight, because he was the last of the six planes that were out. He decided to fly low on the water to keep the ship in view and leaned out his fuel to save gas. Finally he was given the signal to return into the landing circle.

On the next go-around, as his plane approached the flight deck, he sighted the landing signal officer and, even though the plane was coming in pretty hot, he received a cut. He couldn't see very well and hoped to catch an early wire. The plane slammed down on the flight deck, one wheel hitting first, and then the other. He had little fuel and no speed to take off again. The edge of the deck rushed toward him. Suddenly he felt a jolt and his neck snapped back as the plane's hook caught a wire and bounced around the deck.

When he climbed out of the plane the ceiling was less than 500 feet, and the *Saratoga* was taking big waves over her bow. "Glad to have you aboard," said a flight deck crew member.

"I'm glad to be aboard."

22

Night-Flying Combat

When the Japanese Imperial Navy attacked Pearl Harbor on December 7, 1941, they were equipped with the most up-to-date carrier aircraft in the world. The planes were developed from combat experience the Japanese gained in China during the previous four years and gave their pilots a distinct advantage. Admiral Yamamoto, head of the Japanese Imperial Navy, had the vision to foresee the new role that the carrier would play in major sea and land engagements.

This led to the development of the Mitsubishi Zero. A low-wing monoplane, the Zero was fast, could climb rapidly, had good armament and fuel capacity. It was designed to serve as an escort fighter capable of intercepting and destroying enemy attack bombers. The Zero boasted lightness, simplicity, and ease of repair. It had minimal drag, good stability, and control. The cannon in the Zero's nose was a large-caliber weapon and brought a high level of successful kill records for its pilots.

Early in the Pacific War the agile Zero was consistently victorious over obsolete United States aircraft. It was superior to the F4F Wildcat in speed, climbing, service ceiling, range, and turning circles. This gave the Japanese pilots an advantage in dogfights. The

American fighter planes were simply outmoded, ill-equipped, and had insufficient fire power to challenge them.

American pilots had to use what they had until new equipment could be manufactured. They were a tough bunch and were able to become competitive with the Japanese in dogfights over Guadalcanal early in the war as they gained combat experience. The pilots learned to get the most out of their Wildcats, and at the same time found weaknesses in the Zero. They found, for example, that the Japanese planes did not have bullet-proof gas tanks. The .50-caliber machine guns on the F4F often blew up the Zeros.

Tactically, the marine and navy pilots were superior to the Japanese. The Americans used the two-plane flying section as the basic air unit. The F4F was not as agile as the Zero so they used dive-and-run tactics. The pilots learned the hard way not to dogfight with the nimble Zeros. The way to fight was to get above it and dive, gaining speed, and then try to hit it on the first pass. If the Zeros got on your tail you had to roll, dive, and push the throttle to the fire wall to get away. In reality, the Wildcat was no match for the Zero. If the Americans wanted to win the war, this condition could not exist for long.

American military aircraft and engine designers had a lot of catching up to do. The leaders were the Grumman Aircraft Factory on Long Island, New York, and Pratt and Whitney Aircraft in Connecticut. Grumman developed the F6F Hellcat, a big, single-seat fighter. When loaded it was heavier than the Wildcat and had the largest wingspan and lowest wing loading of all United States fighters. This made the plane highly maneuverable and ideally suited for carrier landings.

The plane was designed specifically to take on the Mitsubishi Zero. It had good visibility, rugged construction, and could take a lot of punishment. It had a big, three-bladed prop and a high-powered Pratt and Whitney R-2800-10W engine. It also had super-chargers and a water injection system, to give an extra burst of speed when needed. It could be used as a bomber and could carry six five-inch high-velocity rockets on its underwing racks. Six .50-caliber forward-shooting machine guns, self-sealing fuel tanks, and mounts for carrying two 1,000-pound bombs completed its armament. Its range could be extended by adding belly and wing tanks.

In November 1943 the Grumman Hellcat was brought to the

Pacific. It was a bigger and better Wildcat, but it had not been battle-tested.

Conversely, the agile Zero, considered the dogfighter supreme in the Pacific skies, had never flown against the Hellcat. On November 5, 1943, the first major air confrontation took place in a strike against Rabaul. Rabaul was heavily defended by the Japanese Zero fighters.

The U.S.S. *Saratoga* and a new carrier, the U.S.S. *Princeton,* sailed toward Rabaul with Task Force 38. They launched all their bombers escorted by 52 Hellcats. Japanese radar had picked up the *Saratoga's* strike force and the Zeros were in the air waiting. In the battle that ensued, eleven Japanese Zeros were shot down by the Hellcats.

Later, on November 24, the Hellcats fought the Japanese Zeros over the island of Tarawa. In a roaring battle against Japanese bombers and Zeros, the Hellcats entirely destroyed the Japanese force. No American pilots were lost.

The true coming of the Hellcat was in the largest naval air battle of all time: The Great Marianas Turkey Shoot in the Philippine Sea on June 19, 1944. In this battle, the Japanese Naval Air Force was wiped out. The Hellcat pilots had a kill ratio of better than ten-to-one. Over 350 Japanese planes were shot down and two carriers sunk.

Domkowski, P.G.'s fighter-pilot friend, was in the Marianas Turkey Shoot. His code name was Cobra Seven. Flying in his Hellcat he shot down two Zeros. When he went after a third, he was approached from behind by another Zero.

"Cobra Seven, you've got company. There's a Zero on your ass directly at six o'clock," said Cobra Ten.

Dom swallowed hard. The Zeros had a well-earned reputation for not missing from behind. Several bullets ripped through his so-called shatterproof glass canopy and destroyed a huge chunk of the instrument panel. He pushed the stick forward and dove the plane to get away.

The glass fragments cut his face and he felt a burning in his chest. He looked down and there was blood on his flight suit. Luckily his eyes weren't damaged by the glass, his arms and legs seemed to be functioning, and he didn't lose consciousness. The flight controls didn't seem to be damaged. He hit his superchargers and water injection controls to get an extra burst of speed. The air rushed through the hole in the plane's canopy.

The Zero continued to track Dom. A minute later, a huge explosion ripped through the sky. The Zero had been caught from above by Cobra Ten, and his gas tank had been penetrated and the plane destroyed. Dom pulled out of his dive. He put his goggles down over his eyes as the wind continued to whistle through the broken glass of the canopy. The engine seemed to be running all right but there was a small hole in the fuselage near the cockpit. He radioed to his fighter group commander; "Cobra One, this is Cobra Seven. I've been hit. My canopy is knocked out. I have a chest wound. I'm going to try to get back to the carrier."

Dom stuffed a handkerchief into the tear in his flight suit and this seemed to slow down the flow of blood. Using his right hand to control the stick and his feet to control the rudders, he set his throttle at cruising speed and compressed his left fist against his chest. He felt some glass particles on his flight suit.

"Cobra Seven, this is Cobra One. One of our fighter planes will escort you back. Vector to base is 160 degrees and distance 170 miles. Good luck."

Domkowski decided to put his plane on automatic pilot so he could tend to his injuries. He set his compass headings and turned it on.

Over the radio came; "Cobra One to Cobra Six. Escort Cobra Seven back to base. Acknowledge."

"Cobra Six to Cobra One. Roger. We've knocked most of the bastards out of the sky anyway."

"Cobra Seven, this is Cobra Six. Drop your landing gear so I can tell which one is you."

After Dom put his wheels down, Cobra Six used his fuel injection mechanism to catch up. "Cobra Seven, this is Cobra Six. Follow me in. You okay, Dom?"

"Cobra Six, this is Cobra Seven. I think so. My motor seems okay, the fan is still going around, and I don't seem to be losing fuel."

"Good, hang in there."

As Dom headed back to his carrier, he noticed the bleeding from his chest wound had slowed down considerably and finally stopped. When he arrived back at the base he was given priority to land and, fortunately, he was able to get aboard the carrier's deck safely. He climbed out of the cockpit to survey the damage to his plane and to himself. The plane had been shot up pretty bad. He had scratches on his face and a wedge of glass had penetrated his flight suit and was sticking out of the pocket over his heart. He removed the glass, reached into the pocket, and pulled out a small book of psalms that he always carried with him. The book was punctured straight through and there was blood on it. Dom looked at the book of psalms, and said, "The next time I fly, I'm going to remember to carry a hardcover edition of the Old Testament."

The Hellcat could take a lot of damage and return the pilots home safely to their carrier. The versatility of the Hellcat was demonstrated still further when, shortly after the Marianas Turkey Shoot, the navy decided that a night fighter plane had to be developed. The Hellcat was modified for this purpose.

The F6F-3N and F6F-5N were produced because the Japanese had shown a remarkable aptitude for staging air attacks against surface fleets at night. At Guadalcanal they had shown they could be equally adept in attacking island bases after dark. Having no airborne radar, the Japanese employed pathfinder aircraft and a highly efficient system of flares and illuminating devices to mark the target for their bombers. Torpedo planes often used float lights to indicate the course to the target.

The navy realized they had to devise an aerial defense against such attacks. This led to the development of the Hellcat and the radar-equipped Avenger as a night-fighting team.

The night fighter version of the Hellcat flying off the decks of the U.S.S. *Saratoga* in February 1945 was the F6F-5N. The plane had a pod attached to the right wing which enclosed a radar antenna. It carried a new AN-APS-6 radar system and a redesigned instrument panel with red lighting so as not to interfere with the pilot's night vision.

As the *Saratoga* steamed toward Tokyo, 34 of these planes were on her flight and hangar decks, carrying some of the most effective radar equipment used during the war.

Flying at night, it is difficult for the pilot to determine wind velocity and the location of suspected storms. Even if navigation skills are excellent, a pilot can be blown off course on his return to the carrier and not realize it. This problem was solved somewhat by the addition of the radar on the wing so the pilot could home in on the carrier.

It was also difficult for the enemy to score a hit on the night-flying airplanes. Still, antiaircraft sometimes shot up the planes so severely that the pilot struggled just to keep his plane in the air. If a hit did not transform a plane into a ball of fire, the pilot was forced to make an important decision; bail out or land the plane in the sea.

P.G. had decided that if he ever had the choice between bailing out of a plane or riding the plane into the water he would choose the latter. Both choices had their risks, however. Riding a plane into the water took more skill and courage than bailing out. The pilot had to guess which direction the wind was coming from and try to hit the crest of a wave. P.G. was determined never to bail out, because while flying as a cadet he had seen a terrible accident; a mid-air collision in which one of the cadet pilots was able to get out of his plane but his parachute failed to open. P.G. had been watching from the ground that day, and heard the planes collide high above the runway. He saw the doomed cadet fall to earth.

In the combat area, planes were sometimes damaged or shot up and had to be repaired aboard the carrier, where repair jobs were often jury-rigged. One day, P.G. was assigned an aircraft that had been badly shot up. He down-checked the plane because the magnetos dropped off too much. The day after he down-checked the plane he was given the same plane again and he refused to fly it because he lacked confidence in the ability of the mechanics to fix the plane's engine in such a short time. As he checked out the magnetos, one dropped off 130 rpm. The other magneto wasn't much better so he downed the plane a second time. This fouled up the launch and the captain bellowed over the bullhorn, "Have that pilot report to the bridge."

When P.G. got to the bridge, he saluted the captain

The captain appeared agitated. "What the hell's going on here, Ensign? Have you lost your nerve?"

"No sir," P.G. replied. "It's just that the plane I was assigned to is a clunker. It won't fly, sir."

"How do you know?" asked the captain. "You didn't give it a chance."

"The mags dropped off," answered P.G.

The captain turned and barked at his executive officer, "You tell air operations to get this pilot back in the air this evening!"

He abruptly turned his back to P.G. "Dismissed."

That afternoon P.G. was assigned a different plane for a long search line. He returned after a night-flight setting his plane down on the carrier's deck around midnight. The captain's comments had pissed him off.

Two days later, while P.G. was still stewing, Williams, one of the senior pilots, was assigned the clunker P.G. had down-checked. Williams wasn't too happy about flying the plane either. One of the mags seemed to check out all right, however. When William's plane was hooked onto the catapult, he thought the engine sounded like it was missing. He pushed the throttle all the way forward as he received the signal for launch. The plane's engine cut out completely just as it got over the bow and hit a big wave in front of the carrier. The crash alarm sounded, and the helmsman on the bridge turned the wheel sharply to avoid the plane. The wake created by the carrier as it passed by almost flipped the plane over onto its back. Williams quickly released his seat belt when he hit the water and got out. His radioman got out the back door of the plane, which was sticking up out of the water, and as he emerged the hooks on his parachute harness got caught on the edge of the door. The turret gunner, who was in the water, saw his plight, swam over to him, and released his parachute attachment. Swimmers from the destroyer following behind the carrier rescued the occupants of the plane.

That evening, the air operations officer came into the ready room where P.G. was playing acey-ducey with another pilot. "Grant, I'd like to talk to you," said Commander Rice. P.G. got up and went to the back of the ready room. "The captain sends his apologies. That plane wasn't fit to fly garbage."

"Thanks," said P.G. "Was the captain too busy to apologize in person or too hard-headed?"

"Both," said Rice. "But I won't tell him you asked."

"Thanks again," said P.G.

The next day search lines continued en route to Japan. As the task force got closer the *Sara* and the *Big E* flew both day and night flights. The number of search lines multiplied.

Most were boring, although the radar operators in the bellies were getting workouts watching the scopes. The search lines were flown about 150 feet off the water, monitored by a radio altimeter. Some of the pilots flew on automatic pilot. Usually a Hellcat would fly cover on a torpedo bomber's tail.

Late one afternoon, approaching one of the islands near the coast of Japan, Domkowski was flying fighter cover over P.G.'s tail on the sundown patrol. The sky was cloudy but the water looked calm. Suddenly, out of the blue, P.G. saw tracer bullets flash in front of his plane and a couple of bullets zinged through his wings. Dominic, his gunner, quickly fired back with his turret guns. P.G. picked up his microphone and hollered. "Dom, bogey at 5:00. For God's sake get that guy off my back."

Dom put on his fuel injection to get an extra burst of speed while P.G. headed for the clouds to try and hide. When the Jap pilot saw the Hellcat, he dove for cover. Dom chased him into the clouds.

"Get his ass," screamed P.G.

There was a burst of gunfire in the clouds but the Jap got away. P.G. was pissed because Dom hadn't seen the bogey. When Domkowski emerged from the clouds he pulled his fighter plane up on P.G.'s wing. P.G. hollered at him over the radio, "What the hell were you doing, listening to Tokyo Rose?"

"I didn't see him coming out of the sun," responded Dom.

"Keep alert," said P.G. "He almost made me a new asshole, for God's sake. If that had happened you'd be one hell of an asshole, and I'd haunt you for the rest of your life."

P.G. was still grateful for Dom on his wing. He knew the Avenger was no match for the Japanese fighter plane. "Let's head for home," he said.

The next night Chuck Strong, P.G.'s friend, was sent out on a long search line at sundown with a landing anticipated around 1:00 A.M. The task force had encountered suspected enemy submarines, so the fleet had to change its course and Point Option. When Chuck returned to Point Option in the dead of night no ships were in sight. His radar hadn't been working well and he had to rely on his radio to get back to the carrier.

Pilots get a heavy, sick feeling in the pit of their stomachs when this happens. Chuck climbed his plane to a higher altitude to try to pick up the YE radio signal. His radio was only picking up a weak signal and it was hard to decipher. He continued to climb. When he got to 11,000 feet he picked up a stronger signal and decided to home in on it. As his plane got closer the signal got louder. He was getting more tense because he was running out of fuel.

There were no night lights on the ship when he got close to the signal, so he decided to make a pass over what he thought was the deck of the carrier. At night, the large propellers of the ship created a wake that appeared like phosphorescence in the water and helped Chuck line up in the groove in the flight pattern.

As Chuck made a pass following one of these phosphorescence wakes he couldn't see the flight deck very well and decided to try again even though the landing signal officer hadn't given him the signal to land. He brought his plane back around for another pass but there still was no L.S.O. He was getting worried. Lights out on a ship could mean they were hiding from an approaching enemy attack. That could be bad news. He was afraid to break radio silence if the ships were getting ready to go into action. He knew he had to do something because his gas gauge was approaching empty. What could he do?

Suddenly, the answer came. Radio silence was broken. "Get that goddamned plane out of here or I'll have my crew shoot you down," said a booming voice. "You almost knocked the mast off my destroyer. If you're in trouble the carrier *Essex* is about ten miles off the port bow."

"Thanks," Chuck responded sheepishly. A few minutes later he found the *Essex* and received permission to land. He returned to the *Saratoga* the next morning feeling foolish, but alive and well.

23

Night Fighters Over Tokyo

Task Force 58 moved closer to the shores of Japan under cloud cover and darkness. Below the flight deck, machinists and aircraft maintenance personnel were diligently preparing the planes for the impending battle. Engines that needed check-outs or repairs were worked on and guns were loaded with ammunition. The fighter planes had .50-caliber ammunition loaded and MK rockets mounted on their wings. Some had napalm bombs attached to their bellies. The torpedo bomber planes had their bomb bays filled with 500-pound bombs or napalm bombs. Some of the bomb bays were filled with extra fuel tanks for flying search lines.

The *Saratoga* and *Enterprise* were in the forefront of Task Force 58, their aircraft flying day and night air patrol over the mammoth fleet. Night search lines using the radar-equipped torpedo bomber planes were out in front. Some of the ships' gun crews were at battle stations constantly.

Task Force 58 was heading for Tokyo at a speed of 25 knots. The plan was to surprise the enemy and dare the remnants of the Japanese fleet to come out and fight. When Task Force 58 was 24 hours away from Tokyo, *Sara's* air group commander called a meeting of the night-carrier pilots in the ready room. P.G., Chuck, and Domkowski would not forget that meeting.

The air group leader was Commander Jack Stewart, an experienced combat pilot who had earned the Navy Cross. He was an Annapolis graduate, short in stature, with a reputation as a hard-nosed, strict disciplinarian.

"Gentlemen, the air operations officer of the *Saratoga,* Commander Rice, is going to outline our missions and brief us about the latest intelligence reports obtained by the B-29 bomber crews flying over Tokyo. I want your undivided attention."

Commander Rice, a heavy-set man with a black mustache spoke. "Tomorrow evening some of you will participate in the first night-carrier raids over Tokyo. This will be the navy's first coordinated attack on the Japanese homeland. Our intelligence is that the Japanese do not expect an attack at night but will be waiting for an early dawn attack. The United States Navy has a surprise in store for them.

"The large night carriers, the *Saratoga* and *Enterprise,* will launch coordinated night-fighter attacks using napalm and rockets. The attacks will be centered on those airfields that protect Tokyo. The next day the Japanese will feel the brunt of the entire task force. Fifteen hundred naval aircraft will be launched from the largest United States armada ever assembled. Our mission is to destroy any ships in Tokyo Bay and to crush the morale of the Japanese people. The details of the role that each of you will play will be discussed by Air Group Commander Stewart. Good luck to you and good hunting."

Commander Stewart got up from his chair and turned to face the group of night pilots. "Eighteen fighter planes from the *Saratoga* have been assigned to hit one of the largest Japanese airfields south of Tokyo. It will be a long flight, so auxiliary wing tanks will be attached. You will use the fuel in the wing tanks first and then drop them. The distance to the target is approximately 300 miles, so fuel conservation is of the utmost importance. Each pilot will receive a radar picture of the anticipated target to aid bombing accuracy. Because this is considered a particularly dangerous mission, I have decided to ask for volunteers. Please raise your hands."

The entire fighter squadron raised their hands.

"I thought that would happen," said Commander Stewart. "I'll have to assign the pilots." He then announced, "Lieutenant Ross, the executive officer, will lead the flight. Lieutenant Doty will lead the second section and Lieutenant Wilson the last section. There will be 18 planes in all. Our Night Fighter Group 53 has been assigned to hit Hammamatsu Airfield, south of Tokyo. The air operations officer will review the targets with you and show you the aerial photographs."

There was a buzz in the ready room when the air group commander stopped talking. The commander turned, strode to the door, and left.

"Why isn't Commander Stewart going on the flight?" Chuck asked P.G.

"How the hell would I know?" replied P.G. "Maybe he wants to let the rest of the boys have a shot at a Navy Cross."

"Is Domkowski going to fly this one?" asked Chuck.

"Yeah," said P.G., "and he's crapping in his flight suit."

"He's one hell of a pilot," replied Chuck. "If anybody can make it back, he can."

It became obvious as the pilots' discussion continued that the fighter pilots were less afraid of being shot down by enemy aircraft than returning in the dead of night to a carrier bobbing around off the coast of Japan.

Dom approached Chuck and P.G. He had overheard some of their conversation. "I'm going to fly my plane on lean all the way to the target and back," he said.

"Good idea," said P.G. "But remember to bring a change of underwear. Just to be safe."

"And don't forget, we'll be checking on you here at the home base," said Chuck, smiling comfortably.

"Is that right?" said Dom. "I hear the torpedo bomber pilots are going to be hitting the Yokasuka Naval Base."

"Shit," Chuck said. "Talk about dropping bombs, I wonder when they plan on dropping that one on us?"

As the *Saratoga* and *Enterprise* approached the Japanese coastline, the weather deteriorated. The seas were rough. There was no horizon. Rain pelted the task force. There was some question as to whether the night fighters and torpedo planes would be launched at all that evening; it was finally decided that the fighters would be launched ahead of the bombers.

The tension in the pilot's ready room was reaching a fever pitch. The 18 pilots going on the mission had their red goggles on, adapting their eyes to the darkness. The teletype rattled like a machine gun as it printed out the latest latitude and longitude of the ship's position. The pilots scribbled the numbers on their navigation boards. The task force had gotten closer to the Japanese mainland. Last-minute instructions were shouted by Lieutenant Ross, the executive officer of the fighter squadron. "After the launch, we'll rendezvous and proceed to the target. We won't be able to wait for any stragglers. The weather is piss-poor, so keep a tight formation."

Finally, the announcement: "Pilots, man your planes."

The pilots not going on the mission remained in the ready room, listening to the roar of the plane's engines and the snap of the catapult as each plane was launched. It was like a countdown. The pilots listened and counted, one, two, three . . . finally 18. Some of the pilots ambled up to the combat information center to watch the rendezvous on the radar screen. The three sections of six planes assembled symmetrically and headed on their vector to the target. A cheer went up in the combat information center as the fighter squadron headed for Japan.

The launch of the night torpedo planes was delayed because of bad weather. P.G. and Chuck decided to wait in the combat information center for the return of the fighter squadron. The fighter group had a difficult target that night. The plan was to have the squadron come in low on the water to evade radar and drop parachute flares to illuminate the target. That night the Japanese lit up the sky themselves with a hail of antiaircraft fire as the planes approached Hammamatsu Airfield.

It was the most concentrated antiaircraft fire the pilots had ever encountered. Star shells were fired into the air to light up the sky so the Japanese gunners on the ground could see what they were shooting at. It was a pyrotechnic display beyond comprehension.

As the planes got over the target, all hell broke loose. The three sections of six aircraft split off to box the target in. They worked like a group of professional assassins. First one plane, then another peeled off and dove at the target. Some of the pilots dropped their napalm bombs to start fires. Others fired MK rockets at the hangars and at the planes lined up on the runways. The radio was a lunatic blend of cursing and war cries.

"Oil tank! Oil Tank! Look at that thing blow!" shouted one of the pilots.

"Knock their fucking guts out," shouted another.

"Blast that gun battery by the tower," shouted Doty.

"Got it! Got it! I got it!"

"Watch your altitude. Watch it. Keep your ass away from the batteries on the right."

Screams of murderous frenzy filled the pilots' headsets until it was impossible to tell if a pilot was hit, injured, or attacking.

"Express from Brooklyn," shouted Domkowski, as he pulled the trigger to fire his rockets. Another oil tank erupted and blew to smithereens.

"This here's for Pearl. She sends her tender, loving regards," shouted Wilson, as he released a 500-pound bomb.

Massive balls of fire lit up the sky as the fighter squadron continued to hit their targets. It looked like the Fourth of July. The runways were obliterated by the 500-pound bombs. The enemy's planes that were lined up along the runways were picked off like sitting ducks by the Hellcat pilots.

"Three for a quarter," hollered someone as a triad of enemy fighters were shredded by machine gun fire.

"You win a teddy bear for knocking that one down," said another.

The entire squadron got into the act; oil tanks exploded, hangars were destroyed, most of the enemy's planes on the ground were demolished, and all of the antiaircraft gun batteries were silenced. The attack on Hammamatsu Airfield by Night Fighter Squadron 53 was a complete success. The Japanese thought a full-scale invasion was taking place. They did not realize that night-fighter planes from the *Saratoga* had been the culprits.

Lieutenant Ross picked up his microphone: "Beaver Squadron, this is Beaver One, job well done. Let's head for home. Check in." All 18 night-fighter planes checked in one by one. They survived the attack, rendezvoused, and headed back to sea together in search of the *Saratoga*. War cries settled into sighs as they regrouped, and eyes became riveted on wing lights and fuel gauges.

24

Doty

That night the air plot room of the *Saratoga* was busy. Lieutenant-Commander Stubbs, who was in charge of air plot, and Commander Stewart watched all the action unfold on the ship's radar scope. They watched the flight leave the ship, rendezvous, and vector toward the target. The blip on the radar screen disappeared when the planes were 70 miles away.

"That's one mission I wish I'd been on," said Commander Stewart.

"I suspect there will be many more," said Commander Stubbs. "Those night pilots are true pioneers. The navy should be proud of them."

Just then a radio transmission came in from one of *Sara*'s torpedo bomber planes. It was out on a night search line.

"Beaver Base, this is Beaver 34. I have an unidentified blip on the surface of the water 30 miles away bearing 94 degrees. I'm approximately 174 miles from base."

Commander Stubbs got on the mike, "Orbit and await instructions." He turned to one of the junior officers and said, "Notify the bridge and the captain that our air search has detected possible enemy ships or submarines approaching the task force."

A few minutes later the order came from the captain to change course to avoid the enemy ships. The pilot of the torpedo bomber on the search line was ordered to return to base.

The air group commander knew a problem was developing. The fleet would have to change Point Option. The returning pilots, whose planes were already low on fuel, would now have to remain in the air even longer than planned. The consequences were obvious— pilots could be lost. Stewart called the bridge and asked to speak to the captain.

"Sir, this is Commander Stewart. I'm worried about changing Point Option. The fighter squadron will be approaching the limit of their fuel capacity."

"I understand the problem," said the captain, "but the task force must be protected first. We'll limit the change in Point Option as much as possible. I'll notify the fleet command."

Sara's night-fighter squadron had rendezvoused off the coast of Japan. Two of the fighter planes had been hit by small flak but were not seriously damaged. As the planes flew out to sea to meet the *Saratoga* the weather took a turn for the worse. The rain intensified, and cloud cover increased. There was also a swirling wind, and visibility was approaching zero.

"Lean out your fuel as much as possible," said Lieutenant Ross. "You'll need every ounce to get back."

Domkowski had already leaned out his fuel so much that his plane sounded like a popcorn machine.

Lieutenant Doty, who was leading the second section, was an experienced combat pilot. He reflected on some of his previous combat flights. He knew there would be cheering and laughing and interesting descriptions of how the attack evolved by those who returned safely. There would also be sadness for those who didn't return. So far, however, everyone was okay.

Doty was on his second tour of duty in the Pacific and was getting a little war-weary. He was a fatalist, like most of the other pilots, and considered it pure luck if he survived. He'd noticed recently that he had become more cautious with the night-fighter squadron. He'd become careful, something he never thought would happen. He had recently become engaged to a pretty nurse named Margie. Sometimes while flying the plane on automatic pilot he'd daydream about her and imagined what it would be like to be in her arms. She was the sweetest and most beautiful woman he had ever known and the best thing that had ever happened to him. As the weather worsened, he was quickly brought back to reality. He got on his microphone; "Beaver section two, tighten up the formation. The weather is closing in."

He didn't want any stragglers. Inexperienced pilots might panic and get lost. He knew his night-flying buddies weren't superhuman. They had the proven ability to function effectively in the night alone if necessary. The pilots were highly motivated, stable individuals who really knew how to fly their planes using their instruments. Each plane had radar on its wing so the pilot could home in on the carrier.

Before the night was over, they would all be called on to exhibit their uncanny ability to get aboard the *Saratoga* under extreme adverse weather conditions.

Nobody, of course, was home when the fighter squadron arrived at Point Option. Lieutenant Ross broke radio silence. "I think we're lost. I've circled the area and I can't pick up the *Sara*."

Doty picked up his microphone and made radio contact with the fighter squadron. "Beaver Six to Beaver Group, I'll fly upstairs to pick up the *Sara*'s radio or radar signal. We may be too far away to pick them up or for them to pick us up. Don't break from formation. Stick together. I'll drop a float light in the water for a reference point. Orbit in position over the float light."

He pointed the nose of his plane upward and put on his oxygen mask. At 22,000 feet he picked up the YE radio signal from the *Sara*. The ship was 80 miles further away from Point Option than the pilots had anticipated. Doty flew down to where the rest of the night fighter group was orbiting.

"Beaver Six to all Beaver planes. Vector to the ship is 110 degrees, 80 miles. When you get 30 miles away from the ship you should be able to detect the *Sara* on your own radar. Keep your fuel leaned out. No midnight swims. Good luck. Acknowledge."

Each pilot solemnly acknowledged the message. They all knew they had a big problem.

The weather socked in tight with a zero ceiling. They were on their own. The weather got so bad they couldn't fly formation. This was the final test for the night-carrier pilots. Could they make it back?

The tension grew in the air plot center.

"They should have been overhead by now. Where the hell are they?" asked Commander Stewart. "Aren't there any blips on that screen?"

"No, Sir," replied the seaman doing the plotting.

The *Saratoga* was rolling and bobbing, being pushed around the Pacific as the squalls increased their intensity. The Combat Information Center had difficulty locating the squadron, so they couldn't turn the ship to shorten their return. The unthinkable—that all the planes had been shot down or were lost—became more plausible with every passing minute.

Finally, a blip 30 miles out appeared on the *Sara*'s radar screen. The captain ordered the helmsman to direct the carrier toward the returning planes. Most of the pilots who were not flying were on the flight deck or bridge waiting for their buddies. One by one the planes' engines could be heard in the distance and one by one they appeared through the clouds. As each plane touched down, a cheer went up from the onlookers.

"Whose plane is that?" was the consistent question. Fuel and time were running out and only ten planes had landed safely aboard. The *Sara*'s air plot had the remaining planes on the radar screen. Radio silence was broken to vector them home. Finally there were 16 planes that had been taken aboard. There were two stragglers: Domkowski and Doty.

P.G. and Chuck were on the bridge, silently praying. Another fighter plane entered the groove. The engine was sputtering, and the landing signal officer gave it a wave-off. The pilot didn't take it. He dropped the plane over the edge of the fantail. It slammed down on the flight deck, crushing the landing gear. Domkowski looked bewildered as he climbed out of the cockpit of the damaged aircraft. P.G. and Chuck gave a big shout.

All but one plane of the night fighters who flew that evening returned safely to land on the *Saratoga* or *Enterprise*. Lieutenant Doty never made it back. His blip went off the screen 20 miles from the carrier. He had used his fuel climbing to the higher altitude to pick up the signal from the *Saratoga* and had to ditch his plane in the cold waters off Tokyo. He gave his position before going into the water. An intensive search failed to find him.

That night the pilots all spoke of Doty. Those close to him knew he'd become wary, careful, intent upon ending his part in the war alive. But being careful didn't get Doty killed. Courage did.

His courage exemplified the highest qualities of the Naval Air Corps in risking his own life to save the lives of his fellow pilots.

25

Night Avengers Over Tokyo

When war tactics changed to make the carrier the prime weapon, they became the prime targets, and preventing the carriers from launching their aircraft became the goal. It soon became apparent that while United States dive bombers could cripple enemy ships, they had difficulty in sinking them. This led to the development of torpedo bomber planes that could deliver the knockout blow.

Before Pearl Harbor, the United States Navy high command had engineers and designers already at work. Plans were made to develop a large bomber-type plane built expressly to destroy opposing carriers, battleships, cruisers, and destroyers. A large prototype torpedo bomber plane, the XTB-1, was constructed by Grumman Aircraft. While it was being tested, it had an in-flight fire in the bomb bay and the pilot and engineer had to bail out. A month after the crash and a week after the dastardly attack on Pearl, the navy successfully tested a second plane of the same design. The plane was aptly named "The Avenger."

As the war progressed in the Pacific, Wildcat fighter planes on most carriers were replaced by Hellcats, and the SBD Dauntless dive bomber was replaced by the Avenger.

The TBF-TBM Avengers with their ASB air-to-surface radar

and, later, with their ASD-1 radar, were credited with eliminating the German submarine fleet that was destroying merchant vessels in the Atlantic.

In the Pacific, the TBF Avengers had their baptism of fire at the Battle of Midway. It was their first strike against Japanese carriers. The Avenger's debut was a disaster. All eight Avengers were shot down. Before long, however, the true value of the plane became clear.

By December 1943, Grumman Aircraft and General Motors had begun to mass-produce the Avengers. A more powerful Wright R-2600-20 engine with a supercharger had replaced the previous engine. The plane now weighed 17,000 pounds when fully loaded and was the largest and heaviest single-engine carrier-based plane used by the navy during World War II. It had a service ceiling above 23,000 feet and a range of 1,130 miles. It could also fly as a scout and extend its search line with a drop tank. Another type of gas tank, which could be rigged in the bomb bay, increased its range even more. The new Avengers were equipped to fight back. They had .50-caliber wing machine guns and eight five-inch rockets on racks below the wings. There were a fancy mobile turret gun and rear-firing aft machine guns. The Avenger would become a true battleship of the skies.

Pilots enjoyed flying the plane. It was easy to catapult fully loaded from the decks because it had a large wingspan and a powerful engine. The plane was also heavy, and when landing aboard the carrier would alight softly and settle in, catching the wire in the roughest of weather. It could also withstand heavy combat damage.

The latest radar equipment made the Avenger a formidable detector of subs or surface craft. Its pilots were comforted in knowing that after participating in a battle and not knowing where they were, the fancy radar gear in the belly of the plane would help them home in on their own carrier.

The torpedo bomber squadron on the *Saratoga*, Air Group 53, had the latest planes equipped for night-flying, the TBM-3Ns. It also had six special planes with radar countermeasure equipment containing electronic jamming equipment in the radome on the wing.

The Avenger was capable of carrying a 2,000-pound torpedo. However, because of problems with the torpedo's performance, glide- and skip-bombing techniques were used instead. The plane would attack in a 30- to 45-degree dive, and then a stack of four bombs, spaced 75 feet apart, would be dropped from an altitude of 500 feet or lower. This tactic would practically guarantee one or more hits.

The planes of VTN-53 were to be used on the night raids over Tokyo. Some would be dropping napalm bombs to light up the targets for the day-flying torpedo bomber pilots from the other carriers. They would be launched in the early morning darkness and would return to land on their carriers in the daylight. P.G.'s friend and flight instructor from Memphis, Brad Hayes, was assigned to a day-flying unit that was to take part in the massive raids over Tokyo.

Hayes, who had flown TBF-1s early in the Pacific War and F6F fighters in the Philippine Sea Battle, took command of a torpedo squadron based on one of the Essex-class carriers. He had received a promotion after the Philippine Sea Battle, and because he had flown both fighters and torpedo bombers, he was considered an excellent choice to command a squadron of TBM torpedo bomber pilots.

As commander, Hayes had to train and prepare his group of 25 pilots for the assault on Tokyo. The group he would lead was assigned to hit Yokasuka Naval Base in Tokyo Bay. It would be one of the most difficult targets to hit and get out of safely. Mt. Fuji protected Tokyo on the southern edge; to the north were jutting cliffs almost 6,000 feet above sea level. Tokyo Bay was in the center of the city.

The pilots of Lieutenant-Commander Hayes' torpedo squadron had practiced night-carrier takeoffs and landings just in case they would need to perform them in the anticipated return from the raids over Tokyo.

His group had been told that night pilots flying off the *Saratoga* and *Enterprise* would help by lighting up the targets with napalm bombs. Some B-29 Superfortresses from Tinian would also help. Hayes had been told that more than 1,500 navy planes would participate in the attack. Admiral Marc Mitscher would lead the carrier force, the largest ever assembled. Admiral Spruance was to handle the support of battleships, cruisers, and destroyers. Revenge for Pearl Harbor was in the offing. Prevailing sentiment was that what was left of the Japanese Fleet in Tokyo Bay would come out and fight, and the Japanese people would beg for surrender.

On February 16, 1945, after the night raids by the *Saratoga* and *Enterprise,* Task Force 58 arrived off Tokyo to make the first daytime fleet attack on Japan since the Jimmy Doolittle Raids over Tokyo in 1942. The fleet had come in under a bad weather front and was unopposed.

Hayes told his pilots that 18 torpedo bomber planes from his carrier would participate in the attack on Yokasuka Naval Base. At 2:00 A.M. the pilots were rousted out of their bunks and assembled in the ready room. They were given the confidential codes for submarine air-sea rescue and the position that the carrier would be in before takeoff. The plan was to launch some of the torpedo bombers in darkness. The fleet would be about 200 or 300 miles off the Japanese coastline; the planes would be over Tokyo at sunrise.

The pilots put on their red goggles when they got to the ready room. Most drank coffee and smoked while being briefed by the intelligence officers concerning the targets and alternate targets. The weather was not the best for the night takeoff, so each pilot had to know the vectors in case the group was unable to rendezvous. Hayes would lead. He would fly low on the water and when the coastline was picked up on the radar scope, he would fly up to 10,000 feet and then dive at the Japanese Naval Base. The torpedo bomber squadron was to arrive on the north side of Tokyo Bay at 6:00 A.M.

The catapult launching of the planes went smoothly in the darkness. The weather was bad, but the ceiling was high enough to allow the formation to rendezvous. Once together, the planes flew about 200 feet off the water, using their radio altimeters in the darkness. When they got to the coastline, the planes climbed up to 10,000 feet. It was not difficult to find Tokyo.

B-29 Superfortresses flying from Tinian had done their job well the previous two nights. Hayes noticed as Tokyo emerged through the clouds that the target had been lit up for the navy carrier planes by napalm strikes.

The defense of Tokyo did not go well for the Japanese. American navy pilots shot down over 300 Japanese planes and almost 200 more were destroyed on the ground. The Japanese antiaircraft guns didn't know which planes to shoot at because the American planes were single-engine carrier planes—they had been accustomed to seeing four-engine B-29 bombers.

Commander Hayes and his torpedo bomber squadron arrived

over the target just as the sun was rising—a cruel irony for the Japanese. Four 500-pound bombs were in the bomb bays of each plane. The pilots had turned on the switches to arm their bombs and were now north of the Yokasuka Naval Base. A coordinated attack had been planned—MK5 zero-length rockets would be fired first by the entire squadron, to destroy the Japanese antiaircraft crews, or at least put the fear of God into them. The four 500-pound bombs were to be dropped over the base after the rockets were launched.

Just before the attack was to begin, antiaircraft guns that had been dug into the side of Mt. Fuji lit up the sky like a Christmas tree. Bursts of shells and tracer bullets were targeted at the Americans. There were a few major vessels in the harbor—battleships and cruisers—that would soon join the attack. Lieutenant George Shepard, flying on Commander Hayes' wing, let all his rockets go at one of the oil tankers anchored near the base. There was a massive explosion as the rockets hit. Lighted debris was blown into the sky. The battleships in the harbor returned the fire.

As Brad Hayes was pulling his torpedo bomber out of a dive and weaving back and forth low on the water, he saw Shepard's plane take a direct hit, burst into flames, and fall like tinsel into Tokyo Bay. He said a prayer for his wingman's soul and poured his throttle to the fire wall. "Shit, we've got to get the hell out of here, you pregnant beast," he hollered.

He glanced out over his right wing and saw another torpedo plane hit the water and burst into flames. Bullets started to zing through his own plane's wings and fuselage.

"God bless self-sealing gas tanks," he said to no one. "Come on turkey, flap your wings," he shouted as he flew the plane down lower over the bay. The lower he got, the harder it would be for the Japanese guns to hit him. Suddenly, a ship's mast loomed in front of him. Hayes dipped his left wing to avoid it, and immediately dipped his right to miss another.

Hayes had told his squadron that once they dropped their bombs, they were to skim low on the surface of the water and fly out by way of Tokyo Bay. That would be the safest way out because the cruisers and battleships wouldn't want to fire low and hit their own ships. The only other exit was over Mt. Fuji, which was well protected, not only by its height, but by numerous antiaircraft guns.

The attack on Yokasuka Naval Base by Hayes' torpedo squadron was over in minutes. Fires were raging and there was mass bedlam. Oil tanks were burning and vessels were damaged.

As the planes retreated outside the confines of the bay, the anti-aircraft gunfire stopped. The sun was now up, but the sky was overcast. Twelve planes from the squadron joined up in formation on Hayes' wing. As they were heading back to their carrier, they saw the enormous flotilla of ships. Another wave of navy aircraft was in the sky and flying toward Tokyo.

Some of Hayes' returning planes were badly shot up. The damaged planes were given priority to land, and did so on the first carrier they came to, the U.S.S. *Bunker Hill*. Some planes' hydraulic systems were impaired, and hand cranks had to be used to lower the wheels. One plane's wheels collapsed on landing, but the pilot stepped out unhurt. Six planes from Hayes' squadron failed to return to their own carrier. Four pilots and their crews had been lost in combat over Tokyo Bay.

The next day, February 17, 1945, the pilots were in the air, bombing Tokyo again. There was little or no opposition that day. All the pilots in Brad's group returned safely.

Night and day, the Avengers were evening the score for Pearl Harbor.

26

Missing

Two days after the night fighters had returned from their mission over Tokyo, P.G. met Domkowski in the junior officer's ward room having breakfast. Dom looked depressed.

"Where's the shrimp?" asked P.G.

"I knew you'd ask me that," said Domkowski. "He's missing in action."

"Chuck's missing in action?"

"That's right. I checked with air plot."

"Oh God, I can't believe it," said P.G. "What the hell happened? I just saw him the day before yesterday."

"I don't know all the details, but he's on the missing list of *Sara*'s Air Group 53. I asked communications to find out more, but they don't have any more news to tell."

"Shit, I can't believe it! Have you talked to the air operations officer?"

"I'm way ahead of you. I talked to him and I'll tell you what I know. Chuck volunteered to do a message drop to the fleet admiral about the night operations. He completed the message drop but the weather socked in and he was told to land aboard one of the carriers nearby, which he did."

"He's all right, then?" asked P.G.

"He's not all right. Let me finish," said Domkowski. "Some of the pilots didn't make it back to that carrier from the Tokyo raids. The air group on that carrier went back in to finish the job the next day, and Chuck volunteered to substitute for one of the lost pilots."

"You've got to be kidding. I don't believe they'd let him do that."

"Well, Chuck either knew the air group commander, or convinced him in his infinitely subtle manner that he could help, so they allowed him to go on the attack."

"Well, what happened?"

"He went but he didn't return," said Domkowski. "Either he was shot down over Tokyo or he bailed out over the water. He didn't return to the carrier. He's missing and presumed dead."

"I won't accept that," said P.G. "Chuck ain't going to die that way. If he dies it'll be in the rack with some broad."

He started praying for Chuck, hoping that what he heard wasn't true. They'd been through a lot together, and if Chuck was going to die in combat, he'd like to be alongside fighting with him. Tears ran from Domkowski's eyes. P.G. felt the tug of emotion but denied himself. To cry now would be to admit Chuck's death. No way. Not yet.

"Hang in there, Dom," said P.G. as he grabbed his shoulder. "If he's dead, and we don't know he is, I'm sure he took plenty of Japs with him. It's not true. He's not dead. I won't believe it. We both ought to get some shuteye because we may be flying tonight."

"I don't think I'll be able to sleep," said Dom.

"Give it a try."

The weather socked in even worse that morning and the fleet admiral decided to withdraw from Tokyo. P.G. and Domkowski tried to sleep. At 4:00 P.M., P.G. went up to the flight deck to watch the combat air patrol being launched. The *Sara* was about 400 miles from Tokyo, and heading south into better weather.

After the fighters were launched, the *Sara* continued sailing into the wind. Out of the sky a dark blue Avenger with *Sara*'s numbers on it appeared, approached the carrier, and landed aboard. P.G. watched intently. The pilot who got out looked a lot like Chuck. He ran closer to get a better look. It was! He caught up to him, grabbed him from behind, spun him around, and gave him a big hug.

"You bastard. You almost gave me a heart attack. You've got a heap of explaining to do."

"Would you kindly get your hands off me?" asked Chuck. "The boys might get the wrong idea."

"They said you were missing. What the hell happened?"

"Well, I almost was, but then again I almost wasn't," said Chuck grinning sheepishly. "I'm glad to be here, but I think I'm going to stick to night-flying. Day-flying is a bitch, what with all those fuckers shooting at you. You're too good a target in the daylight."

Suddenly Domkowski appeared on deck. He stopped, stared at Chuck, and then ran over and pounded him so hard on the back Chuck looked like he might take a swing at him. "Where the hell did you come from?" Dom bellowed. "Did one of the sharks cough you up?"

"It's a long story," said Chuck.

"I'll bet it is," said P.G. "Why don't you tell us about it?"

"Well, if you insist, I will," he replied with a smile. "Two days ago, the air operations officer, Commander Rice, asked me to do some message drops. The commander was unable to use radio transmission because the fleet was so close to Tokyo. So I took off early in the morning and made three message drops. Then the weather got bad, so I decided to set down on the nearest carrier and ended up on the *Hornet*. I met a few of my old flying buddies there. After the raids over Tokyo, a few of their torpedo bomber pilots didn't make it back to the carrier. I heard later they landed on other carriers. The bomber skipper was a guy I knew from Pensacola, and I asked him if I could fill in for one of his missing boys. He said, "It's okay with me, if you've got the guts to do it.""

"So I thanked him and told him what a warm individual he was and asked him where I could find out about the mission. He told me the air operations officer would be briefing the pilots in the ready room in about an hour. I felt great. I was now going to see real action. I mean *see* it! With the sun above the horizon. I went to the briefing session and was assigned a position in the formation. I felt like the cat's ass sitting in my plane, ready to head for the target. The ground crew had put four 500-pound bombs in the bomb bay and I was pumped up. I mean, I was ready."

"Keep talking," said Domkowski, "the story's getting better all the time."

"You're right Dom, which is unusual for you. But anyway, there was a reception party waiting for us when we got there," said Chuck.

"I decided I had made a poor decision. The sky was lit up with shells and tracers like a maze. I was supposed to drop the bombs at 500 feet, but because of the antiaircraft fire, it was closer to 20,000 feet. I felt like I needed oxygen. I think my bombs killed a lot of fish. I know I didn't hit any battleships. All I wanted to do was to drop my load and get the hell out of there."

"Incredible. I see the Navy Cross in your future. Dom, remind me to tell the reporters at Stars and Stripes," said P.G.

"I know one thing," said Chuck, "I'm glad I'm in a night outfit. You're an easier target in the daytime. So what can I say? I shit my pants. I thought the executive officer of the torpedo squadron was going to shoot me down. I learned something, though. The skipper always leads the attack. No shit. He sticks his nose right in the middle of the action. He also has a good wingman who can continue to lead if he's shot down and then the executive officer brings up the rear. The rest of the pilots have to account to that guy for their actions. I'm sure I didn't get an A for effort. The biggest problem I had was returning to the fleet after the attack."

"What do you mean?" asked P.G.

"Well, I didn't have any trouble getting back. Shit, if you can find a carrier at night, daytime's a walk in the park. But the plane felt heavy and was using up more fuel than I thought it would. I wondered if I had dropped all four bombs. I knew I had armed them before dropping them. So, I decided to open the bomb bay doors, and Rosie, my radar man, says, 'There's a bomb still hung up in the belly.' I said, 'Damn it, I knew this plane was flying heavy.' There was still one 500-pound bomb still in the bomb bay, armed and fucking dangerous."

"What did you do?" asked Domkowski.

"I took the plane up to 10,000 feet, made a dive bombing attack, and tried to shake it loose. It didn't budge. I tried it four or five times. Still no go. I radioed the carrier and requested instructions from the bridge. They told me I couldn't come aboard, but that I could bail out with my gunner and radar operator and they'd have a destroyer try to pick us up. I love the navy. The water looked awfully cold to me, but I gave my airmen the option of bailing out. They weren't eager to jump, either. Then I remembered one of the veteran pilots saying that if you were ever in big trouble to head for the *Essex*. The skipper was a former pilot and he might take me aboard. I requested a vector to the *Essex* and headed in that direction. It was about 20 miles due east. Sure enough, they said they'd take me aboard but they'd have to make preparations first.

"The problem was deciding whether to open the bomb bay doors before landing and when I caught a hook hope the bomb wouldn't shake loose, roll down the deck, and blow up the ship; or leave the bomb bay doors closed and hope it stayed in place.

"I turned all the arming switches off. But they had already been on for a while. Arming devices can get screwed up too, you know. The plan was to evacuate the plane immediately after it landed. The air ops officer told me to leave the bomb bay doors shut and try for a soft landing. It was like playing Russian Roulette. You guys know me. I brought that plane in as soft as a pussycat, caught the second wire, and the bomb didn't drop. Before I knew it I was pulled out of the plane, along with my gunner and radar operator, and the plane was shoved off the fantail. A few seconds later there was a blast in the ocean behind the carrier. Boy, was I lucky! I bent down and kissed the flight deck. I would have kissed the captain if he let me."

"That's a bunch of bullshit," said Domkowski. "How could they have pushed your plane overboard if you flew it back to the *Sara*? I saw the plane with the radar bubble on it's wing."

"I knew you would ask me that," said Chuck. "For the volunteer attack I flew one of the torpedo planes from the *Hornet* so some dumb shit wouldn't shoot me down. I was later transferred back to pick up my own plane and flew it back to the *Sara*. That's what took me so long."

"Is that all?" asked P.G. "What did you do in your spare time?"

27

One-Way Journey to Death

After the raids over Tokyo, the *Saratoga* and *Enterprise* headed back
to open sea with their escort vessels, the battle cruiser *Alaska*, heavy
cruiser *Baltimore*, antiaircraft light cruiser *Flint*, and nine destroyers. The *Saratoga*'s crew was told that it was going to join an
amphibious force supporting the landing of marines on the island
of Iwo Jima. Admiral Blandy's force of gunnery vessels and escort
carriers had opened fire on Iwo Jima on February 16 to soften
Japanese encampments dug in there.

It was now obvious that the Tokyo Raids were intended only to
distract the Japanese away from the amphibious landing on Iwo
Jima, 750 miles to the south. The marines had been given the
assignment to take the island at all costs. Iwo Jima, if captured,
would be a vital refueling spot for B-29s that had to fly all the way
from Saipan or Tinian to hit their targets. Capture of the island
would neutralize the base from which Japanese bombers harassed
American B-29 fields in the Marianas.

The American amphibious force had six battleships, five cruisers,
and several jeep carriers. Each of the gunnery vessels was assigned
the responsibility of destroying a specific area of the island. The

escort carrier aircraft spotted gunfire and dropped napalm bombs to burn off vegetation and camouflage.

D-Day had been determined to be February 19, and planes from Task Force 58 and the escort carrier group roared over the island.

Pilots flying air support on February 19 saw an unusual sight. Below, headed for the beach, were 500 landing craft carrying battalions of the Fourth and Fifth Marine Divisions. Unforeseen at the shoreline was volcanic ash so soft that the amphibious landing craft sank, and some marines loaded with armaments drowned. The momentum of the assault came to a virtual halt. The marines were not to be denied. They scrambled ashore, clawing their way up the beach to face the enemy.

Wave after wave of landing craft moved onto the beaches, discharged their human cargo, and shuttled back to the troop transports. The antiaircraft fire on the island had been neutralized by the battleships, and the enemy's return fire was concentrated on the marine troops that were trying to get a foothold. As the sun descended, the bright flare of the flame throwers licked at the hillsides of the island, where the marines were working on enemy pillboxes. The air support planes would dive at flashes of gunfire along the shoreline, trying to rouse the enemy forces still dug in.

Pilots above the fighting said prayers for the poor bastards fighting their hearts out down below. They prayed the fight would end quickly and successfully. At night, the ships of the task force reduced the opportunities for ambush by using Starshell and searchlight illumination. Night-carrier air support was unusually effective with parachute float lights. The night pilots of the *Saratoga* and *Enterprise* participated in reconnaissance flights and air attack support. The torpedo bomber pilots were the most active in this phase because they had larger planes and could carry a marine gunnery observer in the gun turret.

On February 21, the *Saratoga*, with three accompanying destroyers, was detached from Task Force 58 to join the escort carrier group under command of Rear Admiral Durgin. The *Sara's* night air group would provide the night cover for the amphibious support force and the escort carriers en route to aid the marines assaulting Iwo Jima.

At 4:00 P.M., the *Saratoga* was at latitude 25 degrees, 10' n., longitude 141 degrees 30' east and proceeding eastward. There were five fighter planes airborne, two serving as ASP, two as combat air patrol over base at mattress and one awaiting recovery after an afternoon of message drops. Eight pilots were in "Condition Ten." Domkowski was one of them. At the time the scramble was requested, "Condition Ten" had been released and the flight deck was being respotted for the launch of the Target Dusk Combat Air Patrol for Iwo Jima.

Domkowski left the ready room and went to get some sack time in his bunk when "Condition Ten" was released.

At 4:28 P.M. the SK radar on the *Sara* reported a bogey at 055 degrees, 75 miles from the *Saratoga*, estimated to be four to six planes, heading 180 degrees at angels 10 (10,000 feet). This contact was immediately broadcast on the 2096 Kc and received by the delegate base on one of the command ships. It was not received by the commander of the task group. The bogey appeared to be slowly losing altitude. The commander of the air support group evaluated the contact as "returning itinerant friendlies."

Seven minutes after sighting the bogey on the *Sara*'s radar screen the body split into two groups. Ten minutes after the first sighting, the outboard bogey turned in toward the *Sara* and closed base at a heading of 270 degrees. At the time of the split, it was now estimated that the bogies' size had increased to ten to fifteen planes. No enemy airborne radar was detected; they had turned their radar off.

The bogies were now flying at high speed, diving from 10,000 feet and when they were 35 miles away were at an altitude of angels 4 (4,000 feet).

General Quarters sounded. Domkowski, who was sleeping in his flight gear since he had been in "Condition Ten," jumped out of the rack and ran to the ready room. When he got there, he heard the order, "Man your planes."

The pilots ran up to the flight deck. Quite a few of the fighter pilots who were in the ready room when General Quarters was sounded beat Domkowski to the front planes on the catapult.

At 4:53 P.M., 25 minutes after the sighting of the initial bogey, the first VF(N) fighter plane was airborne, and by 5:03 P.M., when the first suicide plane hit, 14 VF(N) fighter planes were up and directed toward the raid. Fourteen fighter planes were launched in approximately ten minutes.

Domkowski was one of the fighter pilots waiting to be launched off the deck of the *Saratoga* before the attack. He was number 14 in line on the flight deck. A few seconds after he was launched off the right catapult, the *Sara* took three direct bomb hits by kamikazes. His plane was the last to be airborne. Both of the front launching catapults were disabled by bombs and the two planes sitting on the catapults were blown up. The deck of the *Sara* was a cauldron of fire, with aviation gasoline spewed all over its surface. There were screaming men; sprinting to get out of the remaining planes, racing to battle stations, and trying to find cover.

Dom flew his plane up to 5,000 feet, and called air plot for instructions. "Beaver Base, this is Beaver eight. Request instructions."

"Beaver eight, this is Beaver Base. Wait for vectors."

As Dom orbited his plane over the *Sara*, he had a front-row seat to see the action from the air. Suddenly he saw and heard antiaircraft fire from the *Sara*'s 40 mms, and decided he'd better get the hell out of there. He didn't want the *Sara*'s guns shooting him down. The antiaircraft fire didn't last very long, however, as the *Saratoga* took multiple bomb hits and the flight deck was lit up by fires from the aviation gasoline. He cursed, virtually helpless. There were no planes for Domkowski to chase—the Japanese kamikaze pilots had blown themselves up.

The air plot center and CIC in the *Sara* was not directly hit by the initial attack but the men working there knew they had a big problem. As the *Sara* took on water, she slowly listed six degrees to starboard. The damage control officer ordered the hatches closed beneath the waterline on the posterior starboard side to prevent the ship from sinking.

Air plot radioed all the *Sara*'s Beaver fighter planes that had gotten airborne and vectored them toward new bogies. "Beaver pilots, this is Beaver Base. Ten to 15 enemy planes on a heading of 270 degrees approaching Beaver Base at high speed. Intercept and destroy. Acknowledge."

"Great." Dom felt the effect of adrenalin in his body. "This is Beaver eight heading toward enemy planes closing toward base at 270 degrees."

He put his water injection mechanism on and started combing through the clouds, looking for the enemy planes. He recognized another Hellcat off his right wing doing the same thing. They saw four bogies at the same time. "Tally-Ho, four chickens at 084 degrees, 35 miles, angels 4," Dom radioed to base. "Am closing."

Dom and the other Hellcat pilot dove through the clouds. As the two pilots boxed in the enemy, Dom recognized the Japanese planes as Zekes. He put full power on the Hellcat and used his boosters. He knew he would have one quick pass at the Zekes. Suddenly a plane came into his gun sight. He squeezed the pistol grip on his stick and felt the .50-caliber guns rattle. One enemy plane became a ball of fire. He rolled over to cut back and try to get a second plane, but to no avail. His flying partner beat him to it. The other Jap planes were diving toward the *Sara* and escort jeep carriers at such incredible speed that they were impossible to catch.

"Splash, two chickens," Dom reported back to Beaver Base. There was no reply. He understood. Back at base they were getting the crap knocked out of them.

The Beaver fighter pilots who were still in the air were left to fend for themselves. They had front-row seats for the action that was taking place at the waterline, powerless to interfere.

Dom could see that the entire flight deck of the *Sara* was on fire and that most of the 40 mm antiaircraft guns were strangely silent. He swore to himself. He decided to call the air plot center of the Combat Air Support Group to see if they could vector him to intercept any more enemy planes.

Admiral Durgin's flag was on one of the escort carriers. Dom radioed in. There was mass confusion in their Central Intelligence Center and air plot and there was a lag time in responding.

From the air, Dom could see that the Japanese kamikazes were out to sink the *Saratoga*. It was starting to get dark but he had no difficulty seeing the ship. It was lit up like a torch. He could see the three destroyers around her firing their five-inch guns and 40 mm antiaircraft guns. They had not been hit. There were still a few guns on the *Sara* firing against enemy planes as they approached. The gunners who were killed had been replaced. Ten to 15 miles off the port bow were three escort carriers also under attack.

He saw a Japanese kamikaze fly down the stack of one of them and blow. The jeep escort carrier rolled over on her side and went down like a lead slug. As she was rolling over on her side, Dom could see sailors trying to hang onto ropes. The suction of the sinking ship dragged many of the men to their death.

"Shit," Dom thought to himself. "Where the hell am I going to land?"

One escort carrier was down and another was on fire. The *Sara* was in deep trouble. He was running out of landing fields. His fuel was low after chasing the Zekes, and he was beginning to get nervous. He had jettisoned his auxiliary gas tanks before entering the fight and his fuel tank registered half full. He decided to lean out his gas mixture and bide his time. He was not about to set his plane down on one of the carriers that was under attack. He felt safer in the air. He wondered whether the air plot center on the *Sara* had been knocked out. They weren't responding to his calls. "Beaver Base, this is Beaver eight. Do you read me?"

There was still no reply. Either they were too busy or out of commission. He decided to orbit his plane at 10,000 feet and contemplate his next move. He saw three more Japanese kamikaze planes hit the *Sara*. New fires started on her decks and the 40 mm antiaircraft guns on the port side of her flight deck were silent.

Dom knew that Chuck and P.G. might still be down there on that ship and he prayed for his buddies. As it got darker, it was still easy for Domkowski to see the *Sara*. She was lit up like a firecracker. The Queen of the Flattops was struggling to survive.

He felt alone and powerless in the sky. The only land-based runway nearby was at Iwo Jima and he wasn't about to try landing there. What should he do? He thought about flying close to Iwo Jima where the marines and the American battleships were. Maybe they'd pick him up if he parachuted into the water.

Dom continued to lean out his fuel. He watched from the air as the *Sara*'s flight deck crew fought the fires. They seemed to be getting them under control and the deck wasn't burning as much. There were still fires burning on the flight deck of the jeep escort carrier the *Lingayen Gulf*.

It was completely dark now and it looked like the fires were being put out on the *Sara*. Damage control was doing their job. Dom had to make a decision. His plane couldn't stay in the air much longer. He decided to try to call air plot on the *Saratoga* again to see if they were back in business. "Beaver Base, this is Beaver eight. Do you read me?"

To his surprise, he received a response. "Beaver eight, this is Beaver Base. We read you loud and clear."

"Beaver Base, I need a vector to the nearest carrier that can take me aboard. I have about 30 minutes of fuel left."

"Beaver eight, this is Beaver Base. Nearest healthy jeep carrier is approximately 70 miles away. Stand by and wait for instruction."

"Seventy miles? Why don't I just ditch the thing now?" he

thought. It looked like he had a date with the Pacific Ocean. He didn't like his options. It was black as hell, except for the burning ships.

Over the left wing of his plane, he saw the lights of another aircraft in the distance. Could it be another Japanese kamikaze? He decided to douse his wing lights.

Beaver Base quickly relieved some of his anxieties. "Beaver eight, this is Beaver Base. We have other friendlies circling around us. All our flight deck fires are now out. We're checking the back of the flight deck and the landing cables. We may try to take you aboard."

"Either land me or fish me out of the water, Beaver Base," said Dom. "I've got no fuel for a 70-mile hike."

"Hold your water," said air plot. "We'll take you aboard as soon as we can."

Down on the flight deck, the landing signal officer was uninjured and some of the flight deck crew were still alive. They were mustered quickly and told that some of the pilots were still in the air and running out of gas. They took their stations. The air operations officer got permission from the bridge to begin maneuvering for landing. The helmsman of the *Saratoga* pointed the ship into the wind to get ready to land aircraft aboard. The *Sara* responded slowly because one of her four screws wasn't functioning.

"Beaver eight, this is Beaver Base. You have permission to enter the landing circle."

Dom blew out a breath he seemed to have been holding for two hours. "Beaver Base, this is Beaver eight. Roger. Many thanks."

He entered the downwind leg but had difficulty seeing the *Sara* now that the fires were out. "Here goes nothing," he said. He turned his plane into the cross leg and faintly saw the phosphorescence made by the wake of the *Sara*. He pointed his plane in that direction. As the plane turned into the groove and as he got closer to the fantail, he saw the lighted wands of the L.S.O. His plane was coming in too hot and he got a wave-off.

Radio silence was broken by the landing signal officer. "Slow your plane down, Dom. You're coming in too fast. We can't make much forward speed with a hole in our side."

"Okay, okay. It's gotta be next time or I'm taking a bath," he hollered.

He swung the plane around again and got it into the groove. This time, when the L.S.O. was about to give him the signal to cut he didn't have to. The engine cut out. The plane dropped onto the deck, its wheels bouncing crazily. He felt the left landing gear fold and the tail spin around. Men dove for cover as the tail of the fuselage slammed into the remains of a gun battery. Dom scrambled out of the cockpit onto the wing, and jumped to the deck below. He felt good to be aboard the old, valiant ship even if she had just been put through the wringer.

28

Death and Its Mystery

P.G. flew a long search line with Hellcat protection a few days after returning from the raids over Tokyo. He was worn out and totally exhausted. His neck was in spasm and pulled into tight cords that would not unwind. He was trying to get sack time in his bunk. At about 3:30 P.M. noise on the flight deck above brought him bolt upright as the catapults launched fighter air cover. He swung his legs over the bunk and yawned, stretching his arms. The knuckles on his hands made a subdued pop as he spread them. He felt the calluses on his hands. Well, he mused, at least I'm not using them in hand-to-hand combat, and I thank God for that. He shuddered, figuring his chances of getting through the war were better in the air than on the beach. He was happy he was a pilot. All he could think about were those poor marines he saw in the water trying to gain a foothold on the beach at Iwo Jima. Many marines were dying. "Oh, hell," he muttered. "I could burn to a crisp one of these days missing a night-carrier landing or my plane could flip over the side into the water. Who knows? You live one day at a time. War sure is hell."

He wiped the saliva from the corner of his mouth as his feet hit the deck. A glance in the mirror told him what he expected. He looked dead tired. The stress of combat and night-flights over Japan were taking their toll. Even the color of his eyes looked faded. "Hell, war makes you look old," he thought, "and I'm too young to die."

As he shaved off his three-day growth, he pondered about just why he had volunteered for this mess. He realized he had no choice. A weak smile reflected back at him from the cracked mirror, breaking the somber cast of his face as he completed his shaving. "Oh, well, I've got a job to do," he said, "and things could be worse. I could have been one of those marines on the beach."

As he counted his blessings, he realized he was fortunate to be flying off this carrier, the U.S.S. *Saratoga*. The flight deck was big, and it gave him a shot at making a good night landing. Those small jeep carriers that he had been on bounced around more and were tougher to land on. Besides, he was sailing on a piece of naval history. He had heard all about the *Sara*'s legend. She was one of the first and one of the largest carriers built for the navy. Then too, she was one of the most battle worn, often referred to as the "Queen of the Flattops." The *Sara* also had the distinction of being the first carrier to launch the torpedo bomber, the Avenger. Many admirals had flown their flags on her bridge: Fletcher, Ramsey, and others. Admiral Halsey once said, "The *Saratoga*, when given the chance, is deadly." She certainly was deadly, and the Japanese knew it. They had tried to sink her on two or three occasions and had almost succeeded. She was still one of their prime targets. On February 21, 1945, the U.S.S. *Saratoga* would face one of her biggest battles to survive as she cruised off the coast of Iwo Jima to support the marine landings.

P.G. had been topside the day before when the ship passed within sight of Kita Iwo Jima, a fog-shrouded rock that was supposedly uninhabited. The air operations officer was standing next to him.

"Commander Rice, why are we passing so close to that Japanese Island?" asked P.G.

"I don't know, Ensign. I'm not the fleet commander. You certainly have to wonder whether the natives will be reporting our position."

"It sounds to me like we're being too cocky," P.G. said. "I don't think the enemy has rolled over and died."

Commander Rice responded, "Ours is not to reason why—ours is but to do and die."

P.G. didn't like his answer. "Lousy platitudes," he muttered as he walked away. He contemplated relaxing on the flight deck for awhile. After all, he reasoned, the biggest fleet in the world had just blasted Tokyo and there had been a feeble response from the Japanese. They just had the crap knocked out of them.

The pilots were somewhat relieved that they would not have to immediately face heavy antiaircraft fire again. Most ships' personnel were putting the Tokyo raids out of mind as the hours and miles rolled by. The task force was 700 miles from Tokyo, and it was thought improbable that Japanese bombers could fly to Iwo and return to their homeland on one tank of fuel. There was still the fear of submarine attack, but the fleet was alert. Routine air fighter cover was continuous over the *Saratoga*, and there were no encounters from opposing forces. The general feeling was that the small island of Iwo Jima would be easily neutralized.

P.G. ambled down to the Central Intelligence Center (CIC) to see if anything was going on. Like many of the other pilots in the night air group, he liked to hang out in air plot because that was where all the action was. The CIC had a large plastic screen showing the position of the ship with its support ships around it. Air plot showed the number of planes in the air and their positions, which were constantly changed and updated on the screen. The CIC was under control of the air plot officer and ship's control officer. The ship's radar antenna constantly searched 360 degrees on the surface and in the air. Anyone in the room could listen to the constant chatter from the pilots.

Around 4:30 that afternoon, while P.G. was in the CIC, a lieutenant-commander monitoring the SK radar screen noticed a small blip 75 miles from the task force. He telephoned his immediate superior and notified the fighter planes covering to investigate. The captain was informed, and the carrier with the task force began to turn into the wind in case launching was necessary. The loudspeaker announced, "Pilots report to the ready room."

Only minutes separated the sounding of General Quarters, with bells ringing and men sent running to their battle stations. A bogey was now 22 miles away and approaching at top speed. The bullhorn blared: "Pilots, man your planes." There were no specific instructions as to what to do, just get the planes off the deck of the carrier as fast as possible. The fighters were to try to intercept the enemy and the torpedo bombers were to get airborne, since the planes were loaded with bombs for the assault on Iwo.

P.G. ran to his plane, which was tied down on the flight deck near the fantail, and climbed into the cockpit. He was 25th in line for launching; as usual, the fighter planes had been placed in the front. He started his engine and began to maneuver his plane up the deck. While the fighter planes were being launched, the planes on the back of the deck moved up. Many of the planes had their wings folded like bats to allow for more room on the flight deck. When the planes got to the catapult, the wings spread out and locked in place. The pilots sitting in the cockpits of those planes were hoping they could get airborne. They would rather take their chances in the air than sitting on the deck of a carrier, waiting to be hit by a bomb.

P.G.'s team was in place. Dominic, the gunner, was in the gun turret and Skeeter, the radar and radio operator, was in the belly with the electronic equipment. "Come on, come on, come on, launch those planes," P.G. hollered. "Get a move on. I want to get off this fucking carrier!"

Suddenly, all hell broke loose. At about 5:00 P.M., 30 minutes after the initial identification of the bogey, six Japanese aircraft emerged from the clouds at a range of 6,500 yards.

The *Sara* took three direct hits. The first kamikaze plane, hit and blazing, flew into and penetrated the starboard side of the carrier. The bombs on the plane exploded, blowing the remaining parts of the plane through to the hangar deck, starting fires. Almost simultaneously, another kamikaze blew himself up at the waterline near the rear of the ship, tearing a hole in the *Sara*'s starboard side. The plane had glanced off the water before striking the ship. The *Saratoga* took a six-degree list as she took on water. At the same time, the front of the carrier deck was hit by another kamikaze, knocking out the catapults and preventing any further launch. Planes and pilots sitting on the catapults were blown up. Aviation gasoline was spread all over the flight deck and caught fire. Airplane parts blew sky high and many of the flight deck crew and pilots were killed.

"Oh my, God," said P.G., sitting in the cockpit of his torpedo bomber on the back of the flight deck. He watched entranced by the action going on around him. He had a front-row seat. He and the other pilots still in the planes that weren't hit folded the wings, cut engines, and got out of their cockpits, certain the ship was about to be sunk or already sinking. The *Sara* listed further to starboard. P.G. looked over the side of the flight deck to the ocean 200 feet below and contemplated jumping. He rejected the idea. He didn't think he would survive the leap. He would rather fight to keep the *Sara* afloat.

The pilots on the back of the flight deck realized that because their planes were loaded, it was only a matter of time before the ship would be destroyed by its own bombs. P.G. joined the surviving pilots and crew on the back of the flight deck and pushed the remaining planes into the water.

Fires were raging out of control and someone had to put them out. Since planes frequently caught fire when they crashed, multiple fire hoses were available along the side of the flight deck and gun mounts. Some of the pilots ran to get the hoses, which were heavy and required a lot of effort as they were pulled toward the fires. "Somebody's got to get a spanner wrench," an enlisted man hollered. "Pass it along." The request went all the way down the line of personnel holding the hose.

"What the hell's a spanner wrench?" someone asked.

"You need it to hook up the hose," a chief petty officer yelled. Soon the wrench was found and the water flowed, helping to fight the fires on the flight deck.

The *Sara* continued to come under attack. The Japanese suicide bombers continued to dive at her, sensing the kill. The burning gasoline on the deck and her own ammunition added to the pyrotechnics and made the *Sara* a sitting target. P.G. watched as the gunners on the gun mounts fired at the enemy planes. The rapid firing and noise of the antiaircraft guns made his ears ring. He was fascinated by the fireworks. This was a fight to the finish. He never dreamed he would participate in something like this during his lifetime. He stood mesmerized as he watched a kamikaze plane approach low on the water on the port side. It was only a few hundred yards away, coming straight at him. If it continued its path unobstructed, he would die. The antiaircraft gunners concentrated their guns on the attacking plane. Suddenly it blew up, hit by a 40 mm antiaircraft cannon, and turned into a fiery heap of shredded metal. There was a loud cheer from the gun mounts. P.G. added his voice to the cheer—he had been seconds away from death.

It was beginning to get dark, and he could see that the *Sara* wasn't the only ship under fire. Off the port side forward, escort carriers were also under attack. He saw a kamikaze dive straight down the stack of one of the jeep carriers and blow up. The ship quickly rolled over on her side, taking most of her men with her. He later found out that the ship was the *Bismark Sea*.

P.G. felt that he couldn't just stand there. He had to do something. He ran to the nearest antiaircraft cannon battery. There were two men operating it, one loading shells, the other firing.

"What can I do?" he screamed over the bedlam to the man loading the shells.

"Bring me up the rest of those shells at the bottom of the battery," the gunner shouted.

P.G. found two crates of 40 mm shells. God, they were heavy. He carried them to the loader.

"What else, what else do you need?" Peter asked.

"Nothing," he said. "Just get the fuck out of my way." Peter meekly did as he was told.

He started searching the deck for Chuck. He wondered whether he was dead or alive. Peter had heard that only one torpedo plane had gotten airborne. Odds were it wasn't Chuck. If he was alive, he could still be below deck. P.G. had a horrible headache and a nosebleed from the concussion he'd received from the first bomb and kamikaze hits. Things weren't going too well for the *Sara*'s crew.

He kept searching for Chuck. If the order was given to abandon ship, they'd want to be together. Working his way forward to the ready room, he sensed the fighting was getting fierce topside and it was hot as hell. He looked for Chuck below deck. One of the gunners on the flight deck told him damage control had sealed off some of the compartments below where holes had been torn in the side of the ship. The hatchways had to be sealed to prevent the ship from taking on too much water. He knew men were still in those sealed-off quarters and would drown in the icy vault.

He walked forward on the flight deck and went below and entered the captain's quarters on the port side. Water was sloshing back and forth on the deck of the captain's quarters and it was dark. Only a few lights were still working below deck and they were battery operated. It was like going into a cave without a flashlight.

"Chuck! Chuck! Where the hell are you?" P.G. hollered into the darkness.

From about 15 feet away, P.G. heard, "Could you lower your fucking voice, please? My ears are ringing and they hurt."

P.G.'s eyes adjusted to the darkness and he saw Chuck squatting in the water. "Thank God you're alive. What the hell happened to you, anyway? Are you okay?"

"I got knocked on my ass by a bomb and I can't stand up. I've got no balance," Chuck said.

"Take it easy. Where are the rest of the pilots? Where's Dom?" asked P.G.

"Some got into the air. I wish to hell I had."

"Did Dom get off the deck?"

"I don't know," said Chuck. "I saw him in one of the fighter planes trying to get off before the bastards hit us."

"I hope he made it," said P.G.

"If he got off the deck, he'll have a better shot than we do," said Chuck.

Just then a Japanese Betty dropped a bomb two compartments over from theirs, and the bomb blew four decks below. At first there was a bright flash, then tremendous thunder as the initial shock of the blast reverberated throughout the ship. Then there was a sucking sensation from the concussion. P.G. and Chuck were blown off their feet and were knocked unconscious.

When P.G. came to, there was a ringing in his ears, a constant buzz, and he couldn't hear. He wondered if his eardrums had been punctured. The buzzing finally stopped, and then he heard Chuck talking beside him saying, "Let's get the hell out of here. I think this fucking ship's going down."

P.G. and Chuck went up to the flight deck. There was a strange silence there. Most of the antiaircraft gunners were unconscious, hanging on the gun mounts like discarded rag dolls. A few moments before they had been cheering and P.G. had been cheering with them. Some of them didn't have a scratch on them. It was frightening to see these young men unconscious, no longer working their guns. Others on the flight deck, who had been hit by shrapnel and flying debris, were still alive but were helpless and bleeding.

The sounds of the injured, the mangled, crying like babies for mom in the still of night was very disturbing and echoed across the deck. It is as though the injured and defenseless baby is still in the womb, seeking help—grown men crying, "Momma, Momma." It's a horrible sound. "We come into the world as babes crying and go out of the world the same way," thought P.G. "That is—if there's time to cry. Death was never meant to be easy and one never knows when death will knock at the door."

Death can be sudden and sweet if a major injury occurs. If a vital organ is destroyed or a major blood vessel severed or broken, the rapid blood loss and severe body damage takes away the mental anxiety and pain often associated with dying.

A survivor seeing or hearing such a catastrophe feels completely helpless. One can never forget it. It is eerie, pathetic, sad, and emasculating. The silence that is final with death is permanently imprinted on the memory of the survivors. Massive injury and destruction of life is overwhelming. What do you do? Where do you start? How do you to try to help the injured? Some people get sick and vomit when they see young bodies destroyed by shrapnel or fire. Others just stand there in shock. Adaptation to the stress of seeing someone die is also unpredictable.

P.G. and Chuck decided to get a stretcher and carry the wounded below for medical care. That is, if they could find a sick bay or a place to take the wounded. They finally found a stretcher and decided to take those that were conscious first. Getting a stretcher with a body on it around the ship's tight quarters was difficult. Only a few lights were on below deck, as most of the electrical circuits had been destroyed. They had to hand-carry some of the wounded, bleeding and moaning, feet first, down the hatchways. Medical corpsmen were working in the ready room that was being used as a sickbay triage area.

Most of the doctors had been killed, and chaos still reigned; no one gave orders to tell them what to do with the injured. They felt lost and helpless. Some of the pilots went topside to fight the fires, knowing that the medics needed room to tend the injured. There would be a hell of a lot more dead if the fires weren't extinguished. The way they were burning, it looked as if the ship was a goner anyway.

When P.G. and Chuck went back up to the flight deck to get the unconscious wounded from the gun mounts, they had a tremendous shock. The gunners had no outward evidence of bleeding. There was no crying. All of these young men were cold, stiff, and dead. P.G. and Chuck were stunned and mystified by what they saw. How did they die? What happened to these young men?

Later, they found out that the probable cause of death was the shock wave produced by the bomb blast. The shock wave hits the little air sacs in the lungs and makes a big air embolism that travels through the large veins to the heart and coronary vessels, stopping the heart and causing cardiac arrest. Instead of blood in the veins being pumped by the heart, there's just air. Death for the young men on the gun mounts was sudden.

The fight wasn't over. The Japanese kamikaze pilots were determined to sink the Saratoga. Thirty minutes after the first wave of six kamikazes, more bogies were reported. An hour after the initial attack, five more planes approached the *Sara*, now a sitting target. The ship was struggling and hardly moving. The Japanese returned to finish the job. Gun crewmen on the *Sara* who had been killed were replaced. Using the few guns that had not been destroyed, the men opened fire. Two more enemy planes were shot down, one on the port beam and one astern. Another plane, however, approached unopposed and unobserved ahead of the ship where most of the forward gun mounts had been knocked out from previous attacks. It dropped a bomb on the flight deck and then crashed into the water on the port side. The five-inch gun batteries and more 40 mm quads were put out of commission. Additional fires were started on the deck. The heat and smoke from the fires were getting oppressive and scalding. The continuous fires on the flight deck made the metal so hot it could be felt in one's shoes. The crew valiantly and frantically continued their work to save her. They all knew if the ship went down, they would go down with her.

The *Saratoga* remained afloat after taking seven major bomb hits by the kamikaze pilots. Although the front of the carrier was damaged beyond repair, the fantail was solid enough to permit a few of her homing eagles to land on what was left of her great flight deck; these planes had gotten off and had attacked and downed some of the enemy planes. The sole torpedo bomber pilot who had gotten off the deck landed on the U.S.S. *Bismark Sea,* only to go down with the ship when it sank. The *Sara*, like the survivors aboard her, never gave up. She had been damaged as no other ship had been before and yet remained afloat.

And so the *Sara*'s legend grew. Other ships were as big or bigger, but few had participated in wartime action as much as she had. Rare ships like the *Sara* turn out to be the fire horses of the sea. They don't miss a fight, no matter how far or how fast they may have to go. Often the enemy will concentrate on them because they have fought them before. Sometimes they come out of battle unscathed. Ships like the *Sara* snub their noses at the enemy. Even when they take punishment that could sink a fleet, they keep fighting and set sail again in quest of trouble, as if to say, "Come try and get me if you dare." The *Sara* had originally been constructed as a cruiser with a heavy, thick inner metal hull that made her almost impossible to sink. The Japanese had tried at least three times before to sink her and were unable to. They had hit her with everything they had, putting torpedoes into her and now sacrificing their young kamikaze pilots in a last, desperate, effort. They were unsuccessful. It seemed as though God had put a shroud over her to protect her and the men who fought on her decks.

There is more than oak and iron to ships like the *Saratoga*. The courage of the men who sailed and fought on her and the men who gave their lives to keep her afloat are what make up the spirit of the United States Navy. The men striving to save the *Sara* off the coast of Iwo Jima were heroes. The battle to save the ship was won.

When Chuck and P.G. saw the sun coming up, they were blackened, battered, and completely exhausted. They realized now that the fires were out and the ship would survive. They stretched out on the flight deck and fell sound asleep in broad daylight.

29

Kamikaze Post Mortem

More than 3,000 men were aboard the U.S.S. *Saratoga* when the ship was hit off the coast of Iwo Jima. The morale of the ship's crew had been shattered by the attack. The next day, there was a strange silence aboard ship and the attitudes of the men had changed. The cockiness was gone. Why did it happen? No answer was forthcoming. The pilots stewed in their bitterness and anger; they had been prevented from entering the fight—only a few fighter planes and one torpedo bomber plane had been launched before the *Saratoga* became totally disabled.

P.G. was particularly upset because he had been on the bridge of the *Sara* en route to Iwo Jima when the ship had sailed by that Japanese-held island. Anyone with a telescope could have seen the fleet and identified the ships. It was arrogant and foolish for the command of the task force to feel secure from attack. Kamikazes had been used before in the Philippines, and they had been very successful. The attack should have been anticipated and preparations to repel any attack should have been complete. Combat air patrol should have been out in force. The pilots and crew were sullen. They had been defeated in a battle they could have won.

Burial services were conducted the day after the kamikaze attack

217

on the *Saratoga*. Those who had been killed had to be committed to the deep six the day after battle. For some, it took days to learn a good friend had been lost. Identification had to be established first. Metal dogtags were checked, because some of the bodies were burned beyond recognition. Then the roster was checked to see who was missing. Accounting for everyone was not completely possible because when a kamikaze had torn a large hole below the waterline, the bulkhead doors around the hole had to be slammed shut and locked to prevent the ship from sinking. There were some men still alive inside, screaming, when the doors were shut. They were now entombed.

The odor of death aboard ship is a repulsive, sickening stench. When men are killed in battle, the burial work detail is difficult. The day after the kamikaze attack, the burial chutes on the *Saratoga* worked constantly. Bodies slid down the chutes in canvas bags with five-inch shells in them to make them sink. Prayers were said, religious songs were sung, rifle salutes were fired, and the bugler sounded "Taps."

Four canvas bags with five-inch shells lay on the flight deck separated from the rest of the dead; these were the remains of the Japanese kamikaze pilots. Although the remains were present at the burial service, the hostility of the surviving *Saratoga* crew was so great that they did not allow the four bodies to be given the privilege of the chute.

P.G. viewed the proceedings with his jaw set. He looked at the remains of the suicide pilots and thought: "What manner of man could do what they had done? They had made the supreme sacrifice for their country. They must have been fanatics. They knew that when they went into battle they would not return. How could the Japanese recruit the flower and talent of their youth to do such a deed?"

Kamikaze pilots derived their name, meaning "divine wind," from a storm that blew the enemy fleet of Kublai Khan away from Japan in 1281. In order to try to understand this legacy, one must understand the Japanese code of patriotic self-sacrifice and the homage paid to the emperor. They were obeying the orders of Emperor Hirohito. In the Japanese code, when a person dies bravely, his or her ancestors will benefit from that death. The young Japanese pilots, knowing they were losing the battle, were willing to act as human missiles for their country and their ancestors.

The kamikaze attacks were substantially more effective than conventional weapons. No bombsight was needed, just a pilot to point the nose of his plane at the target. Many times the attacking plane would be set on fire by antiaircraft guns, but it would still hit the target.

The Japanese first used kamikaze pilots during the United States landing on the Philippines, at the Battle of Leyte Gulf. In that battle, the kamikazes damaged the American warships considerably and caught the United States Navy unprepared.

In order to stem the tide of the war, the kamikaze pilot corps was conceived by Admiral Ohnishi, who assumed command of the First Air Fleet in the Philippine Theatre in 1943. He met with another Japanese admiral, Admiral Teraoka, in Manila on October 18, 1943, and discussed the role of "special attacks" against the American enemy.

Twenty-three Japanese pilots who had been lucky enough to survive the Marianas Turkey Shoot were asked to serve as human missiles in the impending Battle of Leyte Gulf. The Japanese pilot selected to lead this suicide mission was Lieutenant Yukio Seki, a graduate of the naval academy at Etajima. The Zero fighters would be loaded with 250-kg bombs and would crash-dive on the enemy warships. Lieutenant Seki, a young naval career officer, had been married just before leaving his homeland. It is incredible to the American mind that he would be asked to lead the group, knowing that he would give up his life. However, he was willing and strongly motivated to do this. His superiors impressed upon him that the Japanese did not want the Americans to return to the Philippines, because that would cause them a great loss of face. Seki understood.

Nevertheless, the Americans returned. The Battle of Leyte Gulf lasted four days. On October 25, 1944, the Japanese carried out the first successful operation of their special attack forces led by Lieutenant Seki. The carriers *Suwannee* and *Santee* were struck by kamikaze planes and the *Kitkun Bay* and *Kalinin Bay* were also hit. Another kamikaze pilot hit the American carrier *St. Lo*, which caught fire and sank.

The Japanese realized they had a new highly effective weapon. They began using anything that could take off from an airfield with a bomb load and reach the target area on a no-return mission. There were three essential ingredients: First, a plane that was capable of getting off the ground; second, a fanatical pilot with sufficient courage to complete the attack; and third, enough fuel in the plane to get to the target. The Japanese were rapidly running short of all three of these essential ingredients.

They used any aircraft that could fly—from Zeros to training planes that could be patched together for one last mission. The attacks were made singly or in groups. To fly as a kamikaze pilot was considered a great honor, and there were many volunteers.

In January 1944, the last kamikaze attacks from the Philippine bases took place. Fifteen Japanese fighter bombers took off from the Philippines and blew themselves up at Lingayen Gulf. One American cruiser and four transports were hit and seriously damaged.

The kamikaze attack on the U.S.S. *Saratoga* and the sinking of the *Bismark Sea* on February 21, 1945, were the next major successes. As word of this great triumph spread through Japan, the number of volunteers skyrocketed.

As the *Saratoga* limped back to Eniwetok, there was time for the pilots and crew to think about what had happened. Those who survived were grateful to be alive.

The *Sara* arrived at Eniwetok in late February and divers surveyed the underwater damage. There was a 40-foot hole beneath the waterline on the starboard quarter. It had been known that there was damage to the hull in that vicinity, but the exact location and extent were not known. From the Marshall Islands she limped back toward Pearl Harbor. The return was interrupted for two days while a search was conducted for Lieutenant-General Harmon, Army Air Force, who was reported lost during a flight near the Marshalls. Two planes were launched, but nothing was sighted. The *Sara* had to back into the wind and launch her planes over the stern because flight deck damage prevented turning into the wind.

As the *Saratoga* got closer to Pearl, there was an almost desperate hope that the tremendous repair job would be done at Bremerton on the west coast.

But the war was not over—the Japanese had just made that clear—and the pilots worried that they would be reassigned to more duty in the Pacific. They knew there weren't many night-carrier pilots and their efforts would be needed. Still, the hope remained that they would be able to spend a few days in the States with their families and friends. P.G. longed for Sarah. She was his link to a life of reality, without shrapnel or lifeless rag-doll bodies strewn across a flaming deck. How could he explain to her what had happened? Those ugly thoughts? Or should he try to completely forget them? He had no answer, but that answer might come when they were together again.

As the *Saratoga* approached the dock, the crew's prayers were answered. Ford Island Marine Band was on shore blaring out "California Here I Come" and a tremendous cheer went up. There was relief and joy from all hands on topside as the music was recognized.

After the *Sara* docked at Pearl Harbor, it was difficult for anyone to see the surface and flight deck damage that had been inflicted by the Japanese kamikaze pilots. Carpenters on Eniwetok had covered the holes with wood and had painted the areas gray to match the *Sara*'s color. This was done so that if spies were watching at the docks, it would be difficult for them to assess the damage and report their success back to Japan.

Back in the States, the news media learned what had happened to the *Saratoga* and how valiantly the men and the ship had fought. The folks at home heard before the crew could notify their next of kin that they were still alive. Sarah was one who heard. She was beside herself. She didn't know if Peter was alive. She demanded that her father call the Navy Department to see if he was. Since the kamikaze attacks on the *Saratoga* were initially top secret, it was difficult to break the umbrella of secrecy until the navy issued its official press release.

P.G. tried to call Sarah from Hawaii many times. At one time, he waited in line at a phone booth for three hours. All the lines to the States were busy. He didn't have a high-priority call. He was frustrated. The girl he had dreamed about while flying planes in the Pacific was within his reach but out of touch. Spending six to eight months away from someone you love is difficult enough, but dodging bullets on a navy carrier wasn't the greatest job in the world. He was mad at the system and Sarah, and he wanted to strangle the phone operator; "Sorry, we are unable to complete your call. Your call cannot be placed at this time."

He finally decided to write her a letter. Hell, he'd probably be back in San Francisco before the letter got to her, he thought, but he wrote anyway.

Dearest Sarah,

It's ironic the name of the ship I wake up on bears your name. This ship, like our love, has survived the war, so far.

By now you've probably read about the battle we were in. I'm alive and well. Sarah, even though I've only known you for a short time, I hate it when I'm away from you; a part of my heart is missing. I think about you and I wonder what you are doing and if you miss me as much as I miss you. I feel insecure and lost without you.

I find it difficult to express my love to you in a letter. I love you very much. I feel awkward writing these words to you. I'm afraid your feelings for me may have changed. I pray they haven't. Someday, when you are mine, all of this will be a memory. You will be mine and I will be yours. I hope time will fly and hasten that moment.

This ship scares me. Its guns and planes are built to kill, to take life; while you give it. God brought us together to help make our life a happy one and I am forever grateful for that blessing.

When the ship is silent at night there is only the creaking of the hulls and bulkheads, and I think of you. I think of your touch, your scent, the curve of your waist, the small of your back. I think of the time we've spent together, and how much it means to me.

These are the thoughts of a man that death approached. I was one of the lucky ones. My life was spared. I pray that the war will end so the bloodshed will stop. Death was close by every day. I felt it. I wanted to share my fear with you as I wanted to share everything with you, but I couldn't because I knew you'd worry.

So instead I'll tell you again that I love you. Why do I love you? There are so many reasons. You know why I love you, because there is only one you.

I'm doing a job here. I'm trying my best. I hope the war ends soon. When it's done, I want you in my arms. I want our love renewed and nurtured. My dreams will disappear and your presence will make me feel alive again. I want you to be mine forever, Sarah.

All my love,
Peter

He sent the letter airmail and hoped Sarah would get it before he arrived in San Francisco.

After five days at Pearl picking up provisions for the trip to San Francisco, the *Saratoga* headed for the States.

The pilots and crew were told the trip would be time-consuming because the *Saratoga* could not travel at full steam. The men were going in the right direction, though, and they needed a respite from combat action. They relaxed on what remained of the flight deck, exercised, played cards—acey deucy, poker, and gin. They slept. Slowly the bags under their eyes diminished, but the hardened lines remained on their faces.

Each crew member had lost someone during the battle, and there was sadness on board. The injured were ever-present reminders of the battle. The more seriously injured had been picked up and transferred to hospital ships.

The existing medical personnel were extremely busy with the ill and injured, especially the serious burn cases that were caused by the aviation gasoline fires. The treatment of burns was still quite primitive. Usually some kind of Vaseline dressing or oil would be applied, and sulfa would be sprinkled on the wound. Penicillin would be given if it was available. Open wounds were not treated adequately immediately after the kamikaze attack because there weren't enough personnel. The medical corpsmen who knew how to do some stitching tried their best. Many of the surviving crew and pilots had severe headaches from concussions and persistent ringing in their ears. They slowly got better. Nightmares were not infrequent, with screams tearing through the night air on board ship. The mental toughness of some had simply crumbled, and it was difficult to treat these people; treatment of mental illness and combat fatigue was also primitive.

Some of the pilots and crew were outspoken about the failure to launch enough aircraft for the *Sara* to put up a better fight. It was their job to protect the ship, and they felt they had not been given a proper opportunity to do so. Some of the senior ships' officers told them to be quiet because the war wasn't over yet. Some felt the *Saratoga* was poorly protected, with only three destroyers accompanying her task force. The cruiser *Alaska* had left her. At the time of the attack, only five fighter planes were airborne, four acting as combat air patrol and one awaiting recovery after an afternoon message drop.

There was no doubt that the radar was helpful in detecting the bogey 75 miles away from the *Saratoga*. However, a radar blip shows only that there is something out there, it doesn't always identify what it is. It doesn't tell you how fast the planes are coming or what altitude they are at. When planes are diving at a ship they can be traveling at 500 mph or faster, and when they're 75 miles away, that means the defense has about 15 minutes or less to react.

The pilots were later told that when the contact was made, it was assessed as four to six planes heading south. A warning broadcast was sent on the I.F.D. frequency to the commander of the air support group, who evaluated the blip and bogey as *returning itinerant friendlies*. This was the first major mistake. It showed that a blip on a radar screen can be falsely identified. As the blip rapidly approached the *Saratoga*, General Quarters should have been sounded and the carrier turned into the wind to launch all her aircraft.

Along with several pilots, P.G. was in the *Saratoga*'s CIC at the time the blip was spotted and remembered hearing the message sent back to the *Saratoga* from Admiral Durgin's staff, "Wait for instructions." A scramble was requested, but the flight deck was being respotted for the launch of the dusk combat air patrol for Iwo Jima, so the scramble didn't happen.

In air plot, it was soon recognized that a large group of aircraft was approaching. The planes had separated into two groups, with one heading for the *Saratoga*. What followed is now history.

Later, in Puget Sound Navy Yard, where the *Saratoga* was repaired, the yard superintendent said the *Saratoga* was the most extensively damaged vessel that his navy yard had ever received for repairs. She was the recipient of more types of damage than any other ship. Her airplane crane had been sheered off at its base by a bomb that had hit the forward flight deck. Another kamikaze had demolished the hangar windlass, motor room controller, and catapults.

Gasoline-fed fires had burned out some areas completely. A large, gaping hole had been blown in the forward flight deck, penetrating four decks, and demolished most of the living quarters for the officers and men. Another area extending on one side of the port bow back one hundred feet on the flight deck, had also been completely wiped out. The worst damage, however, was near the aft waterline. A Japanese plane, knocked down by the ship's gunfire, hurtled over the waves and slammed the starboard side of the ship.

The resulting explosion tore a 40-foot hole in the *Sara's* side and sprayed gasoline onto the hangar deck, setting off fires and explosions.

The *Sara* had bulging and bent bulkheads, heat-melted and bomb-blasted decks, broken pipe lines, burned cables, and demolished machinery. She slowly sailed toward San Francisco. The armchair admirals discussing the attack felt that the *Saratoga* should have had cruiser protection and that there was undue delay in launching the fighter planes. There was definitely delay in opening fire. Only 42 rounds of ammunition were fired during the first attack, in which four kamikaze planes crashed into the side of the *Saratoga*. There was also poor communication between the U.S.S. *Saratoga* and the admiral's flagship when the bogey was initially reported.

A young sailor on the flight deck described the attack on the *Saratoga* best when he said that a big SNAFU occurred: "Situation Normal All Fucked Up."

30

Return to the States

P.G., Chuck, and Domkowski decided that when they reached San Francisco they were going to raise hell for a few days before they headed home on leave. P.G. was not as interested as the other two were in meeting new girls. He'd given it a lot of thought, and planned to give Sarah an engagement ring. He had decided she was the girl for him. She was the reason he was driven to stay alive. Domkowski and Chuck were a couple of young, healthy guys with no commitments looking for female companionship. They were just out for a good time—a one-night stand.

When the sailors and pilots finally saw the west coastline, there was a cheer from all hands topside. The Golden Gate Bridge, from the flight deck of the damaged carrier, loomed like a golden arch, highlighted by the setting sun. "This is what we're fighting for," someone said softly.

As soon as the ship docked, P.G. placed a call to Georgia to try to reach Sarah, but all the lines were busy. He tried three or four times to call her, but to no avail.

The pilots of Night Air Group 53 had been told that they would get 30 days' leave when they reached the States and they would all be reassigned. A small group of the torpedo bomber pilots were notified that they were to report to Alameda Naval Air Station off the coast of San Francisco after their leave. P.G. and Chuck were in that group, along with their torpedo bomber skipper. Some of the pilots were ordered to Pensacola, Florida, or Corpus Christi, Texas, for instructor duty. A few others were ordered to Norfolk Naval Air Station or Washington, D.C. P.G. and Chuck were glad they were not going back to Norfolk to be thrown back into the pilot replacement pool.

The pilots knew they would probably blow a lot of cash in San Francisco, but would have a good time doing it. Most of them who had survived the night raids over Tokyo and the air support over Iwo Jima had received promotions and were now lieutenants. P.G., Chuck, and Domkowski were in that group. The three new lieutenants knew a little about San Francisco and what they had seen briefly before heading out to war in the Pacific was all good. It was an international, cosmopolitan city with quaint shops, beautiful hotels, fabulous restaurants, and many lovely women.

After disembarking from the *Sara*, they headed for Union Square, a park right across from the St. Francis Hotel. Close by was the Sir Francis Drake Hotel and rows of chic shops and art galleries. The park was always filled with flowers and an occasional street musician or soapbox orator. A nearby pet shop attracted passersby with its window full of exotic birds and puppies. The pilots weren't looking for puppies or birds, however. They were more interested in what San Francisco had to offer in the way of bars and young ladies. With Neiman Marcus, I. Magnin, Gumps, Saks Fifth Avenue, and Tiffany's all nearby, the young damsels would be out shopping, and the three aviators went looking for evening companionship. They had money and time. All they needed now were dates. They rode the cable car to Union Square and were disappointed, because all they saw were hungry pigeons being fed by some old men. A lot of ships must have been in port because sailors, marines, and navy officers were all over the place. They suddenly realized that there might be competition for dates that evening.

As they strolled through town, they found that late afternoon was not an ideal time to look for company. The only females available were the working girls out to earn a living, along with a few pimps trying to sell their wares. They were interested in picking up girls, not gonorrhea or syphilis. They had been repeatedly lectured by the flight surgeon before going ashore about the hazards of impropri-

ety. "If you don't know what you're getting, you might get an un-
pleasant surprise," was the flight surgeon's comment.

They decided to go out to dinner first and then look for companionship. They were undecided whether to go to Fisherman's Wharf
and look for a seafood restaurant that served dungeness crab, a
delicious delicacy, or to try some Italian food at North Beach.
Ghirardelli Square was at North Beach, and there were beautiful
views of the bay. Domkowski, however, wanted to go to Chinatown at
Portsmouth Square and eat Chinese food. Chuck and P.G. finally
agreed. After they checked into the Sir Francis Drake, they took a
cab to Chinatown.

Domkowski claimed he was an expert on Chinese cuisine and
declared himself tour director. He had a list of Chinese restaurants,
his first choice being the Empress of China, his second the Forbid-
den City. The pilots were immediately impressed, and not neces-
sarily with the restaurant selections.

"P.G., would you look at that?" Chuck exclaimed.

P.G. turned around and saw one of the most beautiful women he
had ever laid eyes on. In fact, the pilots began to notice that the
Chinese-American women had a dress and style all their own, and it
was both intriguing and alluring. Domkowski, ever the expert on
the Chinese, pointed out that the women dressed to emphasize, as
he delicately put it, "asses and legs."

P.G. and Chuck found it hard to disagree.

After standing in line for a long time and having a few cocktails in
the lounge, the pilots got into the Empress of China. After a few
more drinks each one ordered a different course so they could
share: Peking duck, broiled lobster in ginger sauce, and Mongolian
lamb were their choices. "Hey, this is just like we got aboard ship,"
said Domkowski.

"Yeah, right!" replied Chuck.

The food and service were excellent. When the main courses were
finished, they had tea and fortune cookies. Cracking the cookies
open to get their fortunes, P.G.'s said, "You're about to go on a long
sea journey."

"This is a bunch of crap," he said. "I just completed one."

Domkowski's said, "You're going to meet a stranger, beware!"

"Nothing could be stranger than meeting you two assholes," said
Dom.

Chuck's said, "Romance is in your future, keep your guard up."

His reply was "Hell, I don't want to keep my guard up, I'm ready now."

They left the restaurant and decided to travel around San Francisco's bars and joints to see what type of companionship might be available. Eventually, they went to Nob Hill and the cocktail lounges of the high-class hotels. They took the elevator to the Top of the Mark and looked at the stunning 360-degree view of San Francisco Bay. There weren't any available women there so they went across the street to the Fairmont Hotel and hit a dinner show at the Venetian Room. No luck finding any girls there, either. They finally took the cable car down to the Sir Francis Drake and asked the Beefeater-costumed doorman where the action was.

"Three beautiful WAVES just went into our hotel, gentlemen," he said. "They were going up to the Starlight Room to look for dancing partners."

"Great," said Chuck. "Let's hit the place. I'll do a tap dance to get their attention."

"I'll do you one better," said Domkowski, "I'll drop my pants. After seeing you in that pissing contest, I know you'd never match me. I'd win hands down."

When they got to the Starlight Room they got a table and surveyed the crowd. Quite a few women were present, and there was a good 11-piece band playing. It was obvious the girls who had come were there to dance. P.G. spotted the three WAVES sitting at the bar having drinks. They were all attractive, but the uniforms didn't do their figures justice.

He said he'd go over and ask them to join their table. After spending ten minutes talking to them, he struck out. They weren't interested. He didn't even get a dance. Domkowski was next. He had no luck either. "They're a bunch of cold fish," said Domkowski. "I'd like to crawl into bed with that tall brunette and see what makes her tick. I bet I could warm her up!"

Quite a few other naval officers were hanging around the three girls. Chuck finally said, "You fellas want to watch and see how it's done?" He wedged himself between two of the WAVES sitting at the bar and didn't say a word to them but ordered a "stinger" from the bartender. He knocked it down in one gulp as the shorter WAVE, a blonde, watched. He still said nothing. "I'll have another stinger," he told the bartender. He knocked that one down, too, still ignoring the girls.

Then, a breakthrough. The blonde smiled at him and said, "What's in that drink, anyway?"

"Ingredients mean nothing," he said. "Taste is everything." Calling the bartender over, he ordered two stingers and gave one to the blonde. He found out her name was Mabel Jensen, a Swede from Minnesota. Mabel drank the drink.

"That's neat," she said. "I'll have another." After finishing the second drink, she smiled at Chuck and said, "Do you dance?"

"Do I dance?" he asked. "Incredulous that so obvious a question would be asked. Just watch me. I know all the steps." The band was playing a fast number and the two went out on the dance floor. Before long they were jitterbugging and having a good time. "Why don't you talk your two girlfriends into joining us for a cocktail?" asked Chuck. "I've got two flying buddies with me. They're really harmless," he said.

"I'll bet they're harmless, just like you," she said. She pulled him closer.

When she sat down with Chuck she called her two friends over. The tall brunette immediately sat next to Domkowski, probably because he was six feet five. Her name was Pam Jablonski, and she was quite attractive, with long, slender legs. Domkowski found out she had been a model in Detroit.

By elimination and social constraint, P.G. ended up with the third WAVE, a dirty blonde with a little red tinge to her hair. She was cute, about five feet four, and slim. Her name was Mim Stevens. He immediately compared her with Sarah, but felt to put her in Sarah's shadow wasn't fair to either. Sarah was in a league of her own. But could it be called a league with only one person in it? P.G. was devoted, but didn't want to kill a good time for his pals. He decided to play along. It would hurt no one.

The three pilots drank and danced with the girls until midnight and then Chuck invited the girls up to their rooms. Chuck's and Domkowski's girls were willing to go, but Mim said she had a curfew and had to return to base by 1:00 A.M. Then she told P.G. she wanted to get together the next evening. The other two girls had weekend passes. "That's the luck of the draw," said P.G. "I'll take you back to the base." He hailed a cab and took her back to Alameda Naval Air Base.

On the way to the base, in the back seat of the cab, she undid her jacket and turned to P.G. She kissed him. He froze. She pressed herself to him. He awkwardly embraced her, uncertain. Her advances were insistent, and constant. P.G. was on defense—a new experience. But he felt that to give in would be to denigrate and diminish the love he had made with Sarah.

When they reached the base, she gave him another big kiss. "I can hardly wait to see you tomorrow night. Pick me up at 6:30, all right?"

"Sure. But listen," he said. "I didn't come across tonight for two reasons. One is that this cab is too small. The other is that my heart, as they say, is far away."

She paused, and then locked her eyes to his. "Peter, my heart is far away, too. It's in Pittsburgh. But right now I'm in the middle of a war and I'm lonely and I want to see you tomorrow."

On the way back the cab driver remarked, "That's a real cute little girl you had there. I thought she was giving you CPR at one point, or was it you giving it to her?"

"Both," said P.G. "We were keeping each other alive. I thought I might need some oxygen, however."

The three pilots had reserved a suite of three bedrooms with a living room for the weekend. P.G. felt there wouldn't be any problem if he returned to the hotel. He decided to have a few drinks at a corner bar before going back; he didn't want to catch his buddies in compromising positions.

Shortly after having one drink, a Mai-Tai, his stomach started to get queasy, so he decided to go back to the hotel suite. When he arrived no one was in the living room. The bathroom, which was between the two occupied bedrooms was empty, and female voices could be heard from within the bedrooms. He went into the bathroom, got sick to his stomach, and ended up sitting on the john. The walls were so thin that he could hear the conversations taking place in the bedrooms, word for word. It was obvious that Chuck and Domkowski had their companions in various stages of undress.

Pam was the first one to succumb. Dom told her what a magnificent body she had as she resisted his advances. "I'm a virgin," she said, "and unless you're willing to marry me someday, you can't have me." He continued to caress her, grunting some kind of incoherent reply. He kept telling her how beautiful she was and how he was madly in love with her.

About three minutes later, in a cacophony of oohing, ahing, and sighing, Pam caved in. P.G. could hear the bedsprings squeaking and bodies thrashing around. Suddenly there was silence. P.G. considered giving a loud round of applause but did not. Later, he regretted his decision.

Chuck, in the next room, was having a little more difficulty with Mabel. She too said she was a virgin. "I don't want to get pregnant," she said.

"Mabel, I'm in love with you," said Chuck. "I'll do anything you want me to do."

"Tell him to shit a pile of .50-caliber slugs," P.G. thought.

"Well, if we get engaged, I'm willing to go all the way," she said.

"The girl knows how to play the game," thought Peter.

"I'll tell you what," said Chuck. "I'll give you my navy wings. In the Navy Air Corps that means you're engaged, and then when I get enough money, I'll get you a ring." When he heard this, P.G. almost fell off the john. He knew Chuck was loaded with cash. He had been at sea for six months.

All Mabel wanted, in her own passion, was a little insurance. She quickly took off all her clothes. Chuck had been known for his previous experiences. Within a few minutes, Mabel taught him a few new tricks. All Chuck could think about was "This girl's no virgin! She couldn't have learned all these tricks from a book." P.G. could hear Chuck getting his ass handed to him as the bedsprings rocked to an ever-quickening rhythm. P.G., sitting on the john, couldn't stop laughing. Hell, San Francisco couldn't have *that* many virgins!

When he got out of the bathroom, he decided to try to call Sarah again. Maybe she had another boyfriend. P.G. felt betrayed. He'd been getting his ass shot up on the other side of the world and needed to hear the voice of the girl he loved. He went downstairs and sat in a pay phone in the corner of the lobby. On the third ring, Sarah's mother answered.

"This is Peter Grant, Mrs. Tomkins. Is Sarah there?"

There was a pause on the other end of the phone. P.G. thought for a moment he had dialed the wrong number. Then, her mother spoke up.

"No, Peter, I'm sorry. She's not here."

"Excuse me, ma'am, could you tell me where she is?"

Another pause followed. P.G. could feel a knot beginning to form in his stomach, and he thought he might get sick again. He began to perspire lightly. He again asked where she was.

"Oh, Peter, I'm so sorry. . . ." Her voice trailed off and the phone clattered to the floor. P.G. froze. What was going on? Where was she?

A few seconds later, her mother was back on the line. "Peter, we tried to reach you. I've got some terrible news to tell you. It was raining. Her convertible was hit by a truck. . . ."

He was now sweating heavily. "Is she all right? Where is she? *Where is she?*"

Her mother finally blurted out the two words he dreaded. "She's dead. She was conscious for a while but she only lived for 48 hours. She was asking for you."

P.G. felt dizzy and sick all at the same time. Tears ran down his cheeks. He dropped to his knees and began to sob, then to cry uncontrollably. "Oh, no, it can't be. Sarah and I were talking about getting engaged."

"I know," said Sarah's mother. "There's something else you should know about, too. You'll find out about it later anyway. Sarah was seven months pregnant. The doctors tried to save the baby. It was a boy. Sarah told me that if she had a boy she wanted to name him Peter. They did a caesarean but the baby died. He's buried next to Sarah."

Tears continued to flow. He was speechless. He didn't know what to say. On the other end of the line, he heard, "Are you there, Peter?"

P.G. slammed down the phone. He was furious and upset. Sarah was what he lived for, what had helped him get through the war, what drove him to succeed. He slumped onto a couch, and buried his head into a pillow. He finally got up, and called Sarah's mother back. They talked for an hour.

The next day, he decided to fly to Atlanta to see Sarah's family before heading home. Now he understood why Sarah hadn't seen him after the Virginia Beach episode seven months earlier. They had planned to get engaged when he returned to the States and get married when the war was over. In all her letters she seemed to be apprehensive about his surviving combat. It was now clear that she had good reason. If only she had told him she was pregnant with his baby, he would have kept in touch with her more often. He would have prayed more. He wouldn't have looked at another woman. He would have . . . yes, if only . . . he could have made it better for them both.

When he arrived at the airport in Atlanta, her mother and father were there to meet him. They went to the cemetery to see the burial plot, freshly dug. Many wilted flowers lay on the grass, and next to Sarah's grave was baby Peter's. He broke down, fell to his knees, and cried. Sarah's parents were beyond sharing his emotion. They were fractured; it was in the set of their jaws, their eyes, a bitterness that Peter, for his emotion, could not see.

After several minutes, he got up and went with her parents to their home. He spent two days there, numb to their comforts, numb to himself. Before he left, he went to the cemetery again and arranged for a perpetual flower program for Sarah's and Peter's graves.

P.G. flew home to New England and saw his family. Before he left home, his father said, "I don't think I'll see you again if the war keeps going on."

"Thanks, Dad," replied P.G.

His mother was more optimistic and said that her Peter would come back to her someday. There was nothing to say to his father. He was up to his old tricks. Peter took cold comfort in his isolation; it was so much easier than trying.

He discussed privately with his mother what had happened to Sarah. She was reassuring and helpful to him. She said, "What has happened to you, Peter, is like a deep scar on your heart that will take time to heal. Someday you will find someone to take Sarah's place, and since she is gone now, I'm sure she would want it that way."

He was with his family for about 20 days and then received orders to report to Alameda Naval Air Station in the San Francisco area. He didn't relish the thought of going back into combat.

P.G. took a plane back to San Francisco three days before he had to report to duty. Chuck and Domkowski were waiting for him. They knew what had happened to Sarah. When they met P.G. in the lobby of their old hotel for drinks, they silently embraced him, together.

Chuck and Domkowski knew they had their work cut out for them—trying to make P.G. forget about Sarah.

31

Spring 1945

When their leave was up, P.G., Domkowski, and Chuck reported to the Naval Air Station in Alameda. They checked into the Bachelor Officer's Quarters. Quite a few fighter and torpedo bomber pilots from Night Air Group 53 were already there. There was back-slapping and handshaking as the pilots were reunited. They were told that a new night air group was being formed, with the combat-conditioned pilots of 53 making up the nucleus. It was to be known as Night Air Group 63, and replacement pilots would be added to complete the unit. Since a majority of the group had been in combat, they would be shipping out in a short time in order to catch up with the fleet.

The three pilots didn't like that part of the deal, because they were looking forward to perpetual leave in San Francisco. In fact, they would have enjoyed being permanently assigned to the Alameda Naval Air Station. During the next couple of weeks, the Three Musketeers got to know San Francisco and Oakland quite well, and the young women around town got to know them. Chuck was consistently getting the pilots into trouble, however, and if Domkowski hadn't been six-five and 245 pounds of muscle and P.G. six feet and 210, Chuck would have been pounded into sawdust within a short period of time. Still, P.G. and Dom marveled at the small guy. He weighed 135 pounds soaking wet with his pockets full of change, but he was as fearless fighting on the ground as he was in the air.

One evening, they went into a joint in Ghirardelli Square and after a few drinks, Chuck tried to pick up a chief petty officer's girlfriend. He asked her for a dance, and she accepted. One dance led to another and then another. Before long he began to monopolize all of the girl's time. It was obvious that the chief who was with her was getting disturbed and didn't care whether Chuck was an officer or not.

P.G. approached Chuck through the din of the bar. "There's a lot more like her where she came from," he said. "Lay off, or we're going to have to fight our way out of here."

"I like her," said Chuck, "and, besides, she knows how to dance."

"She's taken," said Domkowski. "Shrimp, lay off."

"Fellas, this is still a free world, right? That's what we're fighting for, right? As long as I'm fighting for her freedom, I may as well see she gets to exercise it, right?" Then he went out dancing with the girl again and she cuddled up to him. There seemed to be a mutual physical attraction.

The chief had had it. He went up to Chuck on the dance floor, spun him around, and landed a crushing right fist high on his forehead. The blow knocked Chuck on his ass. Two of the chief's buddies got into the act and started kicking Chuck. Domkowski heard him screaming for help. He grabbed P.G. and said, "Let's go. The shrimp's started another fight."

When they got to Chuck, two of the chief's buddies were pummeling him. Domkowski grabbed them by the napes of their necks and bounced their heads together. There was a dull, sickening thud and they went down. P.G. cold-cocked the chief with a right uppercut and he fell to the floor. The other enlisted men watching the fight were getting angry, grumbling and slowly closing a circle around Dom and Peter.

"We'd better get the hell out of here before we have to fight the whole fucking navy," said Domkowski, as he grabbed Chuck by the seat of his pants.

"Let me at them," said Chuck, as he swung his fists. "I'll knock the shit out of all of them."

"No more fighting for you," said Dom, as he lifted Chuck easily and carried him toward the door.

P.G. led the way through the crowd of irate onlookers. "His parents dropped him on his head . . . a lot," he explained as they made their way to the door.

The Three Musketeers made a hasty exit, hailed a cab in front of the dive, and took off. Chuck had a big mouse over his left eye. Dom told him it would take at least three weeks to get rid of it.

"What happened to you?" the other pilots asked Chuck the following day. Chuck was known as a ladies' man who sometimes let his libido get the best of him.

"I had to bail P.G. and Dom out of a fight," he replied smoothly.

"Next time, pick out a girl that isn't already taken," said P.G.

Getting into a fight in a dive in San Francisco wasn't the only trouble Chuck instigated.

The new torpedo bomber squadron VTN-63 practiced formation flying, gunnery, and day- and night-carrier landings on a couple of carriers that were being used for training in the area. The carriers operating off the West Coast at that time were the U.S.S. *Bataan* and the U.S.S. *Cabot*.

After a day of shooting carrier landings, Chuck was leading a group of six torpedo planes back to the Alameda Naval Air Station when he decided to fly underneath the San Francisco bridge. It was late afternoon as he led the six planes under the bridge, buzzing some fishing trawlers and pleasure boats. The next day the newspapers described how traffic on the bridge had stopped, and civilians driving their cars on the bridge thought the Japanese were bombing the West Coast, just as they had Pearl Harbor. All the Army Air Force planes in the area were subsequently grounded because the planes that went under the bridge were described as Army Air Corps Thunderbolts. The Army Air Corps quickly denied their planes were the culprits, and an investigation of the incident was launched. The heat was on. Fortunately, two days later they received orders to proceed to Hawaii and Ulithi aboard the *Bataan*, a CVL carrier returning to combat.

While the pilots of Night Air Group 63 were in the States on leave and had their sojourn at Alameda, the capture of Iwo Jima was completed. It had taken a month of brutal, bloody fighting. Once the island was captured, the SeaBees came in to make the airfields on Iwo Jima functional. No longer would Japanese fighter planes, flying off the airfields of Iwo, attack the B-29 Superfortresses as they headed to Japan on their raids. P.G., Domkowski, and Chuck heard about this and praised the marines whose tenacity and guts took the island.

The Army Air Force's VII Fighter Command arrived on Iwo Jima in March of 1945. The pilots were equipped with new P-51D Mustangs. The Mustang, fast and agile, was considered one of the best fighter planes in the world. It was the ideal plane for the job. It could fly more than 450 mph and with wing tanks had a range of 2,000 miles. The plane was fully capable of flying from Iwo Jima to Japan and back, and still have enough fuel for fighting or dropping bombs before returning home. Mustangs were aptly called Sunsetters—built to finish off the Land of the Rising Sun.

With Iwo Jima in American hands, Army Air Corps fighters would now be able to escort B-29 Superfortresses on their raids over Japan. If the Superfortresses were damaged and couldn't make it back to the airfields at Tinian, they had an airfield they could set down on; they could prevent ditching or capture by the Japanese on their homeland. This gave the pilots and crews of the damaged planes a greater chance to survive.

The pilots knew the Japanese frequently took revenge on American airmen who had to bail out. B-29 crews who bombed Japan did not go unscathed. In just one year of operation, more than 300 Superfortresses were shot down or lost, and most of the crewmen did not live once they were captured. Japanese army officers were known to first torture the airmen and in some cases practice karate and sword cuts before decapitating them.

The Joint Chiefs of Staff decided that bombing Japan and using naval blockades would not bring the war to an end. To achieve that goal, an invasion of Japan was essential. Precision bombing of Japanese aircraft construction sites was the first priority. The idea was to cripple the Japanese air defenses before the American invasion.

In January 1945, General Curtis LeMay was put in charge of the army air force at Tinian. He was a tough bomber pilot, hard-driving, and he had more than 350 B-29s at his command in the Marianas when he took over. He had many problems, not the least of which was the weather. The B-29s flew at high altitudes when they came in at night and bad weather diminished the accuracy of the bombing. Japanese searchlights would sweep the sky for intruders, but ack-ack bursts from their antiaircraft guns did little damage because their shells usually fell short.

Despite the relative impunity with which American forces attacked, General LeMay was not pleased with the results he was getting in the high-altitude bombing. He decided to try a new tactic; low-altitude bombing at night and the use of firebombs (napalm). Standard Oil and E.I. DuPont, the chemical company, had developed napalm, a compound of jellied gasoline, which stuck to anything it hit and started extremely hot fires. LeMay knew a lot of lives would be lost and many of them would be Japanese civilians, but the awesome will of the Japanese had to be destroyed. Weapons factories had to be wiped out, along with the people who made the weapons, or the invasion would cost millions of lives on both sides.

On March 9, 1945, Superfortresses took off from Guam and Tinian for Tokyo's commercial and industrial districts, loaded for the first time with napalm bombs that were rigged to fall automatically at regular intervals. More than 300 B-29 bombers took part in the raid. One hundred twenty thousand people were killed or injured, and most of the industrial buildings were destroyed. Approximately two million people were made homeless, and the populace left the cities for the hills. The area was a huge crematorium. Bodies were charred beyond recognition, and if it hadn't been for the Sumida River, which gave some relief from the firestorm, an even greater area of Tokyo would have been destroyed. The water became so hot, however, that people seeking refuge in it literally boiled or steamed to death.

Following the firebombing, there was a mass exodus of survivors. Tokyo had no gas, electricity, water, or any public transportation to take the people out of the charred ruins. Emperor Hirohito left his palace to view the damage to the city and stated, "Tokyo has become no more than scorched earth." General LeMay's firebombing was taking its toll, and the capacity of Japan's industries was being diminished.

LeMay was eager to get on with the job. Four more fire raids were launched in the next eight days; against Nagoya on March 11, Osaka on March 13, Kobe on March 16, and Nagoya again on March 19. The napalm bombs were then used with similar results against many other Japanese industrial cities. The panic-stricken Japanese people fled. Morale was shattered, and absenteeism in the war industries increased. At this time the Joint Chiefs of Staff decided that in order to invade Japan, an island close by had to be captured and used as a staging area for the invasion. The island of Okinawa was chosen.

April 1, 1945, had been designated D-Day. Admiral Nimitz, the theater commander in charge of the Okinawa invasion, was extremely wary of kamikaze planes. He ordered LeMay to help prevent the attacks by having his Superfortresses bomb airfields within kamikaze range of Okinawa. Five days before the invasion, more than 17 airfields were pummeled. Although the bombings were successful, LeMay wasn't happy with his new assignment. He wanted to continue firebombing the industrial cities—he thought he could end the war faster that way.

American forces invaded Okinawa on April 1, with 1,300 ships, and nearly 200,000 assault troops. Kamikazes continued to harass the American fleet off Okinawa, in a last-ditch effort to hold the island. Many American vessels—two battleships, three cruisers, an escort carrier, destroyers, and landing craft—were destroyed. The carriers *Enterprise*, *Yorktown*, *Franklin*, and *Wasp* were all hit. The *Franklin* was the most seriously damaged, and 800 of her crew lost their lives. Enemy dive bombers attacked the *Franklin*, and she was hit so hard that her fueled and armed aircraft contributed to the damage. Fires raged out of control. The ship survived the attack but could only move under tow by the cruiser *Pittsburgh*.

Five thousand tons of shells were fired by amphibious support forces to soften the opposition for the invading forces. On Okinawa, there were 160,000 Japanese; the majority were regular Imperial Japanese Army troops. Their main defensive positions were in the steep hills and narrow ravines of southern Okinawa, northeast of Naha. It took almost two months for the Americans to capture the island, and 13,000 Americans were killed. Nearly 5,000 navy personnel and 3,500 marines were killed. Most of the navy's casualties were the result of air attacks by kamikaze planes.

On April 7, Admiral Mitscher's carrier force intercepted the giant Japanese battleship *Yamato*, the light cruiser *Yahagi*, and accompanying destroyers as they headed for Okinawa. Mitscher's carrier planes struck the enemy in overwhelming force, sinking the *Yamato*, the *Yahagi*, and two destroyers.

An extremely valuable and versatile part of the American fleet in the battle for Okinawa was the CVE, or escort carrier. Escort carriers had been highly effective in the Atlantic with their Hunter

Killer Groups and were now demonstrating their worth in the battle for Okinawa. Many of their planes worked with the army and marine fighting forces in the amphibious support groups, and some provided combat air support to protect the ground forces. Most of the jeep carriers weighed about 10,000 tons and carried 24 fighter planes and torpedo bomber planes with their pilots. The pilots were young, averaging 20 years of age, and had little combat experience, although there were a few veteran pilots tossed in with the youngsters. The Okinawa Campaign duty was rigorous and the pilots had to fly several missions each day. The small jeep carriers were difficult to land on, were subject to numerous kamikaze attacks, and many were hit. The jeep carriers stood fast in the battle for Okinawa, and the loss of that island to the American forces meant that soon American land-based planes would be right at Japan's doorstep.

Once Okinawa was secured, the B-29 Superfortresses resumed their firebombing of Japan. Although the Superfortresses were getting some opposition, the Japanese had few aircraft and no radar to intercept the American planes. The Superfortresses, flying at high altitudes in good weather, would suddenly appear over the targets. Even the best Japanese fighter planes had difficulty reaching high altitudes rapidly in time to intercept the Americans. When the Japanese fighter planes received orders to scramble, getting planes in the air took time, and then flying to 35,000 feet to intercept would take another hour or so. In all, it was a crucial and deadly delay for the Japanese.

Eventually, kamikaze attacks were made directly on the Superfortresses. They usually used the Japanese twin-engine plane called the "Dragon Killer," a night-fighter plane with twin 20 mm cannons mounted in its nose. Their tactic was to fly under the belly of the Superfortress and then fire upward with the cannon. One Japanese pilot was credited with shooting down four Superfortresses, before sacrificing his life.

The Japanese were also having trouble getting enough fuel for their air force, and trained pilots were scarce. Qualified pilots were demoralized and air defense forces decimated. As the number of Japanese planes decreased, in desperation the Japanese pilots started daytime attacks, ramming their planes into the Superfortresses. The kamikaze pilot would dive at the B-29's nose, trying to cripple the bomber by killing the pilot and the co-pilot or injuring the bombardier, who was seated directly behind the cockpit.

Germany surrendered in May 1945, and American strength was now concentrated on forcing an end to the war in the Pacific. Powerful factions in Japan's government and armed forces favored a war to the bitter end, and both people and rulers would not accept a peace that did not preserve the Imperial System. The Japanese would not consider unconditional surrender.

In preparation for the invasion they knew was forthcoming, Japanese engineers had blasted a pit in the side of Mount Minakami, 110 miles northwest of Tokyo. The installation was a chambered tunnel six miles long and was to serve as the nation's command post in preparation for the Allied invasion. One section, lined with cypress wood, was to serve as the emergency home of the Imperial Family. The other adjoining caverns were to house the Imperial General Headquarters.

In June of 1945, it was time for Japan to surrender or be completely annihilated. At a meeting of the Supreme Japanese War Council, Emperor Hirohito stated what others had been afraid to state officially: "Japan must find a way to end the war." All of its cities were being turned to ashes, and the Japanese people were being wiped out.

By this time, P.G., Domkowski, and Chuck were flying off the U.S.S. *Bataan*, heading for Japan. Night Air Group 63 would eventually fly off the U.S.S. *Block Island* (106) and the U.S.S. *Kula Gulf* CVE (108). They would see Leyte Gulf, participate in mopping up Okinawa, and be detached and placed at Marpi Naval Air Field on Saipan at about the time the atomic bombs would be dropped over Hiroshima and Nagasaki.

32

The Atomic Bomb

In the summer of 1945, Night Air Group 63 arrived at Marpi Airfield on Saipan. Saipan was ideal for teaching pilots and marines the coordinated attacks for the invasion of Japan. The marines who had fought at Guadalcanal, Saipan, and Iwo Jima knew the Japanese were cleaver and tenacious fighters. The Japanese showed themselves to be adept at jungle combat. They gave no quarter and expected no quarter. They hid in dug-out caves, which they always built with more than one entrance and exit. The only way the Americans could get them out was to burn them out with flame throwers, or to detonate dynamite in the caves and follow with submachine gunfire. Those who had fought against them believed the Japanese would not crack even when defeat stared them in the face. The only way they could be beaten was through the annihilation of their troops and destruction of their factories.

The marines had fought a bloody battle in taking Saipan and Tinian a year before, with 13,000 American casualties. More than 30,000 Japanese defenders on Saipan died. The most grotesque slaughter, however, took place among Saipan's civilians.

Some Japanese civilians defected to the American side. Emperor Hirohito was greatly disturbed by this. He sent out an imperial order encouraging the civilians still at large to commit suicide, promising them equal spiritual status in the afterlife with that of soldiers perishing in combat.

Japanese propaganda advised that if the island was lost there would be rape, torture, castration, and murder, and that death would be sweet compared to American atrocities. As a result, when it appeared the island would be lost, 22,000 Japanese civilians, including women and children, made their way to the two highest sea cliffs above jagged rocks and, despite appeals from Japanese-American interpreters, flung themselves to their deaths. Some women held babies in their arms as they leaped. Whole families jumped together. Those who resisted were pushed or shot by Japanese soldiers. The ocean surrounding the cliff became a red cauldron of mangled and broken bodies.

The mass suicide on Saipan provided the Americans with further evidence that they were fighting a crazed enemy. The suicide on Saipan demonstrated that the Japanese would choose death over surrender. The pilots of Air Group 63 knew where the suicide cliffs were, and curiosity led most of them to visit the sight.

They had also heard that bamboo spears, to be used in the defense of their homeland, had been issued to the entire Japanese populace. What would they do if a Japanese woman or young child came at them with one of those bamboo spears? Would they shoot? The pilots, navy personnel, and marines training on the coast of Saipan and Tinian for the invasion of Japan hoped the war wouldn't get to that stage. Many prayed that God would help prevent the deaths of people fighting on both sides. There would be numerous casualties and needless bloodshed. Was anything to be gained by all this killing? The morality of the war was questioned for the first time in the hearts of the American men. They hoped the B-29 bombings would force the Japanese Imperial Hierarchy to consider surrender and that the invasion of Japan might not be necessary.

The Americans had an ace up their sleeve. Unknown to many of the military leaders of the United States, was a secretly funded two-billion-dollar operation called the Manhattan Project. Under the auspices of this project, leading physicists such as Enrico Fermi, J. Robert Oppenheimer, Hans Boethe, Ernest Lawrence, Leo Szilard, Walter Zinn, and others had been covertly developing an atomic bomb.

The physicists, under the leadership of Oppenheimer, had devised a uranium bomb that had virtually unlimited and unpredictable destructive potential. They had discovered the special nature of the chain reaction and the unique problems of critical mass. They figured out how to bring two elements of Uranium 235 into contact so quickly that the combined mass would reach the critical point, and an atomic explosion would occur. There were also unanswered questions about how to control the detonation time. The unpredictability of the whole operation gave each of the scientists reason for concern and fear.

The military man chosen to coordinate the Manhattan Project was Brigadier General Groves. It was his job to coordinate civilian tycoons and world-renowned physicists with the military. His dedication had brought the splitting of the atom from the blueprint stage to the point where military use of an atomic bomb to end the war was feasible.

The development of the atomic bomb was a major factor in the war effort at this time. In April 1945, President Franklin D. Roosevelt passed away. His successor, Harry Truman, was the recipient of some startling news on the day of his inauguration. Secretary of War Henry L. Stinson explained the Manhattan Project in detail to him.

On the first day of his presidency, Truman was briefed by his cabinet and then met with Secretary of State James Byrnes, who reiterated Stinson's position. He informed the President that an explosive great enough to destroy the world was being perfected by the government. The decision to use it would have to be made by the new President.

Another development was Germany's surrender on May 8, 1945. The victory in Europe against Germany would now enable the United States to direct all its efforts toward the war against Japan. Harry Truman had given Japan a lot of thought and deemed only unconditional surrender acceptable.

Most Americans believed that Pearl Harbor and Japanese atrocities against American prisoners of war (POWs) had yet to be atoned for. American POWs who survived the Philippines and other islands told horrible stories of cruelty and suffering, fueling the anti-Japanese sentiment. Truman had made his decision. He spoke to the Japanese people by short-wave radio with a clear statement of the American government's position: Surrender unconditionally or be wiped out.

During the months of June and July 1945, with utmost secrecy, civilian, scientific, and military personnel met to consider the future of the atomic bomb. The debate was heated. Some of the scientists were trying to block its use, and some felt Japan should be pre-warned. Others suggested that a public demonstration of the power of the bomb might suffice. Still others felt it wasn't needed and that the Japanese would surrender without its use. On July 16, 1945, the world's first atomic explosive was set off at Alamogordo, New Mexico. Shortly thereafter, the first atomic bomb was loaded aboard the Fifth Fleet Flagship, the U.S.S. *Indianapolis*. The ship carried the bomb from San Francisco to the Marianas Islands.

Secretary of War Stinson felt that a tremendous blow still had to be dealt to the Japanese military in order to save millions of lives. General Groves had selected four prospective targets: Kokura, Hiroshima, Nagasaki, and Kyoto.

The military faction of the Manhattan Project still felt there was no proof the atomic bomb would work, so plans for the invasion of Japan were to continue under the code names Olympic and Coronet. Olympic called for the initial invasion against the southern part of Japan—Kyushu on November 1, 1945, with 815,000 troops participating. Coronet was the plan for invasion of Honshu, in the Tokyo area, with a contingent of more than one million American men. Scuttlebutt was that battleships, cruisers, escort carriers, and the *Kula Gulf* 108, with Night Air Group 63, were to participate in the Tokyo invasion.

In June 1945, General Curtis LeMay was told that part of North Field on Tinian would be taken over to house a special bombing group. The man chosen to drop the first atomic bomb was Lieutenant-Colonel Paul Tibbets, one of America's best bomber pilots. He had flown General Dwight D. Eisenhower and General Mark Clark to Gibraltar to plan the Allied Invasion of North Africa. He also led the first American raid on North Africa and was involved with the flight testing of the B-29 Superfortress. Colonel Tibbets was an outstanding pilot willing to take great risks to defend his country. His pilots and air crewmen were to be completely isolated from the other groups on Tinian, and when they arrived word spread that something big was up.

"I hear something is cooking over at North Field," said P.G. "Why don't we go over there and have lunch in the army air force dining room? Maybe we can find something out."

"How are we going to do that?" asked Chuck.

"We'll fly there and exchange our old movies for theirs," said P.G. "I'll talk to the skipper."

"Okay," said Domkowski. "Count me in. I have a flying buddy over there, too. He's a bombardier on one of those Superfortresses and he might know something."

The next day the three pilots flew to North Field. They arranged to have lunch with Domkowski's friend, Captain Frank Donahue.

"What the fuck is going on over here, Frank?" asked Dom. "My bones tell me something's brewing, and it ain't coffee."

"I don't know, but it's something big, whatever it is," said Donahue. "There's a group at one end of the field who have been isolated from the rest of us. They fly every day but they don't eat with us and they have their own living quarters. Their mail is delivered separately. Everything is hush-hush. There are rumors all over the island. Someone said they invented a light beam that can wipe out a city."

"I don't believe it," said Chuck. "But if they have, when are they going to use it?"

"No way of telling. They fly every day in their own planes and a lot of the brass go down there to see what's going on."

"Well, I hope they really do have something," said Domkowski, "because I'm sick of this fucking war. I don't like getting shot at. Incidentally, one of the movies we traded with you has a weak area in the film. Don't get mad at us. When you see it, you'll know what I mean."

"It's probably the best part of the movie," said Donahue.

"Yeah, it's the part where the girl takes her clothes off," said Chuck smiling. "It's kind of faded and you can't see it too good."

"Thanks a lot!"

On August 6, 1945, with the approval of President Truman, the B-29 Superfortress Enola Gay, named after Colonel Tibbets' mother, dropped the first atomic bomb over Hiroshima, a city of 350,000. When the device went off, four square miles of the city and its inhabitants were completely destroyed within seconds. One-hundred thousand people were killed instantly, and the rest were left to die from radiation exposure. One-third of the casualties were soldiers. Buildings were vaporized. Most of the physicians and nurses in the city were killed. All of the firefighting equipment was destroyed. It would have been useless anyway because of the destruction of the water mains. The heat generated by the blast melted trolley cars, trucks, and railroads.

After the bomb was dropped, the Enola Gay was hit by the shock wave created by the compressed air. The plane and crew were tossed about but survived and then headed for home. The bomb unleashed destruction beyond comprehension and radiation from the cloud would persist for a long time and add to the damage.

When President Truman described the destructive power of the new bomb to the world, many politicians thought it propaganda; the Soviet Union treated the announcement as ordinary news. Very little information concerning the atomic bomb was released in Japan. The Japanese cabinet was told about the bomb, and scientists were selected and sent to Hiroshima to investigate. They were slow to realize its implications.

What it meant for P.G.'s group, however, was quite clear. The enlisted men and officers on Tinian and Saipan, along with the pilots of Night Air Group 63, realized this awesome bomb would hasten the end of the war. P.G. and his cohorts were ecstatic. All the preparations for the invasion of Japan would be scrapped. Millions of American and Japanese lives would be saved, for until the atomic bomb was dropped, many believed the Japanese would fight to the last man.

Although President Truman had given a clear cut warning to the Japanese, they were unwilling to accept the terms of unconditional surrender. Three days after the first, a second bomb was dropped to force their hand—this time on Nagasaki. The pilot was Sweeney flying "Bock's Car," carrying a plutonium bomb. It caused fewer casualties and did less damage than the one dropped on Hiroshima, but the carnage was massive and the message was clear—an unbelievable new weapon was in the hands of the United States. Even after the second atomic bomb, the inner cabinet of the Japanese did not want to surrender. Millions of Japanese soldiers still wanted to fight.

Prime Minister Suzuki felt that Japan would be completely destroyed. He met with Emperor Hirohito and, with his help, convinced the Japanese leaders to agree to unconditional surrender.

Hirohito personally informed his people by radio, and the Japanese surrender was made known to the American public on August 14, 1945. When the announcement came over the radio, wild celebrations took place in the United States. On Saipan, prayers had been answered—enough blood had been shed.

33

Fat Lady Sings

The American troops on Saipan were among the first to know about the atomic bomb drop. The Enola Gay, flying from the island next door, had returned there after the mission. Rumors travel almost as fast as short-wave radio, and within minutes of the plane's landing, news of the successful bomb drop became known.

P.G., Chuck, and Domkowski were playing cards in the hangar at the airfield, waiting for flights late that afternoon, when they heard what happened. The news was intercepted by the control tower at the airport. Most of the flights were canceled immediately and joyous bedlam prevailed.

Chuck commandeered a Jeep from the transport pool that had belonged to a marine colonel who had been transferred back to the States. He quickly removed all identification from the vehicle so they wouldn't be nailed for stealing it. "The shrimp's up to his old tricks again, trying to get us into trouble. He's really incorrigible, you know," Dom said to P.G. as they sped toward the Officer's Club.

Chuck was the only one not flying that night, and had made a date with Molly Martin, one of the navy nurses at the base hospital. She was to meet him at the Officer's Club at 6:30. Peter and Dom figured they'd play it like they always did with Chuck—fast and loose.

Shore Patrol, along with their German shepherds, were still patrolling the beaches, and Combat Air Patrol was still flying. The number of flights had been decreased however, because it was felt that the Japanese would soon agree to surrender. All the pilots still carried their sidearms, .38-caliber Smith and Wesson pistols.

The chef at the Officer's Club had made up plates of hors d'oeuvres, and when the pilots got there the revelry, singing, and drinking was going full force. Chuck was the only one who wasn't drinking. He wanted to stay sober for Molly, he said, and P.G. and Dom raised their eyebrows and exchanged looks.

Molly was a Lieutenant in the Nurse Corps and was in charge of the base hospital's recovery room. She was very pretty, petite, and well built. It was obvious she was working on Chuck. P.G. and Domkowski noticed that he was combing his hair more often. The beard was gone, although there was still a cookie duster above his lip. The gleam in his eye was still there, particularly when Molly was around.

Domkowski remarked one day: "Chuck, P.G., and I are not quite ready to make this group a foursome."

"Our relationship is strictly platonic," said Chuck.

"I'll bet it is," said P.G. "Why are you throwing all that cologne on your face?"

"So I don't have to smell you guys," said Chuck.

P.G. and Dom raised their arms in a gesture and gave a good sniff under their armpits.

"Well, she certainly is cute," said Domkowski. "How the hell tall is she anyway?"

"About five feet."

"She's too short for me," said Dom.

A five-piece band was playing. "Happy Days Are Here Again" was being sung, along with a few other sing-along songs like "Row, Row, Row Your Boat," and occasionally a dirty ditty. The pall of death and tragedy the men had lived under for so long was being vanquished as booze flowed and music played. P.G. felt himself retreating inwardly as he thought of Sarah.

A group of nurses arrived from the base hospital. Not all of them were dressed in their uniforms. Some had put on high heels and dresses. Molly was in the group, looking sharp. There was a lot of whistling and hooting. Chuck told Dom and P.G. he was taking the Jeep and they'd have to find some other way of getting back to the barracks.

"Where you going?" asked P.G.

"It's none of your business. Molly and I are going to really celebrate."

"Yeah," said Domkowski, "you're going to try to ring the bell."

"Bullshit! Molly's not like the others. She's a nice girl."

"Nice? Hey, my *mom's* nice. That girl is *ready!*" said Domkowski.

"You're just jealous," said Chuck.

"Well, if she were a foot taller, I'd give you some competition."

Chuck and Molly took off in the Jeep. Chuck had brought along a blanket from the barracks. He drove the Jeep along the coastline highway to an isolated beach. The night was perfect for making love. He parked the Jeep and then spread the blanket near some bushes, so they couldn't be seen. It was obvious Molly was ready to accept his advances. In fact, she had some permanent plans in mind for him. He fondled her gently as she responded to his kisses.

"Oh, Chuck, I could easily fall in love with you," she said.

"I think I could with you too, Molly." It was a moonlit night and the temperature was in the mid seventies. They rolled together on the blanket as she responded to his advances.

Suddenly, Molly became rigid. "Chuck, there's somebody in the bushes over there," she whispered.

He looked and sensed motion in the darkness. He had already taken his belt and trousers off. He reached for his revolver. It had fallen out of the holster and he couldn't find it.

"Molly," he whispered, "I want you to get up slowly and run down the beach as fast as you can. Once you get down there, start hollering. Move. Do it. Now!"

The dark figure emerged from the bushes and started to come closer.

"I'm not leaving," said Molly.

"Do what I say," said Chuck. "It's our only chance." He saw a knife gleam in the moonlight as the figure came closer. "I can't find my sidearm," said Chuck, as he felt around in the sand for the gun. "Go now," he growled.

He stood up between the darkened figure and Molly. Molly got up and ran down the beach. He heard her screaming in the distance.

The assailant suddenly ran toward him, the knife held high above his head. Chuck grabbed a handful of sand and threw it at his face. He then drove his shoulder into the stomach of his attacker and pushed forward, his legs pumping.

Chuck felt the knife hit his left shoulder. He tried to grab it out of his assailant's hands as they went down in the sand. Chuck rolled away from him. The Jap came back at him. Chuck tried to kick him in the balls. There was a big grunt as he partially succeeded. The Jap grabbed Chuck's leg and Chuck went down. The knife blade flashed and Chuck felt his skin split open high on his right arm. He screamed with pain.

Molly was screaming too, in panic, as she ran down the beach. She finally ran into the Marine Shore Patrol. "There's a Jap up there trying to kill my boyfriend," she gasped.

The marine sentries released two attack dogs and they took off in Chuck's direction.

Chuck was in big trouble. He scrambled away from the Jap. The man lunged, reaching out with the knife. Chuck rolled backward, out of reach, his heart pounding. The man advanced again in a crouch, the blade outstretched. Chuck staggered backwards and fell to the ground. The man jumped on him and stabbed him in the chest. Chuck collapsed. He knew he was going to die. The man stood above him holding the knife, ready to strike again.

Just then the two dogs arrived and leaped on the assailant. The Japanese slashed at one of the dogs as the other tore into his knee. He injured the second dog, then took off into the bushes, bleeding. The dogs went after him. He fell and the shepherds started tearing him to pieces.

When Molly and the two marines arrived, Chuck was in a pool of blood, gasping for air. He was barely conscious. One of the marines called out a command and the dogs backed off. The marine shot his Colt .45 at the assailant, emptying his revolver.

"You all right, Molly?" Chuck gasped.

"Yes, Chuck." She saw the stab wound in his chest, sucking air. She quickly removed one of her silk stockings and pushed it against the hole in his chest. There was blood all over the place. He was coughing up blood.

"One of you guys go get the Jeep on the road," she hollered to the marines.

Chuck was getting cold and clammy.

"Chuck, hold on!" she screamed.

"Thirsty," wheezed Chuck.

The other marine looked on, helpless. The Jeep finally arrived. The marines lifted Chuck and put him in the back while Molly compressed the hole in his chest. She knew she had to prevent air from getting into his chest and collapsing his lungs. The marine slammed the accelerator to the floor as they raced down the highway to the base hospital.

"Hurry! Drive as fast as you can!" yelled Molly. "I hope all the doctors aren't out celebrating and getting drunk."

They pulled into the hospital's emergency entrance as one of the nurses dashed out to meet them.

"Chest wound, stab wound!" screamed Molly as they rushed Chuck inside.

He was slipping away, going into shock. The ride from the beach had increased his bleeding.

"Get a cut-down set and a chest tube!" hollered Molly. "Who's on call?"

"Dr. Jones. He's in the house."

"Get him—*now*. Stat!" said Molly. Jones was a chest surgeon. He'd know how to stop the bleeding. He had a good reputation.

Over the loudspeaker came the call, "Dr. Jones, Dr. Jones, Emergency Room, stat!"

Jones was nearby and came running down the hallway to the emergency room.

Chuck was fading. His blood pressure was way down and his color was bad. He was gasping for air, and blood was running from his mouth. One of the nurses was trying to suction it while giving him nasal oxygen.

"Chest tube," Jones shouted. Molly handed it to him and he quickly put the tube into Chuck's chest through the stab wound and hooked it up to underwater suction. A lot of air and blood came out of the tube as Chuck's lung slowly started to expand. His breathing improved. Jones pulled the chest tube taut against the wound to help stop the bleeding.

"Call the Officer's Club and get the anesthesiologist and Dr. Moran to assist me," said Jones. "Get on the hotline. We're going to have to go in to see where he's bleeding from. Alert the blood bank that we'll need six pints of O negative."

Chuck's main injuries were stab wounds to his left upper chest and the left side of his neck. He also had a minor wound high on his right arm. Cut-downs were put in place in his veins in both arms and blood and plasma pumped in rapidly. His blood pressure slowly improved, although his pulse was rapid and continued to run around 180.

"Where the hell is that anesthesiologist?" hollered Jones.

"We found him. He's on his way."

"Give Chuck massive doses of intravenous antibiotics," said Jones. "Now!"

The nurses quickly injected penicillin into the intravenous tubing. Chuck was wheeled to the operating room, and a large chest incision was rapidly made. Rib retractors were put in place by Dr. Jones to get better exposure. The anesthesiologist pumped three or four units of blood into his veins, while Jones sucked the blood out of Chuck's chest. The left upper lobe of the lung was completely collapsed, and a constant flow of blood was coming from the area. "I'm going to remove his left upper lung," said Jones as he clamped the air tube to the lung. He quickly oversewed the stump with silk sutures. After the upper lobe was removed, he could now see where all the bleeding was coming from. The left subclavian vein in the chest had a big hole in it. Jones irrigated the area with sterile saline and decided to oversew it. He took about 30 seconds to sew up the hole. Molly looked on in amazement. The only sign of stress Jones showed was in his jaw. It was clenched tight.

The chest bleeding stopped. "Stick a Foley catheter into him," said Jones. "We're going to have to monitor his output."

"He doesn't have much urine," said the anesthesiologist.

"Push the fluids. What's his hematocrit doing?"

"It's 23."

"It's still low. Give him another two units of blood," said Jones. "Is he still bleeding from his mouth?"

"No, but he's got a lot of blood-tinged mucus," reported the anesthesiologist.

"We're going to trach him when we get through closing the thoracotomy wound," said Jones. "Get a trach tube. We need to keep his airway clear."

Chuck's blood pressure slowly started to come back. His urinary output was poor. They got him off the operating table. He didn't look good and didn't respond, although his blood pressure and respiration were returning to normal. His pulse was still rapid.

Molly and Dr. Jones stayed with him all night in the recovery room. He continued to have a poor urinary output. Jones was afraid he wouldn't make it. He was worried that Chuck was going into kidney shutdown, something he could not prevent.

"When he was in shock, he probably didn't have enough blood flowing through his kidneys to make them function properly," said Jones. "We have to wait and watch."

The next morning, P.G. and Domkowski heard about the attack. They drove to the hospital and found Molly.

"Molly, what happened?" asked Peter.

"Chuck was stabbed by a Jap who didn't know the war might be over," said Molly. "He may be dying," she cried. "He's still unconscious, and he's not putting out much urine. Oh, God! Why did this have to happen?" she said blankly. There was blood streaked over her blouse. She stared at the floor. P.G. decided not to press her for details.

"We'll just have to hope for the best, Molly," said Dom.

During the next 72 hours, P.G. and Dom kept a vigil outside Chuck's room. Molly never left. She suctioned the mucous out of his tracheotomy to keep his airway clear and rubbed his legs and back, constantly talking to him. "Chuck, you've got to wake up. Do it for me! Do it for P.G. and Dom. But do it," she hollered into his ears, trying to reach him.

His urine output continued to be sparse. It seemed to be concentrated. He remained in a coma. His blood pressure, pulse, and respiration seemed to return to normal, although he had a sharp temperature rise the day after his surgery. He had been given as much antibiotics as he could tolerate.

"Put some booze in his intravenous and I bet he'll wake up," said Domkowski.

"That'll kill him," said Jones flatly.

"What's the big problem, Doc?" asked P.G.

"Well, when he was stabbed and lost all that blood, his body went into shock. He lost so much blood there wasn't enough to go to his brain. There also wasn't enough to go to his kidneys. The kidneys were damaged and have stopped functioning. He could also be brain dead," said Jones.

"Impossible," said Domkowski. "His brain is preserved in alcohol."

"What can we do?" asked P.G.

"Pray that his kidneys open up," said Jones. "In some ways he's lucky. The stab wound didn't get him in the heart."

"I'll tell you smart guys something," said Domkowski. "The shrimp's going to make it and his kidneys are going to open up. Anybody who can win a pissing contest on Mog Mog will start pissing if anyone can. Trust me."

"I hope you're right," said Jones. "He's only putting out a shot glass full of concentrated urine every eight hours now. We're going to give him a special intravenous cocktail tonight that some kidney specialist in Guam has radioed in. We've got nothing to lose."

"Cocktail . . . now you're on the right track," said Dom. But P.G. didn't see any hope. First Sarah, now Chuck.

"Keep working on that little guy!" said Domkowski.

P.G. and Dom fell asleep in the waiting room on hospital couches. When they awoke the next morning, they shared a sullen breakfast and went back to the recovery room. Molly was waiting for them. She had on fresh clothes and a big smile.

"He's up. Chuck woke up this morning," she said, "and he's pissing up a storm."

P.G. and Dom hugged and slapped each other on the back. "I told you he would," said Domkowski. "The shrimp is tougher than a dozen Japs."

"He wants to see you guys but you can't stay too long. He's going to make it," Molly said with tears in her eyes.

When they saw Chuck he still looked pale but had a sheepish grin on his face. He put his finger over his trach so he could talk and said, "No animals allowed."

"Then what the hell are you doing here?" answered Domkowski.

"How do you feel?" asked P.G.

"Lousy. I got tubes sticking out of every orifice except my rear end."

Dr. Jones arrived. "We're going to have to ambulate this guy to get his legs in shape, Molly."

"I know, Doctor. I plan to ambulate his whole body when he's up to it." Jones smiled for the first time since the ordeal began.

After four weeks of TLC by Molly, Chuck walked out of the hospital. His flying days were over for a while because the nerves in his neck had been injured by the stab wounds and he was given priority to return to the States. Molly was able to work it out so she could accompany him.

They left on a navy air transport on a sunny Wednesday. Peter and Dom saw them off. They all exchanged addresses.

"Well, what do you know," said Dom to Peter as the plane was loaded. "The shrimp is leaving us in the middle of a job half done."

"Yeah," said Peter. "Somehow I expected more out. . . ."

". . . listen, shitbirds," Chuck cut in. "Two things. One, this job is about seven-eighths done and if you two can't put the finishing touches on it without me around to help you, then the navy should turn you both over to the Japs. In fact, I wish I'd thought of that before. It probably could've ended the war a year ago."

P.G., Dom, and Molly sputtered into laughter as Chuck continued the assault. A month of bed rest had recharged his batteries.

"The other thing is that I'm thankful as hell to be grounded. The goddamned skies aren't safe with either of you numb nuts up there. I'm going home. And it's going to be a welcome change from watching you guys birddog girls and having to bail you both out of bar brawls when you piss off their boyfriends."

Peter and Dom were doubled over, laughing. Chuck was deadpan. Molly turned to him and said, "Sweetheart, together these two guys are about four times your size, couldn't they defend themselves?"

"Not a lick," said Chuck, as Peter and Dom wiped their eyes. They stood awkwardly for a moment. This was it. No more birddogging girls, no more cards, no more flying together.

"Shit," said P.G., and threw his arms around Chuck and Molly. Dom wrapped his enormous wingspan around all of them, and they swayed together on the airstrip, no one saying a word.

P.G. and Dom were reassigned to the U.S.S. *Block Island* with Air Group 63. There was still some peacetime work to be done in the Pacific for some of the pilots. They weren't going home yet.

34

End of Hostilities

On August 9, 1945, after the bomb was dropped on Nagasaki, a meeting of the Japanese Imperial Conference was called with Emperor Hirohito presiding. Premier Suzuki, Foreign Minister Togo, Army Chief of Staff Umezu, and Navy Chief of Staff Toyoda were also present.

Emperor Hirohito got up and spoke: "I have given serious thought to the situation at home and abroad, and I have concluded that continuing the war can only mean destruction for our nation and a prolongation of bloodshed and cruelty for the world. I don't want to see my innocent people suffer. Our country is being totally destroyed. Ending the war is the only way to restore world peace and to relieve our nation from the dreadful distress with which it is burdened."

After the Emperor spoke at length the delegates filed out of the air raid shelter where the meeting was held. An emergency cabinet meeting was called and the cabinet unanimously accepted the Emperor's advice to accept the Potsdam Declaration and surrender unconditionally.

The telegram accepting the Potsdam Declaration was sent from the foreign office in Tokyo on August 10, 1945, but it had a proviso that the Emperor would still rule as a sovereign ruler.

When the telegram was received by the United States and studied by President Truman, Secretary of State Byrnes, and others, a reply was sent via San Francisco radio: "From the moment of surrender, the authority of the Emperor and the Japanese Government to rule the state shall be subject to the Supreme Commander of the Allied Powers. The ultimate form of government of Japan shall, in accordance with the Potsdam Declaration, be established by the freely expressed will of the Japanese people."

This last statement disturbed Foreign Minister Togo and the Japanese military, and on August 14, a second meeting of the cabinet and Supreme War Direction Council was called with Emperor Hirohito. Hirohito spoke again: "I have studied the terms of the allied reply and I conclude that they constitute a virtually complete acknowledgment of the position we maintain in the note dispatched some days ago. In short, I consider the reply to be acceptable."

After this second meeting, it was decided by the Japanese cabinet to accept the conditions as stated by the United States Government and its allies.

Just before noon on August 15, 1945, the Japanese people heard their Emperor speak over the radio for the first time. He told them the war was over. When he concluded, many of the Japanese war leaders committed hari-kari, rather than be indicted as war criminals.

President Truman told the secretaries of the navy and army that the signing of the unconditional surrender would take place on the deck of the battleship U.S.S. *Missouri*. When the battleship *Missouri* was christened, Harry Truman was the principal speaker and Margaret, his daughter, broke the bottle of champagne across the bow. At the end of August, the U.S.S. *Missouri* was instructed to enter Tokyo Bay, just off Yokosuka Naval Base, and the surrender was to take place on board on September 2, 1945. Some American military leaders were apprehensive about the ship entering Tokyo Bay because the bay was laden with extensive mine fields. Many of the American leaders still did not trust the Japanese because of the surprise attack on Pearl Harbor. No chances were taken. Four American minesweepers, the *Revenge, Token, Tumult,* and *Pochard* were the first ships to enter Tokyo Bay before the signing. It was a dangerous undertaking, and there was a lot of apprehension aboard the minesweepers.

In this operation, a minesweeper's cables are set out behind the ship to cut the cables anchoring the mines, so they will float free. A patrol boat following astern spots the mines and fires at them until they explode. Sometimes, when the cables tangle, the sweeper pulls in the lines and a live mine is snarled on the end. The captain then orders all the men to the front of the minesweeper, and they try zigzagging to work the mine free. This seldom works, and the cables are then cut.

American submarines knew where most of the mines were but some feared Japanese fanatics might try to blow up the *Missouri* with kamikaze submarines, or that the ship might take fire from land-based snipers.

The surrender ceremony was to be broadcast throughout the battleship *Missouri* and relayed back to the United States. General Douglas MacArthur would accept the surrender for the United States, and Prime Minister Shigemitsu would sign as representative of the Japanese Empire. Admiral Nimitz would be the senior naval officer present and would sign as the official United States representative.

The surrender went without a hitch, and as the ceremony concluded, a squadron of United States planes flew over the ship in victory.

When the first American troops arrived in Japan on August 26, Japanese families were extremely anxious. Mothers who could afford it packed their daughters off to the country or told them to go into hiding. Their fears were slowly assuaged by the friendliness of the American troops. Soon they were accepting American cigarettes and eating chocolate. The fate of Emperor Hirohito, however, was still in question. He was not sure whether his dynasty would remain or what his fate would be.

When General MacArthur arrived in Tokyo he resolved that no individual, party, or monarch would interfere with his plans for the occupation of Japan. He felt that Emperor Hirohito should come to him. On September 26, the Emperor made arrangements to go to General MacArthur. The meeting was described as cordial. Mac-Arthur dominated the conversation, but the ice had been broken.

With the end of hostilities, the problem of returning equipment and men to the States had to be addressed. Many army units, marine divisions, naval vessels, and tremendous amounts of equipment had to be either destroyed or shipped back. Three million men had to be returned stateside and reacquainted with civilian life. The navy played a big role in this regard. Many of the CVE escort carriers were used in the operation—called "Magic Carpet"—to get all the marines, soldiers, and sailors back to the States.

Unfortunately, Dom's and P.G.'s unit, Night Air Group 63, still had some important duties to perform and would not return to the States until December 1945. This delay interfered with Peter's plans, because it prevented him from returning to college for the spring semester. The group was assigned to the U.S.S. *Block Island* CVE 106 in early September. The ship was directed to sail to Formosa to pick up American prisoners of war. Most of the POWs they would pick up had been captured by the Japanese at Singapore or in the Philippines and were in terrible physical shape.

The TBF pilots did most of the work. Stretchers were put in the back of the planes, so that two or three POWs could be flown back to the carriers and then transported to hospital ships. The captives had been in concentration camps and suffered from severe malnutrition; some weighed less than 70 pounds. They were too weak to walk and couldn't talk above a whisper. There was a lot of anxiety about picking them up and the fighter pilots flew cover flights over the area to make sure there was no treachery. The prisoners were pitifully emaciated and sick with all sorts of diseases. The well-fed Japanese guards who surrendered themselves infuriated the Americans.

Some of the stories the prisoners told about the atrocities committed by the Japanese made the fliers sick. War was hell, this was accepted, but there were various ways to wage war. The marines and navy did not respect the combat methods of the Japanese and when the war ended, a persistent hate remained in the hearts of those who had fought against them.

One day, when the planes went in to pick up some POWs, a stick-figure clad in rags emerged from the compound. He was a six-foot-three former marine officer. He kept pointing to one of the Japanese guards at the camp. In a whisper he said, "Arrest that guard. He was detestable and he killed many American prisoners."

The marine officer in charge looked at his fellow marine and his face hardened as he fought to control his emotions. "Don't worry, let's get you out of here first," he said.

"I want him arrested," insisted the marine prisoner. "He's carrying a pouch around his waist. Look at it, please. You'll know what I mean when you see it."

The officer in charge went to the guard and asked for the leather pouch. An armed marine accompanied him, his Colt .45 drawn and cocked. The Japanese guard would not give up the pouch. The marine grabbed it and pulled it off his waist. He opened it and found a collection of gold-filled teeth that he had accumulated from the prisoners in the camp. He'd taken the prisoners aside when they entered the camp, and if they had gold fillings, he pulled the teeth without any anesthetic and put them in the pouch. Some of those prisoners died from severe infections.

The officer in charge told the marine sergeant to take care of the problem. A short walk was taken. A shot rang out. There would be no more gold teeth pulled from the mouths of American prisoners by that guard.

After picking up the prisoners of war in the camp and getting them medical attention, the air group was detached from the *Block Island* and returned to the States in December 1945.

Dom and P.G. had one final night together when their ship put in at San Diego harbor. They decided to go out for a few drinks to officially celebrate the end of the war. At an outdoor restaurant near Pacific Beach, they ordered shrimp in honor of Chuck and as they drank beer after beer, they swapped memories.

They recalled flight school and their first times aloft. They thought of all the women they'd met and tried to pick up. Peter thought about Sarah. At times they lapsed into silence with the weight of their experiences on their minds. As they recalled the attack on the *Saratoga*, Dom explained what he had seen from the air and Peter told him what it was like on the deck: the chaos, the blood, and the cold, stiff bodies he'd tried to take below.

The next morning they exchanged addresses and went to the airport. Dom was heading home.

Peter was declared essential to the Naval Air Corps and would remain in the service for an additional six months. He was dispatched to BuPers (Bureau of Personnel) in Washington, D.C., for assignment to further flight duty. The Navy Department was eager to keep some of its night-carrier pilots in the service.

When he checked into BuPers, he had to go through the Personnel Assignment Division, where there was a WAVE chief petty officer named Rebecca Parsons.

Rebecca was an attractive brunette with a nice smile and an outgoing personality. She struck up a conversation with P.G. "Lieutenant, I've looked at your war record, and there are quite a few billets that you could be assigned to. Wouldn't you like to stay in Washington for awhile?" she asked with a big smile on her face. "Do you have a place to stay yet?" Her questions were professional but her manner was personal.

"No," said P.G. "But three of my buddies are here, and we plan to get an apartment together."

"Well, we have a housing department that will tell you where to look," she said. "Report back to me tomorrow morning. I'll probably have an assignment for you by then."

The next day, when P.G. reported to Chief Petty Officer Parsons, she said, "There's an opening for an assistant to the Admiral's Board that's selecting the admirals and captains who will remain in the peacetime navy. If you're interested, I can arrange for you to have a temporary assignment to the job. You would be assigned to Admiral McMorris's Board," she explained. "One of your jobs would be to pick up confidential and secret records with marine guards at the Judge Advocate General's Office. This information will be used in considering the candidates. Another part of the job would be to fly members of the Board around the country if necessary. You'd receive flight pay, per diem, and meet a lot of high-ranking naval officers. Another job might be opening later at the Patuxent Naval Air Test Center in Maryland. Besides, I think you'll like Washington," she said. There was that smile again. "There's a lot of interesting things to do in this town and a lot of people to meet."

"What do you think I should do?"

"I think you should take the job with the Admiral's Board."

"Glad to have an advisor," said Peter, "and it sounds like good advice. I'm a little tired of shooting at people. I'd like to meet some for a change." P.G. noticed her beautiful face and smile. Her uniform appeared to confine an interesting figure. It was obvious the uniform didn't flatter her. Once he got settled, he would strongly consider looking her up.

The next weekend he and two of his flying buddies decided to go into town to see what Washington was like. Saturday afternoon they were walking through Woodward and Lathrop's, a department store, when they saw two beautiful girls in high heels. P.G. thought he recognized one of them but he wasn't sure. "Hey, I've seen that doll somewhere before," he said.

"Yeah, in your dreams," said Tex, one of the pilots.

Peter wasn't sure, and he started to walk over to say something to her. She and her girlfriend quickly turned around and took off in a hurry. The three pilots followed the two girls as they went into Garfinkel's Department Store, but eventually lost them when the girls hailed a cab and disappeared. "P.G., if you did know that girl, she didn't seem to want to know you," said Tex.

On Monday morning, when he checked into BuPers, he immediately realized who the girl had been; it was Chief Petty Officer Rebecca Parsons wearing civilian clothes.

"I want to talk to you," said P.G. She had a big smile on her face again. "How about having lunch with me?"

"I'd love to," she said. "Pick me up at 11:30."

"See you then."

They took a cab to a small restaurant called Hammell's. The food was excellent. She told him that a lot of senators and representatives had their lunches there.

"You know, I thought you might report me because I was out of uniform," she said. "We're still in the navy, you know."

"Not a chance," he said. "But maybe I ought to."

Rebecca held his gaze. "Well, Lieutenant, how can I make it up to you?"

"Well, I'll make a deal with you. If you'll go out with me tonight, I won't report you."

"Subterfuge," she said, laughing. "But I'll take the date. Pick me up at 7:00. Is it for dinner?" she asked.

"Dinner, wine, song, my impression of General MacArthur, anything you like."

"Do you do Winston Churchill?"

"Yes, but I'll have to smoke a cigar."

"In that case let's forget Churchill and stick to dinner, wine, and song." Rebecca then wrote her address and phone number on a slip of paper.

"Okay," said Peter. "See you at 7:00."

That evening he took a cab to the address she'd given him. She lived in a fancy apartment on Connecticut Avenue that was well furnished and obviously quite expensive. Her roommate wasn't in.

She was wearing a beautiful gray suit with black high heels and looked very pretty. "You look gorgeous," he said. He took her hands in his and pulled her to him. She turned her head to one side and looked down.

"Not quite so fast," she said. "I hardly know you."

"You're right," he said. "Maybe I'm rushing things. That's what dinner and wine are for."

"What kind of food do you like? Washington's expensive, you know."

"I know nothing about Washington, D.C. I love any food that isn't standard navy issue. I've been at sea for a long time, and my bank account is full. Price is no object. Lead the way."

"I think I'll take you to the raw bar at the Wardman Park down the street," she said. "They have a piano player in the cocktail lounge. We can talk there, and then we can decide where to eat later."

"When you say 'raw bar' I assume you mean one with topless dancers," said Peter.

"Not quite," she said. "Although the clams, oysters, and shrimp are topless."

"Disappointing, but probably better for the appetite. I'm starving."

They each had a couple of glasses of wine and the conversation flowed as readily as the chablis. Peter caught himself feeling guilty. "My God," he thought, "I'm enjoying myself with a woman other than Sarah." But he didn't dwell on his loss; Rebecca was someone new and interesting and he wanted to get to know her better.

Peter finally said, "If we keep drinking wine I'm going to go face-down onto the table, and I don't think you want to carry me home."

"You're right," she said. "Let's go to the Blue Room at the Shoreham. It's right next to the Wardman Park."

"Okay, I'll follow you anywhere."

"Hmmm," she said. "I'll have to think about that one."

While they were eating, many questions were asked and answered. He found out that Rebecca was from Kansas City and that her father was a dentist.

"Ah," said P.G. "That explains the incredible wattage of that smile."

"Braces. My dad insisted. Five years of tinsel teeth. It wasn't fun, but I'm glad for it now," she replied, as her smile got even bigger. "Do you have a steady girlfriend?"

"Well, you are direct, I'll say that," said P.G. He paused and looked at his dinner. "I did at one time, but she was killed in an auto accident a year ago."

"I'm sorry," said Rebecca.

"Not your doing," said P.G.

"Of course not," she said. "I just meant that it's regrettable, and that I feel for you."

"Thanks. And *I'm* sorry. I'm still a little brittle about it all. The irony of me surviving the war and Sarah being killed is still tough to make sense out of."

After they had finished the meal, a small band came onto the bandstand. They had three or four dances together, moving easily, seeing how their bodies fit together. "I love to dance," said Rebecca, "and by the way, all my friends call me Becky."

"Becky," he said, trying it out. "Becky, Becky . . . do you believe that how two people dance together is an indication of how they'll make love?"

"Yes, I do," she said. "But I believe strongly that lovemaking should be done with one's clothes removed." They laughed together as they held each other.

Around midnight they walked back to Becky's apartment. It was only two or three blocks from the Shoreham Hotel, and a temperate breeze blew, pushing Becky's hair from her forehead.

When they got to the door of her apartment, he spun her around and pulled her to him. She didn't resist this time, and he planted a full, warm kiss on her mouth. "You know, Lieutenant, I'm not doing anything this weekend," she said.

"Great," said P.G. "Let's start the weekend right now. Can I come into your apartment?"

"Not tonight, sweetness, we'll save it for later." Then she held his face in her hands and kissed him on each cheek, then full on his lips as he pulled her to him and gave her a big hug. She disappeared inside her apartment. Peter whistled his way down the hall, thinking, "Hey, I'm back."

35

The Admiral's Wife

When P.G. reported to Admiral McMorris' Selection Board at the beginning of the week, he was impressed by the amount of military brass in the office. Besides the chairman, the Board was comprised of vice-admirals, rear-admirals, and commodores. The Board was convened to select those members of the navy who would be allowed to stay in the service with the rank of captain after World War II. With the rapid expansion of the naval service during the war, the navy had too many flag officers and captains at the top. Many would be asked to retire. Rebecca had arranged for P.G. to serve as a junior recorder for the Naval Selection Board. Besides P.G., the officers and enlisted men who made up the staff were a lieutenant-commander, a chief warrant officer, a chief petty officer, and four WAVE secretaries.

P.G.'s main job was to make sure the records of the officers being considered were in proper order. The picture of the candidate would be on the top of the file in the folder. The photographs varied: some were just pictures of faces, others were head-to-toe pictures. Underneath the picture was a summary of the officer's various tours of duty, including the bases he worked at and ships he served on. The rank that the officer had achieved in each job was in his file, with comments and grades given by his commanding officers. Letters from senators, representatives, and cabinet officers were also included, as well as medals received and letters of commendation.

Not all the records were complimentary. In fact, he noticed that many of them contained reprimands; these ranged anywhere from insubordination to abuse of power. He also found that not everyone earned their way to the top. Some files contained letters from very successful and influential politicians. P.G.'s eyes were beginning to be opened to the fact that it's not always what you do, but rather who you know.

He was frequently sent to the judge advocate general's office for records and when he went he was accompanied by two armed marine sergeants. Some of these records were interesting to look at and review; they were stamped confidential, secret, or top secret. A cursory glance revealed that some senior naval and marine officers, like civilians, succumbed to everyday vices. Drugs played a role in the disaster of some potential admirals and sex, either normal or aberrant, was not unusual and caused the downfall of many potential leaders.

A navy captain in the medical corps in the Hawaii area had three navy nurses taking care of him. They were not only giving him daily massages, but they were also giving him all sorts of strange sexual treatments along with drugs—until one of the nurses got pregnant and blew the whistle. The captain tried to hush the whole thing up and arrange for her to have an abortion. Unfortunately, he told his wife about the situation and was later caught in the act of performing the abortion.

In Jacksonville, a prominent navy officer was involved with a stable of homosexual men. What better place to have a harem of men than in the navy? Out at sea, the crew was not co-ed, and their libido had to be taken care of in one way or another. Saltpeter didn't always help. Betty Grable's or Lana Turner's picture on a calendar in a bathing suit would take care of a man for a short period of time and conjured up interesting dreams, but was not the answer to the problem. It wasn't long before the stable was virtually destroyed when one of the sailors acquired a serious venereal disease and was generous in passing it along to the entire group. Treatment for venereal disease was primitive in the 1940s but sometimes it worked. Potent shots of bismuth and arsenical compounds were injected in the rear end, and penicillin was tried for the first time. The guilty parties eventually owned up to their indiscretions; this became part of their record and generally didn't help them get promoted.

Sometimes, senior officers would goof up on the job at sea and bang up their ships, resulting in a reprimand that would become part of their record. When the sea is rough and a storm is brewing, it's the captain's decision either to anchor outside a bay area or take a pilot aboard. If the ship runs aground or is damaged hooking up to the dock, the captain is responsible, not the pilot. Some channels can be treacherous for the big ships, which mandates that the captain always be on the bridge.

Becky had warned P.G. not to get involved with any of the officers whose credentials were being considered. One day, as he arrived for work, a navy captain was waiting for him in the office. "Lieutenant, I'd like to have lunch with you to discuss an important matter."

P.G. recognized the implications of the conversation and said, "Is it about your record?"

"Yes," said the captain.

A red flag went up in his mind, and Peter thought, "Thanks, Becky."

"Whatever you wish to discuss with me, you can discuss right here," he said.

"I wish to discuss it in private," he replied.

"Okay, we'll go sit on that bench over there," said P.G.

When they got into the corner, the captain said, "I'd like you to change the order of the material in my record."

"Sorry," said P.G. "I'm not exceptionally bright. Explain what you mean."

"Well, it's just that I have a reprimand in my record—a misunderstanding, really—and I wish to have it put on the bottom of the file."

"Captain, let's have no misunderstanding here. Do you realize what would happen to you if I report this to the Board?"

"I want a fair shot at being an admiral someday," he said.

"Well, with what you're doing, I'm not so sure that you're admiral material. Nor do I consider what you're suggesting to be fair. I'll forget this conversation if you turn around and walk out of here."

The captain turned and walked away.

That evening, P.G. discussed the incident with Rebecca. "You did the right thing," she said. "But I do feel sorry for some of those guys. I'm not sure they'll all get an even break."

"What do you mean?" he asked.

"Well, the Board is made up of a limited number of admirals and commodores, and if one of them recognizes the name of the candidate, they have a better shot at being selected."

"So the Board, to some degree, sees who and what they want to see."

"Yeah. That's politics," said Becky. "Sometimes if you get the right assignment when you're a captain, you can make admiral. If you get relegated to serve on a barge or some other pissant duty, you're up the creek without a paddle."

The next day the captain's record was discussed by the Board and he was rejected for staying in the navy. An early retirement was in the offing.

One morning, two weeks later, one of the vice-admirals came storming into the board room office. "Who's the officer in charge here?" he asked.

"Commander Hunt," said P.G., "but he's out today. I'm in charge when he's gone."

"Well, Lieutenant, if any phone calls come in for me, I'm not to be disturbed," he said. "Do you understand?"

"Yes, sir," said P.G. as he saluted sharply.

Around 10:30 A.M., the vice-admiral's wife called the office. The chief petty officer took the call.

"Get Vice-Admiral Wycoff to the phone," she screamed, "I have to talk to him right away."

"Is it an emergency?" the chief asked. "The admiral is in the boardroom and he is not to be disturbed."

"You tell him to get his butt out of there," said his wife.

"Please hold," said the chief. He related the conversation to P.G.

"I'll take it," P.G. said. "This is Lieutenant Grant, what can I do for you?" he asked.

"Get my husband out of that boardroom, pronto," she said, "I have to talk to him."

"I'm afraid I can't do that when they're in session," he said. "What's the problem?"

"He took the car with the chauffeur and I need it. It would be healthy for you and your career, Lieutenant, if you get him out of that boardroom and to the phone."

"Hold on," said P.G.

"Chief, put a note in to the lowest-ranking commodore and tell him to pass it along to Vice-Admiral Wycoff. Let's see how far it will travel."

The note was glanced at by the commodore and passed along. They were seated at the board table according to rank. Suddenly, the door shot open and the admiral, steaming, looked P.G. straight in the eye and said, "Lieutenant, I told you not to disturb me. What's the problem?" he asked.

"Your wife is on the phone, sir. She wants to talk to you," he said.

Furious, the admiral snatched up the phone and said, "I'll thank you to respect my . . ." And that was as far as he got. The admiral paused. Then he said, "Yes dear. Yes dear. I understand, dear. I'm sorry, dear. I'll have the car sent over right away." He gently placed the phone in the cradle and turned to P.G. "Lieutenant, are you married?"

"No, sir," said P.G., "but I have someone special."

"Well, Lieutenant, some day, when you get married, you'll understand that rank may have its privileges on the deck of a ship, but at home, all these medals don't add up to a popcorn fart."

"I'll bear that in mind, sir."

36

Cherry Blossom Time

During the next three months, P.G. and Rebecca became inseparable. They ate lunch together every day if navy business didn't interfere. They also spent a great deal of time sightseeing throughout the entire D.C. area. The scenery was gorgeous, and P.G. was particularly impressed with George Washington's former estate, Mount Vernon. His biggest disappointment came when they visited several sessions of the Senate and the House of Representatives. The chambers were half empty. He wondered why soldiers and pilots like himself should put their lives on the line while the people who run the government weren't working full time.

P.G. and Becky climbed to the top of the Washington Monument together and found the view from the top breathtaking. It wasn't a walk they would recommend for everyone. The best part of the climb was that you could see the Lincoln and Jefferson memorials from the top.

"There's a lot of our country's heritage in Washington," said P.G.

"I know," said Rebecca. "If I hadn't enlisted in the service, I wouldn't be seeing it."

"It sounds corny, but seeing all this makes me proud to be an American," said P.G.

As they walked arm-in-arm, they visited the Lincoln Memorial and were moved by the beauty of the tall, magnificent, granite carving. At night the Memorial is even more impressive. The reflecting pool, stretching 350 feet to the Washington Monument, is an awesome sight. As they stood reading the Gettysburg Address they agreed that it demonstrated significant meaning for all Americans—freedom from slavery for Blacks and equality for all.

Rebecca never ceased to be impressed by everything Lincoln stood for. "He was one of our finest presidents, P.G. He really understood what our government was all about, and he tried to make it work for everyone."

P.G. paused for a second, and then said, "Unlike some of the people of today who are supposed to be making the government work."

A strong bond was growing between them. Their conversations were animated and intimate. He wasn't afraid to hold her hand in public and he loved to see her smile. Sometimes she would grab his hand if he didn't take hers. She was becoming very possessive and was not afraid to show it. The memory of Sarah was disappearing from his mind. He knew that Becky, in time, would heal him completely. He knew also that the suddenness of death in the military made a man value life more dearly.

"What are you planning to do when you leave the service?" he asked Becky.

"If I don't get married, I'll go back to college," she said.

"How do you feel about marriage?"

"I'm for it," she replied. "In fact, it may sound like an incredible coincidence, but my parents are married."

"Isn't that interesting. Mine are, too."

"What are your plans, Peter?"

"Well, I'd thought about becoming a doctor, but that takes an awful long time. I also thought about becoming a civilian airline pilot, but there will be thousands of pilots coming out of the service applying for those jobs. I'm not sure. I'm not sure about anything, except that I want us to be together."

They were both quiet for a moment as the weight of those words hung in the air.

"Have you thought about staying in the Naval Air Corps?" she asked. "Admiral White told me you'd have no trouble staying in, because you're a specialist in night-carrier flying. He told me there aren't many pilots who can land planes on the carriers at night."

"I've thought about it, but I don't think I'd live too long if I did," he said. "The planes are getting faster all the time, and as the speed increases, so does the risk."

"We could be together if you stayed in the navy," said Becky.

"I know. I've given that a lot of thought, too. But what if I didn't stay in the navy? What would that do to us?"

"It would make us both civilians, that's all."

"You're really sure of yourself, aren't you?"

"Yes, I am," she replied.

That evening they went to the Fish Market, a restaurant on the banks of the Potomac. Café tables were set up outdoors, and the moon shining over the river was beautiful and romantic. The seafood was brought in daily from Chesapeake Bay. They went dancing until 1:00 A.M., and when they got back to Becky's apartment, she said, "stay with me tonight."

"Are you sure?" asked P.G.

"Yes, I'm sure," Becky said as she opened the door.

They spent the night making love until they were both completely exhausted. In the morning, when they awoke, they had a long conversation about spending the rest of their lives together.

"Becky, listen. There's no pressure here. But I want you to think about spending your life with me."

She started to say something funny, something to mock the gravity of his proposal, but instead said, "I will, Peter."

The next day at BuPers, he got a call from Rebecca.

"Hi, there."

"Well, hello," he said, stretching his legs out. "I was just engaging in some lurid fantasy involving you and me."

"Well, holster that weapon, Lieutenant. Admiral White wants to talk to you. He wants you to fly some night tests on a new plane."

"Any risks involved? I mean, outside of hurtling through the pitch-black night in a beer can with an engine on it?"

"I don't know. I can't answer that. He says there could be a promotion in it for you."

"That means big-time risk. And I don't need a promotion."

"I know."

"How did he get my name?"

"One of the pilots who knew you in the Pacific recommended you."

"What's his name?"

"Commander Brad Hayes. He's a test pilot at Patuxent River."

"Hayes! I can't believe he's still alive. I love it! What's the project, and where's the plane?"

"The plane is at Patuxent River in Maryland. Evidently, the navy is trying to develop a new type of aircraft. They have three experimental planes that are prop planes with a jet engine in the back. It's something like the Avenger you flew in the Pacific, but it's bigger and faster. The jet is supposed to be used as an auxiliary power source to increase its speed in critical combat situations, or something."

"Or something. Right. Listen, tell him I'm not interested. I don't know how to fly jets."

"We've been invited to the Army-Navy Club in Washington tomorrow night to discuss this. I think maybe you ought to listen to the admiral."

"We'll take the free dinner, but I don't want the job."

"You could be the youngest lieutenant-commander in the navy."

"You mean, I could be the youngest dead lieutenant-commander in the navy."

"Will you go if I ask you?"

"I'll go, but the answer is no about the test."

"Listen, Peter, I know you're skeptical, but Admiral White was very nice, and he said they wanted an experienced night-carrier pilot with brains to handle the project. You'd be able to fly the plane in the daytime to get accustomed to it. Commander Hayes recommended you highly and would check you out himself."

"So, do you want me dead?"

"No, I want you just as you are. This is history happening here, and you can help make it."

"Or help Admiral White make it."

"Will you go to the dinner?"

"Okay, but I'm not interested in anymore heroics."

"He said he'll have a navy limousine pick us up."

"That's great. The full treatment. About as subtle as a battleship's 16-inch gun. Okay, what do I wear?"

"Wear your dress blues, and put a couple of your war ribbons on."

"I'm not trying to impress the admiral. Besides, he's probably got so much fruit salad you could choke on it. He can look up my record."

"I know that, but I like them on your chest. Do it for me?"

"Tell me what you're wearing and I might be interested."

"I'm not wearing my uniform. I'm wearing a blue, tight-fitting dress."

"You must have gotten clearance from the admiral."

"I did."

"Okay, Becky, I'll go. But only because I want to see you in that dress."

At 6:30 a navy limousine stopped in front of the Connecticut Avenue apartment with a marine driver and picked up P.G. and Rebecca. They then drove to the Army-Navy Club in tense silence.

The admiral, a navy captain, and a commander, all with their wives, met them at the club. The men were all naval aviators.

"Lieutenant, how do you like Washington, D.C.?" asked the admiral.

"Fine so far. The scenery is incredible," replied P.G. as he gestured toward Becky.

Becky smiled as she put her arm through P.G.'s.

"Rebecca's quite a gal. You've made a good choice," said the admiral. "And I hope you make another tonight."

First they had a couple of drinks, and then the admiral broke the ice about the test project. "Lieutenant, the Navy Department has asked three aircraft companies to develop a prop-jet aircraft with separate engines for future day and night-carrier use. One of them is ready for testing right now at the NATC Systems Test Branch at Patuxent River, Maryland. The navy wants to have a jet engine plane to be able to land on the carrier's deck, but we feel that in order to get aboard, the pilot will have to come in on the prop."

"I think that's a good idea, but why don't you go to the cantilever flight deck, the way the British have? If the pilot misses the deck, he just takes a wave-off and goes around again."

"We're looking into that, Lieutenant, but we have more important projects to investigate. The jet engine produces a bright flame out the back, and for many reasons we're interested in developing flame dampeners to subdue that flame for night-flying and to reduce the heat emission created by the jet."

"What happens if the jet engine flames out?"

"You turn the prop on and land on the prop."

"Sounds interesting. It also sounds crazy. What do you want me to do?"

"Hayes was right about you," said the admiral cryptically. "You don't call your punches. We want you to go up to 38,000 feet, turn the prop off, feather the prop and turn on the jet, and see if we can follow you with speed and flight illumination devices from the ground and from the air. Another plane, an F8F Bearcat, piloted by Commander Hayes, will be following you. The flame dampener will be already placed on the jet engine of your plane. We'll also have some devices in the other plane to measure heat emission reduction. The navy is interested in reducing the amount of heat emission for many reasons. One is that in the near future, they may be developing an air-to-air rocket called a heat-seeking missile."

"Won't that jet engine overheat with the flame dampener on?"

"That's a possibility!" said the admiral.

"The engine has been thoroughly checked out on the ground without any problems. It's not an easy plane to fly. One of the planes to be tested has high-pressure stopcocks that have to be opened to admit fuel to the jet engine when you use the jet. These stopcocks have to be closed when the engine isn't in use, or the fuel will keep on going to the engine. You could have a fire back there if it gets too hot, and the jet could blow up."

"In which case they bury me in a bottle cap. Becky, make sure it's the finest bottle cap money can buy."

"It is risky, but we wouldn't ask you to do it if you weren't the best."

"Okay, what do I get out of it?"

"What would you like?"

"A three-week vacation on a Caribbean island," he replied as he smiled.

"If everything goes according to Hoyle, we'll give you three weeks off at full pay wherever you want to go."

"How about Barbados?"

"You got it."

"Okay, when do I report?"

"Tomorrow morning."

"That doesn't give me much notice. What do you think, Becky?"

"He'll report in 24 hours if I get the three weeks off too, Admiral."

"I think we can arrange that, Chief," replied the admiral.

Peter turned to Becky. "We should've asked for a month."

Tuesday morning, P.G. left for the Patuxent River Test Station in Maryland. When he arrived, he checked into the B.O.Q. and was assigned temporary quarters. He was also given a check-in list to complete. He was fitted for a special flight suit and helmet. There were compressors built into the suit to apply pressure to his legs and abdomen for the high-speed dives and turns he would have to perform. This would help prevent passing out from the blood leaving his head. There would be a lot of Gs acting on him. P.G. was also concerned about the possibility of his jet breaking the sound barrier and disintegrating in the air. The plane he was testing was capable of going faster than the speed of sound.

When he got out to the flight line at Patuxent River, he was met by Commander Hayes. P.G. saluted him stiffly.

"Fuck you. Cut the formalities," said Commander Hayes as they laughed and hugged each other.

"You show up everywhere I go," said P.G. "People are talking."

"I'm keeping an eye on you," said Hayes. "I told Admiral White you were the best pilot for this project."

"Yeah, I heard. Thanks for nothing! Maybe I can repay the favor."

"You're welcome."

"So, let's get to it—is it hard to fly these prop jets?"

"Not really, once you get the hang of it. I'll be doing your blind-fold cockpit check-out. Today you're going to sit in the cockpit and memorize the instruments."

"I feel like I'm back at preflight," said Peter.

"Yeah," said Hayes, "but there's a World War between you and those days."

The next day he took the plane up for the first time and during the next three or four days flew the plane in broad daylight. It was fun to fly, but was heavy and consumed a lot of jet fuel. He was apprehensive when he switched from the prop to the jet, but it worked fine. "Okay, Becky," he thought, "maybe you were right."

The time arrived for the night test. All the big guns showed up—an admiral, a commodore, and two navy captains. He was briefed on the test flight and methods of turning on and off the jet and prop and the gear that was being used to monitor the flight of the plane. He had flown on the prop separately and on the jet in the daytime but not at night. Hayes would be flying wing on him as he did the night flight test.

He got into the cockpit, plugged in his earphones, started the engine, and called the control tower. "Patuxent Tower, this is Navy SR-1X, request runway instructions."

"Navy SR-1X, proceed to runway 4A for takeoff. Hold for permission."

"Roger."

He taxied the experimental plane out to the end of the runway. "Patuxent Tower, this is Navy SR-1X. Request permission for takeoff."

"Navy SR-1X, permission granted."

He pushed the throttle forward and took off on the prop, cut in the jet engine, and soared to 38,000 feet. The sky was beautiful at night, with the stars out, and he felt like king of the universe. He had his oxygen mask on, and plugged in his special compression flight suit. He feathered the prop and used the jet engine for propulsion. He noticed there was no ejection release in the cockpit.

Hayes pulled his plane up on P.G.'s wing. "P.G., vector for first trial run will be 30 degrees north at 450 mph. I'll blink my wing lights when you're supposed to start."

"Roger, Brad."

"Everything is going too smoothly," he thought, as he approached 450 mph. He could see Washington, not far off in the distance. He scanned the sky and thought as he hurtled through space, "The jet engine *is* the future, dangerous or not."

"P.G., this is Admiral White. Turn the plane around and make another pass over the airport while we calibrate our instruments down here on the ground."

"Roger. Another high-speed pass coming up."

As he saw Washington come into view again, suddenly the jet engine flamed out. He immediately called Patuxent Tower.

"Patuxent Tower. This is Navy SR-1X. I have a flame-out. I'm going to have to start the prop."

"What happened, P.G.?"

"Admiral, I'm too busy trying to restart this prop engine."

He frantically tried to find the starter for the prop engine. Suddenly it was a hell of a lot darker in the cockpit. Where the hell is it? He instinctively reached for an area on the instrument panel. He found the starter button and it felt like it was stuck. The plane began to drop out of the sky like a stone. The prop engine and jet engine were both out. He tried to restart the jet. No luck.

"*Mayday!*" P.G. screamed, as he tried to start the prop again. Thirty-eight thousand to 15,000 feet went by in a few seconds.

"P.G., get the hell out of there," screamed Brad.

"Where am I?"

"Not far from Andrews Air Force Base in Washington."

He tried again to get the jet engine to start. No luck. He kept pushing the button to activate the self-starter switch for the propeller. Nothing happened. He struggled to get his foot up on the instrument panel.

"I'm going to leave her at 5,000," he shouted.

"You may be getting close to the White House," the admiral hollered. "Point it out to sea."

"Where the hell is that?" he shouted. "I'm at 8,000 and losing altitude fast."

He put his left foot up and kicked the dashboard of the plane, hitting the prop starter mechanism. He heard a hissing, whining sound. The prop started to sing, and the engine started. He pushed the throttle forward, and the engine took over at 5,000 feet. He slowly pulled the stick back and the plane pulled up just over the treetops. He called Andrews Air Force Base. "Andrews Tower, this is Navy SR-1X. Request emergency landing instructions."

"Navy SR-1X, this is Andrews Tower. You can't land here now. We've got a plane loaded with VIPs coming in from the Middle East on an army transport plane."

"Tell them to kiss my ass. I'm coming in."

"Is this an emergency?"

"What do you think it is? It's a Mayday."

"Use runway 7 east."

When he landed the plane, he was met by a navy captain. "You can be court-martialed for what you just did," he said. "There were three senior senators in that airliner who had to wait for you to land that plane."

"So they had to drink another gin and tonic. So what? You can call Admiral White at Patuxent River, if there are any questions. That prop jet is an experimental plane worth over $10 million." P.G. was livid. The adrenalin was flowing and he was shaking.

"You can't talk like that to a navy captain."

"And you can't fly a jet, so back off."

"I'll have you court-martialed."

"Why don't you go take a crap."

"That does it. Now I know I'm going to recommend a court-martial."

"Recommend what you want, but get lost."

The navy made arrangements to ship the plane back to Patuxent River the next day. P.G. decided to take a bus back. He had a lot of time to think. He met with Admiral White when he arrived.

"What do you think went wrong?" asked the Admiral.

"Two things: The flame dampener has an effect on flame-outs and has to be perfected; also there has to be a back-up to restart that prop engine if the jet engine flames out or else nobody's going to want to fly that airplane.

"Oh, Admiral, by the way, some navy captain gave me a hard time about landing the plane as an emergency at Andrews. I guess I delayed the landing of an air transport carrying three senators and their wives returning from an overseas junket."

"I know," said the admiral. "I heard all about it. You shouldn't have told the captain to go take a crap, but I reminded him that you saved that experimental plane from ending up in some cornfield."

"Is he going through with the court-martial?" asked P.G.

"Don't worry about it, Lieutenant. I told him you were too valuable to be attending court-martial hearings because you would be doing more test work for the navy on that aircraft."

"Do I get the three weeks in Barbados?"

"It will take us that long to correct the bugs in that jet. Of course you do. We still want you to complete the test when you get back."

"Great," thought P.G. "What a deal!"

37

Barbados

Before they left for the Caribbean, Rebecca spent three paychecks at Garfinkels, and Woodward and Lathrops. She bought three summer dresses, four bathing suits with low-cut backs, an assortment of fancy lingerie and white, pink, and emerald green high heels.

When they arrived in Barbados, they got into their bathing suits and went right to the beach. They spent most of their vacation lying on the island's isolated stretches of sand and soaking up the sun. Becky's tan was complete—there were no strap marks on her shoulders.

During the evenings they went out to dinner at the resort hotels. There was one particularly beautiful hotel at James Fort that had a good dance band. The Barbados Yacht Club had sailboats they rented to sail around the island. Becky would have the hotel chef where they were staying prepare picnic lunches. She and Peter would then set out to find an isolated area on the beach.

During their three-week vacation their love grew stronger. They tried new ways of making love. It was the first time either of them had spent three weeks living with a member of the opposite sex.

Some evenings they would go out to dinner at a native restaurant. If Becky wanted to dress up, they'd have dinner at the Yacht Club.

She would get dressed up in one of her low-cut evening gowns and put on high heels. Lieutenant Grant would wear a white jacket and black tie. Becky was a knockout in some of her strapless gowns and caught the eye of many a young man on the island.

Their closeness living together strengthened their bond of love for each other. Becky enjoyed the isolated beaches in the daytime and sharing the same bed at night with her man. She enjoyed being as close as she could with the man she loved and sleeping next to him, even if he did snore quite loudly.

During their last evening together they relaxed in a tangle of bedcovers and considered the immediate future.

"Peter, I don't think I want you to fly that prop jet when we get back to Washington."

"Why not?"

"I think it's too dangerous."

"I don't think I want to either, but I made a commitment to do a job and I have to complete it."

"Not if you're going to complete it by killing yourself. It's too risky. I want you to think about my life, too."

"Becky, I don't want you to get mad; but remember what I once told you about Sarah, the girl I loved. She got killed in an automobile accident. I didn't think I'd ever find anyone to take her place. I was depressed for a long time. I can honestly tell you that my love for you is as great, if not greater, than any love I had for her. I can assure you that I will not take foolish risks. I'm seriously thinking about staying in the Navy Air Corps so we can be together. It would solve a lot of our financial problems."

"I know how much you love to fly. It would solve your problem as to what to do with your life but it wouldn't solve mine."

"What do you mean?"

"I'd be home chewing my fingernails, worrying about you flying in those airplanes. I'm not so sure I could handle that stress for any length of time. I don't want to be a widow. The navy would give us security while it gives us gray hair."

"Someone has to take the risk."

"Sure, but where is it written that it has to be you? I think you'd do very well in the business world. In fact, you'd do well in anything you set your mind to," said Becky.

"I'm not so sure. In the Navy Air Corps at least I'd be assured of a pretty good income and after 20 years I could retire on a decent pension."

"If you crack up an airplane, none of that will matter. I want you and I want us to be together now. We both want children and I want their father around to see them grow up," said Becky, as she stretched her arms above her head languidly.

Their conversation ended abruptly as he watched her breasts become taut and firm with her nipples erect. Her lips were full and moist and her eyes had a glassy, passionate look. She was obviously ready to make love again. He was aware of the beauty of her slender legs as they reached the curve of her buttocks.

She saw the look in his eyes as she slowly rolled on her side to accentuate the beauty of her curvaceous body. "Come here and make love to me, Peter."

"The way you look right now, I might rape you."

"So come over here and I'll help you," she teased, as she raised her buttocks off the bed.

He slowly began to caress her body and palpate her breasts. She could tell he was aroused. She moistened her lips with her tongue and opened her mouth invitingly. She began to caress his back with her long nails. She decided to tease him and not let him have her too easily.

His strong muscular body prevailed, however, as he grabbed her arms and held them behind her back with his left hand. With his other hand he grabbed her buttocks and pulled her body into his. As she was penetrated she arched her back into his, responding fully to his lovemaking. As their passion increased he continued his drive as her body became uncontrollable in response. Their lovemaking seemed to continue for a long time as Becky felt him become more rigid as he penetrated deeper within her. She began to sigh; "Oh, Peter, I love you so." She had never felt like this before and thought she never wanted their lovemaking to end. She wrapped her legs around him, tightening her leg muscles to pull him tighter against her. She wanted every bit of this man. The response of her passion to his ignited the fuse as she felt his entire body become spasmodically rigid in a desperate inward drive to a climax. Suddenly they both became limp as they lay back against the pillows in utter exhaustion.

"Peter, I love you so much."

"I love you too, Becky. There's no woman more beautiful than one who is completely happily exhausted just after she has responded to the fullest in making love to her man."

"Well, I don't know about the beautiful part, but I certainly am completely happily exhausted."

Time passed. They lay side by side, their feelings woven into each other's. Out of a long silence Peter said, "Will you consider marrying me?"

Out of a much shorter silence, Becky said, "Yes. There, I've considered it. Let's get married."

They decided before leaving Barbados that the first thing on their agenda when they got back would be to buy an engagement ring.

38

The Fireball

When Chief Petty Officer Rebecca Parsons arrived at her office at BuPers, there was a large bouquet of flowers on her desk with a small note. "Glad you're back, Becky. We missed you." It was signed by her boss, the vice-admiral in charge, and the three rear-admirals who she worked for as a receptionist.

Becky knew they would miss her because it was her job to set up the daily agenda for the admirals and to determine how to handle the many dignitaries who visited the office. Her job was also to sift out the important material from the minutiae. Her replacement, a male CPO, had not done a good job.

There is nothing more effective than the feminine touch in handling big shots with big egos. Rebecca's personality and smile could disarm anyone, and she had excellent voice recognition. Vice-Admiral Thatcher, the admiral in charge, would often bypass his secretary to discuss office problems with Becky. She was intuitive and had a gift for strategy in human relations.

In the morning Becky always arrived before the admirals. She was in a good mood this day, having just spent three weeks on a Caribbean island with the man she was going to marry. A sparkling diamond engagement ring graced her left hand, and her tan made her face glow. She felt confident and happy.

When Admiral Thatcher arrived, she thanked him for the flowers.

"Becky, sometimes you don't know how good someone is until they go away on vacation. We missed you around here and we're glad you're back."

"Thank you," she replied, thinking, "There's something he's not telling me."

"There's something else I have to talk to you about," said Admiral Thatcher. "Admiral White from Patuxent River Test Station called me about your boyfriend, Lieutenant Grant. He told me that he's quite a pilot. He knew you would know his whereabouts. He wants Lieutenant Grant to call him at Patuxent River."

"I'll call Peter right away and give him the message, Admiral. But, he's not my boyfriend, he's my fiancée," she replied as she held her left hand out to show off her ring.

"Congratulations, Becky. I thought you had a bigger smile than usual. There's no urgency to contact your fiancée," said the admiral. "He's to call Admiral White at Patuxent River when you do reach him."

Becky was meeting P.G. for lunch so she decided to wait until then to tell him. He had told her that he planned on taking it easy and sleeping in to recharge his batteries.

"Poor baby," thought Becky. "Wait 'til he's living with me full time!"

He met Becky at noon and they took a cab to a small restaurant in Arlington. "I have a message for you, Peter. Admiral Thatcher told me that Admiral White is trying to get in touch with you. Would you know what that's about?" she asked, trying to sound breezy and uncaring.

"Maybe it's about that jet they want me to retest. I'm not too eager to get in that flying coffin again."

"Then why don't you just refuse to fly it?" she replied.

"I can't do that unless I feel it's completely unsafe, but you can be damn sure I'll check it out flying over the air base in daylight in case it cuts out on me."

"I was thinking," she said, touching her ring. "Maybe I can ask Admiral Thatcher to get you a different assignment."

"No, don't interfere, Becky. I'll call Brad and see if he knows what's going on."

"Why don't you call him from the phone here at the restaurant?"

Peter smiled. "Okay, if you want me to."

When he got back to the table after making the call he said, "Brad invited me to Patuxent River next weekend for dinner on Saturday night. When I told him I had gotten engaged, he invited you to join us. How does that sound?"

"Great," said Becky. "I'd love to meet Brad." She saw the excitement in Peter's eyes. "He hates risks, but he loves it," she thought. Could he do without it for her sake? That was the question.

P.G. rented a car for the weekend and they drove to Patuxent River. He renewed his friendship with Brad's wife and couldn't get over how big their daughter Amy had gotten. She was five years old and quite talkative. Becky hit it off effortlessly with each of them. Peter watched her play with Amy and thought, "Someday she'll make a wonderful mother." After a delicious meal, Commander Hayes told P.G. why the admiral wanted to talk to him. The two men cleared the dinner plates—standard practice at the Hayes household—and then took a walk outside.

"They're having trouble fixing that plane that almost did you in," said Brad. "They're designing a new starter system for the prop engine. They're not too happy with the jet engine, either and it will be quite a while before they get all the bugs out of it. There's something else he talked to me about. Admiral White wants you and me to do another project for the navy."

"You've got to be kidding! The answer is no if it's anything like that last one," said P.G.

"Well," said Brad, "it's not an easy one. The navy is going to test fly a new plane called the Fireball out in San Diego in two weeks. Admiral White wants us to fly out there and join the air group and report back to him as to how it works out."

"You mean we'll be observers and not flying?"

"Not completely," said Brad. "He wants us to make a few carrier landings with the air group to see how the plane handles coming onto the flight deck. We'll fly the prop-jet planes for a week, shooting field-carrier landings before we fly them aboard the carrier. You can refuse if you want to but I'd consider it a personal favor if you accepted."

"Why a personal favor, Brad?"

"Because you're the only pilot I trust with my life."

P.G. thought about that.

"Think it over for a couple of days and call me on Tuesday," said Brad.

"How do you feel about it?" asked P.G.

"I'm a full-time professional navy man. I do what I'm told," replied Brad.

"I've never been real good at full-time or doing what I'm told," said P.G.

"I know," replied Brad.

"I'll call you Tuesday. I want to discuss it with Becky."

Riding back in the car, P.G. explained everything to Becky and she insisted that he not take the assignment. "You had a bad experience with one plane. You don't need any more," she said.

"If I'm going to stay in the navy, I have to do it," he said. "It will go on my record if I refuse. We both know what goes into the record books."

"It isn't going to do you any good if you kill yourself."

"This is what it's all about, isn't it, Becky? If I stay in the navy, we'll have to go through this same situation over and over again. You don't always have control of your own destiny."

"I don't like it," repeated Becky. "You do. That's where we differ."

"Liking it doesn't enter into it," said Peter. "You do it or you don't. Being in the navy has a price tag on it, and this is it."

"That stinks," replied Becky.

The next couple of days, P.G. and Becky argued about the pros and cons of completing the project. It was P.G.'s long personal relationship and friendship with Commander Brad Hayes that prevailed. He called Brad on Tuesday.

"If you're willing to risk your life flying that jet off a carrier, I'm willing to do it too. I have one stipulation, Brad—no night-carrier landings flying those prop jets."

"That's when I would refuse, too," said Brad.

The following week, P.G. left Becky, frowning and tight-lipped with tears in her eyes, and flew with Brad to San Diego. They checked into the San Diego Naval Air Station. There were 36 Fireball prop-jets parked along the runway at the field. The two pilots spent three days going to ground school to learn about the flying characteristics of the jet. It was an interesting aircraft. It had two types of engines. In the front of the plane was a radial prop engine with a four-bladed propeller. In the tail there was a jet engine; one of the first constructed for aircraft use.

The navy's brass was worried about the jets landing on the carrier's deck because of the heavy weight and high speed necessary to maintain level flight. The plan was to use the propeller to come in for carrier landings at a slower speed and to use the jet engine for combat situations.

The Fireball was a big aircraft and looked different than other navy carrier planes. It had a tricycle landing gear with a nose wheel similar to commercial airliners. It looked like a missile in flight. The wings were very small for its size and weight and this made it unstable at slow speeds.

The plane had a complicated fuel system because of the two different engines. There had to be two separate gas tanks because two different types of fuel were used; gasoline for the prop and kerosene for the jet. The two engines and the weight of the fuel made the plane very heavy.

The weather was consistently beautiful in San Diego—what else was new—and the day arrived for Brad and P.G. to take the Fireball up for a test run. They both had flown similar planes at Patuxent River Base but had never shot field-carrier landings.

P.G.'s plane almost flipped when he got the airspeed too slow on his first pass. The L.S.O. waved him off in a hurry. Brad had trouble getting acquainted with the tricycle landing gear. The tail hook was placed in the center of the understructure of the plane and not on the tail. To catch a wire flying the Fireball required different timing than flying an Avenger.

Turning the jet engine off before doing field-carrier landings on the prop wasn't easy. It didn't take long to realize, because of the small wing surface, that the plane had to be brought in much faster than the Hellcat or Avenger. The pilots wondered whether the increased speed would break the wire cables on the flight deck.

"I definitely don't like the way that plane handles," said Brad, after they had both landed their planes at the base and were walking to the hangar.

"You have to bring it in too fast," replied P.G. "What kind of carrier are we going to be testing these Fireballs on, anyway?"

"We're going to be shooting some day-carrier landings on a jeep carrier called the *Badoeng Strait* for about two weeks. Some of the planes are already loaded on the carrier and some of us will be flying out from the base here in San Diego. I understand there are more than 40 Fireball jets involved in the test. It's supposed to be a group of crack pilots. They're trying to flatter us, aren't they?"

"I don't need my ego stroked," said P.G. "What I need is a stiff drink."

The landing signal officer working with the group on field-carrier landings would be the same one working with the air group on the carrier landings. He would also have a voice-activated microphone to communicate with the pilots. There would also be civilian observers from the aircraft industry.

The day finally arrived for shooting the carrier landings on the *Badoeng Strait.*

The first three Fireball jets that made a pass at landing were given wave-offs because their airspeed was much too fast. They were coming in at 160 knots. The pilots weren't foolish. They knew the plane had a small wing area and they weren't about to flip it into the ocean.

"Slow it down, slow it down," hollered the L.S.O.

"You come up here and try it," shouted one of the pilots.

The L.S.O. wanted to say "no thanks" but decided it would be inappropriate.

Finally, some of the planes received cuts from the landing signal officer. The tail hook on one of the planes came off when it caught a cable wire and the plane hit the barrier. The damaged plane had to be taken below to the hangar deck.

After ten carrier landings, one of the Fireball jets landed with a thud; banging the nose wheel of the tricycle landing gear against the flight deck. The wheel seemed to explode and the rim of the nose wheel became a spinning projectile that almost took the head off one of the flight deck crew.

The nose wheel also seemed to be a big problem with other planes and one of them broke off completely as the plane landed on the deck and bounced over the side into the ocean. On another, the nose wheel shattered into pieces.

Finally, the ship's captain decided to call it quits for the day. He had seen enough. The jets that were still in the air were told to return to the Naval Air Base in San Diego.

Hayes and Grant had each made two safe landings and were still aboard the jeep carrier.

That evening the air operations officer met with the pilots and the L.S.O. in the ready room to discuss the day's activity. "Gentlemen, that was a sorry exhibition out there today with that Fireball. I want some feedback from all of you."

The executive officer of the air group spoke up. He had been retrieved from the water after putting one of the planes overboard. "That plane's unstable. You have to fly it so fast coming into the groove that it's just like a controlled crash. I think it's more difficult to see the L.S.O. flying at that speed."

The L.S.O. spoke up. "Maybe I should use the voice-activated mike more. I've gotten used to relying completely on hand signals."

"Probably a good idea," said the executive officer.

"I don't like the way that hook engages the cable," said Hayes. "That nose wheel should be constructed better, also."

They talked for one-half hour. The pilots vented frustration and offered advice. They weren't happy about flying that plane. Finally, the air skipper said, "Maybe we'll do better tomorrow," and adjourned the meeting.

The next day, 12 of the prop jets took to the air at 9:00 A.M. The catapult launch was uneventful, but the pilots continued to have problems landing the Fireball prop jet safely on the flight deck.

"You're getting too low," screamed the L.S.O. at one of the pilots. He swore he saw the plane's tail hook touch the water as he dove for the safety net and the pilot poured the coals to the plane as it just missed the fantail of the carrier.

Another nose wheel was broken and the rim took off again like a flying saucer. The flight deck crew was getting more scared each time another plane landed; diving for cover became standard for each landing.

Peter was having particular difficulty landing. He received four consecutive wave-offs and he was pissed.

"You've got to slow that plane down or you won't be coming aboard, Lieutenant," said the L.S.O. as he gave him another wave-off.

"If I slow it down too much I'm going to cartwheel across the deck," P.G. muttered. He was determined to make a safe landing. As he turned his plane into the cross leg, he called the L.S.O. "How's my altitude?" he asked.

"Okay, but slow your speed down."

Peter cut back on his throttle. As he came into the groove and approached the flight deck, he picked up the L.S.O. out of the left side of his canopy.

"Easy as you go," said the L.S.O., as he waved his paddles in a cutting motion across his neck. The plane was coming in fast but looked okay for landing.

When Peter pulled back on his throttle, all hell broke loose. The flight deck came rushing up at him. His nose wheel hit the deck like a rock and he heard the fuselage crack as the nose wheel broke. The plane bounced to the left and the cable wire gave as the plane rolled over the side of the ship toward the water. It knocked off a 40 mm antiaircraft battery as it went. He felt the plane flip over on its back as it hit the water. His shoulder harness broke and his left shoulder hit the instrument panel. There was a stabbing pain as his head hit the canopy. He was knocked unconscious.

As he regained consciousness, blood ran into his eyes and water poured in on his feet. He saw the expanse of ocean around him; the plane was going down. He began to fumble for the handle to release the canopy and screamed out in pain. His left shoulder was useless and it hurt. He reached across with his right hand, groping under the brine for the handle. There. He pulled with all he had, but the canopy would not release. The water was at his chest as the nose of the plane dipped below the surface of the sea. He screamed. The two heavy engines sucked the plane below the surface and water filled the cockpit. Peter took a deep breath, he figured it was his last. He raised his left foot up and kicked at the canopy release and heard the hooks in the fuselage unsnap. He was going down. He used his legs to propel himself up, and as his head and broken shoulder hit the canopy, he screamed, letting air out and water in. He clawed toward the surface weakly with his right hand, but it was no good. He slipped silently toward the bottom.

When he next opened his eyes, he saw only darkness. I'm still on the bottom of the ocean, he thought abstractly, and slowly sense returned as he thought, "How am I breathing water?" The pale green of the sickbay ceiling became clear then and he thought, "Hey, I'm alive."

He tried to move. That was a mistake. His left shoulder was in plaster and pain shot down his torso into his legs. He gasped, and a medical corpsman heard him and came over.

"Am I alive?" he croaked.

"By a nose," he said. "A diver went over the side for you with a line attached to his body. When he went under for you no one figured you were still alive, but you surprised us all. Except for probably a lasting fear of saltwater, you're going to be just fine."

"Where's the guy who pulled me out?"

"He's on board. He was transferred over with you. You want me to get him?"

"Yeah, please, right away."

When the seaman came in, Peter shook his hand. "You're a strong son-of-a-bitch, you know that?" he said.

"Used to swim the hundred at Tennessee State," he said, smiling and making a muscle.

"Well, thanks for saving my life."

"Just doing my job, sir, just like you were."

"Can the bilge," said Peter. "I owe you one."

Before the two weeks were over, half a dozen of the experimental planes ended up in the Pacific. Numerous other planes had broken nose wheels, propellers, and damaged wingtips. The executive officer of the squadron eventually put two planes in the drink.

It was finally decided by all those involved that it would be the better part of valor to quit. The *Badoeng Strait* headed back to port.

The pilots who flew the planes felt that the plane was aptly called the Fireball. The aircraft engineers and plane designers would have to go back to the drawing board on that one.

After mending for seven days and letting his head clear, P.G. left the hospital with his mind made up. He called and made arrangements to be on the next flight back to Washington. He called Brad Hayes and asked him to come to the airport. He got cleaned up, his left arm still in plaster and a sling, shaved, and then left the hospital.

Brad was at the airport. He and Peter joked about the Fireball. "You know," said Brad, "why didn't they just slap a pair of wings on a goddamned tank? I'm amazed at what the navy thinks we can actually fly."

"What you can fly," said Peter.

"Say again?"

"What *you* can fly. I'm grounding myself. I'm done."

Brad stared at him, shocked. "Peter, if you do, it'll be the worst waste of flying talent I've ever seen."

"Thanks, pal, but I'd rather have the talent wasted than be killed by it."

"Listen, you're not always going to be a test pilot. Hell, there's lots of other flying assignments. Besides that, you're a goddamned top pilot now, why let that go?"

"Brad, listen." Peter took a deep breath. "I don't need to be a hero. I really don't. At least not a hero to the navy. I don't want to be a dead hero! I want to do it for someone else now. You've got a family. I want one, too. So I'm walking away, while I can, to a girl who loves me, and who I want to marry. I did my part during the war. You must understand that."

Hayes started to say something, then stopped. "Yeah," he smiled. "Yeah, I guess I can. But remember this. Those skills you have are hard to come by. They're valuable. If civilian life starts to bore you like it did me, give me a call. The navy usually knows where I am."

"Well, the navy will have a hard time finding me," said P.G. "I'm going back to school. There's something that has bothered me since that kamikaze attack on the *Saratoga*. I really couldn't understand what happened to those young dead sailors on those gun mounts. Not a scratch on them and yet they were deader than a doornail. When I started college four years ago, I didn't have a pot to piss in so I chose business administration as my major. I really wanted to consider medicine, but had no money. Now with the G.I. Bill of Rights, I might give it a shot. I'm going to talk to Becky about it. I had plenty of time to think while lying in the hospital bed. There will be more sacrifices to achieve that goal. It might be easier with her by my side."

"You, a doctor?" said Brad.

"Yes," said Peter.

"That's quite a switch. Now that I think about it, I bet you'd be great at it."

"I'll be in touch," said Peter, and shook his friend's hand. Then he saluted him.

"Come on, cut the formal bullshit," said Hayes.

"Hey, it's the last one, come on, you've got to. You've earned it!"

So, with great formality, Hayes took two steps back and threw Grant his best salute. They stood facing each other in silence. There were tears in their eyes.

Becky was there at the gate when Peter got off the plane. He'd been cryptic in his message: "Mission completed, please be at the airport, have exciting news to report."

He looked worn and stiff as he ambled through the gate; the cross-country flight hadn't done his aching body any good. When

Becky saw his arm in a sling and a patch on his head, she began to cry. He tried to hold her with his right arm. She raised her arms around his shoulders and buried her face in his chest. When he grunted in pain she recoiled and said, "Oh God, I'm sorry, I'm so sorry," and he tried to laugh so she would know it was okay, and then she put her arms around his waist—this time to get it right—and she held him tenderly. He whispered to her.

"*Really?*" she asked. "You're really quitting? Really? Oh God, Peter, thank you, thank you, you won't regret it, I promise. It'll keep me from getting gray hair and you'll get to live past the age of 30." He laughed and kissed her as they went to get his bags.

"I have some ideas about what I'm going to do in the civilian world," he said. "But I need to talk to you."

"Tell me, tell me."

"I was thinking about maybe being a race car driver, or a fireman, or one of those guys who swallow flaming swords at the circus. I figure it's probably all technique, right? I mean, how tough can it be?"

"You're not funny, not even a little," she said.

"Well, I'm going to be serious now. I told Brad I'm going to study medicine and become a doctor."

"You did what?"

"You heard me. I'm thinking about becoming a doctor."

"What did he think?"

"He encouraged me."

"Well, that makes two of us."

Postscript

Pete Grant (P.G.) returned to college, attended medical school, and became a doctor. At present he is a prominent surgeon practicing in one of the largest hospitals in New England.

The surviving pilots of Night Air Group 53 went on to achieve greater heights. Seventeen remained in the Navy Air Corps or Reserves and most of them became commanders or captains.

The executive officer of Night Fighter Squadron 53 became one of the first commanders of the Blue Angels stunt team. Unfortunately, seven of the pilots pursuing their careers in the active Navy Air Corps or Reserves were killed in aircraft accidents. Four pilots became doctors, three became lawyers, and many of the remaining members became prominent leaders in their business communities.